JOHN WARD, PREACHER

JOHN WARD, PREACHER

BY

MARGARET DELAND
AUTHOR OF " THE OLD GARDEN "

I sent my soul through the invisible,
Some letter of that after-life to spell:
 And by and by my soul returned to me,
And answered, " I myself am Heav'n and Hell."
OMAR KHAYYÁM.

TWELFTH THOUSAND

THE GREGG PRESS / RIDGEWOOD, N. J.

First published in 1888 by Houghton, Mifflin & Co.
Republished in 1967 by
The Gregg Press Incorporated
171 East Ridgewood Avenue
Ridgewood, New Jersey, U.S.A.

Copyright© 1967 by
The Gregg Press, Inc.

Library of Congress Catalog Card Number: 67-29263

Printed in United States of America

AMERICANS
IN
FICTION

INTRODUCTION BY PROFESSOR CLARENCE GOHDES
Editor of *American Literature* Magazine

In the domain of literature the play may once have been the chief abstract
ad chronicle of the times, but during the nineteenth and twentieth centuries
e novel has usurped the chief place in holding the mirror up to the homely
ce of society. On this account, if for no other, the Gregg Press series of reprints
American fiction merits the attention of all students of Americana and of
orarians interested in building up adequate collections dealing with the social
ad literary history of the United States. Most of the three score and ten novels
volumes of short stories included in the series enjoyed considerable fame in
eir day but have been so long out of print as to be virtually unobtainable in
e original editions.

Included in the list are works by writers not presently fashionable in critical
rcles — but nevertheless well known to literary historians — among them Joel
aandler Harris, Harriet Beecher Stowe, Thomas Bailey Aldrich, and William
ilmore Simms. A substantial element in the list consists of authors who are
aown especially for their graphic portrayal of a particular American setting,
ch as Gertrude Atherton (California), Arlo Bates (Boston), Alice Brown (New
agland), Edward Eggleston (Indiana), Mary Wilkins Freeman (New England),
enry B. Fuller (Chicago), Richard M. Johnston (Georgia), James Lane Allen
Kentucky), Mary N. Murfree (Tennessee), and Thomas Nelson Page (Vir-
nia). There is even a novel by Frederic Remington, one of the most popular
ainters of the Western cowboy and Indian — and another, an impressive minor
assic on the early mining region of Colorado, from the pen of Mary Hallock
oote. The professional student of American literature will rejoice in the oppor-
nity afforded by the collection to extend his reading of fiction belonging to
aat is called the "local-color movement" — a major current in the development
the national belles-lettres.

Among the titles in the series are also a number of famous historical novels.
las Weir Mitchell's *Hugh Wynne* is one of the best fictional treatments of the
merican Revolution. John Esten Cooke is the foremost Southern writer of his
y who dealt with the Civil War. The two books by Thomas Dixon are among
e most famous novels on the Reconstruction Era, with sensational disclosures
the original Ku Klux Klan in action. They supplied the grist for the first great
ovie "spectacular" — *"The Birth of a Nation"* (1915).

Paul Leicester Ford's *The Honorable Peter Stirling* is justly ranked amo
the top American novels which portray American politics in action — a subje
illuminated by other novelists in the Gregg list — A. H. Lewis, Frances
Burnett, and Alice Brown, for example. Economic problems are forcefully
before the reader in works by Aldrich, Mrs. Freeman, and John Hay, whe
novels illustrate the ominous concern over the early battles between labor a
capital. From the sweatshops of Eastern cities in which newly arrived immigra
toiled for pittances, to the Western mining camps where the laborers pack
revolvers, the working class of the times enters into various other stories in t
Gregg list. The capitalist class, also, comes in for attention, with an account
a struggle for the ownership of a railroad in Samuel Merwin's *The Short-L*
War and with the devastating documentation of the foibles of the newly ri
and their wives in the narratives of David Graham Phillips. It was Phillips whc
annoying talent for the exposure of abuses led Theodore Roosevelt to put t
term "muck-raker" into currency.

While it is apparent that local-color stories, the historical novel, and the ec
nomic novel have all been borne in mind in choosing the titles for this importa
series of reprints, it is evident that careful consideration has also been giv
to treatments of various minority elements in the American population. T
Negro, especially, but also the Indian, the half-breed, Creoles, Cajuns — a
even the West Coast Japanese — appear as characters in various of these nov
or volumes of short stories and sketches. Joel Chandler Harris's *Free Joe* w
open the eyes of readers who know that author solely as the creator of humoro
old Uncle Remus. And there is a revelatory volume of dialect tales, written
a Negro author, *The Conjure Woman* by Charles W. Chesnutt.

In literary conventions and the dominating attitudes toward life, the wor
in the Gregg series range from the adventurous romance illustrated so well
Mayne Reid or the polite urbanity of Owen Wister to the mordant irony of Ka
Chopin and the grimmer realism of Joseph Kirkland's own experiences on bloo
Civil War battlefields or the depressing display of New York farm life by Haro
Frederic. In short, the series admirably illustrates the general qualities of t
fiction produced in the United States during the era covered, just as it ge
erously mirrors the geographical regions, the people, and the problems
the times.

To ·

LORIN DELAND

𝔗𝔥𝔦𝔰 𝔅𝔬𝔬𝔨,

ALREADY MORE HIS THAN MINE,

IS DEDICATED.

BOSTON, *December 25th, 1887.*

JOHN WARD, PREACHER.

CHAPTER I.

THE evening before Helen Jeffrey's wedding day, the whole household at the rectory came out into the garden.

"The fact is," said Dr. Howe, smiling good-naturedly at his niece, " the importance of this occasion has made everybody so full of suppressed excitement one can't breathe in the house."

And indeed a wedding in Ashurst had all the charm of novelty. " Why, bless my soul," said the rector, " let me see : it must be ten — no, twelve years since Mary Drayton was married, and that was our last wedding. Well, we could n't stand such dissipation oftener ; it would wake us up."

But Ashurst rather prided itself upon being half asleep. The rush and life of newer places had a certain vulgarity ; haste was undignified, it was almost ill bred, and the most striking thing about the village, resting at the feet of its low green hills, was its atmosphere of leisure and repose.

Its grassy road was nearly two miles long, so that Ashurst seemed to cover a great deal of ground, though there were really very few houses. A lane, leading to the rectory, curled about the foot of East Hill at one end of the road, and at the other was the brick-walled garden of the Misses Woodhouse.

Between these extremes the village had slowly grown; but its first youth was so far past, no one quite remembered it, and even the trying stage of middle age was over, and its days of growth were ended. This was perhaps because of its distance from the county town, for Mercer was twelve miles away, and there was no prospect of a railroad to unite them. It had been talked of once; some of the shopkeepers, as well as Mr. Lash, the carpenter, advocated it strenuously at Bulcher's grocery store in the evenings, because, they said, they were at the mercy of Phibbs, the package man, who brought their wares on his slow, creaking cart over the dusty turnpike from Mercer. But others, looking into the future, objected to a convenience which might result in a diminution of what little trade they had. Among the families, however, who did not have to consider " trade " there was great unanimity, though the Draytons murmured something about the increased value of the land; possibly not so much with a view to the welfare of Ashurst as because their property extended along the proposed line of the road.

The rector was very firm in his opinion. " Why," said he, mopping his forehead with his big silk handkerchief, "what do we want with a railroad ? My grandfather never thought of such a thing, so I think I can get along without it, and it is a great deal better for the village not to have it."

It would have cut off one corner of his barn; and though this could not have interfered with the material or spiritual welfare of Ashurst, Dr. Howe's opinion never wavered. And the rector but expressed the feelings of the other " families," so that all Ashurst was conscious of relief when the projectors of the railroad went no further than to make a cut at one end of the Drayton pastures; and that was so long ago that now the earth, which had shown a ragged yellow wound across the soft greenness of the meadows, was sown by sweet clover and wild roses, and gave no sign of ever having been gashed by picks and shovels.

The Misses Woodhouse's little orchard of gnarled and wrinkled apple-trees came to the edge of the cut on one side, and then sloped down to the kitchen garden and back door of their old house, which in front was shut off from the road by a high brick wall, gray with lichens, and crumbling in places where the mortar had rotted under the creepers and ivy, which hung in heavy festoons over the coping. The tall iron gates had not been closed for years, and, rusting on their hinges, had pressed back against the inner wall, and were almost hidden by the tangle of vines, that were woven in and out of the bars, and waved about in the sunshine from their tops.

The square garden which the wall inclosed was full of cool, green darkness; the trees were the growth of three generations, and the syringas and lilacs were so thick and close they had scarcely light enough for blossoming. The box borders, which edged the straight prim walks, had grown, in spite of clippings, to be almost hedges, so that the paths between them were damp, and the black, hard earth had a film of moss over it. Old-fashioned flowers grew just where their ancestors had stood fifty years before. " I could find the bed of white violets with my eyes shut," said Miss Ruth Wood-house ; and she knew how far the lilies of the valley spread each spring, and how much it would be necessary to clip, every other year, the big arbor vitæ, so that the sunshine might fall upon her bunch of sweet-williams.

Miss Ruth was always very generous with her flowers, but now that there was to be a wedding at the rectory she meant to strip the garden of every blossom she could find, and her nephew was to take them to the church the first thing in the morning.

Gifford Woodhouse had lately returned from Europe, and his three years' travel had not prepared his aunts to treat him as anything but the boy he seemed to them when he left the law school. They still " sent dear Giff " here, or " brought him " there, and arranged his plans for him, in entire un-consciousness that he might have a will of his own. Perhaps the big fellow's silence rather helped the impression, for so long as he did not remonstrate when they bade him do this or that, it was not of so much consequence that, in the end, he did exactly as he pleased. This was not often at variance with the desires of the two sisters, for the wordless in-fluence of his will so enveloped them that his wishes were apt to be theirs. But no one could have been more surprised than the little ladies, had they been told that their nephew's intention of practicing law in the lumber town of Lockhaven had been his own idea.

They had cordially agreed with him when he observed that another lawyer in Ashurst, beside Mr. Denner, would have no other occupation than to make his own will; and they had nodded approvingly when the young man added that it would seem scarcely gracious to settle in Mercer while Mr. Denner still hoped to find clients there, and sat once a week, for an hour, in a dingy back office waiting for them. True, they never came; but Gifford had once read law with Mr. Denner, and knew and loved the little gentleman, so he could not do a thing which might appear discourteous. And when he further remarked that there seemed to be a good opening in Lockhaven, which was a growing place, and that it would be very jolly to have Helen Jeffrey there when she became Mrs. Ward, the two Misses Woodhouse smiled, and said firmly that they approved of it, and that they would send him to Lockhaven in the spring, and they were glad they had thought of it.

On this June night, they had begged him to take a message to the rectory about the flowers for the wedding. "He is glad enough to go, poor child," said Miss Deborah, sighing, when she saw the alacrity with which he started; "he feels her marriage very much, though he is so young."

"Are you sure, dear Deborah?" asked Miss Ruth, doubtfully. "I never really felt quite certain that he was interested in her."

" Certainly I am," answered Miss Deborah, sharply. " I 've always maintained they were made for each other."

But Gifford Woodhouse's pleasant gray eyes, under straight brown brows, showed none of the despair of an unsuccessful lover ; on the contrary, he whistled softly through his blonde moustache, as he came along the rectory lane, and then walked down the path to join the party in the garden.

The four people who had gathered at the foot of the lawn were very silent ; Dr. Howe, whose cigar glowed and faded like a larger firefly than those which were beginning to spangle the darkness, was the only one ready to talk. " Well," he said, knocking off his cigar ashes on the arm of his chair, " everything ready for to-morrow, girls ? Trunks packed and gowns trimmed ? We 'll have to keep you, Helen, to see that the house is put in order after all this turmoil ; don't you think so, Lois ? "

Here the rector yawned secretly.

" You need n't worry about *order*, father," Lois said, lifting her head from her cousin's shoulder, her red lower lip pouting a little, "but I wish we could keep Helen."

" Do you hear that, Mr. Ward ? " the rector said. " Yes, we 're all going to miss the child very much. Gifford Woodhouse was saying to-day Ashurst would lose a great deal when she went. There 's a compliment for you, Helen ! How that fellow has changed in these three years abroad ! He 's quite a man, now. Why, how old is he ? It 's hard for us elders to realize that children grow up."

" Giff is twenty-six," Lois said.

" Why, to be sure," said Dr. Howe, " so he is! Of course, I might have known it : he was born the year your brother was, Lois, and he would have been twenty-six if he 'd lived. Nice fellow, Gifford is. I 'm sorry he 's not going to practice in Mercer. He has a feeling that it might interfere with Denner in some way. But dear me, Denner never had a case outside Ashurst in his life. Still, it shows good feeling in the boy ; and I 'm glad he 's going to be in Lockhaven. He 'll keep an eye on Helen, and let us know if she behaves with proper dignity. I think you 'll like him, Mr. Ward, — I would say John, — my dear fellow ! "

There was a lack of sympathy on the part of the rector for the man at his side, which made it difficult for him to drop the formal address, and think of him as one of the family. "I respect Ward," he said once to his sister, — " I can't help respecting him ; but bless my soul, I wish he was more like other people ! " There was something about the younger man, Dr. Howe did not know just what, which irritated him. Ward's earnestness was positively aggressive, he said, and there seemed a sort of undress of the mind in his entire openness and frankness ; his truthfulness, which ignored the courteous deceits of social life, was a kind of impropriety.

But John Ward had not noticed either the apology or the omission ; no one answered the rector, so he went on talking, for mere occupation.

" I always liked Gifford as a boy," he said ; " he was such a manly fellow, and no blatherskite, talking

his elders to death. He never had much to say, and
when he did talk it was to the point. I remember
once seeing him — why, let me see, he could n't have
been more than fifteen — breaking a colt in the west
pasture. It was one of Bet's fillies, and as black as a
coal: you remember her, don't you, Lois? — a beauty!
I was coming home from the village early in the
morning; somebody was sick, — let me see, was n't
it old Mrs. Drayton? yes, — and I 'd been sent for;
it must have been about six, — and there was Gifford
struggling with that young mare in the west pasture. He had thrown off his coat, and caught her
by the mane and a rope bridle, and he was trying to
ride her. That blonde head of his was right against
her neck, and when she reared he clung to her till
she lifted him off his feet. He got the best of her,
though, and the first thing she knew he was on her
back. Jove! how she did plunge! but he mastered
her; he sat superbly. I felt Gifford had the making
of a man in him, after that. He inherits his father's
pluck. You know Woodhouse made a record at
Lookout Mountain; he was killed the third day."

"Gifford used to say," said Helen, "that he
wished he had been born in time to go into the
army."

"There 's a good deal of fight in the boy," said
the rector, chuckling. "His aunts were always begging him not to get into rows with the village boys.
I even had to caution him myself. 'Never fight,
sir,' I 'd say; 'but if you do fight, whip 'em!'
Yes, it 's a pity he could n't have been in the
army."

"Well," said Lois, impatiently, "Giff would have fought, I know, but he's so contradictory! I've heard him say the Southerners could n't help fighting for secession; it was a principle to them, and there was no moral wrong about it, he said."

"Oh, nonsense!" cried the rector; "these young men, who have n't borne the burden and heat of the day, pretend to instruct us, do they? No moral wrong? I thought Gifford had some sense! They were condemned by God and man."

"But, uncle Archie," Helen said, slowly, "if they thought they were right, you can't say there was a moral wrong?"

"Oh, come, come," said Dr. Howe, with an indignant splutter, "you don't understand these things my dear, — you're young yet, Helen. They were wrong through and through; so don't be absurd." Then turning half apologetically to John Ward, he added, "You'll have to keep this child's ideas in order; I'm sure she never heard such sentiments from me. Mr. Ward will think you have n't been well brought up, Helen. Principle? Twaddle! their pockets were what they thought of. All this talk of principle is rubbish."

The rector's face was flushed, and he brought his fist down with emphasis upon the arm of his chair.

"And yet," said John Ward, lifting his thoughtful dark eyes to Dr. Howe's handsome face, "I have always sympathized with a mistaken idea of duty, and I am sure that many Southerners felt they were only doing their duty in fighting for secession and the perpetuation of slavery."

"I don't agree with you, sir," said Dr. Howe, whose ideas of hospitality forbade more vigorous speech, but his bushy gray eyebrows were drawn into a frown.

"I think you are unfair not to admit that," John continued with gentle persistence, while the rector looked at him in silent astonishment, and the two young women smiled at each other in the darkness. ("The idea of contradicting father!" Lois whispered.) "They felt," he went on, "that they had found authority for slavery in the Bible, so what else could they do but insist upon it?"

"Nonsense," said Dr. Howe, forgetting himself, "the Bible never taught any such wicked thing. They believed in states rights, and they wanted slavery."

"But," John said, "if they did believe the Bible permitted slavery, what else could they do? Knowing that it is the inspired word of God, and that every action of life is to be decided by it, they had to fight for an institution which they believed sacred, even if their own judgment and inclination did not concede that it was right. If you thought the Bible taught that slavery was right, what could you do?"

"I never could think anything so absurd," the rector answered, a shade of contempt in his good-natured voice.

"But if you did," John insisted, "even if you were unable to see that it was right, — if the Bible taught it, inculcated it?"

Dr. Howe laughed impatiently, and flung the end

of his cigar down into the bushes, where it glowed for a moment like an angry eye. " I — I ? Oh, I 'd read some other part of the book," he said. " But I refuse to think such a crisis possible ; you can always find some other meaning in a text, you know."

" But, uncle Archie," Helen said, " if one did think the Bible taught something to which one's conscience or one's reason could not assent, it seems to me there could be only one thing to do, — give up the Bible ! "

" Oh, no," said Dr. Howe, " don't be so extreme, Helen. There would be many things to do ; leave the consideration of slavery, or whatever the supposed wrong was, until you 'd mastered all the virtues of the Bible : time enough to think of an alternative then, — eh, Ward? Well, thank Heaven, the war 's over, or we 'd have you a rank copperhead. Come ! it 's time to go into the house. I don't want any heavy eyes for to-morrow."

" What a speech for a minister's wife, Helen ! " Lois cried, as they rose. " What *would* people say if they heard you announce that you ' would give up the Bible ' ? "

" I hope no one will ever hear her say anything so foolish," said Dr. Howe, but John Ward looked at Lois in honest surprise.

" Would it make any difference what people said ? " he asked.

" Oh, I was n't speaking very seriously," Lois answered, laughing, " but still, one does not like to say anything which is unusual, you know, about such things. And of course Helen does n't really mean that she 'd give up the Bible."

" But I do," Helen interrupted, smiling; and she might have said more, for she could not see John's troubled look in the darkness, but Gifford Woodhouse came down the path to meet them and give Miss Ruth's message.

" Just in time, young man," said the rector, as Gifford silently took some of John's burden of shawls and cushions, and turned and walked beside him. " Here 's Helen giving Ward an awful idea of her orthodoxy ; come and vouch for the teaching you get at St. Michael's."

Gifford laughed. " What is orthodoxy, doctor ? " he said. " I 'm sure I don't know ! "

" 'The hungry sheep look up and are not fed,'" quoted the rector in a burlesque despair. " Why, what we believe, boy, — what *we* believe ! The rest of my flock know better, Mr. Ward, I assure you."

" I don't think we know what we do believe, uncle," Helen said lightly.

" This grows worse and worse," said the rector. " Come, Helen, when an intelligent young woman, I might say a bright young woman, makes a commonplace speech, it is a mental yawn, and denotes exhaustion. You and Lois are tired ; run up-stairs. Vanish ! I say. Good night, dear child, and God bless you ! "

CHAPTER II.

ASHURST Rectory, in a green seclusion of vines and creepers, stood close to the lane, — Strawberry Lane it was called, because of a tradition that wild strawberries grew there. The richness of the garden was scarcely kept in bounds by its high fence; the tops of the bushes looked over it, and climbing roses shed their petals on the path below, and cherries, blossoms, and fruit were picked by the passerby. "There is enough for us inside," said the rector.

The house itself was of gray stone, which seemed to have caught, where it was not hidden by Virginia creepers and wistaria, the mellow coloring of the sunset light, which flooded it from a gap in the western hills. Its dormer-windows, their roofs like brown caps bent about their ears, had lattices opening outward; and from one of these Lois Howe, on the evening of Helen's wedding day, had seen her father wandering about the garden, with the red setter at his heels, and had gone down to join him.

"I wonder," she said, as she wound her round young arm in his, which was behind him, and held his stick, "if John Ward has a garden? I hope so; Helen is so fond of flowers. But he never said anything about it; he just went around as though he

was in a dream. He was perfectly happy if he could
only look at Helen ! "

" Well, that 's right," said the rector ; " that 's
proper. What else would you have ? The fact is,
Lois, you don't like Ward. Now, he is a good fellow; yes, good is just the word for him. Bless
my soul, there 's a pitch of virtue about him that
is exhausting. But that 's our fault," he added
candidly.

" Oh, I 'll like him," Lois said quickly, " if he
will just make Helen happy."

The rector shook his head. " I know how you
feel," he said, " and I acknowledge he is odd ; that
talk of his last night about slavery being a righteous
institution " —

" Oh, he did n't say that, father," Lois interrupted.

— " was preposterous," continued Dr. Howe, not
noticing her ; " but he 's earnest, he 's sincere, and I
have a great deal of respect for earnestness. And
look here, Lois, you must not let anybody see you
are not in sympathy with Helen's choice ; be careful
of that tongue of yours, child. It 's bad taste to make
one's private disappointments public. I would n't
speak of it even to your aunt Deely, if I were you."

He stooped down to pull some matted grass from
about the roots of a laburnum-tree, whose dark
leaves were lighted by golden loops of blossoms.
" Thirty-eight years ago," he said, " your mother
and I planted this ; we had just come home from our
wedding journey, and she had brought this slip from
her mother's garden in Virginia. But dear me, I

suppose I've told you that a dozen times. What? How to-day brings back that trip of ours! We came through Lockhaven, but it was by stage-coach. I remember we thought we were so fortunate because the other two passengers got out there, and we had the coach to ourselves. Your mother had a striped ribbon, or gauze, — I don't know what you call it, — on her bonnet, and it kept blowing out of the window of the coach, like a little flag. You young people can go further in less time, when you travel, but you will never know the charm of staging it through the mountains. I declare, I have n't thought of it for years, but to-day brings it all back to me!"

They had reached the rectory porch, and Dr. Howe settled himself in his wicker chair and lighted his cigar, while Lois sat down on the steps, and began to dig small holes in the gravel with the stick her father had resigned to her.

The flood of soft lamplight from the open hall door threw the portly figure of the rector into full relief, and, touching Lois's head, as she sat in the shadow at the foot of the steps, with a faint aureole, fell in a broad bright square on the lawn in front of the house. They had begun to speak again of the wedding, when the click of the gate latch and the swinging glimmer of a lantern through the lilacs and syringas warned them that some one was coming, and in another moment the Misses Woodhouse and their nephew stepped across the square of light.

Miss Deborah and Miss Ruth were quite unconscious that they gave the impression of carrying Gif-

ford about with them, rather than of being supported by him, for each little lady had passed a
determined arm through one of his, and instead of
letting her small hand, incased in its black silk mitt,
rest upon his sleeve, pressed it firmly to her breast.

Ashurst was a place where friendships grew in
simplicity as well as strength with the years, and
because these three people had been most of the
morning at the rectory, arranging flowers, or moving furniture about, or helping with some dainty
cooking, and then had gone to the church at noon
for the wedding, they saw no reason why they
should not come again in the evening. So the sisters had put on their second-best black silks, and,
summoning Gifford, had walked through the twilight
to the rectory. Miss Deborah Woodhouse had a
genius for economy, which gave her great pleasure
and involved but slight extra expense to the household, and she would have felt it a shocking extrav-
agance to have kept on the dress she had worn to
the wedding. Miss Ruth, who was an artist, the
sisters said, and fond of pretty things, reluctantly
followed her example.

They sat down now on the rectory porch, and
began to talk, in their eager, delicate little voices, of
the day's doings. They scarcely noticed that their
nephew and Lois had gone into the fragrant dusk
of the garden. It did not interest them that the
young people should wish to see, as Gifford had
said, how the sunset light lingered behind the hills ;
and when they had exhausted the subject of the
wedding, Miss Ruth was anxious to ask the rector

about his greenhouse and the relative value of leaf
mould and bone dressing, so they gave no thought
to the two who still delayed among the flowers.

This was not surprising. Gifford and Lois had
known each other all their lives. They had quarreled and made up with kisses, and later on had
quarreled and made up without the kisses, but they
had always felt themselves the most cordial and
simple friends. Then had come the time when Gifford must go to college, and Lois had only seen him
in his short vacations; and these gradually became
far from pleasant. " Gifford has changed," she said
petulantly. " He is so polite to me," she complained
to Helen; not that Gifford had ever been rude, but
he had been brotherly.

He once asked her for a rose from a bunch she
had fastened in her dress. " Why don't you pick
one yourself, Giff ? " she said simply; and afterwards,
with a sparkle of indignant tears in her eyes and
with a quick impatience which made her an amusing
copy of her father, she said to Helen, " I suppose he
meant to treat me as though I was some fine young
lady. Why can't he be just the old Giff ? " And
when he came back from Europe, she declared he
was still worse.

Yet even in their estrangement they united in
devotion to Helen. It was to Helen they appealed
in all their differences, which were many, and her
judgment was final; Lois never doubted it, even
though Helen generally thought Gifford was in the
right. So now, when her cousin had left her, she
was at least sure of the young man's sympathy.

She was glad that he was going to practice in Lockhaven; he would be near Helen, and make the new place less lonely for her, she said, once. And Helen had smiled, as though she could be lonely where John was!

They walked now between the borders, where old-fashioned flowers crowded together, towards the stone bench. This was a slab of sandstone, worn and flaked by weather, and set on two low posts; it leaned a little against the trunk of a silver-poplar tree, which served for a back, and it looked like an altar ready for the sacrifice. The thick blossoming grass, which the mower's scythe had been unable to reach, grew high about the corners; three or four stone steps led up to it, but they had been laid so long ago they were sunken at one side or the other, and almost hidden by moss and wild violets. Quite close to the bench a spring bubbled out of the hillside, and ran singing through a hollowed locust log, which was mossy green where the water had overflowed, with a musical drip, upon the grass underneath.

They stood a moment looking towards the west, where a golden dust seemed blown across the sky, up into the darkness; then Lois took her seat upon the bench. "When do you think you will get off, Giff?" she said.

"I 'm not quite sure," he answered; he was sitting on one of the lower steps, and leaning on his elbow in the grass, so that he might see her face. "I suppose it will take a fortnight to arrange everything."

"I 'm sorry for that," Lois said, disappointedly. "I thought you would go in a few days."

Gifford was silent, and began to pick three long stems of grass and braid them together. Lois sat absently twisting the fringe on one end of the soft scarf of yellow crêpe, which was knotted across her bosom, and fell almost to the hem of her white dress.

"I mean," she said, "I 'm sorry Helen won't have you in Lockhaven. Of course Ashurst will miss you. Oh, dear! how horrid it will be not to have Helen here!"

"Yes," said Gifford sympathetically, "you 'll be awfully lonely."

They were silent for a little while. Some white phlox in the girl's bosom glimmered faintly, and its heavy fragrance stole out upon the warm air. She pulled off a cluster of the star-like blossoms, and held them absently against her lips. "You don't seem at all impatient to get away from Ashurst, Giff," she said. "If I had been you, I should have gone to Lockhaven a month ago; everything is so sleepy here. Oh, if I were a man, would n't I just go out into the world!"

"Well, Lockhaven can scarcely be called the world," Gifford answered in his slow way.

"But I should think you would want to go because it will be such a pleasure to Helen to have you there," she said.

Gifford smiled; he had twisted his braid of grass into a ring, and had pushed it on the smallest of his big fingers, and was turning it thoughtfully about. "I don't believe," he said, "that it will make the slightest difference to Helen whether I am there or not. She has Mr. Ward."

"Oh," Lois said, "I hardly think even Mr. Ward can take the place of father, and the rectory, and me. I know it will make Helen happier to have somebody from home near her."

"No," the young man said, with a quiet persistence, "it won't make the slightest difference, Lois. She 'll have the person she loves best in the world; and with the person one loves best one could be content in the desert of Sahara."

"You seem to have a very high opinion of John Ward," Lois said, a thread of anger in her voice.

"I have," said Gifford; "but that is n't what I mean. It 's love, not John Ward, which means content. But you don't have a very high opinion of him?"

"Oh, yes, I have," Lois said quickly; "only he is n't good enough for Helen. I suppose, though, I 'd say that of anybody. And he irritates me, he is so different from other people. I don't think I do — adore him!"

Gifford did not speak; he took another strand of grass, and began to weave it round and round his little ring, to make it smaller.

"Perhaps I ought not to say that," she added; "of course I would n't to any one but you."

"You ought not to say it to me, Lois," he said.

"Why? Is n't it true?" she said. "I don't think it is wrong to say he 's different; it 's certainly true!" Gifford was silent. "Do you?" she demanded.

"Yes," Gifford answered quietly; "and some-how it does n't seem fair, don't you know, to say anything about them, they are so happy; it seems as though we ought not even to speak of them."

Lois was divided between indignation at being found fault with and admiration for the sentiment. "Well," she said, rather meekly for her, "I won't say anything more; no doubt I 'll like him when I know him better."

"See if that fits your finger, Lois," her com-panion said, sitting up, and handing her the little grass ring. She took it, smiling, and tried it on. Gifford watched her with an intentness which made him frown; her bending head was like a shadowy silhouette against the pale sky, and the little curls caught the light in soft mist around her forehead.

"But I 'm glad for my own part, then," she went on, "to think of you with Helen. You must tell me everything about her and about her life, when you write; she won't do it herself."

"I will," he answered, "if you let me write to you."

Lois opened her eyes with surprise; here was this annoying formality again, which Gifford's fault-find-ing seemed to have banished. "Let you write?" she said impatiently. "Why, you know I depended on your writing, Giff, and you must tell me every-thing you can think of. What 's the good of having a friend in Lockhaven, if you don't?"

She had clasped her hands lightly on her knees, and was leaning forward a little, looking at him; for he had turned away from her, and was pulling at a

bunch of violets. " I tell you what it is, Lois," he
said; " I cannot go away, and write to you, and
not — and not tell you. I suppose I 'm a fool to tell
you, but I can't help it."

" Tell me what? " Lois asked, bewildered.

"Oh," Gifford burst out, rising, and standing
beside her, his big figure looming up in the darkness, " it 's this talk of friendship, Lois, that I cannot stand. You see, I love you."

There was silence for one long moment. It was
so still they could hear the bubbling of the spring,
like a soft voice, complaining in the darkness. Then
Lois said, under her breath, " Oh, Gifford ! "

" Yes, I do," he went on, desperately. " I know
you 've never thought of such a thing; somehow, I
could not seem to make you see it, — you would n't
see it; but I do love you, and — and, Lois — if you
could care, just a little ? I 've loved you so long."

Lois shrank back against the silver-poplar tree,
and put her hands up to her face. In a moment
tenderness made the young man forget his anxiety.
" Did I startle you ? " he said, sitting down beside
her; but he did not take her hand, as he might have
done in their old frank friendship. " I 'm so sorry,
but I could n't help telling you. I know you 've
been unconscious of it, but how could a fellow help
loving you, Lois ? And I could n't go away to
Lockhaven and not know if there was any chance
for me. Can you care, a — little ? "

She did not speak until he said again, his voice
trembling with a sudden hope, " Won't you say
one word, Lois ? "

"Why, Giff," she said, sitting up very straight, and looking at him, her wet eyes shining in the darkness, "you know I care — I've always cared, but not that way — and — and — you don't, Giff, you don't really — it's just a fancy."

"It is not a fancy," he answered quietly. "I knew I loved you that first time I came home from college. But you were too young; it would not have been right. And then before I went abroad, I tried to tell you once; but I thought from the way you spoke you did not care. So I did n't say anything more; but I love you, and I always shall."

"Oh, Gifford," Lois cried, with a voice full of distress, "you *must n't!* Why, don't you see? You're just like my brother. Oh, do please let us forget all this, and let's be just as we used to be."

"We cannot," he said gently. "But I won't make you unhappy; I won't speak if you tell me to be silent."

"Indeed, I do tell you to be silent," she said, in a relieved tone. "I — could not, Giff. So we'll just forget it. Promise me you will forget it?"

He shook his head, with a slow smile. "You must forget it, if it will make you any happier; but you cannot ask me to forget. I am happier to remember. I shall always love you, Lois."

"But you must n't!" she cried again. "Why can't we have just the old friendship? Indeed — indeed, it never could be anything else; and," with a sudden break of tenderness in her voice, "I — I really am so fond of you, Giff!"

Here the young man smiled a little bitterly.

Friendship separated them as inexorably as though it had been hate!

"And," the girl went on, gaining confidence as she spoke, for argument cleared the air of sentiment, in which she felt as awkward as she was unkind, "and you know there are a good many things you don't like in me; you think I have lots of faults, — you know you do."

"I suppose I do, in a way," he acknowledged; "but if I did n't love you so much, Lois, I would not notice them."

Lois held her head a little higher, but did not speak. He watched her twist her fingers nervously together; she had forgotten to take off the little ring of braided grass.

"I am so sorry, Giff," she said, to break the silence, — "oh, so sorry. I — I can't forgive myself."

"There is nothing to forgive," he answered gently; "and you must not distress yourself by thinking that I am unhappy. I am better, Lois, yes, and happier, because I love you. It shall be an inspiration to me all my life, even if you should forget all about me. But I want you to make me one promise, will you?"

She hesitated. "If I can, Giff;" and then, with sudden trustfulness, she added, "Yes, I will. What is it?"

She had risen, and was standing on the step above him. He looked at her nervous little hands a moment, but did not touch them, and then he said, "If the time ever comes when you can love me, tell

me so. I ask you this, Lois, because I cannot bear
to distress you again by speaking words of love you
do not want to hear, and yet I can't help hoping;
and I shall always love you, but it shall be in silence.
So if the day ever does come when you can love me,
promise to tell me."

"Oh, yes," she said, glad to grant something.
"But, Gifford, dear, it will never come; I must say
that now."

"But you promise?"

"Yes," she answered, soberly. "I promise."

He looked at her steadily a moment. "God bless
you, dear," he said.

"Oh, Gifford!" cried the girl, and with a sudden
impulse she stooped and kissed his forehead; then,
half frightened at what she had done, but not yet
regretting it, she brushed past him, and went swiftly
up the path to the rectory.

The young man stood quite still a moment, with
reverent head bent as though he had received a benediction, and then turned and followed her.

CHAPTER III.

LOIS HOWE's mind was in a strange tumult that night; the subtile thrill, which is neither pain nor pride, and yet seems both, with which a young woman hears for the first time that she is loved, stung through all her consciousness of grief at having wounded her old friend. Tears came into her eyes once, and yet she did not know why; perhaps it was anger. How could Gifford have been so foolish as to talk that way, and make her have to say what she did? The old friendship was what she wanted. And then more tears came; and for the first time in her simple girlish life, Lois could not understand her own heart.

It was because Helen had gone away, she said to herself, and she was tired; and that gave her the right to cry with all her heart, which was a great relief.

But Lois was young. The next morning, when she pushed back her windows, she felt joy bubble up in her soul as unrestrainedly as though she had never said a word to Gifford which could make his heart ache. The resistance and spring of the climbing roses made her lean out to fasten her lattices back, and a shower of dew sprinkled her hair and bosom; and at the sudden clear song of the robin under the eaves, she stood breathless a moment to listen, with that simple gladness of living which is perhaps a supreme unselfishness in its entire unconsciousness of individual joy.

But like the rest of the world, Lois found that such moments do not last; the remembrance of the night before forced itself upon her, and she turned to go down-stairs, with a troubled face.

Of course there is plenty to do the day after a wedding, and Lois was glad to have the occupation; it was a relief to be busy.

Ashurst ladies always washed the breakfast things themselves; no length of service made it seem proper to trust the old blue china and the delicate glass to the servants. So Lois wiped her cups and saucers, and then, standing on a chair in the china-closet, put the dessert plates with the fine gilt pattern borders, which had been used yesterday, on the very back of the top shelf, in such a quick, decided way Jean trembled for their safety.

The rectory dining-room was low - studded, and lighted by one wide latticed window, which had a cushioned seat, with a full valance of flowered chintz; the dimity curtains were always pushed back, for Dr. Howe was fond of sunshine. In the open fireplace, between the brasses, stood a blue jug filled with white lilacs, and the big punch-bowl on the sideboard was crowded with roses. There were antlers over the doors, and the pictures on the walls were of game and fish, and on the floor was a bearskin, which was one of the rector's trophies.

Lois stood by a side-table which held a great pan of hot water; she had a long-handled mop in her hand and a soft towel over her arm, and she washed and wiped some wine-glasses with slender twisted stems and sparkling bowls, and then put them on their shelves in the corner closet, where they gleamed and glittered in the sunshine, pouring through the open window.

She did not work as fast now, for things were nearly in order, and she dreaded having nothing to do; her aunt, Mrs. Dale, would have said she was dawdling, but Miss Deborah Woodhouse, who had come over to the rectory early to see if she could be of use, said haste was not genteel, and it was a pleasure to see a young person who was deliberate in her movements.

"But you must let me help you, my dear," she added, taking off her gloves, and pulling the fingers straight and smooth.

"Indeed, Miss Deborah, there is nothing more to do," Lois answered, smiling, as she closed the brass-hinged doors of the corner closet.

"Dear me!" said the other absently, "I do trust dear Gifford's china-closet will be kept in proper order. Your shelves do credit to Jean's housekeeping; indeed they do! And I hope he'll have a maid who knows how to put the lavender among the linen; there's always a right and a wrong way. I have written out directions for her, of course, but if there was time I would write and ask Helen to see to it."

"Why, Giff says he won't get off for a fortnight," Lois said, with sudden surprise.

"I thought so," responded Miss Deborah, shaking

her head, so that the little gray curls just above her ears trembled, — " I thought so, too ; but last night he said he was going at once.　At least," stopping to correct herself, " dear Ruth and I think it best for him to go.　I have everything ready for him, so no doubt he 'll get off to-morrow."

Lois was silent.

" The fact is," said Miss Deborah, lowering her voice, " Gifford does not seem perfectly happy.　Of course you would n't be apt to observe it ; but those things don't escape my eyes.　He 's been depressed for some time."

" I had n't noticed it," said Lois faintly.

" Oh, no, certainly not," answered Miss Deborah ; " it would be scarcely proper that you should, considering the reason : but it 's no surprise to me.　I always thought that when they grew old enough, dear Giff and Helen would care for one another ; and so I don't wonder that he has been feeling some disappointment since he came home, though I had written him she was engaged —　Much too young she was, too, in my judgment."

Lois's astonishment was so great that she dropped her mop, and Miss Deborah looked at her reprovingly over her glasses.　" Oh, yes, there 's no doubt Gifford felt it," she said, " but he 'll get over it. Those things do not last with men.　You know I would n't speak of this to any one but you, but he 's just like a brother to you."

" Yes, exactly like a brother," Lois said hurriedly, " and I think I should have known it if it had been — had been that way."

"No," said Miss Deborah, putting down the last glass, "I think not. I only guessed it myself last night; it is all over now; those things never last. And very likely he 'll meet some nice girl in Lockhaven who will make him happy; indeed, I should n't wonder if we heard he was taken with somebody at once; hearts are often caught on the rebound! I don't know," Miss Deborah added candidly, "how *lasting* an attachment formed on a previous disappointment might be; and dear me! he does feel her marriage very much."

Here Sally came in to take away the pan and mop, and Lois looked about to see if there was anything more to do. She was very anxious to bring Miss Deborah's conversation to an end, and grateful that Jean should come and ask her to take some silver, borrowed for yesterday's festivities, back to Mrs. Dale.

"It 's these spoons," the old woman explained to Miss Deborah. "Mrs. Dale, she lent us a dozen. I 've counted 'em all myself; I would n't trust 'em to that Sally. If there was a hair's difference, Mrs. Dale would know it 'fore she set eyes on them, let alone havin' ône of our spoons 'stead of hers."

Miss Deborah nodded her head. "Very likely, Jean," she said; "I 've not a doubt of it. I 'm going now, and Miss Lois will walk along with me. Yes, Mrs. Dale would see if anything was wrong, you can depend upon it."

They set out together, Lois listening absently to Miss Deborah's chatter about the wedding, and vaguely glad when, at the gate of her aunt's house, she could leave her, with a pretty bow, which was half a courtesy.

There was a depressing stateliness about Dale house, which was felt as soon as the stone gateway, with its frowning sphinxes, was passed. The long shutters on either side of the front door were always solemnly bowed, for Mrs. Dale did not approve of faded carpets, and the roof of the veranda, supported by great white pillars, darkened the second-story windows. There was no tangle of vines about its blank walls of cream-colored brick with white trimmings, nor even trees to soften the stare with which it surveyed the dusty highway ; and the formal precision of the place was unrelieved by flowers, except for a stiff design in foliage plants on the perfectly kept lawn.

On the eastern side of the house, about the deep windows of Mr. Dale's sanctum, ivy had been permitted to grow, and there were a few larch and beech trees, and a hedge to hide the stables ; but these were special concessions to Mr. Dale.

" I do dislike," said Mrs. Dale, — " I do dislike untidy gardens ; flowers, and vines, and trees, all crowded together, and weeds too, if the truth's told. I never could understand how the Woodhouse girls could endure that forlorn old place of theirs. But then, a woman never does make a really good manager unless she's married."

Lois found her aunt in the long parlor, playing Patience. She was sitting in a straight-backed chair, — for Mrs. Dale scorned the weakness of a rocking-chair, — before a spindle-legged table, covered with

green baize and with a cherry-wood rim inlaid with
mother-of-pearl and ivory.   On it were thirteen
groups of cards, arranged with geometrical exactness
at intervals of half an inch.

"Well, Lois," she said, as her niece entered.
"Oh, you have brought the spoons back?"   But she
interrupted herself, her eyebrows knitted and her
lower lip thrust out, to lift a card slowly, and decide
if she should move it.   Then she glanced at the girl
over her glasses.   "I'm just waiting here because I
must go into the kitchen soon, and look at my cake.
That Betty of mine must needs go and see her sick
mother to-day, and I have to look after things.   But
I cannot be idle.   I declare, there is something malicious in the way in which the relatives of servants
fall ill!"

She stopped here long enough to count the spoons,
and then began her game again.   She was able, however, to talk while she played, and pointed out various things which did not "go quite right" at the
wedding.

The parlor at Dale house was as exact and dreary
as the garden.   The whole room suggested to Lois,
watching her aunt play solitaire, and the motes
dancing in the narrow streaks of sunshine which
fell between the bowed shutters, and across the drab
carpet to the white wainscoting on the other side,
the pictures in the Harry and Lucy books, or the
parlor where, on its high mantel shelf, Rosamond
kept her purple jar.

She wondered vaguely, as Mrs. Dale moved her
cards carefully about, whether her aunt had ever

been "bothered" about anything. Helen's marriage seemed only an incident to Mrs. Dale; the wedding and the weather, the dresses and the presents, which had been a breathless interest to Lois, were apparently of no more importance to the older woman than the building up a suit.

"Well," Mrs. Dale said, when she had exhausted the subject of the wedding, " I 'm sure I hope it will turn out well, but I really can't say. Ever since I 've seen this Mr. Ward I 've somehow felt that it was an experiment. In the first place, he 's a man of weak will, — I 'm sure of that, because he seems perfectly ready to give way to Helen in everything ; and that is n't as it ought to be, — the man should rule! And then, besides that, whoever heard of his people ? Came from the South somewhere, I believe, but he could n't tell me the first name of his great-grandfather. I doubt if he ever had any, between ourselves. Still, I hope for the best. And I 'm sure I trust," she added, with an uneasy recollection of the cake in the oven, "she won't have trouble with servants. I declare, the happiness of married life is in the hands of your cook. If Betty had not gone off this morning, I should have come over to the rectory to help you. There 's so much to do after a wedding."

" Oh, you 're very kind," said Lois, " but I think Jean and I can see to things. Miss Deborah came to help me, but we were really quite in order."

" Miss Deborah ! " said Mrs. Dale. " Well, I 'm glad if she could be of any use ; she really is so unpractical. But it 's lucky you have Jean. Just wait till you get a house of your own, young lady, and then you 'll understand what the troubles of housekeeping are."

" I 'm in no haste for a house of my own," said the girl, smiling.

" That 's because you 're a foolish child," returned Mrs. Dale promptly. " You 'd be a great deal happier if you were married and settled. Though I must say there is very little chance of it, unless you go away to make a visit, as Helen did. There is only one young man in Ashurst; and now he 's going. But for that matter, Gifford Woodhouse and you are just like brother and sister. Yes, Lois, I must say, I wish I could see you in a home of your own. No woman is really happy unless she 's married."

" I think I 'm the best judge of that," Lois answered. " No girl could be happier than I am; to hear father call me his — Tyrant? I don't want anything better than that."

" Nonsense ! " said Mrs. Dale decidedly. " If you had a husband to call you *his* Tyrant, it would be a thousand times better. I declare, I always think, when we pray for ' all who are destitute and oppressed,' it means the old maids. I 'm sure the ' fatherless children and widows ' are thought of, and why not the poor, forlorn, unmarried women ? Indeed, I think Archibald is almost selfish to keep you at home as he does. My girls would never have been settled if I had let them stay in Ashurst. I 've a great mind to tell your father he is n't doing his duty. You ought to have a winter in town."

" Indeed, I hope you won't tell him anything of the sort ! " cried Lois. " I would n't leave Ashurst for the world, and I 'm perfectly happy, I assure you ! "

" Don't be so silly," said Mrs. Dale calmly, " or think that no one loves your father but yourself. He was my brother for thirty-four years before he was your father. I only spoke for your good, and his too, for of course he would be happier if you were."

She stopped here to gather her cards up, and deal them out again in little piles, and also to reprove Lois, who had made an impatient gesture at her words.

" These little restless ways you have are very unpleasant," she said ; " my girls never did such things. I don't know where you get your unlady-like habits ; not from your father, I 'm sure. I suppose it 's because you don't go out at all ; you never see anybody. There, that reminds me. I have had a letter from Arabella Forsythe. I don't know whether you remember the Forsythes ; they used to visit here ; let me see, fifteen years ago was the last time, I think. Well, they are going to take the empty house near us for the summer. She was a Robinson ; not really Ashurst people, you know, not born here, but quite respectable. Her father was a button manufacturer, and he left her a great deal of money. She married a person called Forsythe, who has since died. She has one boy, about your age, who 'll be immensely rich one of these days ; he is not married. Heaven knows when Ashurst will see an eligible young man again," she added; and then, absently, "Eight on a nine, and there's a two-spot for my clubs!"

"I wonder if I remember Mrs. Forsythe?" Lois said, wrinkling her pretty forehead in a puzzled way. "Wasn't she a tall, thin lady, with a pleasant face?"

"Yes," answered Mrs. Dale, nodding her sleek head, "yes, *rather* pleasant, but melancholy. And no wonder, talking about her aches and pains all the time! But that's where the button manufacturer showed. She was devoted to that boy of hers, and a very nice child he was, too." She looked sharply at her niece as she spoke.

"I remember him," Lois said. "I saw Gifford shake him once; 'he was too little to lick,' he said."

"I 'm afraid Gifford is very rough and unmannerly sometimes," Mrs. Dale said. "But then, those Woodhouse girls could n't be expected to know how to bring up a big boy."

"I don't think Giff is unmannerly," cried Lois.

"Well, not exactly," Mrs. Dale admitted; "but of course he is n't like Mr. Forsythe. Gifford has n't had the opportunities, or the money, you know."

"I don't think money is of much importance," said Lois. "I don't think money has anything to do with manners."

"Oh, you don't know anything about it!" cried Mrs. Dale. "There! you made me make a mistake, and lose my game. Pray do not be silly, Lois, and talk in that emphatic way; have a little more repose. I mean this young man is — he is very different from anybody you have ever seen in Ashurst. But there is no use trying to tell you anything; you always keep your own opinion. You are exactly like a bag of feathers. You punch it and think you 've made an impression, and it comes out just where it went in."

Lois laughed, and rose to go.

" Tell your father what I said about a winter in town," Mrs. Dale called after her; and then, gathering her cards up, and rapping them on the table to get the edges straight, she said to herself, " But perhaps it won't be necessary to have a winter in town ! " And there was a grim sort of smile on her face when, a moment later, Mr. Dale, in a hesitating way, pushed the door open, and entered.

" I thought I heard Lois's voice, my dear," he said, with a deprecating expression.

He wore his flowered cashmere dressing-gown, tied about the waist with a heavy silk cord and tassel, and a soft red silk handkerchief was spread over his white hair to protect his head from possible draughts in the long hall. Just now one finger was between the pages of " A Sentimental Journey."

" She was here," said Mrs. Dale, still smiling. " I was telling her the Forsythes were coming. It is an excellent thing; nothing could be better."

" What do you mean ? " asked Mr. Dale.

" Mean ? " cried his wife. " What should I be apt to mean ? You have no sense about such things, Henry."

" Oh," said her husband meekly, " you want them to fall in love ? "

" Well, really," she answered, leaning back in her chair, and tapping her foot impatiently, " I do not see how my husband can be so silly. One would think I was a matchmaker, and no one detests anything of that sort as I do, — no one ! Fall in love, indeed ! I think the expression is positively indelicate, Henry. Of course, if Lois should be well married, I should be grateful ; and if it should be Mr. Forsythe, I should only feel I had done my duty in urging Arabella to take a house in Ashurst."

" Oh, you urged her ? "

"I wrote her Ashurst was very pleasant," Mrs. Dale acknowledged, " and it was considered healthy. (I understand Arabella !) I knew her son was going abroad later in the summer, but I thought, if he once got here " —

" Ah," responded Mr. Dale.

CHAPTER IV.

JOHN and Helen had not gone at once to Lockhaven; they spent a fortnight in wandering about
through the mountains on horseback. The sweet
June weather, the crystal freshness of the air, and
the melodious stillness of the woods and fields
wrapped those first heavenly days of entire possession in a mist of joy. Afterwards, John Ward felt
that it had blinded the eyes of his soul, and drifted
between him and his highest duty; he had not been
able to turn away from the gladness of living in her
presence to think of what had been, during all their
engagement, an anxiety and grief, and, he had promised himself, should be his earliest thought when
she became his wife : — the unsaved condition of her
soul.

When he had first seen her, before he knew he
loved her, he had realized with distress and terror
how far she was from what he called truth; how indifferent to what was the most important thing in
the whole world to him, — spiritual knowledge. He
listened to what she said of her uncle's little Episcopal church in Ashurst, and heard her laugh good-
naturedly about the rector's sermons, and then
thought of the doctrines which were preached from
his own pulpit in Lockhaven.

Helen had never listened to sermons full of the

hopelessness of predestination ; she frankly said she did not believe that Adam was her federal head and representative, and that she, therefore, was born in sin. " I 'm a sinner," she said, smiling ; " we 're all miserable sinners, you know, Mr. Ward, and perhaps we all sin in original ways; but I don't believe in original sin."

When he spoke of eternal punishment, she looked at him with grave surprise in her calm brown eyes. " How can you think such a thing ? " she asked. " It seems to me a libel upon the goodness of God."

" But justice, Miss Jeffrey," he said anxiously ; " surely we must acknowledge the righteousness and justice of God's judgments."

" If you mean that God would send a soul to hell forever, if you call that his judgment, it seems to me unrighteous and unjust. Truly, I can think of no greater heresy, Mr. Ward, than to deny the love of God ; and is not that what you do when you say he is more cruel than even men could be ? "

" But the Bible says " — he began, when she interrupted him.

" It does not seem worth while to say, ' the Bible says,' " she said, smiling a little as she looked into his troubled face. " The Bible was the history, and poetry, and politics of the Jews, as well as their code of ethics and their liturgy ; so that, unless we are prepared to believe in its verbal inspiration, I don't see how we can say, as an argument, ' the Bible says.' "

" And you do not believe in its verbal inspiration ? " he said slowly.

" No," Helen answered, " I could not."

It was not for John Ward to ask how she had been taught, or to criticise another minister's influence, but as he walked home, with anxious, downcast eyes, he wondered what Dr. Howe's belief could be, and how it had been possible for her soul to have been so neglected. This woman, whose gracious, beautiful nature stirred him with profound admiration, was in the darkness of unbelief; she had never been taught the truth.

As he said this to himself, John Ward knew, with sudden, passionate tenderness, that he loved her. Yet it was months before he came and told her. What right had he to love her? he said to himself, when he knelt and prayed for her soul's salvation: she was an unbeliever; she had never come to Christ, or she would have known the truth. His duty to his people confronted him with its uncompromising claim that the woman whom he should bring to help him in his labors among them should be a Christian, and he struggled to tear this love out of his heart.

John Ward's was an intellect which could not hold a belief subject to the mutations of time or circumstances. Once acknowledged by his soul, its growth was ended; it hardened into a creed, in which he rested in complete satisfaction. It was not that he did not desire more light; it was simply that he could not conceive that there might be more light. And granting his premise that the Bible was directly inspired by God, he was not illogical in holding with a pathetic and patient faith to the doctrines of the Presbyterian Church.

Helen's belief was as different as was her mode
of thought. It was perhaps a development of her
own nature, rather than the result of her uncle's
teaching, though she had been guided by him spiritually ever since he had taken her to his own home,
on the death of her parents, when she was a little
child. " Be a good girl, my dear," Dr. Howe would
say. So she learned her catechism, and was confirmed just before she went to boarding-school, as
was the custom with Ashurst young women, and
sung in the choir, while Mr. Denner drew wonderful chords from the organ, and she was a very well-
bred and modest young woman, taking her belief
for granted, and giving no more thought to the problems of theology than girls usually do.

But this was before she met John Ward. After
those first anxious questions of his, Helen began to
understand how slight was her hold upon religion.
But she did not talk about her frame of mind, nor
dignify the questions which began to come by calling them doubts ; how could they be doubts, when
she had never known what she had believed ? So,
by degrees, she built up a belief for herself.

Love of good was really love of God, in her mind.
Heaven meant righteousness, and hell an absence
from what was best and truest ; but Helen did not
feel that a soul must wait for death before it was
overtaken by hell. It was very simple and very
short, this creed of hers ; yet it was the doorway
through which grief and patience were to come, —
the sorrow of the world, the mystery of sin, and the
hope of that far-off divine event.

There was no detail of religious thought with Helen Jeffrey; ideas presented themselves to her mind with a comprehensiveness and simplicity which would have been impossible to Mr. Ward. But at this time he knew nothing of the mental processes that were leading her out of the calm, unreasoning content of childhood into a mist of doubt, which, as she looked into the future, seemed to darken into night. He was struggling with his conscience, and asking himself if he had any right to seek her love.

"Be not unequally yoked together with unbelievers," he said to himself. To his mind, Helen's lack of belief in certain doctrines — for it had hardly crystallized into unbelief — was sin ; and sin was punishable by eternal death. Here was his escape from conscience. Should this sweet soul, that he loved more than his own, be lost ? No ; surely, it was a sacred right and duty to win her heart and marry her, that he might take her away from the atmosphere of religious indifference in which she lived, and guide her to light and life.

Love won the day. "I will save her soul ! " he said to himself ; and with this purpose always before him to hide a shadow, which whispered, — so he thought, — " This is a sin," he asked her to be his wife.

He did not have to plead long. " I think I have always loved you," Helen said, looking up into his eyes ; and John was so happy that every thought of anxiety for her soul was swallowed up in gratitude to God for her love.

It was one midsummer afternoon that he reached

Ashurst; he went at once to the rectory, though
with no thought of asking Dr. Howe's permission to
address his niece.   It seemed to John as though
there were only their two souls in the great sunny
world that day, and his love-making was as simple
and candid as his life.

" I 've come to tell you I love you," he said, with
no preface, except to take her hands in his.

He did not see her often during their engagement,
nor did he write her of his fears and hopes for her ;
he would wait until she was quite away from
Ashurst carelessness, he thought; and beside, his
letters were so full of love, there was no room for
theology.   But he justified silence by saying when
they were in their own home he would show her the
beauty of revealed religion ; she should understand
the majesty of the truth; and their little house,
which was to be sacred as the shrine of human love,
should become the very gate of heaven.

It was a very little house, this parsonage.   Its
sharp pitch roof was pulled well down over its eyes,
which were four square, shining windows, divided
into twenty-four small panes of glass, so full of
bubbles and dimples that they made the passer-by
seem sadly distorted, and the spire of the church
opposite have a strange bend in it.

John Ward's study had not a great many books.
He could not afford them, for one reason ; but, with
a row of Edwards, and some of Dr. Samuel Hopkins'
sermons, and pamphlets by Dr. Emmons, he could
spare all but one or two volumes of Hodge and
Shedd, who, after all, but reiterate, in a form suited

to a weaker age, the teachings of Dr. Jonathan Edwards.

The dim Turkey carpet was worn down to the nap in a little path in front of his book-shelves, where he used to stand absorbed in reading, or where he walked back and forth, thinking out his dark and threatening sermons. For before his marriage John preached the law rather than the gospel.

"So I am going to hear you preach on Sunday?" Helen said, the Saturday morning after their return. "It's odd that I've never heard you, and we have known each other more than a year."

He was at his desk, and she rested her hand lightly on his shoulder. He put down his pen, and turned to look up into her face. "Perhaps you will not like my sermons;" there was a little wistfulness in his dark eyes as he spoke.

"Oh, yes, I shall," she said, with smiling certainty. "Sermons are pretty much alike, don't you think? I know some of uncle Archie's almost by heart. Really, there is only one thing to say, and you have to keep saying it over and over."

"We cannot say it too often," John answered. "The choice between eternal life and eternal death should sound in the ears of unconverted men every day of their lives."

Helen shook her head. "I didn't mean that, John. I was thinking of the beauty of holiness." And then she added, with a smile, "I hope you don't preach any awful doctrines?"

"Sometimes the truth is terrible, dear," he said gently.

But when she had left him to write his sermon, he sat a long while thinking. Surely she was not ready yet to hear such words as he had meant to speak. He would put this sermon away for some future Sunday, when the truth would be less of a shock to her. " She must come to the knowledge of God slowly, " he thought. " It must not burst upon her; it might only drive her further from the light to hear of justice as well as mercy. She is not able to bear it yet."

So he took some fresh paper, and wrote, instead of his lurid text from Hebrews, " Ye shall be my sons and daughters, saith the Lord Almighty."

But when Helen went out of the study, she thought very little of sermons or doctrines. John filled her mind, and she had no room for wondering about his beliefs ; he could believe anything he chose ; he was hers, — that was enough.

She went into her small kitchen, the smile still lingering upon her lips, and through its open doorway saw her little maid, Alfaretta, out in the sunny garden at the back of the house. She had an armful of fresh white tea-towels, which had been put out to dry on the row of gooseberry bushes at the end of the garden, and was coming up the path, singing cheerily, with all the force of her strong young lungs. Helen caught the words as she drew near : —

> " My thoughts on awful subjects roll,
>   Damnation and the dead.
>   What horrors seize the guilty soul,
>   Upon the dying bed !
>
> " Where endless crowds of sinners lie,
>   And darkness makes their chains,

Tortured with keen despair they cry,
　Yet wait for fiercer pains ! "

" Oh, Alfaretta ! " her mistress cried, in indignant astonishment. " How can you say such terrible words ! " Alfaretta stood still, in open-mouthed amazement, an injured look in her good - natured blue eyes. The incongruity of this rosy-faced, happy girl, standing in the sunshine, with all the scents and sounds of a July day about her, and singing in her cheerful voice these hopeless words, almost made Helen smile ; but she added gravely, " I hope you will not sing that again. I do not like it."

" But ma'am — but Mrs. Ward," said the girl, plainly hurt at the reproof, " I was practicing. I belong to the choir."

Alfaretta had dropped the tea-towels, hot with sunshine and smelling of clover-blossoms, upon her well-scoured dresser, and then turned and looked at her mistress reproachfully. " I don't know what I am going to do if I can't practice," she said.

" You don't mean to say you sing that in church ? " cried Helen. " Where do you go ? "

" Why, I go to your church," said the still injured Alfaretta, — " to Mr. Ward's. We 're to have that hymn on Sabbath " —

" Oh, there must be some mistake," remonstrated Helen. " I 'm sure Mr. Ward did not notice that verse."

" But it 's all like that ; it says " —

" Don't tell me any more," Helen said. " I 've heard enough. I had no idea such awful words were written." Then she stopped abruptly, feeling her position as the preacher's wife in a way of which she had never thought.

Alfaretta's father was an elder in John's church, which gave her a certain ease in speaking to her mistress that did not mean the slightest disrespect.

"Is it the words of it you don't like?" said Alfaretta, rather relieved, since her singing had not been criticised.

"Yes," Helen answered, "it is the words. Don't you see how dreadful they are?"

Alfaretta stood with her plump red hands on her hips, and regarded Mrs. Ward with interest. "I had n't ever thought of 'em," she said. "Yes, ma'am. I suppose they are awful bad," and swinging back and forth on her heels, her eyes fixed meditatively on the ceiling, she said, —

> "'Then swift and dreadful she descends
>   Down to the fiery coast,
>   Amongst abominable fiends'—

Yes, that does sound dreadful. Worst of it is, you get used to 'em, and don't notice 'em much. Why, I 've sung that hymn dozens of times in church, and never thought of the meanin'. And there 's Tom Davis : he drinks most of the time, but he has sung once or twice in the choir (though he ain't been ever converted yet, and he is really terrible wicked ; don't do nothin' but swear and drink). But I don't suppose he noticed the words of this hymn, — though I know he sung it, — for he keeps right on in his sin ; and he could n't, you know, Mrs. Ward, if that hymn was true to him."

Helen left Alfaretta to reflect upon the hymn, and

went back to the study; but the door was shut, and she heard the scratching of her husband's pen. She turned away, for she had lived in a minister's household, and had been brought up to know that nothing must disturb a man who was writing a sermon. But John had hurriedly opened the door.

" Did you want to speak to me, dearest ? " he said, standing at the foot of the stairs, his pen still between his fingers. " I heard your step."

" But I must not interrupt you," she answered, smiling at him over the balusters.

" You never could interrupt me. Come into the study and tell me what it is."

" Only to ask you about a hymn which Alfaretta says is to be sung on Sunday," Helen said. " Of course there is some mistake about it, but Alfaretta says the choir has been practicing it, and I know you would not want it."

" Do you remember what it was, dear ? "

" I can't quote it," Helen answered, " but it began something about ' damnation and the dead.' "

" Oh, yes, I know ; " and then he added, slowly, " Why don't you like it, Helen? "

She looked at him in astonishment. " Why, it 's absurd ; it 's horrible."

John was silent for a few moments, and then he sighed : " We will not sing it, dear."

" But, John," she cried, " how could such a hymn ever have been printed ? Of course I know people used to think such things, but I had no idea anybody thought of hell in that literal way to-day, or that hell itself was a real belief to very many people ;

however, I suppose, if such hymns are printed, the doctrine is still taught ? "

" Yes," John said, " it is as real to-day as God himself, — as it always has been and must be; and it is believed by Christians as earnestly as ever. We cannot help it, Helen."

Helen looked at him thoughtfully. " It is very terrible; but oh, John, what sublime faith, to be able to believe God capable of such awful cruelty, and yet to love and trust Him! "

John's face grew suddenly bright. " 'Though He slay me, yet will I trust Him,' " he said, with the simplicity of assurance. But when he went back again to his sermon, he was convinced that he had been wise to put off for a little while the instruction in doctrine of which his wife's soul stood in such sore need.

" I was right," he thought; " the Light must come gradually, the blaze of truth at once would blind her to the perfection of justice. She would not be able to understand there was mercy, too."

So the choir was told the hymn would be " Welcome, sweet day of rest," which, after all, was much better suited to the sermon.

CHAPTER V.

WHY the Misses Woodhouse, and Mr. Dale, and
Mr. Denner should go to the rectory for their Saturday night games of whist was never very clear to any
of them. The rector did not understand the game, he
said, and it was perhaps to learn that he watched
every play so closely. Lois, of course, had no part
in it, for Mrs. Dale was always ready to take a
hand, if one of the usual four failed. Mrs. Dale
was too impatient to play whist from choice, but
she enjoyed the consciousness of doing a favor.

Lois's only occupation was to be useful. Ashurst
was strangely behind the times in thinking that it
was a privilege, as it ought to be a pleasure, for
young people to wait upon their elders and betters.

True, Mr. Denner, with old-fashioned politeness,
always offered his services when Lois went for the
wine and cake at close of the rubber; but the little
gentleman would have been conscious of distinct surprise had she accepted them, for Lois, in his eyes,
was still a little girl. This was perhaps because Mr.
Denner, at sixty-two, did not realize that he had
ceased to be, as he would have expressed it, " a gentleman in middle life." He had no landmarks of
great emotions to show him how far the sleepy years
had carried him from his youth; and life in Ashurst
was very placid. There were no cases to try; prop-

erty rarely went out of families which had held it
when Mr. Denner's father wrote their wills and drew
up their deeds in the same brick office which his
son occupied now, and it was a point of decency and
honor that wills should not be disputed.

Yet Mr. Denner felt that his life was full of occupation. He had his practicing in the dim organ-
loft of St. Michael's and All Angels; and every day
when dinner was over, his little nephew slipped from
his chair, and stood with his hands behind him to
recite his *rego regere;* then there were always his
flies and rods to keep in order against the season
when he and the rector started on long fishing
tramps; and in the evenings, when Willie had gone
to bed, and his cook was reading "The Death Beds
of Eminent Saints" by the kitchen fire, Mr. Denner
worked out chess problems by himself in his library,
or read Cavendish and thought of next Saturday;
and besides all this, he went once a week to Mercer,
and sat waiting for clients in a dark back office,
while he studied his weekly paper.

But though there seemed plenty to do, sometimes
Mr. Denner would sigh, and say to himself that it
was somewhat lonely, and Mary was certainly severe.
He supposed that was because she had no mistress
to keep an eye on her.

These weekly games of whist were a great pleasure
to him. The library at the rectory was cheerful,
and there was a feeling of importance in playing a
game at which the rector and Mrs. Dale only looked
on. It was understood that the gentlemen might
smoke, though the formality of asking permission of

the ladies, and being urged by them, always took place. Mr. Denner's weekly remark to the Misses Woodhouse in this connection, as he stood ready to strike a match on the hearth of the big fireplace, was well known. " When ladies," he would say, bowing to each sister in turn, with his little heels close together and his toes turned well out, — " when ladies are so charitable to our vices, we will not reform, lest we lose the pleasure of being forgiven." Mr. Denner smoked a cigar, but Mr. Dale always drew from his pocket a quaint silver pipe, very long and slender, and with an odd suggestion of its owner about it; for he was tall and frail, and his thin white hair, combed back from his mild face, had a silvery gleam in the lamplight. Often the pipe would be between the pages of a book, from the leaves of which Lois would have to shake the loose ashes before putting it back in his pocket.

The whist party sat in high-backed chairs about a square mahogany table, whose shining top betokened much muscle on the part of Sally. At each corner was a candle in a tall silver candlestick, because Miss Deborah objected to a shadow on the board, which would have been cast by a hanging lamp. The August night was hot, and doors and windows were open for any breath of air that might be stirring in the dark garden. Max had retreated to the empty fireplace, finding the bricks cooler than the carpeted floor. All was very still, save when the emphatic sweep of a trump card made the candle flames flicker. But the deals were a diversion. Then the rector, who had tiptoed about, to look over the shoulder of each player, might say, "You did n't answer Miss Ruth's call, Denner;" or, "Bless my soul, Dale, what made you play a ten-spot on that second hand round? You ought not to send a boy to take a trick, sir!"

It was in one of these pauses that Mrs. Dale, drawing a shining knitting-needle out of her work, said, "I suppose you got my message this morning, brother, that Arabella Forsythe did n't feel well enough to come to-night? I told her she should have Henry's place, but she said she was n't equal to the excitement." Mrs. Dale gave a careful laugh; she did not wish to make Mrs. Forsythe absurd in the eyes of one person present.

"You offered her my place, my dear?" Mr. Dale asked, turning his blue eyes upon her. "I did n't know that, but it was quite right."

"Of course it was," replied Mrs. Dale decidedly, while the rector said, "Yes, young Forsythe said you sent him to say so."

Mrs. Dale glanced at Lois, sitting in one of the deep window-seats, reading, with the lamplight shining on her pretty face.

"I asked him to come," continued the rector, "but he said he must not leave his mother; she was not feeling well."

"Quite right, very proper," murmured the rest of the party; but Mrs. Dale added, "As there 's no conversation, I 'm afraid it would have been very stupid; I guess he knew that. And I certainly should not have allowed Henry to give up his seat to him." As she said this, she looked at Mr. Denner, who felt, under that clear, relentless eye, his would have been the seat vacated, if Dick Forsythe had come. Mr. Denner sighed; he had no one to protect him, as Dale had.

" I wonder," said Miss Deborah, who was sorting her cards, and putting all the trumps at the right side, "what decided Mr. Forsythe to spend the summer here? I understood that his mother took the house in Ashurst just because he was going to be abroad."

Mrs. Dale nodded her head until her glasses glistened, and looked at Lois, but the girl's eyes were fastened upon her book.

" I think," remarked Mr. Dale, hesitating, and then glancing at his wife, " he is rather a changeable young man. He has one view in the morning, and another in the afternoon."

" Don't be so foolish, Henry," said his wife sharply. " I hope there 's nothing wrong in the young man finding his own country more attractive than Europe? To change his mind in that way is very sensible." But this was in a hushed voice, for Mr. Denner had led, and the room was silent again.

At the next deal, Miss Deborah looked sympathetically at Mr. Dale. " I think he is changeable," she said; "his own mother told me that she was constantly afraid he 'd marry some unsuitable young woman, and the only safety was that he would see a new one before it became too serious. She said it really told upon her health. Dear me, I should think it might."

Mrs. Dale tossed her head, and her knitting-nee-
dles clicked viciously ; then she told Lois that this
was the rubber, and she had better see to the tray.
The young girl must have heard every word they
said, though she had not lifted her bright eyes from
her book, but she did not seem disturbed by the
charge of fickleness on the part of Mr. Forsythe.
He had not confided to her his reasons for not
going abroad ; all she knew was that the summer
was the merriest one she had ever spent. " I feel
so young," little Lois said ; and indeed she had
caught a certain careless gayety from her almost
daily companion, which did not belong to Ashurst.
But she gave no thought to his reason for staying,
though her father and Mrs. Dale did, and with
great satisfaction.

" What do you hear from Helen, brother ? " Mrs.
Dale asked, as Lois rose to do her bidding. Mrs.
Dale was determined to leave the subject of Dick
Forsythe, " for Henry has so little sense," she
thought, " there is no knowing what he 'll say next,
or Deborah Woodhouse either. But then, one could
n't expect anything else of her."

" Ah, — she 's all right," said Dr. Howe, frowning at Miss Ruth's hand, and then glancing at Mr.
Dale's, and thrusting out his lower lip, while his
bushy eyebrows gathered in a frown.

" What is Ward ? " asked Mr. Dale, sorting his
cards. " Old or new school ? "

" I 'm sure I don't know the difference," said Dr.
Howe ; " he 's a blue Presbyterian, though, through
and through. He did n't have much to say for him-

self, but what he did say made me believe he was consistent ; he does n't stop short where his creed ceases to be agreeable, and you know that is unusual."

" Well," remarked the older man, " he might be consistent and belong to either school. I am told the difference consists merely in the fact that the old school have cold roast beef on the Sabbath, and the new school have hot roast beef on Sunday. But doubtless both unite on hell for other sects."

The rector's quick laugh was silenced by the game, but at the next pause he hastened to tell them what John Ward had said of slavery. " Fancy such a speech ! " he cried, his face growing red at the remembrance. " Under the circumstances, I could n't tell him what I thought of him ; but I had my opinion. I wonder," he went on, rattling a bunch of keys in his pocket, " what would be the attitude of a mind like his in politics ? Conservative to the most ridiculous degree, I imagine. Of course, to a certain extent, it is proper to be conservative. I am conservative myself ; I don't like to see the younger generation rushing into things because they are new, like Gifford, — calling himself a Democrat. I beg your pardon, Miss Deborah, for finding fault with the boy."

" Ah, doctor, ladies don't understand politics," answered Miss Deborah politely.

" But really," said the rector, " for a boy whose father died for the Union, it 's absurd, you know, perfectly absurd. But Ward ! one can't imagine that he would ever change in anything, and that sort of conservatism can be carried too far."

" Well, now," said Mr. Denner, "I should say, I should be inclined to think, it would be just the opposite, quite — quite the contrary. From what you say, doctor, it seems to me more likely that he might be an anarchist, as it were. Yes, not at all a conservative."

" How so ? " asked the rector. " A man who would say such a thing as that the Bible, his interpretation of it, was to decide all questions of duty (a pretty dangerous thing that, for a man must have inclinations of his own, which would be sure to color his interpretation ! What?), and who would bring all his actions down to its literal teachings without regard to more modern needs ? No, Denner ; you are wrong there."

" Not altogether," Mr. Dale demurred in his gentle voice. " Ward would believe in a party only so long as it agreed with his conscience, I should suppose, and his conscience might make him — anything. And certainly the Bible test would not leave him content with democracy, doctor. Communism is literal Christianity. I can fancy he would leave any party, if he thought its teachings were not supported by the Bible. But I scarcely know him ; my opinion is very superficial."

" Why do you express it, then ? " said Mrs. Dale. "Don't you see Deborah has led? You are keeping the whole table waiting ! "

They began to play. Mr. Denner, who was facing the open door, could see the square hall, and the white stair-rail across the first landing, where, with the moon and stars about its face, the clock

stood; it was just five minutes to nine. This made
the lawyer nervous; he played a low trump, in spite
of the rector's mutter of, "Look out, Denner!"
and thus lost the trick, which meant the rubber, so
he threw down his cards in despair. He had scarcely
finished explaining that he meant to play the king,
but threw the knave by mistake, when Lois entered,
followed by Sally with the big tray, which always
carried exactly the same things: a little fat decanter, with a silver collar jingling about its neck,
marked, Sherry, '39; a plate of ratifia cakes, and
another of plum-cake for the rector's especial delec-
tation; and a silver wire basket full of home-made
candy for Mr. Dale, who had two weaknesses, candy
and novels. Of late Mrs. Dale had ceased to in-
veigh against these tastes, feeling that it was hopeless to look for reformation in a man nearly seventy
years old. "It is bad manners," she said, "to do
foolish things if they make you conspicuous. But
then! it is easier to change a man's creed than his
manners."

The candles stood in a gleaming row on the mantelpiece, where Lois had placed them to make room for
the tray on the whist-table; for it was useless to think
of putting anything on the rector's writing-table, with
its litter of church papers, and sporting journals,
and numbers of Bell's "Life," besides unanswered
letters. The ladies, still sitting in the high-backed
chairs, spread white doilies over their laps, and then
took their small glasses of wine and delicate little
cakes, but the gentlemen ate and drank standing, and they all discussed the last game very ear-

nestly. Only Lois, waiting by the tray, ready to
hand the cake, was silent. It was a peculiarity of
Ashurst that even after childhood had passed young
people were still expected to be seen, and not heard;
so her silence would only have been thought decorous, had any one noticed it. By and by, when she
saw she was not needed, she slipped out to the front
porch, and sat down on the steps. Max followed
her, and thrust his cold nose under her hand.

She propped her chin upon her little fist, and
began to think of what had been said of Ashurst's
visitors. With a thrill of subtile satisfaction, she
remembered how pleased Mrs. Forsythe always was
to see her. " She won't have any anxiety this summer which will injure her health!" And then she
tried to disguise her thought by saying to herself
that there were no girls in Ashurst who were not
" suitable."

" Good-evening," some one said gayly. It was
Mr. Forsythe, who had come so quietly along the
path, dark with its arching laburnums and syringas,
she had not heard him.

" Oh," she said, with a little start of surprise,
" I did not know we were to see you to-night. Is
your mother " —

" I 'm like the man in the Bible," he interrupted,
laughing. " He said he would n't, then he did!"
He had followed her to the library, and stood,
smiling, with a hand on each side of the doorway.
" I started for a walk, doctor, and somehow I found
myself here. No cake, thank you, — yes, I guess
I 'll have some sherry. Oh, the whist is over?

Who is to be congratulated, Mrs. Dale? For my part, I never could understand the fascination of the game. Euchre is heavy enough for me. May I have some of Mr. Dale's candy, Miss Lois?"

Except Mrs. Dale, the little party of older people seemed stunned by the quick way in which he talked. His airy manner and flimsy wit impressed them with a sense of his knowledge of life. He represented the world to them, the World with a capital W, and they were all more or less conscious of a certain awe in his presence. His utter disregard of the little observances and forms which were expected from Ashurst young people gave them a series of shocks, that were rather pleasant than otherwise.

Mr. Dale looked confused, and handed him the candy with such nervous haste, some of it fell to the floor, which gave the young man a chance for his frequent light laugh. Miss Deborah began in an agitated way to pick up the crumbs of cake from her lap, and ask her sister if she did not think Sarah had come for them. Mr. Denner stopped talking about a new sort of fly for trout, and said he thought — yes, he really thought, he had better be going, but he waited to listen with open-mouthed admiration to the ease with which the young fellow talked.

Mr. Forsythe's conversation was directed to Mrs. Dale, but it was for Lois; nor did he seem aware of the silence which fell on the rest of the company. Mrs. Dale enjoyed it. She answered by nods, and small chuckles of approval, and frequent glances about at the others, as much as to say, " Do you

hear that? Is n't that bright?" and a certain air
of proprietorship, which meant that she thoroughly
approved of Mr. Forsythe, and regarded him as her
own discovery.

"This is the time we miss Gifford," said Miss
Deborah, who had gone out into the hall to put on
her overshoes. "He was such a useful child." Lois
came to help her, for Mr. Denner was far too timid
to offer assistance, and the rector too stout, and
Mr. Dale too absent-minded. As for Mr. Forsythe,
he did not notice how Miss Deborah was occupied,
until Lois had joined her; and then his offer was not
accepted, for Miss Deborah felt shy about putting
out her foot in its black kid slipper, tied about the
ankle with a black ribbon, in the presence of this
young man, who was, she was sure, very genteel.

Mr. Forsythe's call was necessarily a short one,
for, charming as he was, Ashurst custom would not
have permitted him to stay when the party had
broken up. However, he meant to walk along with
the Dales, and hear her aunt talk about Lois.

The Misses Woodhouse's maid was waiting for
them, her lantern swinging in her hand. Mr. Denner had secretly hoped for a chance of " seeing them
home," but dared not offer his unnecessary services
in Sarah's presence.

Dr. Howe and his daughter went as far as the
gate with their guests, and then stood watching
them down the lane, until a turn in the road hid the
glimmer of the lantern and the dark figures beside it.

" Bless my soul!" said the rector, as they turned

to go back to the house. " This gayety has made
me almost forget my sermon. I must not put it off
so, next week."

This remark of Dr. Howe's was almost as regular
as the whist party itself.

Miss Deborah and Miss Ruth trotted behind
Sarah, whose determined stride kept them a little
ahead of the others ; Dick Forsythe had joined Mrs.
Dale at once, so Mr. Dale and Mr. Denner walked
together. They were only far enough behind to
have the zest one feels in talking about his neighbors when there is danger of being overheard.

" He is a very fine conversationalist," said Mr.
Denner, nodding his head in Dick's direction; " he
talks very well."

" He talks a great deal," observed Mr. Dale.

" He seems to feel," Mr. Denner continued, " no
— ah, if I can so express it — timidity."

" None," responded Mr. Dale.

" And I judge he has seen a great deal of the
world," said Mr. Denner; " yet he appears to be satisfied with Ashurst, and I have sometimes thought,
Henry, that Ashurst is not, as it were, gay." As he
said this, a certain jauntiness came into his step, as
though he did not include himself among those who
were not " gay." " Yet he seems to be content.
I 've known him come down to the church when Lois
was singing, and sit a whole hour, apparently meditating. He is no doubt a very thoughtful young
man."

" Bah ! " answered Mr. Dale, " he comes to hear
Lois sing."

Mr. Denner gave a little start. " Oh," he said —
" ah — I had not thought of that." But when he
left Mr. Dale, and slipped into the shadows of the
Lombardy poplars on either side of his white gate-
posts, Mr. Denner thought much of it, — more with
a sort of envy of Mr. Forsythe's future than of
Lois. " He will marry, some time (perhaps little
Lois), and then he will have a comfortable home."

Mr. Denner sat down on the steps outside of his
big white front door, which had a brass knocker and
knob that Mary had polished until the paint had
worn away around them. Mr. Denner's house was
of rough brick, laid with great waste of mortar, so
that it looked as though covered with many small
white seams. Some ivy grew about the western
windows of the library, but on the north and east
sides it had stretched across the closed white shutters, for these rooms had scarcely been entered since
little Willie Denner's mother died, five years ago.
She had kept house for her brother-in-law, and had
brought some brightness into his life; but since her
death, his one servant had had matters in her own
hands, and the house grew more lonely and cheerless
each year. Mr. Denner's office was in his garden,
and was of brick, like his house, but nearer the
road, and without the softening touch of ivy; it was
damp and mildewed, and one felt instinctively that
the ancient law books must have a film of mould
on their battered covers.

The lawyer's little face had a pinched, wistful
look; the curls of his brown wig were hidden by a
tall beaver hat, with the old bell crown and straight

brim; it was rarely smooth, except on Sundays, when
Mary brushed it before he went to church. He took
it off now, and passed his hand thoughtfully over
his high, mild forehead, and sighed; then he looked
through one of the narrow windows on either side of
the front door, where the leaded glass was cut into
crescents and circles, and fastened with small brass
rosettes; he could see the lamp Mary had left for
him, burning dimly on the hall table, under a dark
portrait of some Denner, long since dead. But he
still sat upon what he called his " doorstones; " the
August starlight, and the Lombardy poplars stirring
in the soft wind, and the cricket chirping in the
grass, offered more companionship, he thought, than
he would find in his dark, silent library.

The little gentleman's mind wandered off to the
different homes he knew; they were so pleasant and
cheerful. There was always something bright about
the rectory, and how small and cosy Henry Dale's
study was. And how pretty the Woodhouse girls'
parlor looked! Mr. Denner was as slow to recognize the fact that Miss Deborah and Miss Ruth were
no longer young as they were themselves. Just now
he thought only of the home-life in their old house,
and the comfort, and the peace. What quiet, pleasant voices the sisters had, and how well Miss Deborah managed, and how delightfully Miss Ruth
painted! How different his own life would have
been if Gertrude Drayton — Ah, well! The little
gentleman sighed again, and then, drawing his big
key from his pocket, let himself into the silent hall,
and crept quietly up-stairs.

CHAPTER VI.

It did not take Gifford Woodhouse very long to get settled in Lockhaven. His office and bedroom constituted his household, and Miss Deborah never knew that her bags of lavender were not even taken out of the trunk, and that the hard-featured Irishwoman who "came in by the day" never saw the paper of directions, written, that she might be able to read it easily, in Miss Deborah's small, neat hand.

But Miss Deborah was right in thinking Helen would look after his comfort, and Gifford soon felt that his real "home" in Lockhaven was at the parsonage, though he had not time to drop in half as often as the master and mistress urged him to do.

He did not tell Helen of that talk with Lois, which had brought a soberer look to his face than she had ever seen there. But she had noticed it, and wondered at it, and she felt his reserve, too, in speaking of her cousin; she even asked herself if he could have cared for Lois? But the thought was too absurd. "Probably they 've quarreled again," she said regretfully; she never had been able to understand her cousin's impatience with him.

Perhaps Gifford thought that she had an intuitive knowledge of the ache there was in his heart when she talked of Lois, for he was comforted in a vague way by the sympathetic look which was always on Helen's face when she spoke to any one who seemed troubled. So he was glad to come to the parsonage as often as he could, and hear the Ashurst news, and have a cup of tea with the preacher and his wife.

John and Helen often walked home with him, though his rooms were quite at the other end of the town, near the river and the mills; and one night, as they stood on the shaking bridge, and looked down at the brown water rushing and plunging against the rotten wooden piers, Helen began to ask him about Mr. Forsythe.

"Tell me about him," she said. "You have seen him since he left college. I only just remember him in Ashurst, though I recall Mrs. Forsythe perfectly: a tall, sick-looking lady, with an amiably melancholy face, and three puffs of hair on each side of it."

"Except that the puffs are white now, she is just the same," Gifford answered. "As for her son, I don't know anything about him. I believe we were not very good friends when we were boys, but now — well, he has the manners of a gentleman."

"Does n't that go without saying?" said Helen, laughing. "From the letters I 've had, I fancy he is a good deal at the rectory."

"Yes," Gifford admitted. "But he is one of those people who make you feel that though they may have good manners, their grandfathers did not, don't you know?"

"But what difference does that make," John asked, "if he is a good man?"

"Oh, of course, no difference," Gifford replied with an impatient laugh.

"But what is the attraction in Ashurst, Giff?" Helen said. "How can he stay there all summer? I should not think he could leave his business."

"Oh, he is rich."

"Why, you don't like him!" said Helen, surprised at his tone.

"I don't know anything about the fellow," the young man answered. "I have n't seen enough of him to have an opinion one way or the other. Judging from aunt Ruth's letters, though, I should say Lois liked him, so I don't think he will be anxious for my approval, or anybody else's."

Helen looked at him with sudden questioning in her eyes, but they had reached his house, and John began to speak to him of his plans and of Lockhaven.

"I 'm afraid you will have only too much to do," he said. "There is a great deal of quarreling among the mill-owners, and constant disagreements between the hands."

"Well," Gifford answered, smiling, and straightening his broad shoulders, "if there is work to do, I am glad I am here to do it. But I 'm not hopeless for the life it indicates, when you say there 's much to be done. The struggle for personal rights and advantages is really, you know, the desire for the best, and a factor in civilization. A generation or two hence, the children of these pushing, aggressive fathers will be fine men."

John shook his head sadly.   " Ah, but the present evil ? "

But Gifford answered cheerfully, " Oh, well, the present evil is one stage of development; to live up to the best one knows is morality, and the preservation of self is the best some of these people know; we can only wait hopefully for the future."

" Morality is not enough," John said gently. " Morality never saved a soul, Mr. Woodhouse."

But Helen laughed gayly : " John, dear, Gifford does n't understand your awful Presbyterian doctrines, and there is no use trying to convert him."

Gifford smiled, and owned good-naturedly that he was a heathen. " But I think," he said, " the thing which keeps the town back most is liquor."

" It is, indeed," John answered, eagerly. " If it could be banished ! "

" High license is the only practical remedy," said Gifford, his face full of interest; but John's fell.

" No, no, not that; no compromise with sin will help us.   I would have it impossible to find a drop of liquor in Lockhaven."

" What would you do in case of sickness ? " Gifford asked curiously.

" I would n't have it used."

" Oh, John, dear," Helen protested, " don't you think that 's rather extreme ?   You know it 's life or death sometimes : a stimulant has to be used, or a person would die.   Suppose I had to have it ? "

His face flushed painfully.   " Death is better than sin," he said slowly and gently; " and you, if you — I don't know, Helen; no one knows his weakness until temptation comes." His tone was so full of trouble, Gifford, feeling the sudden tenderness of his own strength, said good-naturedly, " What do you think of us poor fellows who confess to a glass of claret at dinner ? "

" And what must he have thought of the dinner-table at the rectory ? " Helen added.

" I don't think I noticed it," John said simply. " You were there."

" There, Helen, that 's enough to make you sign the pledge ! " said Gifford.

He watched them walking down the street, under the arching ailantus, their footsteps muffled by the carpet of the fallen blossoms; and there was a thoughtful look on his face when he went into his office, and, lighting his lamp, sat down to look over some papers. " How is that going to come out ? " he said to himself. " Neither of those people will amend an opinion, and Ward is not the man to be satisfied if his wife holds a belief he thinks wrong." But researches into the case of McHenry *v.* Coggswell put things so impractical as religious beliefs out of his mind.

As for John and Helen, they walked toward the parsonage, and Gifford, and his future, and his views of high license were forgotten, as well as the sudden pain with which John had heard his wife's careless words about his " awful doctrines."

" It is very pleasant to see him so often," John said, " but how good it is to have you all to myself ! "

Helen gave him a swift, glad look; then their talk drifted into those sweet remembrances which happy husbands and wives know by heart: what he thought when he first saw her, how she wondered if he would speak to her. "And oh, Helen," he said, "I recollect the dress you wore, — how soft and silky it was, but it never rustled, or gleamed; it rested my eyes just to look at it."

A little figure was coming towards them down the deserted street, with a jug clasped in two small grimy hands.

"Preacher!" cried a childish voice eagerly, "good-evenin', preacher."

John stopped and bent down to see who it was, for a tangle of yellow hair almost hid the little face.

"Why, it is Molly," he said, in his pleasant voice. "Where have you been, my child? Oh, yes, I see, — for dad's beer?"

Molly was smiling at him, proud to be noticed. "Yes, preacher," she answered, wagging her head. "Good-night, preacher." But they had gone only a few steps when there was a wail. Turning her head to watch him out of sight, Molly had tripped, and now all that was left of the beer was a yellow scum of froth on the dry ground. The jug was unbroken, but the child could find no comfort in that.

"I 've spilt dad's beer," she said, sobbing, and sinking down in a forlorn heap on the ground.

John knelt beside her, and tried to comfort her. "Never mind; we 'll go and tell dad it was an accident."

But Molly only shook her head. "No," she said, catching her breath, as she tried to speak, " 't won't do no good. He 'll beat me. He 's getting over a drunk, so he wanted his beer, and he 'll lick me."

John looked down sadly at the child for a moment. " I will take you home, Helen, and then I will go back with Molly."

"Oh," Helen answered quickly, " let me go with you ? "

" No," John replied, " no, dear. You heard what Molly said ?   I — I cannot bear that your eyes should see — what must be seen in Tom Davis's house to-night. We will go to the parsonage now, and then Molly and I will tell dad about the beer." He lifted the child gently in his arms, and stooped again for the pitcher. " Come, Helen," he said, and they went towards the parsonage. Helen entered reluctantly, but without a protest, and then stood watching them down the street. The little yellow head had fallen on John's shoulder, and Molly was almost asleep.

Tom Davis's house was one of a row near the river. They had been built on piles, so as to be out of the way of the spring " rise," but the jar and shock of the great cakes of ice floating under them when the river opened up had given them an unsteady look, and they leaned and stumbled so that the stained plastering had broken on the walls, and there were large cracks by the window frames. The broken steps of Molly's home led up to a partly open door. One panel had been crushed in in a fight, and the knob was gone, and the door-posts were dirty and greasy. The narrow windows were without shutters, and only a dingy green paper shade hid the room within.

Molly opened her sleepy eyes long enough to say, " Don't let dad lick me ! "

"No, little Molly," John said, as he went into the small entry, and knocked at the inner door. " Don't be afraid."

" Come in," a woman's voice answered.

Mrs. Davis was sitting by the fireless stove, on which she had placed her small lamp, and she was trying by its feeble light to do some mending. Her face had that indifference to its own hopelessness which forbids all hope for it. She looked up as they entered.

" Oh, it 's the preacher," she said, with a flickering smile about her fretful lips ; and she rose, brushing some lifeless strands of hair behind her ears, and pulling down her sleeves, which were rolled above her thin elbows.

" Molly has had an accident, Mrs. Davis," John explained, putting the child gently down, and steadying her on her uncertain little feet, until her eyes were fairly opened. " So I came home with her to say how it happened."

"She spilt the beer, I reckon," said Mrs. Davis, glancing at the empty jug John had put on the table. " Well, 't ain't no great loss. He 's asleep, and won't know nothing about it. He 'll have forgot he sent her by mornin'." She jerked her head towards one side of the room, where her husband was lying upon the floor. " Go get the preacher a

chair, Molly. Not that one; it 's got a leg broke.
Oh, you need n't speak low," she added, as John
thanked the child softly ; " he won't hear nothing before to-morrow."

The lumberman lay in the sodden sleep with
which he ended a spree. He had rolled up his coat
for a pillow, and had thrown one arm across his
purple, bloated face. Only the weak, helpless, open
mouth could be seen. His muscular hands were
relaxed, and the whole prostrate figure was pathetic
in its unconsciousness of will and grotesque un-
humanness. Fate had been too strong for Tom
Davis. His birth and all the circumstances of his
useless life had brought him with resistless certainty
to this level, and his progress in the future could
only be an ever-hastening plunge downward.

But the preacher did not consider fate when he
turned and looked at the drunken man. A stern
look crept over the face which had smiled at Molly
but a moment before.

" This is the third time," he said, " that this has
happened since Tom came and told me he would try
to keep sober. I had hoped the Spirit of God had
touched him."

" I know," the woman answered, turning the coat
she was mending, and moving the lamp a little to
get a better light ; " and it 's awful hard on me, so
it is ; that 's where all our money goes. I can't get
shoes for the children's feet, let alone a decent rag to
put on my back to wear of a Sabbath, and come
to church. It 's hard on me, now, I tell you, Mr.
Ward."

" It is harder on him," John replied. " Think of his immortal soul. Oh, Mrs. Davis, do you point out to him the future he is preparing for himself ? "

" Yes," she said, " I 'm tellin' him he 'll go to hell all the time ; but it don't do no good. Tom 's afraid of hell, though ; it 's the only thing as ever did keep him straight. After one o' them sermons of yours, I 've known him swear off as long as two months. I ain't been to church this long time, till last Sabbath ; and I was hopin' I 'd hear one of that kind, all about hell, Mr. Ward, so I could tell Tom, but you did n't preach that way. Not but what it was good, though," she added, with an evident wish to be polite.

John's face suddenly flushed. " I — I know I did not, but the love of God must constrain us, Mrs. Davis, as well as the fear of hell."

Mrs. Davis sighed. Tom's spiritual condition, which had roused a momentary interest, was forgotten in the thought of her own misery. " Well, it 's awful hard on me," she repeated with a little tremor in her weak chin.

John looked at her with infinite pity in his eyes. " Yes," he said, " hard on you, because of the eternal suffering which may come to your husband. Nothing can be more frightful than to think of such a thing for one we love. Let us try to save him ; pray always, pray without ceasing for his immortal soul, that he may not slight the day of salvation, and repent when it is too late to find the mercy of God. Oh, the horror of knowing that the day of grace has gone forever ! ' For my spirit shall not always strive with man.' "

He went over to the drunken man, and, kneeling down beside him, took one of the helpless hands in his. Mrs. Davis put down her sewing, and watched him.

Perhaps the preacher prayed, as he knelt there, though she could not hear him; but when he rose and said good-night, she could see his sad eyes full of trouble which she could not understand, a pity beyond her comprehension.

Molly came sidling up to her protector, as he stood a moment in the doorway, and, taking his hand in hers, stroked it softly.

" I love you, preacher," she said, " 'cause you 're good."

John's face brightened with a sudden smile ; the love of little children was a great joy to him, and the touch of these small hands gave him the indefinable comfort of hope. God, who had made the sweetness of childhood, would be merciful to his own children. He would give them time, He would not withdraw the day of grace ; surely Tom Davis's soul would yet be saved. There was a subtle thought below this of hope that for Helen, too, the day of grace might be prolonged, but he did not realize this himself; he did not know that he feared for one moment that she might not soon accept the truth. He was confident, he thought, of her, and yet more confident of the constraining power of the truth itself.

He looked down at Molly, and put his hand

gently on her yellow head. " Be a good girl, my little Molly ; " then, with a quiet blessing upon the dreary home, he turned away.

But what Mrs. Davis had said of going to church to hear a sermon on hell, and her evident disappointment, did not leave his mind. He walked slowly towards the parsonage, his head bent and his hands clasped behind him, and a questioning anxiety in his face. " I will use every chance to speak of the certain punishment of the wicked when I visit my people," he said, " but not in the pulpit. Not where Helen would hear it — yet. In her frame of mind, treating the whole question somewhat lightly, not realizing its awful importance, it would be productive of no good. I will try, little by little, to show her what to believe, and turn her thoughts to truth. For the present that is enough, that is wisest." And then his heart went back to her, and how happy they were. He stopped a moment, looking up at the stars, and saying, with a breathless awe in his voice, " My God, how good Thou art, how happy I am ! "

CHAPTER VII.

THE little stir which the arrival of the Forsythes
made in Ashurst was delightful.

"Of course," as Mrs. Dale said, "Arabella Forsythe had not been born there, and could not be expected to be just like Ashurst people; but it was
something to have a new person to talk to, even if
you had to talk about medicines most of the time."

Lois Howe enjoyed it, for there were very few
young people in Ashurst that summer; the two
Drayton girls had gone away to visit a married
brother, and there were no young men now Gifford
had gone. So it was pleasant to have a person of
her own age to talk to, and sometimes to walk with,
though the rector never felt quite sure what his sister would say to that. However, Mrs. Dale had
nothing to say; she shut her eyes to any impropriety, and even remarked severely to Miss Deborah
Woodhouse that those old-fashioned ideas of a girl's
being always under her mother's eye, were prim and
old maidish; "and beside, Lois's mother is dead,"
she added, with a sort of triumph in her voice.

As for Lois, she almost forgot that she had
thought Ashurst lonely when Helen had gone, and
Gifford; for of course, in so small a place, every one
counted. She had wondered, sometimes, before the
Forsythes came, with a self-consciousness which was

a new experience, if any one thought she missed Gifford. But her anxiety was groundless, — Ashurst imagination never rose to any such height; and certainly, if the letters the young man wrote to her could have been seen, such a thought would not have been suggested. They were pleasant and friendly; very short, and not very frequent; mostly of Helen and what she did; there was almost nothing of himself, and the past, at least as far as a certain night in June was concerned, was never mentioned. At first this was a relief to Lois, but by and by came a feeling too negative to be called pique, or even mortification at having been forgotten; it was rather an intangible soreness in her memory of him.

" It is just as Miss Deborah says," she said to herself : " young men always forget those things. And it is better that they do. Gifford never thinks of what he said to me, and I 'm sure I 'm glad he does n't — but still ! " And then that absurd suggestion of Miss Deborah's about Helen would creep into her mind ; she might banish it, because it was silly and impossible, yet she did not utterly forget it. However, she really thought very little about it ; the presence of Mrs. Forsythe and her son gave her plenty of occupation. There was the round of teas and dinners which Ashurst felt it incumbent to give to a new arrival, and Lois was to have two new gowns in consequence of so much gayety.

She spent a good deal of time with Mrs. Forsythe, for the elder lady needed her, she said. It was not altogether the companionship which fascinated Lois : the sunny drawing-room of the house the Forsythes had hired was filled with dainty things, and light, graceful furniture, and many harmlessly silly novels; there was a general air about it of belonging to a life she had never seen which made it a pleasure to come into it. The parlors in Ashurst had such heavy, serious chairs and tables, she said to herself, and the pictures were all so dark and ugly, and she was so tired of the carpets.

So she was very glad when Mrs. Forsythe begged her to come and read aloud, or fix her flowers, or even stroke her soft white hair when she had a headache. "Dick may be at home, my dear," Mrs. Forsythe would say in her deprecating voice, "but you won't mind him?" And soon Lois did not mind him at all.

At first she was very shy in the presence of this light-hearted young fellow, whose indifference to Ashurst opinion was very impressive; but by and by that wore off, and Mrs. Forsythe's drawing-room echoed with their young laughter. Lois began to feel with Dick the freedom and friendliness which had once been only for Gifford. "Why couldn't Giff have been like this?" she thought; yet she did not say that she and Mr. Forsythe were like "brother and sister," for she was always conscious of a possibility in their friendship; but it was enough that Mr. Forsythe was very interesting, and that that summer, life was very delightful.

After all, love is frequently a matter of propinquity.

Dick found himself going often to the rectory, and Lois fell into the habit of making her plans

with the reservation, " In case Mr. Forsythe calls ; "
and it generally happened that he did call. " Mother
sends her love, and will Miss Lois come and read
to her a little while this afternoon, if she is not too
busy ? " or, " Mother returns this dish, and begs
me to thank you for the jelly, and to tell Jean how
good it was."

It was easy for Dick to manufacture errands like
these. Dr. Howe began to think young Forsythe
spent the greater part of his time at the rectory.
But this did not trouble him at all ; in fact it was a
satisfaction that this lively young man liked the rectory so much. Dr. Howe did not go very far into the
future in his thoughts ; he was distinctly flattered in
the present. Of course, if anything came of it (for
the rector was not entirely unworldly), why, it would
be all for the best. So he was quite patient if Lois
was not on hand to hunt up a book for him or to
fetch his slippers, and he fell into the habit of spending much time in Mr. Denner's office, looking over
the " Field " and talking of their next hunting trip.
He was not even irritated when, one morning,
wishing to read a letter to his daughter, he had gone
all over the house looking for her, and then had
caught a glimpse of her through the trees, down in
the sunny garden, with Dick Forsythe. " I 'll just
let that letter wait," he said, and went and stretched
himself comfortably on the slippery, leather-covered
sofa in the shaded library, with a paper in his hand
and a satisfied smile on his lips.

The garden was ablaze with color, and full of all
sorts of delicious scents and sounds. The gay old-

fashioned flowers poured a flood of blossoms through all the borders : hollyhocks stood like rockets against the sky; sweet-peas and scarlet runners scrambled over the box hedges and about the rose-bushes ; mallows and sweet-williams, asters and zinias and phlox, crowded close together with a riotous richness of tint; scarlet and yellow nasturtiums streamed over the ground like molten sunshine ; and, sparkling and glinting through the air, butterflies chased up and down like blossoms that had escaped from their stems.

Lois had come out to pick some flowers for the numerous vases and bowls which it was her delight to keep filled all summer long. She was bareheaded, and the wind had rumpled the curls around her forehead ; the front of her light blue dress — she wore light blue in a manner which might have been called daring had it implied the slightest thought — was caught up to hold her lapful of flowers ; a sheaf of roses rested on her shoulder, and some feathery vines trailed almost to the ground, while in her left hand, their stems taller than her own head, were two stately sunflowers, which were to brighten the hall.

Mr. Forsythe caught sight of her as he closed the gate, and hurried down the path to help her carry her fragrant load. He had, as usual, a message to deliver. " Mother sends her love, Miss Lois, and says she is n't well enough to go and drive this afternoon ; but she 'll be glad to go to-morrow, if you 'll take her ? "

" Oh, yes, indeed ! " Lois cried, in her impetuous voice. " But I 'm sorry she 's ill to-day."

Dick gave the slightest possible shrug of his square shoulders. " Oh, I guess she 's all right," he said. " It amuses her. But won't you give me some flowers to take home to her ? "

Of course Lois was delighted to do it, but Dick insisted that she should first put those she had already gathered in water, and then get some fresh ones for his mother. " You see I 'm very particular that she should have the best ; " then they both laughed. Now mutual laughter at small jokes brings about a very friendly feeling.

They went up to the side porch, where it was shady, and Lois and Sally brought out all the vases and dishes which could be made to hold flowers, and put them in a row on the top step. Then Dick brought a big pitcher of fresh, cold water from the spring, and Lois went for the garden scissors to clip off the long stems ; and at last they were ready to go to work, the sweet confusion of flowers on the steps between them, and Max sitting gravely at Lois's elbow as chaperon.

The rector heard their voices and the frequent shouts of laughter, and began to think he must bestir himself ; Mr. Forsythe should see that Ashurst young women were under the constant oversight of their parents ; but he yawned once or twice, and thought how comfortable the cool leather of the lounge was, and had another little doze before he went out to the porch with the open letter in his hand.

Dick had his hat full of white, and pink, and winecolored hollyhocks, which he had stripped from their stems, and was about to put in a shallow dish, so he did not rise, but said " Hello ! " in answer to the rector's " Good-morning," and smiled brightly up at him. It was the charm of this smile which made the older people in Ashurst forget that he treated them with very little reverence.

" Lois," her father said, " I have a letter from Helen ; do you want to send any message when I answer it ? Mr. Forsythe will excuse you if you read it."

" Why, of course," Dick replied. " I feel almost as though I knew Mrs. Ward, Miss Lois has talked so much about her."

" How funny to hear her called ' Mrs. Ward ! ' " Lois said, taking the letter from her father's hand.

" I should think she 'd hate Lockhaven," Dick went on. " I was there once for a day or two. It is a poor little place ; lots of poverty among the hands. And it is awfully unpleasant to see that sort of thing. I 've heard fellows say they enjoyed a good dinner more if they saw some poor beggar going without. Now, I don't feel that way. I don't like to see such things ; they distress me, and I don't forget them."

Lois, reading Helen's letter, which was full of grief for the helpless trouble she saw in Lockhaven, thought that Mr. Forsythe had a very tender heart. Helen was questioning the meaning of the suffering about her ; already the problem as old as life itself confronted her, and she asked, Why ?

Dr. Howe had noticed this tendency in some of her later letters, and scarcely knew whether to be

annoyed or amused by it. " Now what in the
world," he said, as Lois handed back the letter, —
" what in the world does the child mean by asking
me if I don't think — stay, where is that sentence ? "
The rector fumbled for his glasses, and, with his
lower lip thrust out, and his gray eyebrows gathered
into a frown, glanced up and down the pages. "Ah,
yes, here : ' Do you not think,' she says, ' that the
presence in the world, of suffering which cannot pro-
duce character, irresponsible suffering, so to speak,
makes it hard to believe in the personal care of
God ? ' It 's perfect nonsense for Helen to talk in
that way ! What does she know about ' character '
and ' irresponsible suffering ' ? I shall tell her to
mend her husband's stockings, and not bother her
little head with theological questions that are too
big for her."

" Yes, sir," Lois answered, carefully snipping off
the thorns on the stem of a rose before she plunged
it down into the water in the big punch-bowl ; " but
people cannot help just wondering sometimes."

" Now, Lois, don't you begin to talk that way,"
the rector cried impatiently ; " one in a family is
enough ! "

" Well," said Dick Forsythe gayly, " what 's the
good of bothering about things you can't understand ? "

" Exactly," the rector answered. " Be good ! if
we occupy our minds with conduct, we won't have
room for speculation, which never made a soul better
or happier, anyhow. Yes, it 's all nonsense, and I
shall tell Helen so ; there is too much tendency

among young people to talk about things they don't understand, and it results in a superficial, skin-deep sort of skepticism that I despise! Besides," he added, laughing and knocking his glasses off, " what is the good of having a minister for a husband? She ought to ask him her theological questions."

" Well, now, you know, father," Lois said, " Helen is n't the sort of woman to be content just to step into the print her husband's foot has made. She 'll choose what she thinks is solid ground for herself. And she is n't superficial."

" Oh, no, of course not," the rector began, relenting. " I did n't mean to be hard on the child. But she must n't be foolish. I don't want her to make herself unhappy by getting unsettled in her belief, and that is what this sort of questioning results in. But I did n't come out to scold Helen; it just occurred to me that it might be a good thing to send her that twenty-five dollars I meant to give to domestic missions, and let her use it for some of her poor people. What?"

" Oh, yes, do!" Lois replied.

" Let me send twenty-five dollars, too!" Dick cried, whipping out a check-book.

Dr. Howe protested, but Mr. Forsythe insisted that it was a great pleasure. " Don't you see," he explained, smiling, " if Mrs. Ward will spend some money for me, it will make my conscience easy for a month; for, to tell you the truth, doctor, I don't think about poor people any more than I can help; it 's too unpleasant. I 'm afraid I 'm very selfish."

This was said with such a good-natured look, Dr.

Howe could only smile indulgently. "Ah, well, you 're young, and I 'm sure your twenty-five dollars for Helen's poor people will cover a multitude of sins. I fancy you are not quite so bad as you would have us believe."

Lois watched him draw his check, and was divided between admiration and an undefined dissatisfaction with herself for feeling admiration for what really meant so little.

"Thank you very much," the rector said heartily.

"Oh, you 're welcome, I 'm sure," answered the other.

Dr. Howe folded the check away in a battered leather pocket-book, shiny on the sides and ragged about the corners, and overflowing with odds and ends of memoranda and newspaper clippings; a row of fish-hooks was fastened into the flap, and he stopped to adjust these before he went into the house to answer Helen's letter.

He snubbed her good-naturedly, telling her not to worry about things too great for her, but beneath his consciousness there lurked a little discomfort, or even irritation. Duties which seem dead and buried, and forgotten, are avenged by the sting of memory. In the rector's days at the theological school, he had himself known those doubts which may lead to despair, or to a wider and unflinching gaze into the mysteries of light. But Archibald Howe reached neither one condition nor the other. He questioned many things; he even knew the heartache which the very fear of losing faith gives. But the way was too hard, and the toil and anguish

of the soul too great; he turned back into the familiar paths of the religion he knew and loved; and
doubt grew vague, not in assured belief, but in the
plain duties of life.   After a little while, he almost
forgot that he ever had doubted.   Only now and
then, when some questioning soul came to him,
would he realize that he could not help it by his own
experience, only by a formula, — a text-book spirit-
uality; then he would remember, and promise himself that the day should come when he would face
uncertainty and know what he believed.   But it was
continually eluding him, and being put off; he could
not bear to run the risk of disturbing the faith of
others; life was too full; he had not the time for
study and research, — and perhaps it would all end
in deeper darkness.   Better be content with what
light he had.   So duty was neglected, and his easy,
tranquil life flowed on.

Writing his careless rebuke to Helen brought this
past unpleasantly before his mind; he was glad
when he had sanded his paper and thrust the folded
letter into its envelope, and could forget once more.

Dick Forsythe had prolonged his call by being
very careful what flowers were picked for his
mother, and he and Lois wandered over the whole
garden, searching for the most perfect roses, before
he acknowledged that he was content.   When they
parted at the iron gate, he was more in love than
ever, and Lois walked back to the rectory, thinking
with a vague dissatisfaction how much she would
miss the Forsythes when they left Ashurst.

But Mr. Forsythe's was not the sort of love which

demanded solitude or silence, so that when he saw
Mr. Dale coming from Mr. Denner's little law office,
he made haste to join him. Conversation of any
sort, and with any person, was a necessity to this
young man, and Mr. Dale was better than no one.

"I've just been to the rectory," he said, as he
reached the older man's side.

"I suppose so," Mr. Dale answered shortly. Perhaps he was the only person in Ashurst who was not
blinded by the glamour of that World which Mr.
Forsythe represented, and who realized the nature
of the young man himself. Dick's superficiality was
a constant irritation to Mr. Dale, who missed in him
that deference for the opinions of older people
which has its roots in the past, in the training of
fathers and mothers in courtesy and gentleness, and
which blossoms in perfection in the third or fourth
generation.

There was nothing in his voice to encourage Dick
to talk about Lois Howe, so he wisely turned the
conversation, but wished he had a more congenial
companion. Mr. Dale walked with hands behind
him and shoulders bent forward ; his wide-brimmed
felt hat was pulled down over his long soft locks of
white hair, and hid the expression of his face.

So Dick rattled on in his light, happy voice, talking of everything or nothing, as his hearer might
happen to consider it, until suddenly Mr. Dale's attention was caught: Dick began to speak of John
Ward. "I thought I'd seen him," he was saying.
"The name was familiar, and then when Miss Lois
described his looks, and told me where he studied

for the ministry, I felt sure of it. If it is the same man, he must be a queer fellow."

"Why?" asked Mr. Dale. He did not know John Ward very well, and had no particular feeling about him one way or the other ; but people interested Mr. Dale, and he had meant some time to study this man with the same impersonal and kindly curiosity with which he would have examined a new bug in his collection.

"Because, if he 's the man I think he is, — and I guess there is no doubt about it — thin, dark, and abstracted-looking, named Ward, and studying at the Western Theological Seminary that year, — I saw him do a thing — well, I never knew any other man who would have done it !"

"What was it, sir ?" said Mr. Dale, turning his mild blue eyes upon the young man, and regarding him with an unusual amount of interest.

Dick laughed. "Why," he answered, "I saw that man, — there were a lot of us fellows standing on the steps of one of the hotels ; it was the busiest street and the busiest time of the day, and there was a woman coming along, drunk as a lord. Jove ! you ought to have seen her walk ! She could n't walk, — that was about the truth of it ; and she had a miserable yelling brat in her arms. It seemed as though she 'd fall half a dozen times. Well, while we were standing there, I saw that man coming down the street. I did n't know him then, — somebody told me his name, afterwards. I give you my word, sir, when he saw that woman, he stood still one minute, as though he was thunderstruck by the sight of her, — not hesitating, you know, but just amazed to see a woman looking like that, — and then he went right up to her, and took that dirty, screeching child out of her arms; and then, I'm damned if he did n't give her his arm and walk down the street with her!"

Mr. Dale felt the shock of it. " Ah!" he said, with a quick indrawn breath.

" Yes," continued Dick, who enjoyed telling a good story, " he walked down that crowded street with that drunken, painted creature on his arm. I suppose he thought she 'd fall, and hurt herself and the child. Naturally everybody looked at him, but I don't believe he even saw them. We stood there and watched them out of sight — and — but of course you know how fellows talk! Though so long as he was a *minister* " — Dick grinned significantly, and looked at Mr. Dale for an answer; but there was none.

Suddenly the old man stood still and gravely lifted his hat: " He 's a good man," he said, and then trudged on again, with his head bent and his hands clasped behind him.

Mr. Forsythe looked at him, and whistled. " Jove! " he exclaimed, " it does n't strike you as it did Dr. Howe. I told him, and he said, ' Bless my soul, had n't the man sense enough to call a policeman ? ' "

But Mr. Dale had nothing more to say. The picture of John Ward, walking through the crowded street with the woman who was a sinner upheld by his strong and tender arm, was not forgotten; and when Dick had left him, and he had lighted his slender silver pipe in the quiet of his basement study, he said again, " He 's a good man."

CHAPTER VIII.

It was one of those deliciously cold evenings in early autumn. All day long the sparkling sunshine-scented air had held an exhilaration like wine, but now night had folded a thin mist across the hills, though the clear darkness of the upper sky was filled with the keen white light of innumerable stars.

A fire in the open grate in John Ward's study was pure luxury, for the room did not really need the warmth. It was of that soft coal which people in the Middle States burn in happy indifference to its dust-making qualities, because of its charm of sudden-puffing flames, which burst from the bubbling blackness with a singing noise, like the explosion of an oak-gall stepped on unawares in the woods.

It had been a busy day for John, ending with the weekly prayer-meeting; and to sit now in front of the glowing fire, with Helen beside him, was a well-earned rest.

In the afternoon he had taken a dozen of the village children to find a swamp whose borders were fringed with gentians, which seemed to have caught the color of the wind-swept October skies. He would not let Helen go. "The walk would tire you," he said; but he himself seemed to know no

weariness, though most of the time he carried one
of the children, and was continually lifting them
over rough places, and picking their flowers and
ferns for them.

Helen had seen them start, and watched them as
they tramped over the short, crisp grass of an up-
land pasture, and she could just distinguish the
words of a hymn they sung, John's deep, sweet tenor
leading their quavering treble: —

> " His loving kindness, loving kindness,
> His loving kindness, oh, how free ! "

After they had gathered gentians to their hearts'
content, they crowded about John and begged for a
story, for that was always the crowning bliss of an
afternoon with the preacher. But, though prefaced
with the remark that they must remember it was
only a story and not at all true, their enjoyment of
gnomes and fairies, of wondrous palaces built of
shining white clouds, with stars for lamps, was never
lessened. True, there was generally a moral, but in
his great desire to make it attractive John often
concealed it, and was never quite sure that his
stories did the good he intended. But they did
good in another way ; the children loved him, as
most of them loved nothing else in their meagre,
hungry little lives. And he loved them ; they stirred
the depths of tenderness in him. What did the
future hold for them ? Misery, perhaps, and surely
sin, for what hope was there of purity and holiness
in such homes as theirs ? And the horror of that
further future, the sure eternity which follows sin,
cast a dreary shadow over them, and lent a sup-

pressed passion to the fervor with which he tried to
win their love, that he might lead them to righteousness.

But it was his gentleness, and a childlike simplicity which they themselves must early lose, which
attracted and charmed the children, and made them
happy and contented if they could but be with the
preacher.

They had left him reluctantly at the parsonage
gate, clamoring for another afternoon, which was
gladly promised.   Then John had had a quiet half
hour for further thought upon his evening talk to
his people, which had been prepared the day before.   Helen had laughed at the amount of study
given to every address.   " I wish you could see how
uncle Archie manages his sermons."

" He has not the sort of people I have," John
said, with kindly excuse.   " Yet think of the importance of speaking to any one in Christ's name! We
preach for eternity, Helen, — for eternity."

She looked at him gravely.   " John," she answered, " you take these things too much to heart.
It is not wise, dear."

He hesitated, and then said gently, " These are
the only things to take to heart.   We only live to
prepare for that other life.   Can we be too earnest
dear, when eternity hangs upon the use we make of
time ?   That thought is a continual spur to make
me eager for my duty to my people."

" Oh, I know it," Helen responded, laying her
head upon his shoulder ; " but don't work too hard."

He put his arms about her, and the impulse which

had been strong a moment before to speak to her of her own soul was forgotten.

These prayer-meetings were trials to Helen Ward. She missed the stately Liturgy of her own church. " I don't like to hear Elder Dean give the Almighty so much miscellaneous information," she said, half laughing, yet quite in earnest. But she always went, for at least there was the pleasure of walking home with John. Beside, practice had made it possible for her to hear without heeding, and in that way she escaped a great deal of annoyance.

This especial Wednesday evening, however, she had not been able to close her ears to all that was said. She had grown restless, and looked about the narrow whitewashed room where the lecture was given, and longed for the reverence of the starlit silence outside.

John had begun the meeting by a short prayer, simple and direct as a child's request to his father, and after a hymn he said a few words on the text he had chosen. Then the meeting was open, and to some of the things said, Helen listened with indignant disapproval. As they walked home, rejoicing in the fresh cold air and the sound of their quick footsteps on the frosty ground, she made up her mind what she meant to do, but she did not speak of it until they were by their own fireside.

The room was full of soft half-darkness ; shadows leaped out of the corners, and chased the gleams of firelight ; the tall clock ticked slowly in the corner, and on the hearts of these two fell that content with life and each other which is best expressed by silence.

John sat at his wife's feet; his tired head was upon her knee, and he could look up into her restful face, while he held one of her hands across his lips. It was a good face to see: her clear brown eyes were large and full, with heavy lids which drooped a little at the outer corners, giving a look of questioning sincerity, which does not often outlast childhood. Her bronze-brown hair was knotted low on her neck, and rippled a little over a smooth white forehead.

John had begun to stroke her hand softly, holding it up to shield his eyes from the firelight, and twisting the plain band of her wedding ring about.

" What a dear hand," he said ; " how strong and firm it is ! "

" It is large, at least," she answered, smiling. He measured it against his own gaunt thin hand, which always had a nervous thrill in the pale fingers. " You see, they are about the same size, but mine is certainly much whiter. Just look at that ink-stain ; that means you write too much. I don't like you to be so tired in the evenings, John."

" You rest me," he said, looking up into her face. " It is a rest even to sit here beside you. Do you know, Helen," he went on, after a moment's pause, " if I were in any pain, I mean any physical extremity, I would have strength to bear it if I could hold your hand ; it is so strong and steady."

She lifted her hand, and looked at it with amused curiosity, turning it about, " to get the best light upon it."

" I am in earnest," John said, smiling. " It is the

visible expression of the strength you are to me. With your help I could endure any pain. I wonder," he went on, in a lower voice, as though thinking aloud, " if this strength of yours could inspire me to bear the worst pain there could be for me, — I mean if I had to make you suffer in any way ? "

Helen looked down at him, surprised, not quite understanding.

" Suppose," he said, — " of course one can suppose anything, — that for your best good I had to make you suffer : could I, do you think ? "

" I hope so," she answered gravely ; " I hope I should give you strength to do it."

They fell again into their contented silence, watching the firelight, and thinking tenderly each of the other. But at last Helen roused herself from her reverie with a long, pleasant sigh of entire peace and comfort.

" John, do you know, I have reached a conclusion ? I 'm not going to prayer-meeting any more."

John started. " Why, Helen ! " he said, a thrill of pain in his voice.

But Helen was not at all troubled. " No, dear. Feeling deeply as I do about certain things, it is worse than useless for me to go and hear Elder Dean or old Mr. Smith ; they either annoy me or amuse me, and I don't know which is worse. I have heard Mr. Smith thank the Lord that we are not among the pale and sheeted nations of the dead, ever since I came to Lockhaven. And Elder Dean's pictures of the eternal torments of the damned, ' souls wreathing in sulphurous flames ' (those were

his words to-night, John !), and then praising God
for his justice (his justice!) right afterwards, — I
cannot stand it, dear. I do not believe in hell,
such a hell, and so it is absurd to go and listen
to such things. But I won't miss my walk with
you," she added, " for I will come and meet you
every Wednesday evening, and we 'll come home together."

John had risen as she talked, and stood leaning
against the mantel, his face hidden by his hand.
Her lightly spoken words had come with such a
shock, the blood leaped back to his heart, and for a
moment he could not speak. He had never allowed
himself to realize that her indifference to doctrine
was positive unbelief; had his neglect encouraged
her ignorance to grow into this?

At last he said very gently, " But, dearest, I believe in hell."

" I know it," she answered, no longer carelessly,
but still smiling, " but never mind. I mean, it does
not make any difference to me what you believe. I
would n't care if you were a Mohammedan, John, if it
helped you to be good and happy. I think that
different people have different religious necessities.
One man is born a Roman Catholic, for instance,
though his father and mother may be the sternest
Protestants. He cannot help it; it is his nature !
And you " — she looked up at him with infinite tenderness in her brown eyes, — " you were born a
Presbyterian, dear; you can't help it. Perhaps you
need the sternness and the horror of some of the
doctrines as a balance for your gentleness. I never
knew any one as gentle as you, John."

He came and knelt down beside her, holding her face between his hands, and looking into her clear eyes. " Helen," he said, " I have wanted to speak to you of this; I have wanted to show you the truth. You will not say you cannot believe in hell (in justice, Helen) when I prove " —

" Don't prove," she interrupted him, putting her hand softly across his lips, " don't let us argue. Oh, a theological argument seems to me sacrilege, and dogma can never be an antidote for doubt, John. I must believe what my own soul asserts, or I am untrue to myself. I must begin with that truth, even if it keeps me on the outskirts of the great Truth. Don't you think so, dear? And I do not believe in hell. Now that is final, John."

She smiled brightly into his troubled face, and, seeing his anxiety, hastened to save him further pain in the future. " Do not let us ever discuss these things. After all, doctrine is of so little importance, and argument never can result in conviction to either of us, for belief is a matter of temperament, and I do so dislike it. It really distresses me, John."

" But, dearest," he said, " to deliberately turn away from the search for truth is spiritual suicide."

"Oh, you misunderstand me," she replied quickly. " Of course one's soul always seeks for truth, but to argue, to discuss details, which after all are of no possible importance, no more part of the eternal verities than a man's — buttons are of his character! Now, remember," with smiling severity, " never again!" She laid her head down on his shoulder.

" We are so happy, John, so happy; why should we disturb the peace of life? Never mind what we think on such matters; we have each other, dear ! "

He was silenced; with her clinging arm about him, and her tender eyes looking into his, he could not argue; he was the lover, not the preacher.

He kissed her between her level brows; it was easy to forget his duty! Yet his conscience protested faintly. " If you would only let me tell you"—

" Not just now," she said, and Helen's voice was a caress. " Do you remember how, that first time we saw each other, you talked of belief ? " It was so natural to drift into reminiscence, kneeling there in the firelight by her side, John almost forgot how the talk had begun, and neither of them gave a thought to the lateness of the hour, until they were roused by a quick step on the path, and heard the little gate pushed hurriedly open, shutting again with a bang.

" Why, that 's Gifford Woodhouse," John said, leaning forward to give the fire that inevitable poke with which the coming guest is welcomed.

" No, it can't be Giff," Helen answered, listening; " he always whistles."

But it was Gifford. The quick-leaping flame lighted his face as he entered, and Helen saw that, instead of its usual tranquil good-nature, there was a worried look.

" I 'm afraid I 'm disturbing you," he said, as they both rose to welcome him, and there was the little confusion of lighting the lamp and drawing up a chair. " Have n't I interrupted you ? "

" Yes," John replied simply, "but it is well you
did. I have some writing I must do to-night, and I
had forgotten it. You and Helen will excuse me
if I leave you a little while? "

Both the others protested : Gifford that he was
driving Mr. Ward from his own fireside, and Helen
that it was too late for work.

" No, you are not driving me away. My papers
are up-stairs. I will see you again," he added, turning to Gifford ; and then he closed the door, and
they heard his step in the room above.

The interruption had brought him back to real
life. He left the joy which befogged his conscience,
and felt again that chill and shock which Helen's
words had given him, and that sudden pang of remorse for a neglected duty; he wanted to be alone,
and to face his own thoughts. His writing did not
detain him long, and afterwards he paced the chilly
room, struggling to see his duty through his love.
But in that half hour up-stairs he reached no new
conclusion. Helen's antipathy to doctrine was so
marked, it was, as she said, useless to begin discussion ; and it would be worse than useless to urge her
to come to prayer-meeting, if she did not want to; it
would only make her antagonistic to the truth. She
was not ready for the strong meat of the Word,
which was certainly what his elders fed to hungry
souls at prayer-meetings. John did not know that
there was any reluctance in his own mind to disturb
their harmony and peace by argument ; he simply
failed to recognize his own motives ; the reasons he
gave himself were all secondary.

"I ought not to have come so late," Gifford said, "and it is a shame to disturb Mr. Ward, but I did want to see you so much, Helen!"

Helen's thoughts were following her husband, and it was an effort to bring them back to Gifford and his interests, but she turned her tranquil face to him with a gracious gentleness which never left her. "He will come back again," she said, "and he will be glad to have this writing off his mind to-night. I was only afraid he might take cold; you know he has a stubborn little cough. Why did you want to see me, Giff?"

She took some knitting from her work-table, and, shaking out its fleecy softness, began to work, the big wooden needles making a velvety sound as they rubbed together. Gifford was opposite her, his hands thrust moodily into his pockets, his feet stretched straight out, and his head sunk on his breast. But he did not look as though he were resting; an intent anxiety seemed to pervade his big frame, and Helen could not fail to observe it. She glanced at him, as he sat frowning into the fire, but he did not notice her.

"Something troubles you, Gifford."

He started. "Yes," he said. He changed his position, leaning his elbows on his knees, and propping his chin on his fists, and still scowling at the fire. "Yes, I came to speak to you about it."

"I wish you would," Helen answered. But Gifford found it difficult to begin.

"I 've had a letter from aunt Ruth to-day," he said at last, "and it has bothered me. I don't know how to tell you, exactly; you will think it 's none of my business."

" Is there anything wrong at the rectory? " Helen asked, putting down her work, and drawing a quick breath.

" Oh, no, no, of course not," answered Gifford, " nothing like that. The fact is, Helen — the fact is — well, plainly, aunt Ruth thinks that that young Forsythe is in love with Lois."

Gifford's manner, as he spoke, told Helen what she had only surmised before, and she was betrayed into an involuntary expression of sympathy.

" Oh," cried the young man, with an impatient gesture and a sudden flush tingling across his face, " you misunderstand me. I have n't come to whine about myself, or anything like that. I 'm not jealous ; for Heaven's sake, don't think I am such a cur as to be jealous! If that man was worthy of Lois, I — why, I 'd be the first one to rejoice that she was happy. I want Lois to be happy, from my soul! I hope you believe me, Helen? "

" I believe anything you tell me," she answered gently, " but I don't quite understand how you feel about Mr. Forsythe ; every one speaks so highly of him. Even aunt Deely has only pleasant things to say of ' young Forsythe,' as she calls him."

Gifford left his chair, and began to walk about the room, his hands grasping the lapels of his coat, and his head thrown back in a troubled sort of impatience. " That 's just it," he said ; " in this very letter aunt Ruth is enthusiastic, and I can't tell you anything tangible against him, only I don't like

him, Helen. He's a puppy, — that's the amount
of it. And I thought — I just thought — I'd come
and ask you if you supposed — if you — of course
I've no business to ask any question — but if you
thought" —

But Helen had understood his vague inquiry.
" I should think," she said "you would know that
if he is what you call a *puppy* Lois could n't care
for him."

Gifford sat down, and took her ball of wool, beginning nervously to unwind it, and then wind it up
again.

" Perhaps she would n't see it," he said tenta-
tively.

" Ah, you don't trust her !" Helen cried brightly,
" or you would not say that. (Don't tie my worsted
into knots !) When you write to Lois, why don't
you frankly say what you think of him ? "

" Oh, I could not," he responded quickly. " Don't
you see, Helen, I'm a young fellow myself, and —
and you know Lois did not care for me when I —
told her. And if I said anything now, it would only
mean that I was jealous, that I wanted her myself.
Whereas, I give you my word," striking his fist
sharply on his knee, " if he was fit for her, I'd rejoice ; yes, I — I love her so much that if I saw her
happy with any other man (who was worthy of
her !) I'd be glad ! "

Helen looked doubtful, but did not discuss that ;
she ran her hand along her needle, and gave her
elastic work a pull. " Tell me more about him,"
she said.

But Gifford had not much to tell; it was only his vague distrust of the man, which it was difficult to put into words. " A good out-and-out sinner one can stand," he ended; " but all I saw of this For-sythe at the club and about town only made me set him down as a small man, a — a puppy, as I said. And I thought I 'd talk to you about it, because, when you write to Lois, you might just hint, you know."

But Helen shook her head. " No, Gifford, that never does any good at all. And I do not believe it is needed. The only thing to do now is to trust Lois. I have no anxiety about her; if he is what you say, her own ideal will protect her. Ah, Giff, I 'm disappointed in you. I should n't have thought you could doubt Lois."

" I don't! " he cried, " only I am so afraid! "

" But you should n't be afraid," Helen said, smil-ing; " a girl like Lois could n't love a man who was not good and noble. Perhaps, Gifford," she ven-tured, after a moment's pause, — " perhaps it will be all right for you, some time."

" No, no," he answered, " I don't dare to think of it."

Helen might have given him more courage, but John came in, and Gifford realized that it was very late. " Helen has scolded me, Mr. Ward," he said, " and it has done me good."

John turned and looked at her. " Can she scold ? " he said. And when Gifford glanced back, as he went down the street, he saw them still stand-ing in the doorway in the starlight; Helen leaning back a little against John's arm, so that she might see his face. The clear warm pallor of her cheek glowed faintly in the frosty air.

Gifford sighed as he walked on. " They are very happy," he thought. " Well, that sort of happiness may never be for me, but it is something to love a good woman. I have got that in my life, anyhow."

Helen's confidence in her cousin's instinct might perhaps have been shaken had she known what pleasure Lois found in the companionship of Mr. Forsythe, and how that pleasure was encouraged by all her friends. That very evening, while Gifford was pouring his anxieties into her ear, Lois was listening to Dick's pictures of the gayeties of social life; the " jolly times," as he expressed it, which she had never known.

Dr. Howe was reading, with an indignant exclamation occasionally, a scathing review of an action of his political candidate, and his big newspaper hid the two young people by the fire, so that he quite forgot them. Max seemed to feel that the responsibility of propriety rested upon him, and he sat with his head on Lois's knee, and his drowsy eyes blinking at Mr. Forsythe. His mistress pulled his silky ears gently, or knotted them behind his head, giving him a curiously astonished and grieved look, as though he felt she trifled with his dignity; yet he did not move his head, but watched, with no affection in his soft brown eyes, the young man who talked so eagerly to Lois.

" That brute hates me," said Mr. Forsythe, " and yet I took the trouble to bring him a biscuit to-day.

Talk of gratitude and affection in animals. They don't know what it means!"

"Max loves me," Lois answered, taking the setter's head between her hands.

"Ah, well, that's different," cried Forsythe; "of course he does. I'd like to know how he could help it. He would n't be fit to live, if he did n't."

Lois raised the hand-screen she held, so that Dick could only see the curls about her forehead and one small curve of her ear. "How hot the fire is!" she said.

Dr. Howe folded his newspaper with much crackling and widely opened arms. "Don't sit so near it. In my young days, the children were never allowed to come any nearer the fireplace than the outside of the hearth-rug." Then he began to read again, muttering, "Confound that reporter!"

Dick glanced at him, and then he said, in a low voice, "Max loves you because you are so kind to him, Miss Lois; it is worth while to be a dog to have you" —

"Give him bones?" Lois cried hurriedly. "Yes, it is too hot in here, father; don't you think so; don't you want me to open the window?"

Dr. Howe looked up, surprised. "If you want to, child," he said. "Dear me, I'm afraid I have not been very entertaining, Mr. Forsythe. What do you think of this attack on our candidate? Contemptible, is n't it? What? I have no respect for any one who can think it anything but abominable and outrageous."

"It's scandalous!" Dick answered, — and then

in a smiling whisper to Lois, he added, "I'm afraid to tell the doctor I'm a Democrat."

But when Lois was quite alone that night, she found herself smiling in the darkness, and a thrill of pride made her cheeks hotter than the fire had done.

CHAPTER IX.

"Yes," said Miss Deborah Woodhouse, as she stood in the doorway of Miss Ruth's studio, "yes, we must give a dinner party, sister. It is certainly the proper thing to do, now that the Forsythes are going back to the city. It is to be expected of us, sister."

"Well, I don't know that it is expected of us," said Miss Ruth, who never agreed too readily to any suggestion of Miss Deborah's; "but I think we ought to do it. I meant to have spoken to you about it."

Miss Ruth was washing some brushes, a task her soul abhorred, for it was almost impossible to avoid some stain upon her apron or her hands; though, to guard against the latter, she wore gloves. The corners of Miss Ruth's mouth were drawn down and her eyebrows lifted up, and her whole face was a protest against her work. On her easel was a canvas, where she had begun a sketch purporting to be apple-blossoms.

The studio was dark, for a mist of November rain blurred all the low gray sky. The wide southwest window, which ran the length of the woodshed (this part of which was devoted to art), was streaming with water, and though the dotted muslin curtain was pushed as far back as it would go, very little light struggled into the room. The dim engravings of nymphs and satyrs, in tarnished frames, which had been hung here to make room in the house for Miss Ruth's own productions, could scarcely be distinguished in the gloom, and though the artist wore her glasses she could not see to work.

So she had pushed back her easel, and began to make things tidy for Sunday. Any sign of disorder would have greatly distressed Miss Ruth. Even her paint-tubes were kept scrupulously bright and clean, and nothing was ever out of place. Perhaps this made the room in the woodshed a little dreary, certainly it looked so now to Miss Deborah, standing in the doorway, and seeing the gaunt white-washed walls, the bare rafters, and the sweeping rain against the window.

"Do, sister," she entreated, "come into the house, and let us arrange about the dinner."

"No," said Miss Ruth, sighing, "I must wash these brushes."

"Why not let Sarah do it?" asked the other, stepping over a little stream of water which had forced itself under the threshold.

"Now, surely, sister," said Miss Ruth pettishly, "you know Sarah would get the color on the handles. But there! I suppose you don't know how artistic people feel about such things." She stopped long enough to take off her gloves and tie the strings of her long white apron a little tighter about her trim waist; then she went to work again.

"No, I suppose I don't understand," Miss Deborah acknowledged; "but never mind, we can talk here, only it is a little damp. What do you think of asking them for Thursday? It is a good day for a dinner party. You are well over the washing and ironing, you know, and you have Wednesday for the jellies and creams, besides a good two hours in the afternoon to get out the best china and see to the silver. Friday is for cleaning up and putting things away, because Saturday one is always busy getting ready for Sunday."

Miss Ruth demurred. "I should rather have it on a Friday."

"Well, you don't know anything about the house-keeping part of it," said Miss Deborah, promptly. "And I don't believe William Denner would want to come then; you know he is quite superstitious about Friday. Beside, it is not convenient for me," she added, settling the matter once for all.

"Oh, I've no objection to Thursday," said Miss Ruth. "I don't know but that I prefer it. Yes, we will have it on Thursday." Having thus asserted herself, Miss Ruth began to put away her paints and cover her canvas.

"It is a pity the whist was put off to-night," said Miss Deborah; "we could have arranged it at the rectory. But if I see Adele Dale to-morrow, I'll tell her."

"I beg," said Miss Ruth quickly, "that you'll do nothing of the sort."

"What!" exclaimed Miss Deborah.

"We will write the invitations, if you please," said Miss Ruth loftily.

"Fiddlesticks!" retorted the other. "We'll

write the Forsythes, of course, but the people at the rectory and Adele Dale? — nonsense!"

"It is not nonsense," Miss Ruth answered; "it is *proper*, and it must be done. I understand these things, Deborah; you are so taken up with your cooking, you cannot really be expected to know. When you invite city people to a formal dinner, everything must be done decently and in order. It is not like asking the rector and Adele to drop in to tea any time."

"Fudge!" responded Miss Deborah.

A faint color began to show in Miss Ruth's faded cheek, and she set her lips firmly. "The invitations should be written," she said.

It was settled, as usual, by each sister doing exactly as she pleased. Miss Deborah gave her invitations by word of mouth the next day, standing in the rain, under a dripping umbrella, by the church porch, while on Monday each of the desired guests received a formal note in Miss Ruth's precise and delicate hand, containing the compliments of the Misses Woodhouse, and a request for the honor of their company at dinner on Thursday, November 12th, at half past six o'clock.

A compromise had been effected about the hour. Miss Ruth had insisted that it should be at eight, while Miss Deborah contended that as they dined, like all the rest of Ashurst, at noon, it was absurd to make it later than six, and Miss Ruth's utmost persuasion had only brought it to half past.

During these days of preparation Miss Ruth could only flutter upon the outskirts of the kitchen, which just now was a solemn place, and her suggestions were scarcely noticed, and never heeded. It was hard to have no share in those long conversations between Sarah and her sister, and not to know the result of the mysterious researches among the receipts which had been written out on blue foolscap and bound in marbled pasteboard before Miss Deborah was born.

Her time, however, came. Miss Deborah owned that no one could arrange a table like Miss Ruth. The tall silver candlesticks with twisted arms, the fruit in the open-work china baskets, the slender-stemmed glasses for the wines, the decanters in the queer old coasters, and the great bunch of chrysanthemums in the silver punch-bowl in the centre, — no one could place them so perfectly as her sister.

"Ruth," she affirmed, " has a touch," and she contemplated the board with great satisfaction.

"Pray," said Miss Ruth, as she quietly put back in its place a fruit dish which Miss Deborah had "straightened," " pray where are Mr. Dale's comfits? They must be on the tray to be taken into the parlor."

" Sarah will fetch them," answered Miss Deborah; and at that moment Sarah entered with the candy and a stately and elaborate dish, which she placed upon the sideboard.

"Poor, dear man," said Miss Ruth. "I suppose he never gets all the candy he wishes at home. I trust there is plenty for to-night, sister? But what is that Sarah just brought in ?"

" Well," Miss Deborah replied, with anxious pride

in her tone, " it is not Easter, I know, but it does look so well I thought I 'd make it, anyhow. It is Sic itur ad astra."

This dish had been " composed " by Miss Deborah many years ago, and was considered by all her friends her greatest triumph. Dr. Howe had christened it, declaring that it was of a semi-religious nature, but in Miss Deborah's pronunciation the Latin was no longer recognizable.

It consisted of an arrangement of strips of candied orange and lemon peel, intended to represent a nest of straw. On it were placed jellied creams in different colors, which had been run into egg-shells to stiffen. The whole was intended to suggest a nest of new-laid eggs. The housekeeper will at once recognize the trouble and expense of such a dish, as the shells which served for moulds had first to be emptied of their contents through a small hole in one end, hopelessly mixing the whites and yolks, and leaving them useless for fine cookery.

No wonder, then, that Miss Deborah's face beamed with pride. But Miss Ruth's showed nothing but contempt. " That — that — barn-door dish ! " she ejaculated.

" Barn-door ? " faltered Miss Deborah.

" Barn-yard, I mean," said her sister sternly. " The idea of having such a thing ! Easter is the only excuse for it. It is undignified, — it is absurd, — it is — it is preposterous ! "

" It is good," Miss Deborah maintained stoutly.

" I don't deny that," said Miss Ruth, thinking they would have it for dinner the next day, and perhaps the next also, — for it takes more than one day for a family of two to eat up the remnants of a dinner party, — " but you must see it is out of place at a formal dinner. It must not appear."

Discussion was useless. Each was determined, for each felt her particular province had been invaded. And each carried her point. The dish did not appear on the table, yet every guest was asked if he or she would have some "Sicituradastra" — for to the housemaid it was one word — which was on the sideboard.

But the anxieties of the dinner were not over even when the table was as beautiful and stately as could be desired, and Miss Deborah was conscious that every dish was perfect. The two little ladies, tired, but satisfied, had yet to dress. Sarah had put the best black silks on the bed in each room, but for the lighter touches of the toilette the sisters were their own judges. Miss Deborah must decide what laces she should wear, and long did Miss Ruth stand at her dressing-table, wondering whether to pin the pale lavender ribbon at her throat or the silver-gray one.

Miss Deborah was dressed first. She wore a miniature of her great-grandfather as a pin, and her little fingers were covered with rings, in strange old-fashioned settings. Her small figure had an unusual dignity in the lustrous silk, which was turned away at the neck, and filled with point-lace that looked like frosted cobwebs. The sleeves of her gown were full, and gathered into a wristband over point-lace ruffles which almost hid her little hands, folded

primly in front of her. "Little bishops" Miss
Deborah called these sleeves, and she was apt to say
that, for her part, she thought a closely fitting sleeve
was hardly modest. Her full skirt rustled, as, holding herself very straight, she came into her sister's
room, that they might go down together.

Miss Ruth was still in her gray linsey-woolsey
petticoat, short enough to show her trim ankles in
their black open-worked silk stockings. She stood
with one hand resting on the open drawer of her
bureau, and in the other the two soft bits of ribbon,
that held the faint fragrance of rose leaves which
clung to all her possessions. Miss Ruth would never
have confessed it, but she was thinking that Mr.
Forsythe was a very genteel young man, and she
wished she knew which ribbon would be more becoming.

"Ruth!" said Miss Deborah, in majestic disapproval.

The younger sister gave a little jump of fright,
and dropped the ribbons hastily, as though she
feared Miss Deborah had detected her thoughts.
"I — I 'll be ready directly, sister."

"I hope so, indeed," said Miss Deborah severely,
and moved with deliberate dignity from the room,
while Miss Ruth, much fluttered, took her dress from
the high bedstead, which had four cherry-wood posts,
carved in alternate balloons and disks, and a striped
dimity valance.

She still realized the importance of the right
ribbon, and the responsibility of choice oppressed
her; but it was too late for any further thought.

She shut her eyes tight, and, with a trembling little hand, picked up the first one she touched. Satisfied, since Fate so decided it, that gray was the right color, she pinned it at her throat with an old brooch of chased and twisted gold, and gave a last glance at her swinging glass before joining her sister in the parlor. The excitement had brought a faint flush into her soft cheek, and her eyes were bright, and the gray ribbon had a pretty gleam in it. Miss Ruth gave her hair a little pat over each ear, and felt a thrill of forgotten vanity.

"It's high time you were down, Ruth," cried Miss Deborah, who stood on the rug in front of the blazing fire, rubbing her hands nervously together, — "high time!"

"Why, they won't be here for a quarter of an hour yet, sister," protested Miss Ruth.

"Well, you should be here! I do hope they won't be late; the venison is to be taken out of the tin kitchen precisely at five minutes of seven. Do, pray, sister, step into the hall and see what o'clock it is. I really am afraid they are late."

Miss Ruth went, but had scarcely crossed the threshold when Miss Deborah cried, "Come back, come back, Ruth! You must be here when they come," and then bustled away herself to fetch the housemaid to be ready to open the door, though, as Miss Ruth had said, it was a good quarter of an hour before the most impatient guest might be expected.

Miss Ruth went about, straightening a chair, or pulling an antimacassar to one side or the other, or putting an ornament in a better light, and then stop-

ping to snuff the candles in the brass sconces on
either side of the old piano. This and her anxiety
about the venison fretted Miss Deborah so much, it
was a great relief to hear the first carriage, and
catch a glimpse of Mrs. Dale hurrying across the
hall and up the stairs, her well-known brown satin
tucked up to avoid a speck of mud or dust.

Miss Deborah plucked Miss Ruth's sleeve, and,
settling the lace at her own throat and wrists, bade
her sister stand beside her on the rug. " And do,
dear Ruth, try and have more repose of manner,"
she said, breathing quite quickly with excitement.

When Mrs. Dale entered, rustling in her shiny
satin, with Mr. Dale shambling along behind her,
the sisters greeted her with that stately affection
which was part of the occasion.

" So glad to see you, dear Adele," said Miss Deborah and Miss Ruth in turn ; and Mrs. Dale responded with equal graciousness, and no apparent
recollection that they had almost quarreled that
very morning at the post-office, when Mrs. Dale said
that the first cloth to be removed at a dinner should
be folded in fours, and Miss Deborah that it should
be folded in threes.

Mr. Denner was the next to arrive, and while he
was still making his bow the Forsythes came in;
Dick looking over the heads of the little ladies, as
though in search of some one else, and his mother
languidly acknowledging that it was an effort to
come out in the evening. Lois and the rector came
with Colonel Drayton, and Miss Deborah breathed a
sigh of relief that the venison would not be kept
waiting.

Then Miss Deborah took Mrs. Forsythe's arm, while Miss Ruth and Dick closed the little procession, and they marched into the dining-room, and took their places about the table, glittering with silver and glass, and lighted by gleaming wax tapers. It had not occurred to the little ladies to place Dick near Lois. Mrs. Drayton was the lady upon his right, and Lois was between such unimportant people as Mr. Denner and Mr. Dale.

Dick was the lion of the dinner, and all that he said was listened to with deference and even awe. But it was a relief to Lois not to have to talk to him. She sat now at Mr. Denner's side, listening to the small stream of words bubbling along in a cheerful monotony, with scarcely a period for her answers. She was glad it was so; for though her apple-blossom face was drooped a little, and her gray eyes were not often lifted, and she looked the embodiment of maiden innocence and unworldliness, Lois was thinking the thoughts which occupied her much of late; weighing, and judging, struggling to reach some knowledge of herself, yet always in the same perplexity. Did she love Dick Forsythe? There was no doubt in her mind that she loved the life he represented; but further than this she could not go. Yet he was so kind, she thought, and loved her so much. If, then and there, Dick could have whispered the question which was trembling on his lips, Lois was near enough to love to have said Yes.

Dinner was nearly over; that last desultory conversation had begun, which was to be ended by a bow from Miss Deborah to Mrs. Forsythe, and the

ladies were dipping their nuts in their wine, half
listening, and half watching for the signal to rise.

"How much we miss Gifford on such an occasion!" said Mr. Dale to Miss Ruth.

"Yes," replied the little lady, "dear Giff! How
I wish he were here! He would so enjoy meeting
Mr. Forsythe."

Lois smiled involuntarily, and the current of her
thoughts suddenly turned. She saw again the fragrant dusk of the rectory garden, and heard the
wind in the silver poplar and the tremble in a strong
voice at her side.

She was as perplexed as ever when the ladies
went back to the parlor. Mrs. Forsythe came to
her, as they passed through the hall, and took the
young girl's hand in hers.

"I shall miss you very much this winter, Lois,"
she said, in her mildly complaining voice. "You
have been very good to me; no daughter could have
been more thoughtful. And I could not have loved
a daughter of my own more." She gently patted
the hand she held. "Dick is not very happy, my
dear."

"I'm sorry," faltered Lois.

They had reached the parlor door, and Mrs. Forsythe bent her head towards the girl's ear. "I hope
— I trust — he will be, before we leave Ashurst."

Lois turned away abruptly; how could she grieve
this gentle invalid!

"She'll find out what Arabella Forsythe is, one
of these days," Mrs. Dale thought, "but it's just as
well she should love her for the present." Nor did

she lose the opportunity of using her influence to bring about the desired consummation.

Lois had gone, at Miss Deborah's request, to the piano, and begun to sing, in her sweet girlish voice, some old-fashioned songs which the sisters liked.

"Jamie's on the stormy sea!" sang Lois, but her voice trembled, and she missed a note, for Mrs. Dale had left the group of ladies about the fire, and bent over her shoulder.

"You know they go on Saturday, Lois," she said. "Do, now, I beg of you, be a sensible girl. I never saw a man so much in love. You will be perfectly happy, if you will only be sensible! I hope you will be at home alone to-morrow."

When the gentlemen entered, Dick Forsythe was quick to make his way to Lois, sitting in the glimmer of the wax-lights in the sconces, at the old piano.

She stopped, and let her hands fall with a soft crash on the yellow keys.

"Do go on," he pleaded.

"No," she said, "it is too cold over here; let us come to the fire," and she slipped away to her father's side. After that she was silent until it was time to say good-night, for no one expected her to speak, although Dick was the centre of the group, and did most of the talking. Later in the evening they had some whist, and after that, just before the party broke up, Mr. Denner was asked to sing.

He rose, coughed deprecatingly, and glanced sidewise at Mr. Forsythe; he feared he was out of tune. But Miss Deborah insisted with great politeness.

" If Miss Ruth would be so good as to accompany me," said Mr. Denner, " I might at least make the attempt."

Miss Ruth was shy about playing in public, but Mr. Denner encouraged her. " You must overcome your timidity, my dear Miss Ruth," he said. " I — I am aware that it is quite painful ; but one ought not to allow it to become a habit, as it were. It should be conquered in early life."

So Miss Ruth allowed him to lead her to the piano. There was a little stir about finding the music, before they were ready to begin ; then Mr. Denner ran his fingers through his brown wig, and, placing his small lean hands on his hips, rocked back and forth on his little heels, while he sang in a sweet but somewhat light and uncertain voice, —

> " Lassie wi' the lint-white locks,
>   Bonnie lassie ! artless lassie !
> Will ye wi' me tent the flocks,
>   Will ye be my dearie, O ? "

This was received with great applause ; then every one said good-night, assuring each sister that it had been a delightful evening ; and finally the last carriage rolled off into the darkness, and the Misses Woodhouse were left, triumphantly exhausted, to discuss the dinner and the guests.

The rector walked home with Mr. Denner, who was still flushed with the praise of his singing, so Lois had the carriage all to herself, and tried to struggle against the fresh impulse of irresolution which Mrs. Forsythe's whispered " Good-night, Lois ; be good to my boy ! " had given her.

She went into the library at the rectory, and, throwing off her wrap, sat down on the hearth-rug, and determined to make up her mind. But first she had to put a fresh log on the andirons, and then work away with the wheezy old bellows, until a leaping flame lighted the shadowy room. The log was green, and, instead of deciding, she found herself listening to the soft bubbling noise of the sap, and thinking that it was the little singing ghosts of the summer birds. Max came and put his head on her knee, to be petted, and Lois's thoughts wandered off to the dinner party, and Mr. Denner's singing, and what good things Miss Deborah cooked, and how much his aunts must miss Gifford; so that she did not even hear the front door open, or know that Dick Forsythe had entered, until she heard Max snarl, and some one said, in a tone which lacked its usual assurance, " I — I hope I 'm not disturbing you, Miss Lois ? "

She was on her feet before he had a chance to help her rise, and looked at him with the frankest astonishment and dismay.

What would aunt Deely say, what would Miss Deborah think ! A young woman receiving a gentleman alone after ten at night ! " Father is not home yet," she said hastily, so confused and startled she scarcely knew what she was saying. " How dark it is in here ! The fire has dazzled my eyes. I 'll get a light."

" Oh, don't," he said ; " I like the firelight." But she had gone, and came back again with Sally, who carried the lamps, and looked very much sur-

prised, for Sally knew Ashurst ways better than
Mr. Forsythe did : her young man always went home
at nine.

"How pleasant it was at Miss Deborah's!" Lois
began, when Sally had gone out, and she was left
alone to see the anxiety in Dick's face. "Nobody has
such nice dinners as Miss Deborah and Miss Ruth."
Lois's voice was not altogether firm, yet, to her own
surprise, she began to feel quite calm, and almost
indifferent ; she knew why Dick had come, but she
did not even then know what her answer would be.

"Yes — no — I don't know," he answered. "The
fact is, I only seemed to live, Miss Lois, until I could
get here to see you to-night. I heard your father
say he was going home with Denner, and I thought
you'd be alone. So I came. I could not stand any
more suspense!" he added, with something like a
sob in his voice.

Lois's heart gave one jump of fright, and then
was quiet. She thought, vaguely, that she was glad
he had rushed into it at once, so that she need not
keep up that terrible fencing, but she did not speak.
She had been sitting in a corner of the leather-
covered sofa, and his excitement, as he stood looking
at her, made her rise.

He grasped her hands in his, wringing them
sharply as he spoke, not even noticing her little cry
of pain, or her efforts to release herself. "You
know I love you, — you know it! Why have n't you
let me tell you so? Oh, Lois, how lovely you are
to-night, — how happy we shall be!"

He kissed one of her hands with a sudden savage

passion that frightened her. "Oh — don't," she said, shrinking back, and pulling her hands away from him.

He looked at her blankly a moment, but when he spoke again it was gently. " Did I frighten you? I did n't mean to; but you know I love you. That has n't startled you? Tell me you care for me, Lois."

" But — but" — said Lois, sorry and ashamed, " I — don't ! "

The eager boyish face, so near her own, flushed with sudden anger. " You don't? You must ! Why — why, I love you. It cannot be that you really don't — tell me ? "

But there was no doubt in Lois's mind now. " Indeed, Mr. Forsythe," she said, " indeed, I am so sorry, but I don't — I can't ! "

A sullen look clouded his handsome face. " I cannot believe it," he said, at length. " You have known that I loved you all summer; you cannot be so cruel as to trifle with me now. You will not treat me so. Oh, I love you ! " There was almost a wail in his voice, and he threw himself down in a chair and covered his face with his hands.

Lois did not speak. Her lip curled a little, but it was partly with contempt for herself and her past uncertainty. " I am so sorry, so grieved," she began. But he scarcely heard her, or at least he did not grasp the significance of her words.

He began to plead and protest. " We will be so happy if you will only care for me. Just think how different your life will be ; you shall have everything in this world you want, Lois."

She could not check his torrent of words, and when at last he stopped he had almost convinced himself that she loved him.

But she shook her head. " I cannot tell you how distressed I am, but I do not love you."

He was silent, as though trying to understand.

" Won't you try and forget it ? Won't you forgive me, and let us be friends ? " she said.

" You really mean it ? You really mean to make me wretched? Forget it ? I wish to Heaven I could ! "

Lois did not speak. There seemed to be nothing to say.

" You have let me think you cared," he went on, " and I have built on it ; I have staked all my happiness on it ; I am a ruined man if you don't love me. And you coolly tell me you do not care for me ! Can't you try to ? I 'll make you so happy, if you will only make me happy, Lois."

" Please — please," she protested, " do not say anything more ; it never can be, — indeed, it cannot ! "

Dick's voice had been tender a moment before, but it was hard now. " Well," he said, " you have amused yourself all summer, I suppose. You made me think you loved me, and everybody else thought so, too."

The hint of blame kept Lois from feeling the sting of conscience. She flung her head back, and looked at him with a flash of indignation in her eyes. " Do you think it 's manly to blame me ? You had better blame yourself that you could n't win my love ! "

"Do you expect a man to choose his words when you give him his death-blow?" he said; and then, "Oh, Miss Lois, if I wait, can't you learn to care for me? I'll wait, — a year, if you say there's any hope. Or do you love anybody else? Is that the reason?"

"That has nothing to do with it," Lois cried, hotly, "but I don't."

"Then," said Dick eagerly, "you must love me, only you don't recognize it, not having been in love before. Of course it's different with a girl who doesn't know what love is. Oh, say you do!"

Lois, with quick compunction for her anger, was gentle enough now. "I cannot say so. I wish you would forget me, and forgive me if you can. I'm sorry to have grieved you, — truly I am."

There was silence for a few minutes, only broken by a yawn from Max and the snapping of the fire.

"I tell you I cannot forget," the young man said, at last. "You have ruined my life for me. Do you think I'll be apt to forget the woman that's done that? I'll love you always, but life is practically over for me. Remember that, the next time you amuse yourself, Miss Howe!" Then, without another word, he turned on his heel and left her.

Lois drew a long breath as she heard him slam the front door behind him, and then she sat down on the rug again. She was too angry to cry, though her hands shook with nervousness. But under all her excitement was the sting of mortification and remorse.

Max, with that strange understanding which animals sometimes show, suddenly turned and licked her face, and then looked at her, all his love speaking in his soft brown eyes.

"Oh, Max, dear," Lois cried, flinging her arms around him, and resting her cheek on his shining head, "what a comfort you are! How much nicer dogs are than men!"

CHAPTER X.

Dr. Howe, with no thought of Mr. Forsythe's unceremonious call at the rectory, had gone home with Mr. Denner. "One needs a walk," he said, "after one of Miss Deborah's dinners. Bless my soul, what a housekeeper that woman is!"

"Just so," said Mr. Denner, hurrying along at his side, — "just so. Ah — it has often occurred to me."

And when the rector had left him at his white gateway between the Lombardy poplars, Mr. Denner went into his library, and after stumbling about to light his lamp, and stirring his fire to have a semblance, at least, of cheer, he sat down and meditated further on this subject of Miss Deborah's housekeeping.

It was a dreary room, with lofty ceilings and few and narrow windows. The house was much lower than the street, and had that piercing chill of dampness which belongs to houses in a hollow, and the little gentleman drew so close to the smouldering fire that his feet were inside the fender.

He leaned forward, and resting his elbows on his knees, propped his chin on his hands, and stared at the smoke curling heavily up into the cavernous chimney, where the soot hung long and black. It was very lonely. Willie Denner, of course, had

long ago gone to bed, and unless the lawyer chose
to go into the kitchen for company, where Mary was
reading her one work of fiction, "The Accounts of
the Death Beds of Eminent Saints," he had no one
to speak to. Many a time before had he sat.thus,
pondering on the solitude of his life, and contrasting
his house with other Ashurst homes. He glanced
about his cold bare room, and thought of the parlor
of the Misses Woodhouse. How pleasant it was,
how bright, and full of pretty feminine devices!
whereas his library — Mary had been a hard mistress. One by one the domestic decorations of the
late lady of the house had disappeared. She could
not "have things round a-trapin' dust," Mary said,
and her word was law.

"If my little sister had lived," he said, crouching
nearer the fire, and watching a spark catch in the
soot and spread over the chimney-back like a little
marching regiment, that wheeled and manœuvred,
and then suddenly vanished, "it would have been
different. She would have made things brighter.
Perhaps she would have painted, like Miss Ruth;
and I have no doubt she would have been an excellent housekeeper. We should have just lived
quietly here, she and I, and I need never have
thought " — Mr. Denner flushed faintly in the firelight — "of marriage."

Mr. Denner's mind had often traveled as far as
this; he had even gone to the point of saying to
himself that he wished one of the Misses Woodhouse
would regard him with sentiments of affection, and
he and Willie, free from Mary, could have a home

of their own, instead of forlornly envying the rector and Henry Dale.

But Mr. Denner had never said which Miss Woodhouse ; he had always thought of them, as he would have expressed it, " collectively," nor could he have told which one he most admired, — he called it by no warmer name, even to himself.

But as he sat here alone, and remembered the pleasant evening he had had, and watched his fire smoulder and die, and heard the soft sigh of the rising wind, he reached a tremendous conclusion. He would make up his mind. He would decide which of the Misses Woodhouse possessed his deeper regard. " Yes," he said, as he lifted first one foot and then the other over the fender, and, pulling his little coat-tails forward under his arms, stood with his back to the fireplace, — " yes, I will make up my mind ; I will make it up to-morrow. I cannot go on in this uncertain way. I cannot allow myself to think of Miss Ruth, and how she would paint her pictures, and play my accompaniments, and then find my mind on Miss Deborah's dinners. It is impracticable ; it is almost improper. To-morrow I will decide."

To have reached this conclusion was to have accomplished a great deal.

Mr. Denner went to bed much cheered ; but he dreamed of walking about Miss Ruth's studio, and admiring her pictures, when, to his dismay, he found Mary had followed him, and was saying she could n't bear things all of a clutter.

The next morning he ate his breakfast in solemn

haste; it was to be an important day for him. He
watched Mary as she walked about, handing him
dishes with a sternness which had always awed him
into eating anything she placed before him, and
wondered what she would think when she heard —
He trembled a little at the thought of breaking it to
her; and then he remembered Miss Ruth's kind
heart, and he had a vision of a pension for Mary,
which was checked instantly by the recollection of
Miss Deborah's prudent economy.

"Ah, well," he thought, "I shall know to-night.
Economy is a good thing, — Miss Ruth herself would
not deny that."

He went out to his office, and weighed and balanced his inclinations until dinner-time, and again in
the afternoon, but with no result. Night found him
hopelessly confused, with the added grievance that
he had not kept his word to himself.

This went on for more than a week; by and by
the uncertainty began to wear greatly upon him.

"Dear me!" he sighed one morning, as he sat in
his office, his little gaitered feet upon the rusty top
of his air-tight stove, and his brierwood pipe at his
lips — it had gone out, leaving a bowl of cheerless
white ashes, — " dear me! I no sooner decide that it
had better be Miss Deborah — for how satisfying
my linen would be if she had an eye on the laundry,
and I know she would not have bubble-and-squeak
for dinner as often as Mary does — than Miss Ruth
comes into my mind. What taste she has, and
what an ear! No one notices the points in my singing as she does; and how she did turn that carpet
in Gifford's room; dear me!"

He sat clutching his extinguished pipe for many minutes, when suddenly a gleam came into his face, and the anxious look began to disappear.

He rose, and laid his pipe upon the mantelpiece, first carefully knocking the ashes into the wood-box which stood beside the stove. Then, standing with his left foot wrapped about his right ankle and his face full of suppressed eagerness, he felt in each pocket of his waistcoat, and produced first a knife, then a tape measure, a pincushion, a bunch of keys, and last a large, worn copper cent. It was smooth with age, but its almost obliterated date still showed that it had been struck the year of Mr. Denner's birth.

Next, he spread his pocket handkerchief smoothly upon the floor, and then, a little stiffly, knelt upon it. He rubbed the cent upon the cuff of his coat to make it shine, and held it up a moment in the stream of wintry sunshine that poured through the office window and lay in a golden square on the bare floor.

" Heads, " said Mr. Denner, — " heads shall be Miss Deborah ; tails, Miss Ruth. Oh, dear me ! I wonder which ? "

As he said this, he pitched the coin with a tremulous hand, and then leaned forward, breathlessly watching it fall, waver from side to side, and roll slowly under the bookcase. Too much excited to rise from his knees, he crept towards it, and, pressing his cheek against the dusty floor, he peered under the unwieldy piece of furniture, to catch a glimpse of his penny and learn his fate.

At such a critical moment it was not surprising that he did not hear Willie Denner come into the office. The little boy stood still, surprised at his uncle's attitude. "Have you lost something, sir?" he said, but without waiting for an answer, he fell on his knees and looked also.

"Oh, I see, — your lucky penny; I'll get it for you in a minute."

And stretching out flat upon his stomach, he wriggled almost under the bookcase, while Mr. Denner rose and furtively brushed the dust from his knees.

"Here it is, uncle William," Willie said, emerging from the shadow of the bookcase; "it was clear against the wall, and 'most down in a crack."

Mr. Denner took the penny from the child, and rubbed it nervously between his hands.

"I suppose," he inquired with great hesitation, "you did not chance to observe, William, which — ah — which side was up?"

"No, sir," answered Willie, with amazement written on his little freckled face; "it had n't fallen, you know, uncle; it was just leaning against the wall. I came in to bring my Latin exercise," he went on. "I'll run back to school now, sir."

He was off like a flash, saying to himself in a mystified way, "I wonder if uncle William plays heads and tails all alone in the office?"

Mr. Denner stood holding the penny, and gazing blankly at it, unconscious of the dust upon his cheek.

"That did not decide it," he murmured. "I must try something else."

For Mr. Denner had some small superstitions, and it is doubtful if he would have questioned fate again in the same way, even if he had not been interrupted at that moment by the rector.

Dr. Howe came into the office beating his hands to warm them, his face ruddy and his breath short from a walk in the cold wind. He had come to see the lawyer about selling a bit of church land ; Mr. Denner hastily slipped his penny into his pocket, and felt his face grow hot as he thought in what a posture the rector would have found him had he come a few minutes sooner.

" Bless my soul, Denner," Dr. Howe said, when, the business over, he rose to go, " this den of yours is cold ! " He stooped to shake the logs in the small stove, hoping to start a blaze. The rector would have resented any man's meddling with his fire, but all Mr. Denner's friends felt a sort of responsibility for him, which he accepted as a matter of course.

" Ah, yes," replied Mr. Denner, " it is chilly here. It had not occurred to me, but it is chilly. Some people manage to keep their houses very comfortable in weather like this. It is always warm at the rectory, I notice, and at Henry Dale's, or — ah — the Misses Woodhouse's, — always warm."

The rector, taking up a great deal of room in the small office, was on his knees, puffing at the fire until his face was scarlet. " Yes. I don't believe that woman of yours half looks after your comfort, Denner. Can't be a good housekeeper, or she would not let this stove get so choked with ashes."

" No," Mr. Denner acknowledged — " ah — I am

inclined to agree with you, doctor.   Not perhaps a really good housekeeper.   But few women are, — very few.   You do not find a woman like Miss Deborah Woodhouse often, you know."

"True enough," said Dr. Howe, pulling on his big fur gloves.   "That salad of hers, the other night, was something to live for.   What is that ? — 'plunge his fingers in the salad bowl ' — 'tempt the dying anchorite to eat,' — I can't remember the lines, but that is how I feel about Miss Deborah's salad."   The rector laughed in a quick, breezy bass, beat his hands together, and was ready to start.

"Yes," said Mr. Denner, "just so, — quite so. But Miss Deborah is a remarkable woman, an estimable woman.   One scarcely knows which is the more admirable, Miss Deborah or Miss Ruth.   Which should you — ah — which do you most admire ? "

The rector turned, with one hand on the doorknob, and looked at the lawyer, with a sudden gleam in his keen eyes.   "Well, I am sure I don't know. I never thought of comparing them.   They are both, as you say, estimable ladies."

"Oh, yes, yes, just so," said Mr. Denner hurriedly.   "I only mentioned it because — it was merely in the most general way ; I — I — did not mean to compare — oh, not at all — of course I should never discuss a lady's worth, as it were.   I spoke in confidence ; I merely wondered what your opinion might be — not" — cried Mr. Denner, bursting into a cold perspiration of fright to see how far his embarrassment had betrayed him — "not that I really care to know !   Oh, not at all ! "

The rector flung his head back, and his rollicking laugh jarred the very papers on Mr. Denner's desk.

"It is just as well you don't, for I am sure I could not say. I respect them both immensely. I have from boyhood," he added, with a droll look.

Mr. Denner coughed nervously.

"It is not of the slightest consequence," he explained, — "not the slightest. I spoke thoughtlessly; ah — unadvisedly."

"Of course, of course; I understand," cried the rector, and forbore to add a good-natured jest at Mr. Denner's embarrassment, which was really painful.

But when he was well out of hearing, he could not restrain a series of chuckles.

"By Jove!" he cried, clapping his thigh, "Denner! — Denner and Miss Deborah! Bless my soul, — Denner!"

His mirth, however, did not last long; some immediate annoyances of his own forced themselves into his mind.

Before he went to the lawyer's office, he had had a talk with Mrs. Dale, which had not been pleasant; then a letter from Helen had come; and now an anxious wrinkle showed itself under his fur cap, as he walked back to the rectory.

He had gone over to show Mr. Dale a somewhat highly seasoned sketch in "Bell's Life;" in the midst of their enjoyment of it, they were interrupted by Mrs. Dale.

"I want to speak to you about Lois, brother. Ach! how this room smells of smoke!" she said.

"Why, what has the child done now?" said Dr. Howe.

" You need n't say ' What has she done now ? ' as though I was always finding fault," Mrs. Dale answered, " though I do try to do my Christian duty if I see any one making a mistake."

" Adele," remarked the rector, with a frankness which was entirely that of a brother, and had no bearing upon his office, " you are always ready enough with that duty of fault-finding." Mr. Dale looked admiringly at his brother - in - law. " Why don't you think of the duty of praise, once in a while ? Praise is a Christian grace too much neglected. Don't you think so, Henry ? "

But Mrs. Dale answered instead : " I am ready enough to praise when there is occasion for it, but you can't expect me to praise Lois for her behavior to young Forsythe. Arabella says the poor youth is completely prostrated by the blow."

" Bah ! " murmured Mr. Dale under his breath ; but Dr. Howe said impatiently, —

" What do you mean ? What blow ? "

" Why, Lois has refused him ! " cried Mrs. Dale. " What else ? "

" I did n't know she had refused him," the rector answered slowly. " Well, the child is the best judge, after all."

" I am glad of it," said Mr. Dale, — " I am glad of it. He was no husband for little Lois, — no, my dear, pray let me speak, — no husband for Lois. I have had some conversation with him, and I played euchre with him once. He played too well for a gentleman, Archibald."

" He beat you, did he ? " said the rector.

"That had nothing to do with it!" cried Mr. Dale. "I should have said the same thing had I been his partner " —

"Fudge!" Mrs. Dale interrupted, "as though it made the slightest difference how a man played a silly game! Don't be foolish, Henry. Lois has made a great mistake, but I suppose there is nothing to be done, unless young Forsythe should try again. I hope he will, and I hope she will have more sense."

The rector was silent. He could not deny that he was disappointed, and as he went towards the post-office, he almost wished he had offered a word of advice to Lois. "Still, a girl needs her mother for that sort of thing, and, after all, perhaps it is best. For really, I should be very dull at the rectory without her." Thus he comforted himself for what was only a disappointment to his vanity, and was quite cheerful when he opened Helen's letter.

The post-office was in that part of the drug-store where the herbs were kept, and the letters always had a faint smell of pennyroyal or wormwood about them. The rector read his letter, leaning against the counter, and crumpling some bay leaves between his fingers ; and though he was interrupted half a dozen times by people coming for their mail, and stopping to gossip about the weather or the church, he gained a very uncomfortable sense of its contents.

"More of this talk about belief," he grumbled, as he folded the last sheet, covered with the clear heavy writing, and struck it impatiently across his hand before he thrust it down into his pocket. "What

in the world is John Ward thinking of to let her
bother her head with such questions ? "

" I am surprised," Helen wrote, " to see how narrowness and intolerance seem to belong to intense
belief. Some of these elders in John's church, especially a man called Dean (the father of my Alfaretta), believe in their horrible doctrines with all
their hearts, and their absolute conviction make them
blind to any possibility of good in any creed which
does not agree with theirs. Apparently, they think
they have reached the ultimate truth, and never even
look for new light. That is the strangest thing to
me. Now, for my part, I would not sign a creed
to-day which I had written myself, because one lives
progressively in religion as in everything else. But,
after all, as I said to Gifford the other day, the *form*
of belief is of so little consequence. The main thing
is to have the realization of God in one's own soul ;
it would be enough to have that, I should think.
But to some of us God is only another name for the
power of good, — or, one might as well say force,
and that is blind and impersonal ; there is nothing
comforting or tender in the thought of force. How
do you suppose the conviction of the personality of
God is reached ? "

" All nonsense," said the rector, as he went home,
striking out with his cane at the stalks of golden-
rod standing stiff with frost at the roadside. " I
shall tell Gifford he ought to know better than to
have these discussions with her. Women don't understand such things ; they go off at half cock, and
think themselves skeptics. All nonsense ! "

But the rector need not have felt any immediate anxiety about his niece. As yet such questions were only a sort of intellectual exercise ; the time had not come when they should be intensely real, and she should seek for an answer with all the force of her life, and know the anguish of despair which comes when a soul feels itself adrift upon a sea of unbelief. They were not of enough importance to talk of to John, even if she had not known they would trouble him ; she and Gifford had merely spoken of them as speculations of general interest ; yet all the while they were shaping and moulding her mind for the future.

But the letter brought a cloud on Dr. Howe's face ; he wanted to forget it, he was impatient to shake off the unpleasant remembrances it roused, and so engaged was he in this that by the time he had reached the rectory Mr. Denner and his perplexities were quite out of his mind, though the lawyer's face was still tingling with mortification.

Mr. Denner could not keep his thoughts from his puzzle. Supper-time came, and he was still strug-gling to reach a conclusion. He carved the cold mutton with more than usual precision, and ate it in anxious abstraction. The room was chilly ; draughts from the narrow windows made the lamp flare, and the wind from under the closed door raised the car-pet in swells along the floor. He did not notice Willie, who kept his hands in his pockets for warmth, and also because he had nothing for them to do.

When Mr. Denner rang for Mary, the boy said

with anxious politeness, " Was — was the mutton good, sir ? "

Willie had been well brought up, — he was not to speak unless spoken to ; but under the press of hunger nature rebelled, for his uncle, in his absorption, had forgotten to help him to anything.

Mr. Denner carved some meat for the child, and then sat and watched him with such gloomy eyes, that Willie was glad to finish and push his chair back for prayers.

The table was cleared, and then Mary put the Bible in front of Mr. Denner, and Jay's " Morning and Evening Exercises," open at the proper day. Two candles in massive candlesticks on either side of his book gave an unsteady light, and when they flickered threw strange shadows on the ceiling. The frames which held the paintings of Mr. Denner's grandparents loomed up dark and forbidding, and Mary, who always sat with her arms rolled in her apron and her head bowed upon her ample breast, made a grotesque shadow, which danced and bobbed about on the door of the pantry. Mary generally slept through prayers, while for Willie it was a time of nervous dread. The room was so dark, and his uncle's voice so strange and rolling, the little fellow feared to kneel down and turn his back to the long table with its ghastly white cloth ; his imagination pictured fearful things stealing upon him from the mysterious space beneath it, and his heart beat so he could scarcely hear the words of the prayer. But Mr. Denner enjoyed it. Not, however, because prayer was the expression of his soul ; family prayer was merely a dignified and proper observance. Mr. Denner would not have omitted it any more than he would have neglected Sunday morning service; but he was scarcely more aware of the words than Willie or Mary were. It was the reading which gave Mr. Denner so much pleasure.

Perhaps the cases he had never pleaded, the dramatic force which he secretly longed to exert, expended themselves in the sonorous chapters of Isaiah or in the wail of Jeremiah. Indeed, the thought had more than once occurred to Mr. Denner that the rector, who read the service with cheerful haste, might improve in his own delivery, could he listen to the eloquence under which Mary and little Willie sat every evening.

To-night it was the victory of Jephtha. The reading proceeded as usual : Mary slumbered tranquilly at her end of the room; Willie counted the number of panes of glass in the window opposite him, and wondered what he should do if suddenly a white face should peer in at him out of the darkness ; Mr. Denner had reached the vow that whatsoever should first meet Jephtha, — when, with his hand extended, his eyebrows drawn together, and his whole attitude expressing the anxiety and fear of the conqueror, he stopped abruptly. Here was an inspiration !

Mary woke with a start. " Is it a stroke ? " she exclaimed. But Willie, with one frightened look at the window and the long table, slipped from his chair to kneel, thinking the reading was over. The sound of his little copper-toed boots upon the floor aroused Mr. Denner ; he frowned portentously. " *So*

Jephtha passed over unto the children of Ammon," he read on, " *to fight against them, and the Lord delivered them into his hands."*

When prayers were ended, however, and he was sitting in his library alone, he said with a subdued glee, " That is the way to do it, — the one I see first ! " And Mr. Denner went to bed with a quiet mind, and the peace which follows the decision of a momentous question.

CHAPTER XI.

THE cold that winter was more persistent and severe in the mountains than down in Ashurst.

At Lockhaven the river had been frozen over for
a month, even above the bridge and the mills, where
the current was swiftest. Long lines of sawdust,
which had been coiling and whirling in the eddies,
or stretching across the black seething water, were
caught in the ice, or blown about with the powdered
snow over its surface.

Rafts could not come down the river, so the mills
had no work to do, for the logs on hand at the beginning of the cold snap had been sawed into long
rough planks, and piled in the lumber-yards, ready
to be rafted as soon as the thaw came. The cold,
still air was sweet with the fragrance of fresh pine
boards, and the ground about the mills was covered
with sawdust, so that footsteps fell as silently as
though on velvet, instead of ringing sharp against
the frozen ground.

John Ward, walking wearily home from a long
visit to a sick woman, came, as he crossed the lumber-yards, upon a group of raftsmen; they had not
heard his approach, and were talking loudly, with
frequent bursts of drunken laughter.

It was towards evening; the sky had been threatening all day, and when the clouds lifted suddenly in

the west, blown aside like tumultuous folds of a gray
curtain, the red sun sent a flood of color across the
wintry landscape; the bare branches of the trees
were touched with light, and the pools of black, clear
ice gleamed with frosty fire. John's face had caught
the radiance.

He had come up to the men so silently that he
had been standing beside them a moment before
they noticed him, and then Tom Davis, with a start
of drunken fear, tried to hide the bottle which he
held.

" Damn you, mate, you 're spillin' it! " cried one
of the others, making an unsteady lunge forward to
seize the bottle.

" Let up, let up," said Tom thickly. " Don't ye
see the preacher? " Though Davis was not one of
his flock, he had the same reverence for the preacher
which his congregation felt. All Lockhaven loved
and feared John Ward.

John had not spoken, even though a little boy,
building block houses on a heap of sawdust near the
men, had come up and taken his hand with a look
of confident affection.

The man who had saved the whiskey stumbled to
his feet, and leaning against a pile of lumber stood
open - mouthed, waiting for the preacher's rebuke;
but Davis hung his head, and began to fumble for a
pipe in his sagging coat pocket; with clumsy fingers,
scattering the tobacco from his little bag, he tried
to fill it.

" Tom," the preacher said, at last, " I want you
to come home with me, now. And Jim, you will
give me that bottle."

"I can't go home, preacher. I've got to buy some things. She said I was to buy some things for the brats."

"Have you bought them?" John asked. Tom gave a silly laugh.

"Not yet, preacher, not yet."

"Listen, men," John said, with sudden sternness. "You have let this child see you on the road to hell. If he can remember this sight, it will save his soul."

Tom Davis shrank as the preacher said "hell." He gave a maudlin cry, and almost whimpered, "No, sir, no, preacher, I am a-goin' to reform." John had known what note to touch in this debased nature. Not love, nor hope, nor shame, would move Tom Davis, but fear stung him into a semblance of sobriety. "I'll come along wi' you," he went on, swaying back and forth, and steadying himself with a hand on the lumber against which he had been leaning. "This is the last time, preacher. You won't see me this way no more."

Here he hiccoughed, and then laughed, but remembering himself instantly, drew his forehead into a scowl.

The other men slunk away, for the minister had taken the bottle, and Tom Davis was following him through the narrow passages between the great piles of boards, towards his house.

The boy had gone back to his block house; the pile of sawdust in the sheltered corner was more comfortable and not more cheerless than his own home.

John left Davis at his door. The man looked
cowed, but there was no shame in his face, and no
sense of sin. It was unpleasant to be caught by
the preacher, and he was frightened by that awful
word, which it was the constant effort of his numb,
helpless brain to forget.

John went on alone. He walked slowly, with his
eyes fixed absently on the ground, thinking. " Poor
Davis," he said, " poor fellow ! " The man's future
seemed quite hopeless to the preacher, and, thinking
of it, he recalled Mrs. Davis's regret that he had not
spoken of hell in his sermon.

John sighed. His grief at Helen's unbelief was
growing in his silence ; yet he realized the incon-
sistency of his love in hiding his sorrow from her.

" It is robbing her, not to let her share it," he
thought, " but I dare not speak to her yet."

More than once during the winter he had tried to
show her the truth and the beauty of various doctrines, generally that of reprobation, but she had
always evaded discussion ; sometimes lightly, for it
seemed such a small matter to her, but always firmly.

The preacher loitered, stopping to look at the
river and the gaunt line of mills against the sky.
He left the path, and went down to the edge of the
white ice, so full of air bubbles, it seemed like solid
snow, and listened to the gurgle of the hurrying
water underneath.

A shed was built close to the stream, to shelter
a hand fire - engine. It had not been used for so
long that the row of buckets beside it, which were
for dipping up water to fill it, were warped and

cracked, their iron bands rusty, and out of one or two the bottom had fallen. The door of the shed creaked on its one hinge, and John looked up surprised to see how dark it had grown, then he turned towards home.

"Yes," he said to himself, "I must show her her danger. It will grieve her to force an argument upon her, and I don't think she has had one unhappy hour since we were married; but even if it were not for her own soul's sake, I must not let my people starve for the bread of life, to spare her. I must not be silent concerning the danger of the sinner. But it will trouble her, — it will trouble her."

John had dallied with temptation so long, that it had grown bold, and did not always hide under the plea of wisdom, but openly dared him to inflict the pain of grieving his wife upon himself. He still delayed, yet there were moments when he knew himself a coward, and had to summon every argument of the past to his defense. But before he reached the parsonage door he had lapsed into such tender thoughts of Helen that he said again, "Not quite yet; it seems to annoy her so to argue upon such things. I must leave it until I win her to truth by the force of its own constraining beauty. Little by little I will draw her attention to it. And I must gradually make my sermons more emphatic."

Helen met him at the door, and drew him into the house. "You are so late," she said, pressing his chill fingers against her warm cheek, and chafing them between her hands.

He stopped to kiss her before he took his coat off, smiling at her happiness and his own.

"How raw and cold it is!" she said. "Come into the study; I have a beautiful fire for you. Is it going to snow, do you think? How is your sick woman?"

"Better," he answered, as he followed her into the room. "Oh, Helen, it is good to be at home. I have not seen you since noon."

She laughed, and then insisted that he should sit still, and let her bring his supper into the study, and eat it there by the fire. He watched her with a delicious luxury of rest and content; for he was very tired and very happy.

She put a little table beside him, covered with a large napkin; and then she brought a loaf of brown bread and some honey, with a mould of yellow butter, and last a little covered dish of chicken.

"I broiled that for you myself," she explained proudly; "and I did not mean to give you coffee, but what do you think? — the whole canister of tea has disappeared. When Alfaretta went to get it for my supper, it had gone."

"Oh," John said, smiling, while Helen began to pour some cream into his coffee from a flat little silver jug, "I forgot to mention it: the fact is, I took that tea with me this afternoon, — I thought probably they had none in the house; and I wish you could have seen the woman's joy at the sight of it. I cooked some for her, — she told me how," he said deprecatingly, for Helen laughed; "and she said it was very good, too," he added.

But Helen refused to believe that possible. " It was politeness, John," she cried gayly, " and because, I suppose, you presented her with my lacquered canister."

" I did leave it," John admitted; " I never thought of it." But he forgot even to ask forgiveness, as she bent towards him, resting her hand on his shoulder while she put his cup beside him.

" The fire has flushed your cheek," he said, touching it softly, the lover's awe shining in his eyes ; with John it had never been lost in the assured possession of the husband. Helen looked at him, smiling a little, but she did not speak. Silence with her told sometimes more than words.

" It has been such a long afternoon," he said. " I was glad to hurry home ; perhaps that is the reason I forgot the canister."

" Shall I send you back for it ? " She put her lips for a moment against his hand, and then, glancing out at the night for sheer joy at the warmth and light within, she added, " Why, what is that glow, John ? It looks like fire."

He turned, and then pushed back his chair and went to the window.

" It does look like fire," he said anxiously.

Helen had followed him, and they watched together a strange light, rising and falling, and then brightening again all along the sky. Even as they looked the upper heavens began to pulsate and throb with faint crimson.

" It is fire ! " John exclaimed. " Let me get my coat. I must go."

"Oh, not now," Helen said. "You must finish your supper; and you are so tired, John!"

But he was already at the door and reaching for his hat.

"It must be the lumber-yards, and the river is frozen!"

"Wait!" Helen cried. "Let me get my cloak. I will go if you do," and a moment later the parsonage door banged behind them, and they hurried out into the darkness.

The street which led to the lumber-yards had been silent and deserted when John passed through it half an hour before, but now all Lockhaven seemed to throng it.

The preacher and his wife could hear the snapping and crackling of flames even before they turned the last corner and saw the blaze, which, sweeping up into the cold air, began to mutter before it broke with a savage roar. They caught sight of Gifford's broad shoulders in the crowd, which stood, fascinated and appalled, watching the destruction of what to most of them meant work and wages.

"Oh, Giff!" Helen said when they reached his side, "why don't they do something? Have they tried to put it out?"

"It's no use to try now," Gifford answered. "They did n't discover it in time. It has made such headway, that the only thing to do is to see that it burns out, without setting fire to any of the houses. Fortunately the wind is towards the river."

John shook his head; he was too breathless to speak for a moment; then he said, "Something must be done."

"There is no use, Mr. Ward," Gifford explained. But John scarcely heard him; his people's comfort, their morality almost, — for poverty meant deeper sin to most of them, — was burning up in those great square piles of planks.

"Men," he shouted, "men, the engine! To the river! Run! run!"

"Nothing can be done," Gifford said, as the crowd broke, following the preacher, who was far ahead of all; but he too started, as though to join them, and then checked himself, and went back into the deserted street, walking up and down, a self-constituted patrol.

Almost every man had gone to the river. Tom Davis, however, with Molly beside him, stood lolling against a tree, sobered, indeed, by the shock of the fire, but scarcely steady enough on his legs to run. Another, who was a cripple, swaying to and fro on his crutches with excitement, broke into a storm of oaths because his companion did not do the work for which he was himself too helpless. But Tom only gazed with bleared eyes at the fire, and tried to stand up straight.

The little crowd of women about Helen had been silenced at first by the tumult and glare, but now broke into wild lamentations, and entreaties that Heaven would send the engine soon, wringing their hands, and sobbing, and frightening the children that clung about their skirts even more than the fire itself.

"How did it start?" Helen said, turning to the woman next to her, who, shivering with excitement,

held a baby in her arms, who gazed at the fire with
wide, tranquil eyes, as though it had been gotten up
for his entertainment.

"They say," answered the woman, tossing her
head in the direction of Tom Davis, — "they say
him and some other fellows was in 'mong the lumber this afternoon, drinkin', you know, and smokin'.
Most likely a match dropped, or ashes from their
pipes. Drunken men ain't reasonable about them
things," she added, with the simplicity of experience.
"They don't stop to think they 're burnin' up money,
an' whiskey too ; for Dobbs don't trust 'em, now the
mill is shut down."

"Yes," said another woman who stood by, "them
men ! what do they care ? You," she shouted, shaking her fist at Tom, — "you 'll starve us all, will
ye ? an' your poor wife, just up from her sick bed !
I do' know as she 'll be much worse off, though,
when he is out of work," she added, turning to
Helen — "fer every blessed copper he has goes to
the saloon."

"Yer man 's as bad as me," Tom protested, stung
by her taunts and the jeers of the cripple.

"An' who is it as leads him on ? " screamed the
woman. "An' if he does take a drop sometimes, it
was n't him as was in the lumber-yard this afternoon, a-settin' fire to the boards, an' burnin' up the
food and comfort o' the whole town ! "

Tom hurled a torrent of profanity at the woman
and the cripple collectively, and then stumbled towards the road with the crowd, for the fire was approaching the side of the yard where they stood,
and beating them back into the village street.

The air was filled with the appalling roar and scream of the flames; showers of sparks were flung up against the black sky, as with a tremendous crash the inside of one of the piles would collapse; and still the engine did not come.

"Hurry! hurry!" the women shouted with hoarse, terrified voices, and some ran to the edge of the bluff and looked down at the river.

The men were hurrying; but as they drew the long-unused engine from its shed, an axle broke, and with stiff fingers they tried to mend it. Some had had to run for axes to break the ice, and then they pushed and jostled each other about the square hole they had cut, to dip up the dark, swift water underneath; and all the while the sky behind them grew a fiercer red, and the very ice glared with the leaping flames. At last, pulling and pushing, they brought the little engine up the slope, and then with a great shout dragged it into the outskirts of the yard. They pumped furiously, and a small jet of water was played upon the nearest pile of boards. A hissing cloud of steam almost hid the volunteer firemen, but the flames leaped and tossed against the sky, and the sparks were sucked up into the cold air, and whirled in sheets across the river.

John Ward came breathlessly towards his wife. "Are you all right, Helen? You seemed too near; come back a little further." Then, suddenly seeing the woman beside her with the baby in her arms, he stopped, and looked about. "Where's your boy, Mrs. Nevins?" he said. The woman glanced around her.

" I — I 'm not just sure, preacher."

" Have you seen him since six o'clock ? "

" No — I — I ain't," the woman answered. There was something in John's face which terrified her, though the mere absence of her son gave her no uneasiness.

" Go back, Helen," he said, quickly, — " go as far as that second house, or I shall not feel sure you are safe. Mrs. Nevins, we must look for Charley. I am afraid — he was in the lumber-yard this afternoon" —

John did not wait to hear the woman's shriek ; he turned and ran from group to group, looking for the boy whom he had seen building block houses on the pile of sawdust ; but the mother, pushing her baby into a neighbor's arms, ran up and down like a mad woman.

" My boy ! " she cried ; " Charley ! Charley ! He 's in the fire, — my boy 's in the fire ! "

Tom Davis had heard the hurried words of the preacher, and the mother's cries roused all the manhood drink had left. He hesitated a moment, and then pushing Molly towards the cripple whose taunts still rung in his ears, " Take care of the brat ! " he said, and pulling off his coat, which he wrapped about his head to guard himself from the falling boards, he stooped almost double, and with his left arm bent before his face, and his right extended to feel his way, he ran towards the fire, and disappeared in the blinding smoke.

Even Mrs. Nevins was silenced for a moment of shuddering suspense ; and when she tossed her arms into the air again, and shrieked, it was because John Ward came towards her with Charley trotting at his side.

"You should have looked after the child," the preacher said sternly. "I found him on the other side of the yard, near the fire-engine."

Mrs. Nevins caught the boy in her arms in a paroxysm of rage and joy; and then she thought of Tom.

"Oh, preacher," she cried, "preacher! he's run in after him, Tom Davis has!"

"*There?*" John said, pointing to the fire. "God help him!"

There was no human help possible. Tom had run down between two long piles of boards, not yet in flames, but already a sheet of fire swept madly across the open space. They could only look at each other, dumb with their own helplessness, and wait. How long this horror of expectation lasted no one knew, but at last, as if from the very mouth of hell, Tom Davis came, staggering and swaying, — his singed coat still rolled about his head, and his hands stretched blindly out.

John Ward ran towards him, and even the cripple pressed forward to take his hand. But with unseeing eyes he stood a moment, and then fell forward on his face. They lifted him, and carried him back into the street, away from the glare of light; there were plenty of kindly hands and pitying words, for most of the crowd had gathered about him; even the men who had brought the engine followed, for their efforts to subdue the fire were perfectly futile.

They laid him down on the stiff frozen grass by the roadside; but Molly clung so tightly about his neck, that the preacher could scarcely move her to put his hand upon Tom's heart; Helen lifted the little girl, and laid her own wet cheek against the child's.

The group of men and women stood awed and silent about the prostrate form, waiting for John to raise his head from the broad, still breast; when he lifted it, they knew all was over.

Whether the shock of the heat and tumult, coming upon the stupor of intoxication, and paralyzing the action of the heart, or whether a blow from a burning plank, had killed him, no one could know. The poor sodden, bloated body was suddenly invested with the dignity of death; and how death had come was for a little while a secondary thought.

" He is dead," John said. " He has died like a brave man ! "

He stood looking down at the body for some moments, and no one spoke. Then, as there was a stir among those who stood near, and some one whispered that Mrs. Davis must be told, the preacher looked away from the dead man's face.

" Poor soul," he said, " poor soul ! "

A few light flakes of snow were beginning to fall in that still, uncertain way which heralds a storm; some touched the dead face with pure white fingers, as though they would hide the degraded body from any eyes less kind than God's.

Helen, who had gone further back into the street that Molly might not look again at her father, came to John's side.

" I will take Molly home with me," she said ; " tell Mrs. Davis where she is."

" Gifford is here to go with you ? " John asked, with that quick tenderness which never left him. Then he turned away to help in carrying the dead man to his home.

The silent procession, with its awful burden, went back through the streets, lighted yet by the pulsing glare of the fire. John walked beside the still figure with his head bent upon his breast. That first impulse of human exultation in a brave deed was gone; there was a horror of pity instead. Just before they reached Tom's home, he stopped, by a gesture, the men who bore the body.

" Oh, my people," he said, his hands stretched out to them, the snow falling softly on his bared head, " God speaks to you from the lips of this dead man. Listen to his words : the day or the hour knoweth no man ; and are you ready to face the judgment-seat of Christ ? Oh, be not deceived, be not deceived ! Whatsoever a man soweth, that shall he also reap."

It was long past midnight when the knot of men about Tom Davis's door dispersed ; the excitement of the fire faded before that frank interest in death, which such people have no hesitation in expressing. Society veils it with decent reserve, and calls it morbid and vulgar, yet it is ineradicably human, and circumstances alone decide whether it shall be confessed.

But when the preacher came out of the house, all was quiet and deserted. The snow, driving in white sheets down the mountains, was tinged with a faint

glow, where, in a blinding mist it whirled across the
yards; it had come too late to save the lumber, but
it had checked and deadened the flames, so that the
few unburned planks only smouldered slowly into
ashes.

John had told Mrs. Davis of her loss with that
wonderful gentleness which characterized all his
dealings with sorrow. He found her trying to quiet
her baby, when he went in, leaving outside in the
softly falling snow that ghastly burden which the
men bore. She looked up with startled, questioning
eyes as he entered. He took the child out of her
arms, and hushed it upon his breast, and then, with
one of her shaking hands held firm in his, he told
her.

Afterwards, it seemed to her that the sorrow in his
face had told her, and that she knew his message
before he spoke.

Mrs. Davis had not broken into loud weeping
when she heard her husband's fate, and she was
very calm, when John saw her again, after all had
been done which was needful for the dead; only moving nervously about, trying to put the room into an
unusual order. John could not bear to leave her;
knowing what love is, his sympathy for her grief
was almost grief itself; yet he had said all that he
could say to comfort her, all that he could of Tom's
bravery in rushing into the fire, and it seemed useless to stay. But as he rose to go, putting the child,
who had fallen asleep in his arms, down on the bed,
Mrs. Davis stopped him.

She stood straightening the sheet which covered

Tom's face, creasing its folds between her fingers, and pulling it a little on this side or that.

" Mr. Ward," she said, " he was drunk, Tom was."

" I know it," he answered gently.

"He went out with some money this forenoon," she went on; " he was to buy some things for the young ones. He did n't mean to drink ; he did n't mean to go near the saloon. I *know* it. Mrs. Shea, she came in a bit after he went, and she said she seen him comin' out of the saloon, drunk. But he did n't mean it. Then you brought him home. But, bein' started, preacher, he could not help it, an' he 'd been round to Dobbs's again, 'fore he seen the fire."

" Yes," John said.

Still smoothing the straight whiteness of the sheet, she said, with a tremor in her voice : —

" If he did n't want to, preacher — if he did n't mean to — perhaps it was n't a sin? and him dying in it ! "

Her voice broke, and she knelt down and hid her face in the dead man's breast. She did not think of him now as the man that beat her when he was drunk, and starved the children ; he was the young lover again. The dull, brutal man and the fretful, faded woman had been boy and girl once, and had had their little romance, like happier husbands and wives.

John did not answer her, but a mist of tears gathered in his eyes.

Mrs. Davis raised her head and looked at him. " Tell me, you don't think it will be counted a sin to

him, do you? You don't think he died in sin?"
she asked almost fiercely.

"I wish I could say I did not," he answered.

She threw her hands up over her head with a
shrill cry.

"You don't think he's lost? Say you don't,
preacher, — say you don't!"

John took her hands in his. "Try and think,"
he said gently, "how brave Tom was, how nobly he
faced death to save Charley. Leave the judgments
of God to God; they are not for us to think of."

But she would not be put off in that way. Too
weak to kneel, she had sunk upon the floor, leaning still against the bed, with one thin, gaunt arm
thrown across her husband's body.

"You think," she demanded, "that my Tom's
lost because he was drunk to-night?"

"No," he said, "I do not think that, Mrs. Davis."

"Is he saved?" she cried, her voice shrill with
eagerness.

John was silent. She clutched his arm with her
thin fingers, and shook it in her excitement; her
pinched, terrified face was close to his.

"He was n't never converted, — I know that, —
but would the Lord have cut him off, sudden-like,
in his sin, if He was n't goin' to save him?"

"We can only trust his wisdom and his goodness."

"But you think he was cut off in his sins — you
think — my Tom's lost!"

The preacher did not speak, but the passionate
pity in his eyes told her. She put her hands up to

her throat as though she were suffocating, and her face grew ghastly.

"Remember, God knows what is best for his children," John said. "He sends this grief of Tom's death to you in his infinite wisdom. He loves you, — He knows best."

"Do you mean," asked the woman slowly, "that it was best fer Tom he should die?"

"I mean this sorrow may be best for you," he answered tenderly. "God knows what you need. He sends sorrow to draw our souls nearer to Him."

"Oh," she exclaimed, her voice broken and hoarse, "I don't want no good fer me, if Tom has to die fer it. An' why should He love me instead o' Tom? Oh, I don't want his love, as would n't give Tom another chance! He might 'a' been converted this next revival, fer you would 'a' preached hell, — I know you would, then. No, I don't want no good as comes that way. Oh, preacher, you ain't going to say you think my Tom's burning in hell this night, and me living to be made better by it? Oh, no, no, no!" She crawled to his feet, and clasped his knees with her shaking arms. "Say he is n't, — say he is n't!"

But the presence of that dead man asserted the hopelessness of John's creed; no human pity could dim his faith, and he had no words of comfort for the distracted woman who clung to him. He could only lift her and try to soothe her, but she did not seem to hear him until he put her baby in her arms; at the touch of its little soft face against her drawn cheek, she trembled violently, and then came the

merciful relief of tears. She did not ask the preacher
again to say that her husband was not lost; she had
no hope that he would tell her anything but what
she already knew. "The soul that sinneth, it shall
die." She tried, poor thing, to find some comfort in
the words he spoke of God's love for her; listening
with a pathetic silence which wrung his heart.

When John left her, beating his way home
through the blinding snow, his face was as haggard
as her own. He could not escape from the ultimate
conclusion of his creed, — " He that believeth not
shall be damned." Yet he loved and trusted completely. His confidence in God's justice could not
be shaken; but it was with almost a groan that he
said, " O my God, my God, justice and judgment are
the habitation of thy throne ; mercy and truth shall
go before thy face! But justice with mercy, — justice first! "

CHAPTER XII.

THE snow fell all that night, but the day broke exquisitely clear upon a white and shining world. The sky was blue and sparkling, and the keen north wind had carved the drifts into wonderful overhanging curves, like the curling crests of breakers.

John Ward went early to Mrs. Davis's. The sharp agony of the night before was over; there was even a momentary complacency at the importance of death, for the room was full of neighbors, whose noisy sympathy drove her despair of her husband's fate from her mind. But when she saw John, her terror came back, and she began to be silent, and not so ready to tell the story of the dead man's bravery to each one that entered. But with the people who were not immediately affected, the excitement of Tom's death could scarcely last.

By the afternoon his widow was for the most part alone. Helen had thought it would be so, and waited until then to go and see her. But first she went into her kitchen, and she and Alfaretta packed a little basket with cold meat, and sweet, snowy bread, and some jam, for the children.

"They do say," Alfaretta said, as she tucked the corners of the napkin under the wicker cover, — "they do say Tom Davis went straight to the bad place, last night. He was n't never converted, you know; but somehow, seein' as he really thought he was going to save that Charley, seein' as he died for him, as you might say, it don't seem like as if it was just " — Alfaretta lowered her voice a little — " as if it was just — fair. Do you think he went there, Mrs. Ward?"

"I know he did not," Helen answered promptly. "I don't think about hell quite as you do, Alfaretta. I cannot believe God punishes people eternally; for if He is good, He could not be so cruel. Why, no human being would be so cruel as that, and do you think we ought to believe that men are better and kinder than God?"

Alfaretta looked confused. "Well, but justice?"

"Justice!" Helen said. "Would it be just if I put a little child where it was certain to fall down, and then punish it for falling? The child did not ask to be put there. So God puts us here, where we must sin; would it be just to punish us eternally for his own work?"

Alfaretta shook her head, and sighed. "Well, I don't know but yer right, though the preacher don't say so."

Helen did not speak for a moment, and then said quietly, "Perhaps not, — not yet ;˙ but he will say so some day. He is so good himself, you know, Alfaretta, he cannot bear to think every one else does not love and serve God, too ; and it seems to him as though they ought to be punished if they don't."

This was a very lame explanation, but it closed the discussion, and she hurried away from the honest, searching eyes of her servant, which she felt must

see through the flimsy excuse. Her eyes burned
with sudden tears that blurred the white landscape ;
it hurt her to excuse her husband's belief even to
herself, and gave her a feeling of disloyalty to him ;
for a moment she weakly longed to creep into the
shelter of the monstrous error in which she felt he
lived, that they might be one there, as in everything
else. " Yet it does not matter," she said to herself,
smiling a little. " We love each other. We know
we don't think alike on doctrinal points, but we love
each other."

She stopped a moment at the lumber-yard. The
ghastly blackness of the ruin glared against the
snow-covered hills and the dazzling blue of the sky ;
here and there a puff of steam showed where the
melting snow on the cooler beams dripped on the
hot embers below. Some scattered groups of lumbermen and their forlorn wives braved the cold,
and stood talking the fire over, for, after all, it was
the immediate interest ; death would not come to
them for years, perhaps, but where were they going
to get money for their families during the spring ?
There could be no rafting down the river until after
the loggers had brought their rafts from up in the
mountains, to be sawed into planks.

Alfaretta's father, who stood contemplating the
ruins, and moralizing when any one would stop to
listen to him, had pointed this out. Mr. Dean was
a carpenter, and kept a grocery store as well, so he
could pity the lumbermen from the shelter of com-
parative affluence. When he saw the preacher's
wife, he came over to speak to her.

"Well, ma'am," he said, "the dispensations of Providence is indeed mysterious, — that the river should have been froze last night!"

Mr. Dean had a habit of holding his mouth open a moment before he spoke, and looking as though he felt that his listener was impatient for his words, which were always pronounced with great deliberation. Helen had very little patience with him, and used to answer his slowly uttered remarks with a quickness which confused him.

"It would be more mysterious if it were not frozen, at this time of year," she replied, almost before he had finished speaking. She was in haste to reach Mrs. Davis, and she had no time to hear Elder Dean's platitudes.

He began to open his beak-like mouth in an astonished way, when a by-stander interrupted him: "I suppose this here sudden death in our midst" (it was easy to fall into pious phraseology in the presence of Elder Dean) "will be made the subject of the prayer-meeting to-night?"

"It will," said Mr. Dean solemnly, — "it will. It is an awful example to unbelievers. An' it is a lesson to the owners not to allow smoking in the yards." Then, with a sharp look at Helen out of his narrow eyes, he added, "I have n't seen you at prayer-meeting, lately, Mrs. Ward. It is a blessed place, a blessed place: the Lord touches sinners' hearts with a live coal from off his altar; souls have been taught to walk in the light, in the light of God." Mr. Dean prolonged the last word in an unctuous way, which he reserved for public prayer and admonition.

Helen did not answer.

But the elder was not rebuffed. " I hope we will see you soon," he said. " A solemn season of revival is approaching. Why have you stayed away so long, Mrs. Ward?"

Annoyed at the impertinence of his questions, Helen's face flushed a little.

" I do not like the prayer-meeting," she answered quietly; but before the elder could recover from the shock of such a statement, Mrs. Nevins had come up to speak to him.

" Have you seen Mrs. Davis yet, Mr. Dean?" she said. " She took on awful, last night; the neighbors heard her. 'T was after twelve 'fore she was quiet."

" Yes, I saw her," responded the elder, shaking his head in a pompous way. " I went to administer consolation. I 'm just coming from there now. It is an awful judgment on that man : no chance for repentance, overtook by hell, as I told Mrs. Davis, in a moment! But the Lord must be praised for his justice : that ought to comfort her."

" Good heavens!" cried Helen, "you did not tell that poor woman her husband was overtaken by hell?"

" Ma'am," said Mr. Dean, fairly stuttering with astonishment at the condemnation of her tone — " I — I — did."

" Oh, shame!" Helen said, heedless of the listeners around them. " How dared you say such a thing? How dared you libel the goodness of God? Tom Davis is not in hell. A man who died to save

another's life? Who would want the heaven of such
a God? Oh, that poor wife! How could you
have had the heart to make her think God was so
cruel?"

There was a dead silence; Elder Dean was too
dumfounded to speak, and the others, looking at
Helen's eyes flashing through her tears of passionate
pain, were almost persuaded that she was right.
They waited to hear more, but she turned and hurried away, her breath quick, and a tightened feeling
in her throat.

The elder was the first to break the spell of her
words, but he opened his lips twice before a sound
came. "May the Lord forgive her! Tom Davis
not in hell? Why, where's the good of a hell at
all, then?"

Helen's heart was burning with sympathy for the
sorrow which had been so cruelly wounded. She
had forgotten the reserve which respect for her husband's opinions always enforced. "It is wicked to
have said such a thing!" she thought, as she walked
rapidly along over the creaking snow. "I will tell
her it is not true, — it never could be true."

The path through the ragged, unkempt garden in
front of the tenement house was so trodden that the
snow was packed and hard. The gate swung back
with a jar and clatter, and two limp frosted hens
flew shrieking out from the shelter of the ash-heap
behind it. The door was open, and Helen could see
the square of the entry, papered, where the plaster
had not been broken away, with pale green castles
embowered in livid trees. On either side was the

entrance to a tenement; a sagging nail in one of the door-posts held a coat and a singed and battered hat. Here Helen knocked.

Mrs. Davis was in the small inner room, but came out as her visitor entered, wiping the soapsuds from her bare arms on her dingy gingham apron. On the other side of the room, opposite the door, was that awful Presence, which silenced even the voices of the children.

"I'm washing," the woman said, as she gave her hand to Helen. "It is Tom's best shirt, — fer to-morrow."

Helen took the hand, wrinkled and bleached with the work it had done, and stroked it gently; she did not know what to say. This was not the grief she had thought of, — a woman working calmly at her wash-tub, while her husband lay dead in the next room. Helen could see the tub, with the mist of steam about it, and the wash-board, and the bar of yellow soap.

She followed Mrs. Davis back to her work, and sat down on a bench, out of the way of a little stream of water which had dripped from the leaking tub, and trickled across the floor. She asked about the children, and said she had brought some food for them; she knew it was so hard to have to think of housekeeping at such a time.

But the widow scarcely listened; she stood lifting the shirt from the water, and rubbing it gently between her hard hands, then dipping it back into the suds again. Once she stopped, and drew the back of her wet hand across her eyes, and once

Helen heard her sigh; yet she did not speak of her sorrow, nor of Elder Dean's cruel words. For a little while the two women were silent.

"Mrs. Davis," Helen said, at last, "I'm so sorry."

It was a very simple thing to say, but it caught the woman's ear; it was different from any of the sympathy to which, in a dull, hopeless way, she had listened all that morning. The neighbors had sighed and groaned, and told her it was "awful hard on her," and had pitied Tom for his terrible death; and then Mr. Dean had come, with fearful talk of justice, and of hell.

A big tear rolled down her face, and dropped into the tub. "Thank you, ma'am," she said.

She made a pretense of turning towards the light of the one small window to see if the shirt was quite clean; then she began to wring it out, wrapping the twist of wet linen about her wrist. When she spoke again, her voice was steady.

"Elder Dean 'lows I ought n't to be sorry; he says I 'd ought to be resigned to God's justice. He says good folks ought to be glad when sinners go to the bad place, even if they 're belonging to them. He 'lows I 'd ought n't to be sorry."

"I am sure you have a right to be sorry Tom is dead," Helen said, — the woman's composure made her calm, too, — "but I do not believe he is in any place now that need make you sorry. I do not believe what Elder Dean said about — hell."

Mrs. Davis looked at her, a faint surprise dawning in her tired eyes, and shook her head. "Oh. I 'm not sayin' that he ain't right. I 'm not sayin' Tom

ain't in the bad place, ner that it ain't justice. I 'm
a Christian woman. I was convicted and converted
when I was n't but twelve years old, and I know my
religion. Tom — he was n't no Christian, he did n't
ever experience a change of heart: it was always
like as if he was just going to be converted, when he
was n't in drink ; fer he was good in his heart, Tom
was. But he was n't no Christian, an' I 'm not sayin' he is n't lost. I 'm only sayin'," — this with a
sudden passion, and knotting her tremulous hands
hard together, — " I 'm only sayin' I can't love God
no more ! Him havin' all the power — and then look
at Tom an' me " —

Helen tried to speak, but Mrs. Davis would not
listen. " No," she cried, " yer the preacher's wife,
but I must say it. He never give Tom a chance,
an' how am I goin' to love Him now ? Tom," — she
pointed a shaking finger at the coffin in the next
room, — " born, as you might say, drinkin'. His father died in a drunken fit, and his mother give it to
her baby with her milk. Then, what schoolin' did he
get ? Nothin', 'less it was his mother lickin' him.
Tom 's often told me that. He had n't no trade
learned, neither, — just rafted with men as bad as
him. Is it any wonder he was n't converted ? "

" I know all that," Helen began to say gently,
but Mrs. Davis could not check the torrent of her
despairing grief.

" He did n't have no chance ; an' he did n't ask to
be born, neither. God put him here, an' look at
the way He made him live ; look at this house ; see
the floor, how the water runs down into that corner :

it is all sagged an' leanin' — the whole thing is rotten
look at that one window, up against the wall; not a
ray of sunshine ever struck it. An' here's where
God's made us live. Six of us, now the baby's come.
Children was the only thing we was rich in, and we
did n't have food enough to put in their mouths, or
decent clothes to cover 'em. Look at the people
'round us here — livin' in this here row of tenements
— drinkin', lyin' swearin'. What chance had Tom ?
God never give him any, but He could of, if He'd
had a mind to. So I can't love Him, Mrs. Ward, —
I can't love Him; Him havin' all the power, and yet
lettin' Tom's soul go down to hell; fer Tom could n't
help it, and him livin' so. I ain't denyin' religion,
ner anything like that — I'm a Christian woman,
an' a member — but I can't love Him, so there's no
use talkin' — I can't love Him."

She turned away and shook the shirt out, hanging
it over the back of a chair in front of the stove, to
dry. Helen had followed her, and put her arm
across the thin, bent shoulders, her eyes full of tears,
though the widow's were hard and bright.

"Oh, Mrs. Davis," she cried, "of course you could
not love a God who would never give Tom a chance
and then punish him; of course you could not love
Him! But he is not punished by being sent to hell;
indeed, indeed, he is not. If God is good, He could
not be so cruel as to give a soul no chance, and then
send it to hell. Don't ever think that Tom, brave
fellow, is there ! Oh, believe what I say to you!"

Mrs. Davis seemed stupefied; she looked up into
these beautiful distressed brown eyes, and her dry
lips moved.

" You don't think," she said, in a hoarse, hurried whisper — "you 're not saying — *Tom is n't in hell?*"

" I know he is not, I know it! Justice? it would be the most frightful injustice, because, don't you see," she went on eagerly, "it is just as you said, — Tom had no chance; so God could not punish him eternally for being what he had to be, born as he was, and living as he did. I don't know anything about people's souls when they die, — I mean about going to heaven, — but I do know this: as long as a soul lives it has a chance for goodness, a chance to turn to God. There is no such place as hell!"

" But — but" — the widow faltered, " he was cut off in his sins. The preacher would n't say but he was lost!" Her words were a wail of despair.

Helen groaned; she was confronted by her loyalty to John, yet the suffering of this hopeless soul! " Listen," she said, taking Mrs. Davis's hands in hers, and speaking slowly and tenderly, while she held the weak, shifting eyes by her own steady look, " listen. I do not know what the preacher would say, but it is not true that Tom is lost; it is not true that God is cruel and wicked; it is not true that, while Tom's soul lives, he cannot grow good."

The rigid look in the woman's face began to disappear; her hopeless belief was shaken, not through any argument, but by the mere force of the intense conviction shining in Helen's eyes.

" Oh," she said appealingly, and beginning to tremble, " are you true with me, ma'am?"

" I am true, indeed I am!" Helen answered, un-

conscious that her own tears fell upon Mrs. Davis's
hands; the woman looked at her, and suddenly her
face began to flush that painful red which comes before violent weeping.

"If you 're true, if you 're right, then I can be
sorry. I would n't let myself be sorry while I
could n't have no hope. Oh, I can be that sorry it
turns me glad!"

The hardness was all gone now; she broke into a
storm of tears, saying between her sobs, "Oh, I 'm
so glad — I 'm so glad!"

A long time the two women sat together, the
widow still shaken by gusts of weeping, yet listening
hungrily to Helen's words, and sometimes even
smiling through her tears. The hardship of loss to
herself and her children was not even thought of;
there was only intense relief from horrible fear; she
did not even stop to pity Tom for the pain of death;
coming out of that nightmare of hell, she could only
rejoice.

The early sunset flashed a sudden ruddy light
through the window in the front room, making a
gleaming bar on the bare whitewashed wall, and
startling Helen with the lateness of the hour.

"I must go now," she said, rising. "I will come
again to-morrow."

Mrs. Davis rose, too, lifting her tear-stained face,
with its trembling smile, towards her deliverer.
"Won't you come in the other room a minute?"
she said. "I want to show you the coffin. I got the
best I could, but I did n't have no pride in it.
It seems different now."

They went in together, Mrs. Davis crying quietly. Tom's face was hidden, and a fine instinct of possession, which came with the strange uplifting of the moment, made his wife shrink from uncovering it.

She stroked the varnished lid of the coffin, with her rough hands, as tenderly as though the poor bruised body within could feel her touch.

"How do you like it ? " she asked anxiously. "I wanted to do what I could fer Tom. I got the best I could. Mr. Ward give me some money, and I spent it this way. I thought I would n't mind going hungry, afterwards. You don't suppose," — this with a sudden fear, as one who dreads to fall asleep lest a terrible dream may return, — " you don't suppose I 'll forget these things you 've been tellin' me, and think *that* of Tom ? "

"No," Helen answered, " not if you just say to yourself that I told you what Mr. Dean said was not true. Never mind if you cannot remember the reasons I have given you, — I 'll tell them all to you again ; just try and forget what the elder said."

"I will try," she said ; and then wavering a little, " but the preacher, Mrs. Ward ? "

"The preacher," Helen answered bravely, " will think this way, too, some day, I know." And then she made the same excuse for him which she had given Alfaretta, with the same pang of regret.

"Yes, ma'am," the woman said, "I see. I feel now as though I could love God real hard 'cause He 's good to Tom. But Mrs. Ward, the preacher must be wonderful good, fer he can think God would send my Tom to hell, and yet he can love Him ! I could n't do it."

" Oh, he is good ! " Helen cried, with a great leap of her heart.

The wind blew the powdered snow about, as she walked home in the cold white dusk, piling it in great drifts, or leaving a ridge of earth swept bare and clean. The blackened lumber-yards were quite deserted in the deepening chill which was felt as soon as the sun set ; the melting snow on the hot, charred planks had frozen into long icicles, and as she stopped to look at the ruin one snapped, and fell with a splintering crash.

One of those strangely unsuggested remembrances flashed into her mind : the gleam of a dove's white wing against the burning blue of a July sky, the blaze of flowers in the rectory garden, and the sub- tle, penetrating fragrance of mignonette. Perhaps the contrast of the intense cold and the gathering night brought the scene before her ; she sighed ; if she and John could go away from this grief and misery and sin, which they seemed powerless to re- lieve, and from this hideous shadow of Calvinism !

" After all," she thought, hurrying along towards home and John. " Mrs. Davis is right, — it is hard to love Him. He does not give a chance to every one ; none of us can escape the inevitable past. And that is as hard as to be punished unjustly. And there is no help for it all. Oh, where is God ? "

Just as she left the lumber-yard district, she heard her name called, and saw Gifford Woodhouse strid- ing towards her. " You have been to those poor Davises I suppose," he said, as he reached her side, and took her empty basket from her hand.

" Yes," she answered, sighing. " Oh, Gifford, how dreadful it all is, — the things these people say, and really believe ! " Then she told him of Elder Dean, and a little of her talk with Mrs. Davis. Gifford listened, his face growing very grave.

" And that is their idea of God ? " he said, as she finished. " Well, it is mine of the devil. But I can't help feeling sorry you spoke as you did to the elder."

" Why ? " she asked.

" Well," he said, " to assert your opinion of the doctrine of eternal damnation as you did, considering your position, Helen, was scarcely wise."

" Do you mean because I am the preacher's wife ? " she remonstrated, smiling. " I must have my convictions, if I am ; and I could not listen to such a thing in silence. You don't know John, if you think he would object to the expression of opinion." Gifford dared not say that John would object to the opinion itself. " But perhaps I spoke too forcibly ; I should be sorry to be unkind, even to Elder Dean."

" Well," Gifford said doubtfully, " I only hope he may not feel called upon to ' deal with you.' "

They laughed, but the young man added, " After all, when you come to think of it, Helen, there is no bigotry or narrowness which does not spring from a truth, and nothing is truer than that sin is punished eternally. It is only their way of making God responsible for it, — not ourselves, — and arranging the details of fire and brimstone, which is so monstrous. Somebody says that when the Calvinists

decided on sulphur they did not know the properties
of caustic potash.   But there are stages of truth;
there 's no use knocking a man down because he is
only on the first step of the ladder, which you have
climbed into light.   I think belief in eternal damnation is a phase in spiritual development."

" But you don't really object to my protest ? " she
said. " Come, Giff, the truth must be strong enough
to be expressed."

" I don't object to the protest," he answered
slowly, " but I hope the manner of it will not make
things difficult for Mr. Ward."

Helen laughed, in spite of her depression. " Why,
Gifford," she said, " it is not like you to be so ap-
prehensive, and over so small a matter, too.   Mr.
Dean has probably forgotten everything I said, and,
except that I mean to tell him, John would never
hear a word about it."

CHAPTER XIII.

The winter was passing very quietly in Ashurst; the only really great excitement was Helen's letter about the fire and Colonel Drayton's attack of gout.

Life went on as it had as far back as any one cared to remember, with the small round of church festivals and little teas, and the Saturday evening whist parties at the rectory. But under monotonous calm may lurk very wearing anxiety, and this was the case in Ashurst.

Mr. Denner endeavored, with but indifferent success, to conceal the indecision which was still preying upon his mind. For the suggestion gained from Jephtha had proved useless. He had, indeed, tried to act upon it. A day or two after the thought had come to him which so interrupted family prayers, Mr. Denner sallied forth to learn his fate. It was surprising how particular he was about his linen that morning, — for he went in the morning, — and he arrayed himself in his best clothes; he saw no impropriety, considering the importance of the occasion, in putting on his evening coat. He even wore his new hat, a thing he had not done more than half a dozen times — at a funeral perhaps, or a fair — since he bought it, three years before.

It was a bright, frosty day, and the little gentleman stepped briskly along the road towards the

house of the two sisters. He felt as light-hearted
as any youth who goes a-wooing with a reasonable
certainty of a favorable answer from his beloved.
He even sang a little to himself, in a thin, sweet
voice, keeping time with his stick, like a drum-
major, and dwelling faithfully on all the prolonged
notes.

"Believe me," sang Mr. Denner, —

> " 'Believe me, if all those endearing young charms
> Which I gaze on so fondly to-day' " —

Mr. Denner's rendering of charms was very elaborate. But while he was still lingering on the last
word, disappointment overtook him.

Coming arm in arm down the road were two small
figures. Mr. Denner's sight was not what it once
was ; he fumbled in the breast of his bottle-green
overcoat for his glasses, as a suspicion of the truth
dawned upon him.

His song died upon his lips, and he turned ir-
resolutely, as though to fly, but it was too late ; he
had recognized at the same moment Miss Deborah
and Miss Ruth Woodhouse. By no possibility could
he say which he had seen first.

He advanced to meet them, but the spring had
gone from his tread and the light from his eye ; he
was thrown back upon his perplexities. The sisters,
still arm in arm, made a demure little bow, and
stopped to say "Good-morning," but Mr. Denner
was evidently depressed and absent-minded.

"I wonder what 's the matter with William Denner, sister ? " Miss Ruth said, when they were out of
hearing.

" Perhaps he 's troubled about his housekeeping," answered Miss Deborah. " I should think he might be, I must say. That Mary of his does keep him looking so ! And I have no doubt she is wasteful ; a woman who is economical with her needle and thread is pretty apt not to be saving in other things."

" What a pity he has n't a wife ! " commented Miss Ruth. " Adele Dale says he 's never been in love. She says that that affair with Gertrude Drayton was a sort of inoculation, and he 's been perfectly healthy ever since."

" Very coarse in dear Adele to speak in that way," said Miss Deborah sharply. " I suppose he never has gotten over Gertrude's loss. Yet, if his sister-in-law had to die, it is a pity it was n't a little sooner. He was too old when she died to think of marriage."

" But, dear Deborah, he is not quite too old even yet, if he found a person of proper age. Not too young, and, of course, not too old."

Miss Deborah did not reply immediately. " Well, I don't know ; perhaps not," she conceded. " I do like a man to be of an age to know his own mind. That is why I am so surprised at Adele Dale's anxiety to bring about a match between young Forsythe and Lois, they are neither of them old enough to know their own minds. And it is scarcely delicate in Adele, I must say."

" He 's a very superior young man," objected Miss Ruth.

" Yes," Miss Deborah acknowledged ; " and yet "

— she hesitated a little — " I think he has not quite the — the modesty one expects in a young person."

" Yes, but think how he has seen the world, sister ! " cried Miss Ruth. " You cannot expect him to be just like other young people."

" True," said Miss Deborah, nodding her head ; " and yet " — it was evident from her persistence that Miss Deborah had a grievance of some kind — " yet he seems to have more than a proper conceit. I heard him talk about whist, one evening at the rectory ; he said something about a person, — a Pole, I believe, — and his rules in regard to ' signaling.' I asked him if he played," Miss Deborah continued, her hands showing a little angry nervousness ; " and he said, ' Oh, yes, I learned to play one winter in Florida ! ' Learned to play in a winter, indeed ! To achieve whist " — Miss Deborah held her head very straight — " to achieve whist is the work of a lifetime ! I 've no patience with a young person who says a thing like that."

Miss Ruth was silenced for a moment ; she had no excuse to offer.

" Adele Dale says the Forsythes are coming back in April," she said, at last.

" Yes, I know it," answered Miss Deborah. " I suppose it will all be arranged then. I asked Adele if Lois was engaged to him ; — she said, ' Not formally.' But I 've no doubt there 's an understanding."

Miss Deborah was so sure of this that she had even mentioned it casually to Gifford, of course under the same seal of confidence with which it had been told her.

It was quite true that Dick and his mother were
to return to Ashurst. After storming out of the
rectory library the night of the Misses Woodhouse's
dinner party, Dick had had a period of hatred of
everything connected with Ashurst; but that did not
last more than a month, and was followed by an
imploring letter to Lois. Her answer brought the
anger back again, and then its reaction of love; this
see-saw was kept up, until his last letter had announced that he and his mother were coming to
take the house they had had before, and spend the
summer.

" We will come early," he wrote. " I cannot stay
away. I have made mother promise to open the
house in April, so in a month more I shall see you.
I had an awful time to get her to come; she hates
the country except in summer, but at last she said
she would. She knows why I want to come, and
she would be so happy if " — and then the letter
trailed off into a wail of disappointment and love.

Impatient and worried, Lois threw the pages into
the fire, and had a malicious satisfaction in watching the elaborate crest curl and blacken on the red
coals. " I wish he'd stay away," she said; " he
bothers me to death. I hate him! What a silly
letter ! "

It was so silly, she found herself smiling, in spite
of her annoyance. Now, to feel amusement at one's
lover is almost as fatal as to be bored by him.
But poor Dick had no one to tell him this, and had
poured out his heart on paper, in spite of some dif-
ficulty in spelling, and could not guess that he was
laughed at for his pains.

Miss Deborah and Miss Ruth were rewarded for their walk into Ashurst by a letter from Gifford, which made them quite forget Mr. Denner's looks, and Mrs. Dale's bad taste in being a match-maker.

He would be at home for one day the next week; business had called him from Lockhaven, and on his way back he would stay a night in Ashurst. The little ladies were flurried with happiness. Miss Deborah prepared more dainties than even Gifford's healthy appetite could possibly consume, and Miss Ruth hung her last painting of apple-blossoms in his bedroom, and let her rose jar stand uncovered on his dressing-table for two days before his arrival. When he came, they hovered about him with small caresses and little chirps of affection, as though they would express all the love of the months in which they had not seen him.

Gifford had thought he would go to the rectory in the evening, and somehow the companionship of his aunts while there had not occupied his imagination; but it would have been cruel to leave them at home, so after tea, having tasted every one of Miss Deborah's dishes, he begged them to come with him to see Dr. Howe. They were glad to go anywhere if only with him, and each took an arm, and bore him triumphantly to the rectory.

"Bless my soul," said Dr. Howe, looking at them over his glasses, as they came into the library, "it is good to see you again, young man! How did you leave Helen?" He pushed his chair back from the fire, and let his newspapers rustle to the floor, as he rose. Max came and sniffed about Gifford's knees, and wagged his tail, hoping to be petted. Lois was the only one whose greeting was constrained, and Gifford's gladness withered under the indifference in her eyes.

" She does n't care," he thought while he was answering Dr. Howe, and rubbing Max's ears with his left hand. " Helen may be right about Forsythe, but she does n't care for me, either."

" Sit here, dear Giff," said Miss Ruth, motioning him to a chair at her side.

" There 's a draught there, dear Ruth," cried Miss Deborah anxiously. " Come nearer the fire, Gifford." But Gifford only smiled good-naturedly, and leaned his elbow on the mantel, grasping his coat collar with one hand, and listening to Dr. Howe's questions about his niece.

" She 's very well," he answered, " and the happiest woman I ever saw. Those two people were made for each other, doctor."

" Well, now, see here, young man," said the rector, who could not help patronizing Gifford, " you 'll disturb that happiness if you get into religious discussions with Helen. Women don't understand that sort of thing ; young women, I mean," he added, turning to Miss Deborah, and then suddenly looking confused.

Gifford raised his eyebrows. " Oh, well, Helen will reason, you know ; she is not the woman to take a creed for granted."

" She must," the rector said, with a chuckle, " if she 's a Presbyterian. She 'll get into deep water if she goes to discussing predestination and original sin, and all that sort of thing."

" Oh," said Gifford lightly, " of course she does not discuss those things. I don't think that sort of theological rubbish had to be swept out of her mind before the really earnest questions of life presented themselves. Helen is singularly free from the trammels of tradition — for a woman."

Lois looked up, with a little toss of her head, but Gifford did not even notice her, nor realize how closely she was following his words.

" John Ward, though," Gifford went on, " is the most perfect Presbyterian I can imagine. He is logical to the bitter end, which is unusual, I fancy. I asked him his opinion concerning a certain man, a fellow named Davis, — perhaps Helen wrote of his death — I asked Ward what he thought of his chances for salvation ; he acknowledged, sadly enough, that he thought he was damned. He did n't use that word, I believe," the young man added, smiling, " but it amounted to the same thing."

There was an outcry from his auditors. " Abominable ! " said Dr. Howe, bringing his fist heavily down on the table. " I should n't have thought that of Ward, — outrageous ! "

Gifford looked surprised. " What a cruel man ! " Lois cried ; while Miss Deborah said suddenly, —

" Giff, dear, have those flannels of yours worn well ? " But Gifford apparently did not hear her.

" Why, doctor," he remonstrated, " you misunderstand Ward. And he is not cruel, Lois ; he is the gentlest soul I ever knew. But he is logical, he is consistent ; he simply expresses Presbyterianism with utter truth, without shrinking from its conclusions."

"Oh, he may be consistent," the rector acknowledged, with easy transition to good-nature, " but that does n't alter the fact that he 's a fool to say such things. Let him believe them, if he wants to, but for Heaven's sake let him keep silent! He can hold his tongue and yet not be a Universalist. *Medio tutissimus ibis*, you know. It will be sure to offend the parish, if he consigns people to the lower regions in such a free way."

" There is no danger of that," Gifford said; "I doubt if he could say anything on the subject of hell too tough for the spiritual digestion of his flock. They are as sincere in their belief as he is, though they have n't his gentleness; in fact, they have his logic without his light; there is very little of the refinement of religion in Lockhaven."

" What a place to live!" Lois cried. " Does n't Helen hate it? Of course she would never say so to us, but she *must!* Everybody seems so dreadfully disagreeable; and there is really no one Helen could know."

" Why, Helen knows them all," answered Gifford in his slow way, looking down at the girl's impulsive face.

" Lois," said her father, " you are too emphatic in your way of speaking; be more mild. I don't like gush."

" Lois punctuates with exclamation points," Gifford explained good-naturedly, meaning to take the sting out of Dr. Howe's reproof, but hurting her instead.

" But, bless my soul," said the rector, " what does Helen say to this sort of talk? "

" I don't think she says anything, at least to him ; "
Gifford answered. " It is so unimportant to Helen,
she is so perfectly satisfied with Ward, his opinions
are of no consequence. She did fire up, though,
about Davis," and then he told the story of Elder
Dean and Helen's angry protest.

Dr. Howe listened, first with grave disapproval,
and then with positive irritation.

" Dean," Gifford concluded, " has taken it very
much to heart ; he told me — he's a client of mine,
a stupid idiot, who never reasoned a thing out in
his life—he told me that ' not to believe in eternal
damnation was to take a short cut to atheism.' He
also confided to me that ' a church which could permit such a falling from the faith was in a diseased
condition.' I don't believe that opinion has reached
Ward, however. It would take more grit than
Dean possesses to dare to find fault with John
Ward's wife to her husband."

" What folly ! " cried the rector, his face flushed
with annoyance. " What possessed Helen to say
such a thing ! She ought to have had more sense.
Mark my words, that speech of hers will make trouble for Ward. I don't understand how Helen could
be so foolish ; she was brought up just as Lois was,
yet, thank Heaven, her head isn't full of whims
about reforming a community. What in the world
made her express such an opinion if she had it, and
what made her have it? "

Dr. Howe had risen, and walked impatiently up
and down the room, and now stood in front of Gifford, with a forefinger raised to emphasize his words.

" There is something so absurd, so unpleasant, in a young woman's meddling with things which don't belong to her, in seeing a little mind struggle with ideas. Better a thousand times settle down to look after her household, and cook her husband's dinner, and be a good child."

Lois laughed nervously. " She has a cook," she said.

" Don't be pert, Lois, for Heaven's sake," answered her father, though Miss Deborah had added, —

" Gifford says dear Helen is a very good house-keeper."

" Pray," continued the rector, " what business is it of hers what people believe, or what she believes herself, for that matter, provided she 's a good girl, and does her duty in that station of life where it has pleased God to put her, — as the wife of a Presbyterian minister? 'Stead of that she tries to grapple with theological questions, and gets into hot water with the parish. 'Pon my word, I thought better of the child! I 'll write and tell her what I think of it." (And so he did, the very next day. But his wrath had expended itself in words, and his letter showed no more of his indignation than the powdery ashes which fell out of it showed the flame of the cigar he was smoking when he wrote it.) " And as for Ward himself," the rector went on, " I don't know what to think of him. Did you know he had given up his salary? Said ' Helen had enough for them to live on,' and added that they had no right to any more money than was necessary for their comfort; anything more than that belonged to the

Lord's poor. Bless my soul, the clergyman comes under that head, to my mind. Yes, sir, he's willing to live on his wife! I declare, the fellow's a — a — well, I don't know any word for him! "

There was a chorus of astonishment from the ladies.

" 'Christian' would be a pretty good word," said Gifford slowly. "Is n't he following Christ's example rather more literally than most of us?"

" But to live on his wife!" cried Dr. Howe.

" I don't believe," Gifford responded, smiling, " that that would distress John Ward at all."

" Apparently not," said the rector significantly.

" He loves her too much," Gifford went on, "to think of himself apart from her; don't you see? They are one; what difference does it make about the money?"

" Could you do it?" asked Dr. Howe.

" Well, no," Gifford said, shrugging his shoulders; "but then, I 'm not John Ward."

" Thank Heaven!" said the rector devoutly.

" But it is a mistake, all the same," Gifford went on; "it is unbusiness-like, to say nothing of being bad for his people to have the burden of support lifted from them; it pauperizes them spiritually."

After the relief of this outburst against John Ward, Dr. Howe felt the inevitable irritation at his hearers. " Well, I only mention this," he said, "because, since he is so strange, it won't do, Gifford, for you to abet Helen in this ridiculous skepticism of hers. If Ward agreed with her, it would be all right, but so long as he does not, it will make trouble between them, and a woman cannot quarrel with an obstinate and bigoted man with impunity. And you have no business to have doubts yourself, sir."

The two sisters were much impressed with what the rector said. " I must really caution Giff," said Miss Deborah to Lois, " not to encourage dear Helen in thinking about things ; it 's very unfeminine to think, and Gifford is so clever, he does n't stop to remember she 's but a woman. And he is greatly attached to her ; dear me, he has never forgotten what might have been," — this in almost a whisper.

Both the sisters talked of Dr. Howe's anger as they went home.

" He 's right," said Miss Deborah, who had dropped her nephew's arm, so that she might be more cautious about the mud, and who lifted her skirt on each side, as though she was about to make a curtsy, — " he 's right : a woman ought to think just as her husband does ; it is quite wrong in dear Helen not to, and it will bring unhappiness. Indeed, it is a lesson to all of us," she added.

Respect was an instinct with Gifford, and he did not stop to think that it was a lesson by which Miss Deborah would have no opportunity to profit.

But he was not listening closely to the chatter of the little ladies ; he was thinking of Lois's indifference. " She even looked bored, once," he thought ; " but that does not necessarily mean that she cares for Forsythe. I will trust her. She may never love me, but she will never care for him."

CHAPTER XIV.

THE feeling in Lockhaven about Helen Ward's unbelief was not confined to Elder Dean; for every one who knew Mrs. Davis knew what the preacher's wife thought of Tom's salvation, and judged her accordingly. As for the widow herself, the hope Helen had given her quite died out under the fostering care of Elder Dean. She grew more bitter than ever, and refused even to speak on the subject.

"No, ma'am," she said wearily, when Helen went to see her after the funeral, — "no, ma'am, 't ain't no use to talk. Elder Dean's been here, and I know there ain't no good hopin'. Even the preacher don't say there's any good hopin'. What you said was a comfort, ma'am, but 't was n't true. 'T was n't religion. It's in the Bible that there's a hell, and there's no use sayin' there is n't; sayin' there is n't won't keep us from it, Elder Dean says, and I guess he's about right. I'm sure I'm much obliged to you, ma'am; but I'm a Christian woman myself, and I can't deny religion."

There was no use arguing; custom and a smattering of logic settled her convictions, and no reasoning could move her dreary hopelessness.

Helen told John of it, her head resting on his breast, and comforted by his mere presence. "I know you believe in hell," she ended, "but, oh, John, it is so horrible!"

He stroked her hair softly. "I am afraid, dearest," he said, "Mrs. Davis is right. I am afraid there is no possibility of hope. The soul that sinneth, it shall die, and shall not the Judge of all the earth do right?"

Helen sprang to her feet. "Oh," she cried passionately, — "that is just it, — He does do right! Why, if I thought God capable of sending Tom to hell, I should hate Him." John tried to speak, but she interrupted him. "We will never talk of this again, never! Believe what you will, dearest, — it does not matter, — but don't speak of it to me, if you love me. I cannot bear it, John. Promise me."

"Oh, Helen," he said, with tender reproach, "would you have me conceal my deepest life from you? It would seem like living apart, if there were one subject on which we dared not touch. Just let me show you the truth and justice of all this; let me tell you how the scheme of salvation makes the mystery of sin and punishment clear and right."

"No," she said, the flush of pain dying out of her face, but her eyes still shining with unshed tears, — "no, I cannot talk of it. I should be wicked if I could believe it; it would make me wicked. Don't ever speak to me of it, John."

She came and put her arms around him, and kissed his forehead gently; and then she left him to struggle with his conscience, and to ask himself whether his delay had caused this feeling of abhorrence, or whether the waiting had been wise and should be prolonged.

But Helen's words to Mrs. Davis were repeated, and ran from mouth to mouth, with the strangest additions and alterations. Mrs. Ward had said that there was no hell, and no heaven, and no God. What wonder, then, with such a leaven of wickedness at work in the church, Elder Dean grew alarmed, and in the bosom of his own family expressed his opinion of Mrs. Ward, and at prayer-meeting prayed fervently for unbelievers, even though she was not there to profit by it. Once, while saying that the preacher's wife was sowing tares among the wheat, he met with an astonishing rebuff. Alfaretta dared tell her father that he ought to be ashamed of himself to talk that way about a saint and an angel, if ever there was one.

Mr. Dean was staggered; a female, a young female, and his daughter, to dare to say such a thing to him! He opened his mouth several times before he was able to speak.

Alfaretta was at home for her evening out, and her young man was with her, anxious for the clock to point to nine, that he might " see her home." They had intended to leave the elder's early, and wander off for a walk by the river, but prayers were delayed a little, and after that Alfaretta had to listen to the good advice given every week; so Thaddeus lost all hope of the river-walk, and only watched for nine o'clock, when he knew she must start. But in this, too, he was doomed to disappointment, for the outburst which so stunned the elder detained Alfaretta until after ten, thereby causing Helen no little anxiety about her prompt and pretty maid.

The elder had closed his admonitions by warning his daughter not to be listening to any teachings of the preacher's wife, for she was a backslider, and she had fallen from grace. " In the first place," said the elder, laying down the law with uplifted hand, " she 's a Episcopalian, — I heard her say that herself, when she first come here; and her letter of dismissal was from a church with some Popish name, — St. Robert or Stephen, — I don't just remember. I 've seen one of those churches. Thank the Lord, there is n't one in Lockhaven. They have candles burnin', and a big brass cross. Rags of Popery, — they all belong to the Scarlet Woman, I tell you! But she 's a backslider even from that, fer they have some truth; she 's a child of the Evil One, with her unbelief ! "

This was more than Alfaretta could bear. " Indeed, pa," she cried, " you don't know how good she is, or you would n't be sayin' that! Look how she 's slaved this winter fer the families that 'a' been in trouble, havin' no work ! "

" 'T ain't what she 's done, Alfaretta," said her father solemnly; " works without faith is of no avail. What says the Scripture? ' A man is justified by faith ' (by faith, Alfaretta!) ' without the deeds of the law.' And what says the confession ? "

Alfaretta, by force of habit, began to stumble through the answer: " ' We cannot by our best works merit pardon of sin, or eternal life at the hand — at the hand — of God, by reason of ' " — Here her memory failed her.

" Well," her father said impatiently, " can't you

remember the rest? 'Works done by unregenerate men are sinful, and cannot please God,' you know. Go on."

But Alfaretta could not go on, and the elder would not betray his own lack of memory by attempting to quote.

"So you see," he continued, "it is n't any use to talk of how good and kind she is, or what she does; it is what she believes that will settle her eternal salvation."

But Alfaretta was unconvinced. "Well, sir," she said stubbornly, "it don't seem to me that way, fer she 's the best woman, except mother, I ever saw. I reckon if anybody goes to heaven, she will; don't you, Thaddeus?"

Thaddeus was tilting back in his chair, his curly black head against the whitewashed wall, and thus suddenly and embarrassingly appealed to — for he was divided between a desire to win the approval of the elder and to show his devotion to Alfaretta — he brought his chair down with a clatter of all four legs on the floor, and looked first at the father and then at the daughter, but did not speak.

"Don't you, Thaddeus?" repeated Alfaretta severely, for the elder was dumb with astonishment.

"Well," said Thaddeus, struggling for some opinion which should please both, — "well, I do suppose we can hope for the best; that is n't against the catechism."

But the elder did not notice his feeble compromise, while Alfaretta only gave him a quick, contemptuous look, for her father, opening and shutting his mouth slowly for a moment, began to say, —

" How sharper than a serpent's tooth it is to have a child that 's ungrateful for the best of teaching and sound doctrine! Many 's the time," said the elder, lifting his eyes and hands, — " many 's the time I 've showed her the truth; many 's the time I 've explained how every other sort of religion is all wrong, and is of its father the Devil! And I 've brought her up faithful to the catechism and the confession, yet now the child would instruct the parent! This comes," he cried, becoming very angry, and beating his hand so violently upon the table that the family Bible fell with a crash to the floor, from which Thaddeus lifted it, — " this comes from your settin' in the seat of the scornful, and bein' in the kitchen of an unbeliever! You 'll leave her; do you hear me, Alfaretta? You 'll leave her this day month. I 'll perform my duty to my child's soul, even if Brother Ward's wife has to do her own cooking. Yes, and I 'll do my duty to Brother Ward, too, though I used to think him a pious young man. I 'll tell him he has got to convert that woman's soul. She 's a corrupter of youth, she 's a teacher of false doctrines, — her tellin' Mrs. Davis there was n't any hell! — she 's a — a Episcopalian, so she is! She 'll experience a change of heart, or the Session will take this matter in hand."

At this terrible threat, even Alfaretta was speechless, and her mother put two shaking hands on her arm, and whispered, " Oh, Retta, I would n't say no more; it makes your pa angry."

" Yes," continued the elder violently, " that woman is the Jonah of the church, and she 's got to be dealt with ; to save her soul, she 's got to be disciplined, for the sake of every one that heard her false and lying tongue. I 'll have her brought before the Session and showed the truth, and she shall be saved. Tom Davis not in hell, indeed ! "

Mr. Dean stopped for breath. Alfaretta's courage came back with a rush.

" Listen to me," cried the young woman, stamping her foot with excitement, for she was as angry as the elder himself, — " listen to me ! How can you say such things about her ? A saint and angel, if ever there was one. The Lord don't send no one to hell, let alone such as her. An' any way, I 'd rather go to the bad place with her than stay with all the golden harps and crowns in the best sort of a heaven with them as would keep her out, so I would ! "

Here Alfaretta broke down, and began to cry. Thaddeus could not stand that ; he edged up to her, murmuring, " I would n't cry, Retta, — I would n't cry."

But she only gave the shoulder he touched a vicious shake, and cried harder than ever, saying, " No — I — I bet you would n't — you 'd never — care."

But Alfaretta's defense changed Mr. Dean's anger at the snub he received from the preacher's wife into real alarm for his child's spiritual welfare. A daughter of his to say the Lord did not send souls to hell !

" Alfaretta," he said, with solemn slowness, " you 'd better get your bunnet and go home. I 'll see Mr. Ward about this; his wife's done harm enough. You've got to leave her, — I mean it. I won't see her send my child to hell before my very eyes."

"Oh, pa," Alfaretta entreated, choking and sobbing, and brushing her tears away with the back of her hand, "don't, — don't say nothin' to Mr. Ward, nor take me away. 'T was n't her made me say those things; it was just my own self. Don't take me away."

"Did she ever say anything to you about the Lord not sendin' people to hell?" asked her father.

"Oh," said Alfaretta, growing more and more frightened, "'t ain't what she talks about; it's her bein' so good, an'" —

"Did she ever," interrupted the elder, with slow emphasis, standing over her, and shaking his stubby forefinger at her, — "did she ever say the Lord did n't send Tom Davis to hell, to you?"

Alfaretta cowered in her chair, and Thaddeus began to whimper for sympathy. "I don't know," she answered desperately, — "I don't know anything, except she 's good."

"Listen to me," said Mr. Dean, in his harsh, monotonous voice: "did Mrs. Ward ever say anything to you about hell, or the Lord's not sendin' people there? Answer me that."

Then the loving little servant-maid, truthful as the blood of Scotch ancestors and a Presbyterian training could make her, faced what she knew would bring remorse, and, for all she could tell, unpardonable sin upon her soul, and said boldly, "No, she

never did. She never said one single blessed word
to me about hell."

The wind seemed suddenly to leave the elder's
sails, but the collapse was only for a moment; even
Alfaretta's offering of her first lie upon the altar of
her devotion to her mistress was not to save her.

"Well," he said, opening his mouth slowly and
looking about with great dignity, "if she has n't
said it to you, she has to other people, I 'll be bound.
Fer she said it to Mrs. Davis, and " — the elder in-
flated his chest, and held his head high — "and me.
It is my duty as elder to take notice of it, fer her
own soul's sake, and to open her husband's eyes, if
he 's been too blind to see it. Yes, the Session
should deal with her. Prayers ain't no good fer
such as her," he said, becoming excited. "Ain't she
heard my prayers most all winter, till she give up
comin' to prayer-meetin', preferrin' to stay outside,

"'Where sinners meet, and awful scoffers dwell'?

An' I 've exhorted; but " — the elder raised his
eyes piously to heaven — "Paul may plant and Apol-
los may water, but it don't do no good."

Alfaretta knew her father's iron will too well to
attempt any further protests. She wiped her eyes,
and, while she put on a hat adorned with an aggressive white feather, she bade the family good-night
in an unsteady voice. Thaddeus, anxious only to
escape notice, sidled towards the door, and stood
waiting for her, with a deprecating look on his round
face.

In spite, however, of the elder's indignation and

his really genuine alarm about the influences which surrounded his child, he had a prudent afterthought in the matter of her leaving the service of Mrs. Ward. It was difficult to get anything in Lock-haven for a young woman to do, and times were hard that year.

"You — ah — you need n't give notice to-night, Alfaretta," he said. "I 'll speak to the preacher about it, myself. But mind you have as little to say to her as you can, and may the Lord protect you ! "

But the elder's plans for cautioning his pastor were doomed to disappointment. He was a prisoner with lumbago for the next fortnight, and even the most sincere interest in some one else's spiritual welfare cannot tempt a man out of the house when he is bent almost double with lumbago. Nor, when John came to see him, could he begin such a conversation as he had planned, for his neck was too stiff to allow him to raise his head and look in Mr. Ward's face. When he recovered, he was delayed still another week, because the preacher had gone away to General Assembly.

But Alfaretta was far too miserable to find in her father's command "not to give notice to-night" any ray of comfort. She choked down her tears as best she might, and started for the parsonage.

Thaddeus had almost to run to keep up with her, such was her troubled and impatient haste, and she scarcely noticed him, though he tramped through the mud to show his contrition, instead of taking his place by her side on the board walk.

It is curious to see how a simple soul inflicts useless punishment upon itself, when the person it has
offended refuses to retaliate.   Had Alfaretta scolded,
Thaddeus would not have walked in the mud.

Her silence was most depressing.

" Retta," he ventured timidly, " don't be mad
with me, — now don't."

He came a little nearer, and essayed to put an arm
about her waist, a privilege often accorded him on
such an occasion.   But now she flounced away from
him, and said sharply, " You need n't be comin'
round me, Mr. Thaddeus Green.   Anybody that
thinks my Mrs. Ward is n't goin' to heaven had
just better keep off from me, fer I 'm goin' with her,
wherever that is ; and I suppose, if you think *that* of
me, you 'd better not associate with me."

" I did n't say *you* was goin'," protested Thaddeus
tearfully, but she interrupted him with asperity.

" Don't I tell you I 'm bound to go where she
goes ?   And if you 're so fearful of souls bein' lost, I
wonder you don't put all your money in the mission-
ary-box, instead of buying them new boots."

Perhaps it was the thought of the new boots, but
Thaddeus stepped on the board walk, and this time,
unreproved, slipped his arm about Alfaretta's waist.

" Oh, now Retta," he said, " I did n't mean any
harm.   I only did n't want the elder thinkin' I
was n't sound, for he 'd be sayin' we should n't keep
company, an' that 's all I joined the church for last
spring."

" Well, then," said Alfaretta, willing to be reconciled if it brought any comfort, " you do think Mrs. Ward will go to heaven ? "

" Yes," Thaddeus answered with great confidence, and added in a burst of gallantry, " She 'll have to, Retta, if she goes along with you, for you 'll go there, sure ! "

CHAPTER XV.

MRS. FORSYTHE did not come to Ashurst until the middle of April, and then she came alone. Dick had been detained, she said, and would come in a week or two. So Lois breathed freely, though she knew it was only a respite, and made the most of her freedom to go and see his mother.

She was very fond of the invalid, who always seemed to her, in her glowing, rosy health, like an exquisite bit of porcelain, she was so fine and dainty, with soft white hair curling around her gentle and melancholy face. Mrs. Forsythe dressed in delicate grays and lavenders, and her fingers were covered with rings, and generally held some filmy fancy-work. Her invalidism had only given her an air of interesting fragility, which made Lois long to put her strong young arms about her, to shield her lest any wind might blow too roughly upon her.

Mrs. Forsythe accepted her devotion with complacency. She had never had this adoring tenderness from her son, who had heard her remark that she was at the gates of death too often to live in a state of anxiety; but to Lois her gentle resignation and heavenly anticipations were most impressive. The girl's affection almost reconciled the elder lady to having been made to come to Ashurst while the snow still lingered in sheltered spots, and before the

crocuses had lighted their golden censers in her garden ; for Lois went to see her every day, and though
she could not always escape without a meaning look
from the invalid, or a sigh for Dick's future, she
thoroughly enjoyed her visits. It was charming to
sit in the dusk, before the dancing flames of an ap-
ple-wood fire, the air fragrant with the hyacinths
and jonquils of the window garden, and listen to tales
of Mrs. Forsythe's youth.

Lois had never heard such stories. Mrs. Dale
would have said it was not proper for young girls to
know of love affairs, and it is presumable that the
Misses Woodhouse never had any to relate ; so this
was Lois's first and only chance, and she would sit,
clasping her knees with her hands, listening with
wide, frank eyes, and cheeks flushed by the fire and
the tale.

" But then, my poor health," Mrs. Forsythe ended
with a sigh, one evening, just before it was time for
Lois to go ; " of course it interfered very much."

" Why, were you ill *then*," Lois said, " when
you used to dance all night ? "

" Oh, dear me, yes," answered the other shaking
her head, " I have been a sufferer all my life, a great
sufferer. Well, it cannot last much longer ; this
poor body is almost worn out."

" Oh, *don't* say it ! " Lois cried, and kissed the
white soft hand with its shining rings, in all the tenderness of her young heart.

All this endeared the girl very much, and more
than once Mrs. Forsythe wrote of her sweetness and
goodness to her son. Miss Deborah, or Miss Ruth,

or even Mrs. Dale, would have been careful in
using the name of any young woman in writing to a
gentleman, but Mrs. Forsythe had not been born in
Ashurst.

However, Dick still lingered, and Lois rejoiced,
and even her anticipation of the evil time to come,
when he should arrive and end her peaceful days,
could not check her present contentment. It was
almost May, and that subtile, inexplainable joy of
the springtime made it a gladness even to be alive.
Lois rambled about, hunting for the first green
spears of that great army of flowers which would
soon storm the garden, and carrying any treasure
she might find to Mrs. Forsythe's sick-room. The
meadows were spongy with small springs, bubbling
up under the faintly green grass. The daffadown-
dillies showed bursting yellow buds, and the pallid,
frightened-looking violets brought all their mystery
of unfolding life to the girl's happy eyes.

One Saturday morning, while she was looking for
the bunch of grape hyacinths which came up each
year, beside the stone bench, she was especially
light-hearted. Word had come from Helen that the
long-promised visit should be made the first week
in June. " It can only be for a week, you know,"
Helen wrote, " because I cannot be away from John
longer than that, and I must be back for our first
anniversary, too."

More than this, Mrs. Forsythe had sighed, and
told her that poor dear Dick's business seemed to
detain him ; it was such a shame ! And perhaps he
could not get to Ashurst for a fortnight. So Lois

Howe was a very happy and contented girl, standing under the soft blue of the April sky, and watching her flock of white pigeons wheeling and circling
about the gable of the red barn, while the little
stream, which had gained a stronger voice since the
spring rains, babbled vociferously at her side. The
long, transparent stems of the flowers broke crisply
between her fingers, as she heard her name called.

Mr. Denner, with his fishing-basket slung under
one arm and his rod across his shoulder, was regarding her through a gap in the hedge.

" A lovely day ! " said the little gentleman, his
brown eyes twinkling with a pleasant smile.

" Indeed it is, sir," Lois answered ; " and look at
the flowers I 've found ! "

She tipped the basket of scented grass on her arm
that he might see them. Mr. Denner had stopped
to ask if Mrs. Forsythe would be present at the
whist party that night, and was rather relieved to
learn that she was not able to come ; he had lost his
hand the week before, because she had arrived with
the Dales. Then he inquired about her son's arrival, and went away thinking what a simple matter a love affair was to some people. Lois and that
young man ! Why, things were really arranged for
them ; they had almost no responsibility in the matter ; their engagement settled itself, as it were.

He walked abstractedly towards his house, wrest-
ling with the old puzzle. Nothing helped him, or
threw light on his uncertainty ; he was tired of
juggling with fate, and was growing desperate.

" I wish they would settle it between themselves,"

he murmured, with a wistful wrinkle on his forehead. Suddenly a thought struck him ; there was certainly one way out of his difficulties : he could ask advice. He could lay the whole matter frankly before some dispassionate person, whose judgment should determine his course. Why had he not thought of it before ! Mr. Denner's face brightened ; he walked gayly along, and began to hum to himself : —

> " Oh, wert thou, love, but near me,
> But near, near, near me,
> How fondly wouldst thou cheer me " —

Here he stopped abruptly. Whom should he ask ? He went carefully through his list of friends, as he trudged along the muddy road.

Not Dr. Howe : he did not take a serious enough view of such things ; Mr. Denner recalled that scene in his office, and his little face burned. Then, there was Mrs. Dale : she was a woman, and of course she would know the real merit of each of the sisters. Stay : Mrs. Dale did not always seem in sympathy with the Misses Woodhouse ; he had even heard her say things which were not, perhaps, perfectly courteous ; that the sisters had been able to defend themselves, Mr. Denner overlooked. Colonel Drayton : well, a man with the gout is not the confidant for a lover. He was beginning to look depressed again, when the light came. Henry Dale ! No one could be better.

Mr. Denner awaited the evening with impatience. He would walk home with the Dales, he thought, and then he and Henry could talk it all over, down in the study.

He was glad when the cool spring night began to close, full of that indefinable fragrance of fresh earth and growing things, and before it was time to start he cheered himself by a little music. He went into the dreary, unused parlor, and pulling up the green Venetian blinds, which rattled like castanets, he pushed back the ivy-fastened shutters, and sat down by the open window; then, with his chin resting upon his fiddle, and one foot in its drab gaiter swinging across his knee, he played mournfully and shrilly in the twilight, until it was time to start.

He saw the Misses Woodhouse trotting toward the rectory, with Sarah walking in a stately way behind them, swinging her unlighted lantern, and cautioning them not to step in the mud. But he made no effort to join them; it was happiness enough to contemplate the approaching solution of his difficulties, and say to himself triumphantly, "This time to-morrow!" and he began joyously to play, "Ye banks and braes o' bonnie Doon," rendering carefully all the quavers in that quavering air.

Mr. Denner's meditations made him late at the rectory, and he felt Mrs. Dale look sternly at him; so he made haste to deal, sitting well forward in his chair, under which he tucked his little feet, and putting down each card with nervous care. His large cuffs almost hid his small, thin hands, and now and then he paused to rub his thumb and forefinger together, that the cards might not stick.

But Mr. Denner did not play well that night; Miss Deborah looked at him with mild reproach, and was almost angry when he answered her with an absent smile.

The evening seemed very long to Mr. Denner, and even when the party had said "Good-night" Mr. Dale was slow about getting off ; he put his wife into the carriage, and then stopped to ask Dr. Howe if he had the first edition of "Japhet in Search of a Father"?

"In search of a father!" Mr. Denner thought, as he stood waiting by the steps, — "how can he be interested in that?"

At last the front door closed, and Mr. Dale and Mr. Denner walked silently down the lane in the starlight, the lawyer's little heart beating so with excitement, that he had a suffocated feeling, and once or twice put his hand to his throat, as though to loosen his muffler.

Mr. Dale, still absorbed in his first edition, took swinging strides, the tails of his brown cloth overcoat flapping and twisting about his long, thin legs. Mr. Denner had now and then almost to break into a trot to keep up with him.

Mr. Dale walked with his hands clasped behind him, and his stick under his arm ; his soft felt hat was pulled down over his eyes, so that his keeping the path was more by chance than sight. He stopped once to pluck a sprig from the hawthorn hedge, to put between his lips. This gave Mr. Denner breath, and a chance to speak.

"I think I will walk home with you, Henry," he said. "I want to have a talk with you."

His heart thumped as he said that ; he felt he had committed himself.

"Well, now, that 's very pleasant," responded Mr. Dale. "I was just thinking I should be alone half the way home."

"But you would not be alone when you got there," Mr. Denner said meditatively; "now, with me it is different."

"Oh, quite different, — quite different."

"Yes," proceeded the other, "I have very little companionship. I go home and sit in my library all by myself. Sometimes, I get up and wander about the house, with only my cigar for company."

"I suppose," said Mr. Dale, "that you can smoke wherever you want, in your house? I often think of your loneliness; coming and going just as you please, quite independently."

Mr. Denner gave him a sudden questioning look, and then appeared to reproach himself for having misunderstood his friend.

"Yes, just so, — just so. I knew you would appreciate it; but you can never know from experience, Henry, how a man feels left quite to himself. You do not think of the independence; it is the loneliness. You cannot know that."

"No," murmured Mr. Dale, "perhaps not, but I can imagine it."

When they reached the iron gate of Dale house, they followed the trim path across the lawn to the north side of the house, where it ended in a little walk, three bricks wide, laid end to end, and so damp with perpetual shade, they were slippery with green mould, and had tufts of moss between them.

Mr. Dale's study was in a sort of half basement,

one went down two steps to reach the doorway, and the windows, set in thick stone walls and almost hidden in a tangle of wistaria, were just above the level of the path.

The two old men entered, Mr. Dale bending his tall white head a little; and while the lawyer unwound a long blue muffler from about his throat, the host lighted a lamp, and, getting down on his knees, blew the dim embers in the rusty grate into a flickering blaze. Then he pulled a blackened crane from the jamb, and hung on it a dinted brass kettle, so that he might add some hot water to Mr. Denner's gin and sugar, and also make himself a cup of tea. That done, he took off his overcoat, throwing it across the mahogany arm of the horse-hair sofa, which was piled with books and pamphlets, and whitened here and there with ashes from his silver pipe; then he knotted the cord of his flowered dressing-gown about his waist, spread his red silk handkerchief over his thin locks, and, placing his feet comfortably upon the high fender, was ready for conversation.

Mr. Denner, meanwhile, without waiting for the formality of an invitation, went at once to a small corner closet, and brought out a flat, dark bottle and an old silver cup. He poured the contents of the bottle into the cup, added some sugar, and lastly, with a sparing hand, the hot water, stirring it round and round with the one teaspoon which they shared between them.

Mr. Dale had produced a battered caddy, and soon the fumes of gin and tea mingled amicably together.

"If I could always have such evenings as this," Mr. Denner thought, sipping the hot gin and water, and crossing his legs comfortably, "I should not have to think of — something different."

"Your wife would appreciate what I meant about loneliness," he said, going back to what was uppermost in his mind. "A house without a mistress at its head, Henry, is — ah — not what it should be."

The remark needed no reply; and Mr. Dale leaned back in his leather chair, dreamily watching the blue smoke from his slender pipe drift level for a moment, and then, on an unfelt draught, draw up the chimney.

Mr. Denner, resting his mug on one knee, began to stir the fire gently. "Yes, Henry," he continued, "I feel it more and more as I grow older. I really need — ah — brightness and comfort in my house. Yes, I need it. And even if I were not interested, as it were, myself, I don't know but what my duty to Willie should make me — ah — think of it."

Mr. Dale was gazing at the fire. "Think of what?" he said.

Mr. Denner became very much embarrassed. "Why, what I was just observing, just speaking of, — the need of comfort — in my house — and my life, I might say. Less loneliness for me, Henry, and, in fact, a — person — a — a female — you understand."

Mr. Dale looked at him.

"In fact, as I might say, a wife, Henry."

Mr. Dale was at last aroused; with his pipe between his lips, he clutched the lion's-heads on the arms of his chair, and sat looking at Mr. Denner in such horrified astonishment, that the little gentleman stumbled over any words, simply for the relief of speaking.

"Yes," he said, "just so, Henry, just so. I have been thinking of it lately, perhaps for the last year; yes — I have been thinking of it."

Mr. Dale, still looking at him, made an inarticulate noise in his throat.

Mr. Denner's face began to show a faint dull red to his temples. "Ah — yes — I — I have thought of it, as it were."

"Denner," said Mr. Dale solemnly, "you 're a fool."

"If you mean my age, Henry," cried the other, his whole face a dusky crimson, that sent the tears stinging into his little brown eyes, "I cannot say I think your — surprise — is — ah — justified. It is not as though there was anything unsuitable — she — they — are quite my age. And for Willie's sake, I doubt if it is not a — a duty. And I am only sixty-one and a half, Henry. You did not remember, perhaps, that I was so much younger than you?"

Mr. Dale pulled off his red handkerchief, and wiped his forehead; after which he said quite violently, "The devil!"

"Oh," remonstrated Mr. Denner, balancing his mug on his knee, and lifting his hands deprecatingly, "not such words, Henry, — not such words; we are speaking of ladies, Henry."

Mr. Dale was silent.

"You have no idea," the other continued, "in your comfortable house, with a good wife, who makes you perfectly happy, how lonely a man is who lives as I do ; and I can tell you, the older he grows, the more he feels it. So really, age is a reason for considering it."

" I was not thinking of age," said Mr. Dale feebly.

" Well, then," replied the other triumphantly, "age is the only objection that could be urged. A man is happier and better for female influence ; and the dinners I have are really not — not what they should be, Henry. That would all be changed, if I had a — ah — wife."

" Denner," said his friend, "there are circumstances where a dinner of herbs is more to be desired than a stalled ox, you will remember."

" That is just how I feel," said the other eagerly, and too much interested in his own anxieties to see Mr. Dale's point. "Mary is not altogether amiable."

Again Mr. Dale was silent.

" I knew you would see the — the — desirability of it," the lawyer continued, the flush of embarrassment fading away, " and so I decided to ask your advice. I thought that, not only from your own — ah — heart, but from the novels and tales you read, you would be able to advise me in any matter of esteem."

Mr. Dale groaned, and shook his head from side to side.

" But, good Lord, Denner, books are one thing, life 's another. You can't live in a book, man."

" Just so," said Mr. Denner, "just so ; but I only want the benefit of your experience in reading these tales of — ah — romance. You see, here is my trouble, Henry, — I cannot make up my mind."

"To do it?" cried Mr. Dale, with animation.

But Mr. Denner interrupted him with a polite gesture. "No, I shall certainly do it. I did not mean to mislead you. I shall certainly do it, but I cannot make up my mind which."

"Which?" said Mr. Dale vaguely.

"Yes," answered the little gentleman, "which. Of course you know that I refer to the Misses Woodhouse. You must have noticed my attentions of late, for I have shown a great deal of attention to both; it has been very marked. Yet, Henry, I cannot tell which (both are such estimable persons) which I — should — ah — prefer. And knowing your experience, a married man yourself, and your reading on such subjects, — novels are mostly based upon esteem, — I felt sure you could advise me."

A droll look came into Mr. Dale's face, but he did not speak.

Feeling that he had made a clean breast of it, and that the responsibility of choice was shifted to his friend's shoulders, the lawyer, taking a last draught from the silver mug, and setting it down empty on the table, leaned comfortably back in his chair to await the decision.

There was a long silence; once Mr. Denner broke it by saying, "Of course, Henry, you see the importance of careful judgment," and then they were still again.

At last, Mr. Dale, with a long sigh, straightened up in his chair. He lifted his white fluted china tea-cup, which had queer little chintz-like bunches of flowers over it and a worn gilt handle, and took a pinch of tea from the caddy; then, pouring some boiling water over it, he set it on the hob to steep.

"Denner," he said slowly, "which advice do you want? Whether to do it at all, or which lady to choose?"

"Which lady, of course," answered Mr. Denner promptly. "There can be but one opinion as to the first question."

"Ah," responded Mr. Dale; then, a moment afterwards, he added, "Well" —

Mr. Denner looked at his friend, with eyes shining with excitement. "It is very important to me, Henry," he said, with a faltering voice. "You will keep that in mind, I am sure. They are both so admirable, and yet — there must be some choice. Miss Deborah's housekeeping — you know there's no such cooking in Ashurst; and she's very economical. But then, Miss Ruth is artistic, and" — here a fine wavering blush crept over his little face — "she is — ah — pretty, Henry. And the money is equally divided," he added, with a visible effort to return to practical things.

"I know. Yes, it's very puzzling. On the whole, Denner, I do not see how I can advise you."

Mr. Denner seemed to suffer a collapse.

"Why, Henry," he quavered, "you must have an opinion?"

"No," Mr. Dale answered thoughtfully, "I cannot say that I have. Now, I put it to you, Denner: how could I decide on the relative merits of Miss Ruth and Miss Deborah, seeing that I have no affection, only respect, for either of them? Affection! that ought to be your guide. Which do you have most affection for?"

" Why, really " — said Mr. Denner, "really " — and he stopped to think, looking hard at the seal ring on his left hand—" I am afraid it is just the same, if you call it affection. You see that does n't help us."

He had identified Mr. Dale's interest with his own anxiety, and looked wistfully at the older man, who seemed sunk in thought and quite forgetful of his presence. Mr. Denner put one hand to his lips and gave a little cough. Then he said : —

" One would think there would be a rule about such things, some acknowledged method; a proverb, for instance ; it would simplify matters very much."

" True," said Mr. Dale.

" Yes," Mr. Denner added, " you would think in such a general thing as marriage there would be. Complications like this must constantly arise. What if Miss Deborah and Miss Ruth had another sister? Just see how confused a man might be. Yes, one would suppose the wisdom of experience would take the form of an axiom. But it has n't."

He sighed deeply, and rose, for it was late, and the little fire had burned out.

Mr. Dale bent forward, with his elbows on his lean knees, and gently knocked the ashes from his silver pipe. Then he got up, and, standing with his back to the cold grate, and the tails of his flowered dressing-gown under each arm in a comfortable way, he looked at the lawyer, with his head a little on one side, as though he were about to speak. Mr. Denner noticed it.

" Ah, you cannot make any suggestion, Henry?"

" Well," said Mr. Dale, " it seems to me I had a thought — a sort of a proverb, you might say — but it slips my memory."

Mr. Denner, with his overcoat half on, stood quite still, and trembled.

" It is something about how to make up your mind," Mr. Dale continued, very slowly ; " let me see."

" How to make up your mind?" cried Mr. Denner. " That's just the thing! I'm sure, that's just the thing! And we cannot but have the greatest confidence in proverbs. They are so eminently trustworthy. They are the concentrated wisdom — of — of the ages, as it were. Yes, I should be quite willing to decide the matter by a proverb."

He looked at Mr. Dale eagerly, but this especial piece of wisdom still eluded the older man.

" It begins," said Mr. Dale, hesitating, and fixing his eyes upon the ceiling, — " it begins — let me see. ' When in doubt' — ah " —

" What is it?" gasped Mr. Denner. " That has a familiar sound, but I cannot seem to finish it. When in doubt, what?"

" Well," answered his friend ruefully, " it is not quite — it does not exactly apply. I am afraid it won't help us out. You know the rest. It is merely — 'take the trick'!"

CHAPTER XVI.

THE morning after John Ward's return from his
two weeks' absence at General Assembly, he found
it hard to settle down to work. Not that there was
very much to talk about, for daily letters had told
of daily doings, but to be with Helen again was an
absorbing joy. She followed him about as he put
his papers away, and he, in turn, came out into the
garden to watch her while she showed Alfaretta
where to plant some flower seeds.

"Come over here," Helen said, "and see these
violets under the big elm! I have been so in hopes
they would blossom in time to welcome you. Let's
pick some for the study."

They pushed the shining, wet leaves aside, and
found the flowers, and then John watched his wife
put them in a shallow dish on his table.

"It is weak in me to come in here," Helen said,
smiling. "I know you ought to work, yet here I
sit."

"This is Thursday," he answered, "and I wrote
my sermon on the train yesterday, so after I have
copied the reports I can afford to be lazy. I cannot bear to have you out of my sight!" He drew
her brown head down on his shoulder, and stroked
her face softly. "When I'm away from you, Helen,
I seem only half alive."

" And in three weeks I have to go to Ashurst,"
she said ruefully. " It is too bad I could n't have
gone while you were at General Assembly, but it
would n't have been right for us both to be away
from the parsonage at once."

" No. Well, we have the three weeks yet. Yes,
I must send you away, and get at the reports. How
you brighten this room, Helen! I think it must be
the sunshine that seems caught in your hair. It
gleams like bronze oak-leaves in October."

" Love has done wonderful things for your eyes,
John," she said, smiling, as she left him.

She put on her heavy gloves and brought her
trowel from under the front porch, and she and the
maid began to dig up the fresh, damp earth on the
sunny side of the house.

" We 'll have some sweet-peas here, Alfaretta,"
she said cheerily, " and I think it would be nice to let
the nasturtiums run over that log, don't you? And
you must plant these morning-glory seeds around
the kitchen windows." Suddenly she noticed that
Alfaretta, instead of listening, was gazing down the
road, and her round freckled face flushing hotly.

" He sha'n't come in," she muttered, — " he sha'n't
come in!" and dropping the hammer, and the box
of tacks, and the big ball of twine, she hurried to
the gate, her rough hands clinched into two sturdy
fists.

Helen looked towards the road, and saw Mr. Dean
come stiffly up to the gate, for lumbago was not altogether a memory. Alfaretta reached it as he did,
and as she stooped to lean her elbows on its top bar
she slipped the latch inside.

"Alfaretta," said her father pompously, "open the gate, if you please." As he spoke, he rapped upon it with his heavy stick, and the little latch clattered and shook.

"Were you coming to see me, pa?" the girl asked nervously. "I — I'm busy this morning. It's my night out, so I'll see you this evenin'."

"Yes, I'll see you," returned Mr. Dean significantly, "but not now. I did n't come to see you now; I'm here to see the preacher, Alfaretta. Come, don't keep me out here in the sun," he added impatiently, shaking the gate again.

"I guess he's too busy to see you this morning, — he's awful busy."

"I guess he's not too busy to see me," said the elder.

Alfaretta's face was white now, but she still stood barring the gateway. "Well, you can't see him, anyhow;" her voice had begun to tremble, and Mrs. Ward, who had joined them, said, with a surprised look, —

"Why, what do you mean, Alfaretta? Of course Mr. Ward will see your father. I hope your lumbago is better, Elder Dean?"

Mr. Dean did not notice her question. "Certainly he will see me. Come, now, open the gate; be spry."

"You can't see him!" cried Alfaretta, bursting into tears. "I say he won't see you, so there!"

Her mistress looked at her in astonishment, but her father put his big hand over the gate, and, wrenching the little latch open, strode up to the front door of the parsonage.

Helen and her maid looked at each other ; Alfaretta's face working convulsively to keep back the
tears, and her mistress's eyes full of disapproval.

"Why did you say that, Alfaretta?" she said.
"It was not true ; you knew Mr. Ward could see
your father." Then she turned back to her planting.

Alfaretta followed her, and, kneeling down by
the border, began to grub at the intruding blades
of grass, stopping to put her hand up to her eyes
once in a while, which made her face singularly
streaked and muddy.

"What is the matter, Alfaretta?" Helen asked,
at last, coldly. She did not mean to be unkind, but
she was troubled at the girl's untruthfulness.

Alfaretta wailed.

"Tell me," Helen said, putting her hand lightly
on her shoulder. "Are you crying because you
said what was not true?"

"'T ain't that!" sobbed Alfaretta.

"I wish, then, you would either stop, or go into
the house." Helen's voice was stern, and Alfaretta
looked at her with reproachful eyes ; then covering
her face with her hands, she rocked backwards and
forwards, and wept without restraint.

"I'm afraid — I'm afraid he's going to take
me away from here!"

"Take you away?" Helen said, surprised.
"Why? Is the work too hard?"

"No — no ma'am," Alfaretta answered, choking.

"I'll go and see him at once," Helen said.

"Oh, no!" Alfaretta cried, catching her mistress's skirt with grimy hands, "don't go; 't won't do any good."

"Don't be foolish," Helen remonstrated, smiling; "of course I must speak to him. If your father thinks there is too much work, he must tell me, and I will arrange it differently."

She stooped, and took the hem of her cambric gown from between the girl's fingers, and then went quickly into the house.

She rapped lightly at the study door. "John, I must come in a moment, please."

She heard a chair pushed back, and John's footstep upon the floor. He opened the door, and stood looking at her with strange, unseeing eyes.

"Go away, Helen," he said hoarsely, without waiting for her to speak, for she was dumb with astonishment at his face, — "go away, my darling."

He put out one hand as if to push her back, and closed the door, and she heard the bolt pushed. She stood a moment staring at the blank of the locked door. What could it mean? Alfaretta's misery and morals were forgotten; something troubled John, — she had no thought for anything else. She turned away as though in a dream, and began absently to take off her garden hat. John was in some distress. She went up-stairs to her bedroom, and tried to keep busy with sewing until she could go to him, but she was almost unconscious of what she did. How long, how very long, the morning was!

. . . .

John had looked up from his writing to see Mr. Dean standing in the doorway.

"Good-morning," he said cordially, as he rose to give his hand to his elder. "I am glad to see you. How have things gone since I have been away?"

But Mr. Dean seemed to have nothing special to report, and let the preacher tell him of General Assembly, while, embarrassed and very uncomfortable, he sat twisting his hat round and round in his big, rough hands.

A bar of sunshine from the south window crept across the floor, and touched the low dish of violets on the table, and then John's face, making a sudden golden glint in his gentle dark eyes.

"Mr. Ward," the elder said, at last, opening his mouth once or twice before he began to speak, "I have a distress on my mind. I think the Spirit of the Lord 's driven me to tell you of it."

"Are you in any trouble, my friend?" The tired look which had fallen upon John's face as he put down his pen was gone in a moment. "I am glad, then, I was not away any longer. I trust sickness has not come to your family?"

"No, sir," answered the other solemnly, "not sickness of body. What does the Good Book say to the Christian? 'He shall give his angels charge over thee.' No, I 'm mercifully preserved from sickness; for, as for me and my house, we serve the Lord. My lumbago was bad while you was away; but it 's better, I 'm thankful to say. Sickness of the soul, Mr. Ward, — that is what is truly awful."

"I hope you are not feeling the power of Satan in doubts?" John said anxiously. "Such sickness of the soul is indeed worse than any which can come to the body."

"No," replied the elder, "no, my feet are fixed. I know whom I have believed. I have entered into the hidden things of God. I am not afraid of doubt, ever. Yet what a fearful thing doubt is, Brother Ward!"

"It is, indeed," John replied humbly. "Through the mercy of God, I have never known its temptation. He has kept me from ever questioning truth."

"What a terrible thing it would be," said Mr. Dean, beginning to forget his awkwardness, "if doubt was to grow up in any heart, or in any family, or in any church! I've sometimes wondered if, of late, you had given us enough sound doctrine in the pulpit, sir? The milk of the Word we can get out of the Bible for ourselves, but doctrines, they ain't to be found in Holy Writ as they'd ought to be preached."

John looked troubled. He knew the rebuke was merited. "I have feared my sermons were, as you say, scarcely doctrinal enough. Yet I have instructed you these six years in points of faith, and I felt it was perhaps wiser to turn more to the tenderness of God as it is in Christ. And I cannot agree with you that the doctrines are not in the Bible, Mr. Dean."

"Well," the elder admitted, "of course. But not so he that runs may read, or that the wayfaring man will not err therein. There is some folks as would take 'God is love' out of the Good Book, and forget 'Our God is a consuming fire.'"

John bent his head on his hand for a moment, and drove his mind back to his old arguments for silence.

Neither of the men spoke for a little while, and then John said, still without raising his head: —

"Do you feel that this — neglect of mine has been of injury to any soul? It is your duty to tell me."

It was here that Helen's knock came, and when John had taken his seat again he looked his accuser straight in the eyes.

"Do you?" he said.

"Sir," answered the elder, "I can't say. I ain't heard that it has — and yet — I 'm fearful. Yet I didn't come to reproach you for that. You have your reasons for doing as you did, no doubt. But what I did come to do, preacher, was to warn you that there was a creepin' evil in the church; and we need strong doctrine now, if we ain't before. And I came the quicker to tell you, sir, because it 's fastened on my own household. Yes, on my own child!"

"Your own child?" John said. "You have nothing to fear for Alfaretta; she is a very good, steady girl."

"She 's good enough and she 's steady enough," returned Mr. Dean, shaking his head; "and oh, Mr. Ward, when she joined the church, two years ago, there was n't anybody (joinin' on profession) better grounded in the faith than she was. She knew her catechism through and through, and she never asked a question or had a doubt about it in her life. But now, — now it 's different!"

"Do you mean," John asked, "that her faith is shaken, — that she has doubts? Such times are apt

to come to very young Christians, though they
are conscious of no insincerity, and the doubts are but
superficial.   Has she such doubts?"

"She has, sir, she has," cried the elder, "and it
breaks my heart to see my child given over to the
Evil One!"

"No, no," John said tenderly; "if she is one of
the elect, — and we have reason to hope she is, —
she will persevere.   Remember, for your comfort,
the perseverance of the saints.   But how has this
come about?   Is it through any influence?"

"Yes, sir, it is," said the elder quickly.

"What is the especial doubt?" John asked.

"It is her views of hell that distress me," answered the elder.   John looked absently beyond
him, with eyes which saw, not Alfaretta, but Helen.

"That is very serious," he said slowly.

"'T ain't natural to her," protested the elder.
"She was grounded on hell; she's been taught better.   It's the influence she's been under, preacher."

"Surely it cannot be any one in our church,"
John said thoughtfully.   "I can think of too many
who are weak in grace and good works, but none
who doubt the faith."

"Yes," replied the elder, "yes, it is in our church.
That's why I came to beg you to teach sound doctrine, especially the doctrine of everlasting punishment.   I could a' dealt with Alfaretta myself, and
I'll bring her round, you can depend on that; but
it is for the church I'm askin' you, and fer that
person that's unsettled Alfaretta.   Convert her,
save her.   It is a woman, sir, a member (by letter,

Brother Ward) of our church, and she 's spreadin'
nets of eternal ruin for our youth, and I came to
say she ought to be dealt with; the Session ought to
take notice of it. The elders have been speakin' of
it while you was away; and we don't see no way out
of it, for her own soul's sake, — let alone other people's souls, — than to bring her before the Session.
If we can't convert her to truth, leastways she 'll be
disciplined to silence."

That subtile distinction which John Ward had
made between his love and his life was never more
apparent than now. Though his elder's words
brought him the keenest consciousness of his wife's
unbelief, he never for an instant thought of her as
the person whose influence in the church was to be
feared. His church and his wife were too absolutely
separate for such identification to be possible.

" And," Mr. Dean added, his metallic voice involuntarily softening, " our feelings, Mr. Ward,
must n't interfere with it; they must n't make us
unkind to her soul by slightin' her best good."

" No," John said, still absently, and scarcely listening to his elder, — " no, of course not. But have
you seen her, and talked with her, and tried to
lead her to the truth? That should be done with
the tenderest patience before anything so extreme
as Sessioning."

" We ain't," the elder answered significantly,
" but I make no doubt she 's been reasoned with
and prayed with."

" Why, I have not spoken to her," John said,
bewildered; " but you have not told me who it is,
yet."

" Mr. Ward," said the other solemnly, " if you ain't spoke to her, you 've neglected your duty ; and if you don't give her poor soul a chance of salvation by bringing her to the Session, you are neglectin' your duty still more. Your church, sir, and the everlastin' happiness of her soul demand that this disease of unbelief should be rooted out. Yes, Brother Ward, if the Jonah in a church was our nearest and dearest — and it don't make no odds — the ship should be saved ! "

They both rose ; a terrible look was dawning in John Ward's face, and, seeing it, the elder's voice sunk to a hurried whisper as he spoke the last words.

" Who is this woman ? " the preacher said hoarsely.

" Sir — sir " — the elder cried, backing towards the door and raising his hands in front of him, " don't look so, — don't look so, sir ! "

" Who ? " demanded the other.

" I spoke fer the sake of Alfaretta's soul, and fer the sake of them that 's heard her say them things about Tom Davis, provin' there was n't any punishment for sinners. Don't look so, preacher ! "

" Tell me her name ! "

" Her name — her name ? Oh, you know it, sir, you know it — it 's — your wife, preacher."

John Ward sprang at the cowering figure of the big elder, and clinched his trembling hands on the man's shoulders, with an inarticulate cry.

" My wife ! " he said, between his teeth. " How dare you speak her name ! " He stopped, struggling for breath.

" My duty ! " gasped the elder, trying to loosen the trembling fingers — " to her — an' you — an' the church you 've starved and neglected, Brother Ward ! "

John blenched. Mr. Dean saw his advantage. " You know your vows when you were ordained here six years ago : do you keep them ? Do you feed your people with spiritual food, or will you neglect them for your wife's sake, and let her example send the souls in your care to endless ruin ? "

John had loosened his hold on the elder, and was leaning against the wall, his head bowed upon his breast and his hands knotted together. A passion of horrified grief swept across his face ; he seemed unconscious of the elder's presence. Mr. Dean looked at him, not certain what to do or say ; he had quite forgotten Alfaretta's " notice." At last the preacher raised his head.

" You have said enough," he said, in a low voice ; " now go," and he pointed with a shaking finger to the door. " Go ! " he repeated.

The elder hesitated, then slowly put on his hat and stumbled from the room. John did not notice his outstretched hand, but followed him blindly to the door, and locked it after him.

The full blaze of sunshine flooded the room with its pitiless mirth ; it was wilting the dish of violets, and he moved it to the shaded end of the table.

.   .   .   .

Alfaretta, peering out of her attic window, and wiping her eyes on the corner of the dimity curtain which hid her, saw the elder walk out of the parsonage and through the little gateway, with shame written on his drooping shoulders and in his hurried, shambling steps. He never once looked back.

CHAPTER XVII.

ALMOST before Elder Dean had left the threshold Helen stood at the bolted door. She turned the knob gently while she knocked.

"John," she said anxiously, — "John, dear!" But there was no answer.

"John!" she said again, a thread of fear in her voice. "What is the matter? Are you ill, dearest? Please let me in!"

Only the rustle of the wind outside and the flickering shadows across the hall answered her. She shook the door slightly, and then listened. "John, John!" she called again, and as she heard a long breath inside the closed room she leaned against the wall, faint with a fright she had not realized. She heard a slow footstep upon the floor, that stopped on the other side of the door.

"Helen," her husband said, in a voice she scarcely knew, "I want to be alone. I am not ill, but I must be — undisturbed. Will you go away, please?"

"Let me in just one moment, darling," she pleaded, still nervously turning the knob. "I won't disturb you, but it terrifies me to be shut out in this way. Please let me just see you, and then I will go right away."

"No," he answered, "I cannot see you. I do not want to see you, Helen. I must be alone just now."

"You are sure you are not ill?" she insisted.

"Quite sure."

"Well," she said reluctantly, "I'll go, but call me just as soon as I can come, will you?"

"Yes," he answered, "but do not come until I do call you."

She heard him walk back to his study table, and then silence seemed to fall like a shadow on her heart. She was more bewildered than before. John was in trouble, and she could not help him. Nevertheless, she did not speak again; she was one of those unusual women who are content to wait until the moment it is needed, to give their sympathy or tenderness. So she went to her own room, and sat wistfully looking out at the sweet spring day; she could not read while this anxiety filled her mind, and her hands were idle in her lap. She did not even summon John to luncheon, knowing he would come if he saw fit; for herself, she could not eat. It was almost five, when she heard John push his chair back (she was sitting on the lowest step of the staircase, which ended at the study door, leaning her head against the frame), and again her ear caught the heavy, long-drawn sigh. Her suspense was to end.

She rose, her hands pressed hard together to check their trembling; she bit her lip lest she might speak and disturb him one moment before he was ready to hear her.

He pushed back the bolt, and slowly opened the door and looked at her. All the words of love and anxiety died on her lips.

"John," she whispered, — "oh, my dear, what is it?"

He came out, and, putting his hands on her shoulders, looked down at her with terrible, unsmiling eyes. "Helen," he said, "I am grieved to have distressed you so, but it had to be. I had to be alone. I am in much trouble. No," laying his hand gently on her lips; "listen to me, dearest. I am in great distress of soul; and just now, just for a few days, I must bear it alone."

Helen felt a momentary sense of relief. Distress of soul? — that meant some spiritual anxiety, and it had not the awfulness to her which a more tangible trouble, such as sickness, would have.

"What is it, John? Tell me," she said, looking at him with overflowing love, but without an understanding sympathy; it was more that feeling which belongs to strong women, of maternal tenderness for the men they love, quite apart from an intellectual appreciation of their trouble.

John shook his head. "I must bear it alone, Helen. Do not ask me what it is; I cannot tell you yet."

"You cannot tell me? Oh, John, your sorrow belongs to me; don't shut me out; tell me, dear, and let me help you."

"You cannot help me," he answered wearily; "only trust me when I say it is best for me not to tell you now; you shall know all there is to know, later. Be patient just a few days, — until after the Sabbath. Oh, bear with me, — I am in great sorrow, Helen; help me with silence."

She put her arms around him, and in her caress-
ing voice, with that deep note in it, she said, " It
shall be just as you say, darling. I won't ask you
another question, but I 'm ready to hear whenever
you want to tell me."

He looked at her with haggard eyes, but did not
answer. Then she drew him out into the fresh coolness of the garden, and tried to bring some brightness into his face by talking of small household hap-
penings, and how she had missed him during his two
weeks' absence, and what plans she had for the next
week. But no smile touched his white lips, or banished the absent look in his eyes. After tea, during
which his silence had not been broken, he turned to
go into his study.

" Oh, you are not going to work to-night? " Helen
cried. " Don't leave me alone again ! "

He looked at her with sudden wistfulness. " I —
I must," he said, his voice so changed it gave her a
shock of pain. " I must work on my sermon."

" I thought you had written it," she said; " and
you are so tired — do wait until to-morrow."

" I am not going to use the sermon I prepared,"
he answered. " I have decided to preach more directly on foreign missions. You know I exchange
with Mr. Grier, of Chester, on the Sabbath ; and he
will preach to our church on the attitude of Assembly towards missions. I had intended to give a
more general sermon to his people, but — I have
decided otherwise."

Helen was surprised at so long an explanation ;
John's sermons were generally ignored by both, but

for different reasons. She followed him into the study, and when she had lighted his lamp he kissed her, saying softly, "May God bless you, Helen," and then he shut her gently from the room.

"Don't lock the door, John," she had said. " I won't come in, but don't lock it." Her lip almost trembled as she spoke.

"No, — no," he said tenderly. " Oh, Helen, I have made you suffer ! "

She was quick to protect him. " No, I was only lonely ; but you won't lock it ? "

He did not, but poor Helen wandered forlornly about the darkened house, an indefinable dread chasing away the relief which had come when her husband spoke of spiritual trouble ; she was glad, for the mere humanness of it, to hear Thaddeus and Alfaretta talking in the kitchen.

The next day, and the next, dragged slowly by. When John was not at his writing - table, he was making those pastoral calls which took so much time and strength, and which Helen always felt were unnecessary. Once, seeing her standing leaning her forehead against the window and looking out sadly into the rainy garden, he came up to her and took her in his arms, holding her silently to his heart. That cheered and lightened her, and somehow, when Sunday morning dawned, full of the freshness of the past rain and the present wind and sunshine, she felt the gloom of the last three days lifting a little. True, there was the unknown sorrow in her heart, but love was there, too. She was almost happy, without knowing it.

They were to go on horseback, for Chester was eight miles off, and the thought of a ride in this sparkling mountain air brought a glow to her cheek, which had been pale the last few days. They started early. The sun seemed to tip the great green bowl of the valley, and make every leaf shine and glisten; the road wound among the circling hills, which were dark with sombre pines, lightened here and there by the fresh greenness of ash or chestnuts; in some places the horse's hoofs made a velvety sound on the fallen catkins. A brook followed their path, whispering and chattering, or hiding away under overhanging bushes, and then laughing sharply out into the sunshine again. The wind was fresh and fickle: sometimes twisting the weeds and flowers at the wayside, or sending a dash of last night's raindrops into their faces from the low branches of the trees, and all the while making cloud shadows scud over the fresh-ploughed fields, and up and across the blue, distant hills.

John rested his hand on her bridle, as she stroked her horse's mane. "How the wind has blown your hair from under your hat!" he said.

She put her gauntleted hand up to smooth it.

"Don't," he said, "it's so pretty; it looks like little tendrils that have caught the sun."

Helen laughed, and then looked at him anxiously; the sunshine brought out the worn lines in his face. "You work too hard, dearest; it worries me."

"I have never worked at all!" he cried, with a sudden passion of pain in his voice. "Oh, my wasted life, Helen, — my life that has wronged and cheated you!"

"John!" she said, almost frightened. Yet it was characteristic that she should think this was only a symptom of overwork and bodily weariness. And when at last they reached the church in Chester, and John lifted her from her saddle, the anxiety had come again, and all the joy of the summer morning had left her face. They fastened their horses to one of the big chestnuts which stood in a stately row in front of the little white church, and then Helen went inside, and found a seat by one of the open windows; she secretly pushed the long inside shutter, with its drab slats turned down, half-way open, so that she might look out across the burying-ground, where the high blossoming grass nodded and waved over the sunken graves.

John had followed her, and folded a coat over the back of the pew. He gave her a long, yearning look, but did not speak. Then he turned, and walked slowly up the aisle, with reverently bent head.

At the first hymn the congregation turned and faced the choir. Helen, with the shadows of the leaves playing across her hymn-book, leaned against the high back of the pew behind her, and sang in a strong, sweet voice, rejoicing in the rolling old tune of "Greenland's icy mountains." She could see the distant line of the hills, and now and then between the branches of the trees would come the flash and ripple of the brown river; and through the open door, which made a frame for the leaves and sky, she caught sight of the row of horses pounding and switching under the chestnuts, and those backsliders outside, who found it necessary to " see to the beasts " rather than attend their religious privileges. But there were not very many of these, for Mr. Ward's fame as a preacher had spread through all the villages near Lockhaven.

Helen, watching John while he read the chapter from the Bible, thought anxiously how tired and worn his face looked, and so thinking, and looking out into the dancing leaves, the short prayer, and the long prayer, and the hymn before the sermon passed, and she scarcely heard them. Then came the rustle of preparation for listening. The men shuffled about in their seats, and crossed their legs; the women settled their bonnet-strings, and gave the little children a peppermint drop, and the larger children a hymn-book to read. There were the usual rustling and whispering in the choir, and the creaking footsteps of the one or two who entered shamefacedly, as though they would explain that the horses had detained them. Then the church was very still.

John Ward rose, and spread his manuscript out upon the velvet cushion of the white pulpit.

" You will find my text," he said, " in the sixth chapter of Romans, the twenty-first verse: ' The end of those things is death.' "

It had been announced that his sermon was to be upon foreign missions, and the people waited patiently while the preacher briefly told them what had been accomplished by the Presbyterian Church during the last year, and, describing its methods of work, showed what it proposed to do in the future.

"That's just a-tunin' up, — he'll set the heathen dancin' pretty soon; you see!" some one whispered behind Helen; and then there was a giggle and "hush-sh," as Mr. Ward began to say that foreign missions were inevitable wherever the sentiment of pity 'found room in a human heart, because the guilt of those in the darkness of unbelief, without God, without hope, would certainly doom them to eternal misery; and this was a thought so dark and awful, men could not go their way, one to his farm, and another to his merchandise, and leave them to perish.

The simple and unquestioning conviction with which the preacher began to prove to his congregation that the heathen were guilty, because Adam, their federal head and representative, had sinned, perhaps hid from them the cruelty with which he credited the Deity. No one thought of disputing his statement that the wrath of God rested upon all unconverted souls, and that it would, unless they burst from their darkness into the glorious light of revealed truth, sink them to hell.

Some of the older Christians nodded their heads comfortably at this, and looked keenly at the sinners of their own families, trusting that they would be awakened to their danger by these trumpet bursts of doctrine. To such hearers, it was unnecessary that John Ward should insist upon the worthlessness of natural religion, begging them remember that for these heathen, as well as for more favored souls, Christ's was the only name given under heaven whereby men might be saved, and appealing to God's people, as custodians of the mercies of Christ, to stretch their hands out into the darkness to these blind, stumbling, doomed brothers. He bade them be quick to answer that cry of "Come and help us!" and to listen for that deeper voice beneath the wail of despair, which said, "Inasmuch as ye have done it unto one of the least of these my brethren, ye have done it unto me."

The possibility of being saved without a knowledge of Christ remained, he said, after eighteen hundred years, a possibility illustrated by no example; and we could only stand in the shadow of this terrible fact, knowing that millions and millions of souls were living without the gospel, the only source of life, and dying without hope, and pray God for the spirit and the means to help them.

Link by link he lengthened the chain of logic till it reached to the deepest hell. He showed how blasphemous was the cry that men must be saved, if for lack of opportunity they knew not Christ; that God would not damn the soul that had had no chance to accept salvation. It had had the chance of salvation in Adam, and had lost it, and was therefore condemned. To the preacher this punishment of the helpless heathen seemed only just.

"Shall not the Judge of all the earth do right?" he cried, and he stopped to suppose, for the sake of argument, that Adam had not sinned: surely no one would have disputed the justice of receiving the blessings which his godliness would have entailed. Then he began to prove the right of the potter over the clay. He had forgotten his congregation; the horror of the damnation of the heathen was lost in the fear that one soul should perish. He saw only Helen; she was in danger, she was far from God, but yet the price of admission to heaven could not be altered, though his heart broke for longing that she should be saved; the requirements of the gospel had not softened, the decrees of Omnipotence were as unchangeable as the eternal past.

His words, glowing with his love and grief, were only for her. The thunders of God's justice shook his soul, while he offered her the infinite mercy of Christ. But he did not shrink from acknowledging that that mercy was only for those who would accept it, nor presume to dictate to God that all sinners should be saved, forced into salvation, without accepting his conditions.

"What right," he said, "have we to expect that mercy should exist at all? What madness, then, to think He will depart from the course He has laid out for himself, and save without condition those who are justly condemned? Yet justice is satisfied, for Christ has died. O Soul, accept that sacrifice!" He had come to the edge of the pulpit, one pale hand clinched upon the heavy cover of the Bible, and the other stretched tremblingly out; his anxious, grieving eyes looked over the solemn, upturned faces of his listeners, and sought Helen, sitting in the dusky shadow by the open window, her face a little averted, and her firm, sweet lips set in a line which was almost stern.

Some of the women were crying: an exaltation purely hysterical made them feel themselves lost sinners; they thrilled at John's voice, as though his words touched some strained chord in their placid and virtuous lives.

" Come," he said, " stand with me to-day under the pierced hands and bleeding side of Infinite Mercy; look up into that face of divine compassion and ineffable tenderness, and know that this blood-stained cross proclaims to all the centuries death suffered for the sin of the world, — for your sin and mine. Can you turn and go away to outer darkness, to wander through the shadows of eternity, away from God, away from hope, away from love? Oh, come, while still those arms are open to you; come, before the day of grace has darkened into night; come, before relentless Justice bars the way with a flaming sword. O Soul, Christ waits!"

He stood a moment, leaning forward, his hands clasped upon the big Bible, and his face full of trembling and passionate pleading. Then he said, with a long, indrawn breath, " Let us pray!"

The people rose, and stood with bowed heads through the short, eager, earnest prayer. Then the preacher gave out the hymn, and there was the rustle of turning to face the choir. The quaint, doleful tune of Windham wailed and sobbed through the words, —

> " The burden of our weighty guilt
>   Would sink us down to flames;
>   And threatening vengeance rolls above,
>   To crush our feeble frames!"

The choir sang with cheerful heartiness; it was a relief from the tension of the sermon, a reaction to

life, and hope, and healthy humanness after these
shadows of death. It all seemed part of a dream to
Helen : the two happy-faced girls standing in the
choir, with bunches of apple-blossoms in the belts of
their fresh calico dresses, and the three young farm-
ers who held the green singing-books open, all singing heartily together, —

> " 'T is boundless, 't is amazing love,
> That bears us up from hell ! "

Helen watched them with fascinated curiosity;
she wondered if they could believe what they had
just heard. Surely not; or how could they know a
moment's happiness, or even live !

After the benediction had been pronounced she
walked absently down the aisle, and went at once to
her horse under the flickering shadows of the chestnuts. Here she waited for John, one hand twisted
in the gray's mane, and with the other switching at
the tall grass with her riding-whip. Only a few of
the people knew her, but these came to speak of the
sermon. One woman peered at her curiously from
under her big shaker bonnet. The stories of Mr.
Ward's wife's unbelief had traveled out from Lockhaven. " Wonderful how some folks could stand
against such doctrine ! " she said ; " and yet they
must know it 's a sin not to believe in everlasting
punishment. I believe it 's a mortal sin, don't you,
Mrs. Ward ? "

" No," Helen said quietly.

CHAPTER XVIII.

THEY rode quite silently to the house of the minister with whom John had exchanged, where they were to dine; after that, the preacher was to go back to the church for the afternoon sermon.

Mrs. Grier, a spare, anxious-looking woman, with a tight friz of hair about her temples which were thin and shining, met them at the door. She had hurried home to " see to things," and be ready to welcome her guests. John she ushered at once into her husband's study, a poor little room, with even fewer books than Mr. Ward's own, while Helen she took to the spare chamber, where she had thoughtfully provided a cambric dress for her, for the day had grown very warm, and the riding-habit was heavy.

She sat down in a splint rocking-chair, and watched her guest brush out her length of shining bronze hair, and twist it in a firm coil low on her neck.

" It was a good gathering," she said; " people came from a distance to hear Mr. Ward. The folks at Lockhaven are favored to listen to such preaching."

" No doubt they feel favored to have Mr. Grier with them to-day," Helen answered, courteously; but there was an absent look in her eyes, and she did not listen closely.

" Well, people like a change once in a while,"
Mrs. Grier admitted, rocking hard. " Mr. Grier's
discourse was to be on the same subject as your husband's, foreign missions. It is one that moves the
preachers, and the people seem to like it, I notice,
though I don't know that it makes much difference
in the collections. But I think they like to get all
harrowed up. You 'll find there won't be such an
attendance in the afternoon. It is ways and means,
then, you know. Yes, seems as if sermons on hell
made them shiver, and they enjoyed it. I 've sometimes thought — I don't know as I 'm right — they
get the same kind of pleasure out of it that worldly
people do out of a play. Not that I know much
about such things, I 'm sure."

Helen smiled, which rather shocked Mrs. Grier ;
but though the guest scarcely listened, the little
sharp babble of talk was kept up, until they went
down to dinner.

There had been no chance for the husband and
wife to speak to each other. John looked at Helen
steadily a moment, but her eyes veiled any thought.
In the midst of Mrs. Grier's chatter, she had gone
into the solitude of her own heart, and slowly and
silently light was beginning to shine into the mysterious darkness of the last few days. John's grief
must have had something to do with this terrible
sermon. She felt her heart leap up from the past
anxiety like a bird from a net, and the brooding
sadness began to fade from her face. The preacher
had come down from the pulpit with a certain exhilaration, as of duty done. He was inspired to

hope, and even certainty, by the greatness of the
theme. Helen should see the truth, his silence should
no longer mislead her, she should believe in the justice of God. He had forgotten his sin of cowardice
in the onward - sweeping wave of his convictions;
he seemed to yield himself up to the grasp of truth,
and lost even personal remorse in the contemplation
of its majesty.

Mrs. Grier had four noisy children, who all spoke
at once, and needed their mother's constant care and
attention, so John and Helen could at least be silent; yet it was hard to sit through the dinner when
their hearts were impatient for each other.

In a little breathing space at the end of the meal,
when two of the children had clambered down from
their high chairs and been dismissed, Mrs. Grier
began to speak of the sermon.

"It was a wonderful discourse, sir," she said;
"seems as if nobody could stand against such doctrine as you gave us. I could have wished, though,
you'd have told us your thoughts about infants being lost. There is a difference of opinion between
Mr. Grier and two of our elders."

"What does Brother Grier hold?" asked the
preacher.

"Well," Mrs. Grier answered, shaking her head,
"he does say they are all saved. But the elders,
they say that the confession of faith teaches that
elect infants are saved, and of course it follows that
those not elect are lost. My father, Mr. Ward, was
a real old-fashioned Christian, and I must say that
was what I was taught to believe, and I hold by it.

There now, Ellen, you take your little sister and go out into the garden, like a good girl."

She lifted the baby down from her chair, and put her hand into that of her elder sister.

"Mrs. Grier," Helen said, speaking quickly, "you say you believe it, but if you had ever lost a child, I am sure you could not."

"I have, ma'am," — Mrs. Grier's thin lip quivered, and her eyes reddened a little, — "but that can't make any difference in truth; besides, we have the blessed hope that she was an elect infant."

It would have been cruel to press the reason for this hope, and Helen listened instead with a breath of relief to what John was saying, — he, at least, did not hold this horrible doctrine.

"No, I agree with your husband," he said. "True, all children are born in sin, and are despised and abhorred as sinners by God. Jonathan Edwards, you know, calls them 'vipers,' which of course was a crude and cruel way of stating the truth, that they are sinners. Yet, through the infinite mercy, they are saved because Christ died, not of themselves; in other words, all infants who die, are elect."

Mrs. Grier shook her head. "I'm for holding to the catechism," she said; and then, with a sharp, thin laugh, she added, "But you 're sound on the heathen, I must say."

Helen shivered, and it did not escape her hostess, who turned and looked at her with interested curiosity. She, too, had heard the Lockhaven rumors.

"But then," she proceeded, "I don't see how a person can help being sound on that, though it is

surprising what people will doubt, even the things
that are plainest to other people. I 've many a time
heard my father say that the proper holding of the
doctrine of reprobation was necessary to eternal life.
I suppose you believe that, Mr. Ward," she added,
with a little toss of her head, " even if you don't go
all the way with the confession, about infants ? "

" Yes," John said sadly, " I must; because not
to believe in reprobation is to say that the sacrifice
of the cross was a useless offering."

" And of course," Mrs. Grier went on, an edge
of sarcasm cutting into her voice, " Mrs. Ward
thinks so, too ? Of course she thinks that a belief
in hell is necessary to get to heaven ? "

The preacher looked at his wife with a growing
anxiety in his face.

" No," Helen said, " I do not think so, Mrs.
Grier."

Mrs. Grier flung up her little thin hands, which
looked like bird-claws. " You *don't !* " she cried
shrilly. " Well, now, I do say ! And what do you
think about the heathen, then ? Do you think
they 'll be damned ? "

" No," Helen said again.

Mrs. Grier gave a gurgle of astonishment, and
looked at Mr. Ward, but he did not speak.

" Well," she exclaimed, " if I did n't think the
heathen would be lost, I would n't see the use of the
plan of salvation ! Why, they 've got to be ! "

" If they had to be," cried Helen, with sudden
passion, " I should want to be a heathen. I should
be ashamed to be saved, if there were so many lost."

She stopped; the anguish in John's face silenced her.

"Well," Mrs. Grier said again, really enjoying the scene, "*I'm* surprised; I would n't a' believed it!"

She folded her hands across her waist, and looked at Mrs. Ward with keen interest. Helen's face flushed under the contemptuous curiosity in the woman's eyes; she turned appealingly to John.

"Mrs. Ward does not think quite as we do, yet," he said gently; "you know she has not been a Presbyterian as long as we have."

He rose as he spoke, and came and stood by Helen's chair, and then walked at her side into the parlor.

Mrs. Grier had followed them, and heard Helen say in a low voice, "I would rather not go to church this afternoon, dearest. May I wait for you here?"

"Well," she broke in, "I should n't suppose you would care to go, so long as it's just about the ways and means of sending the gospel to the heathen, and you think they're all going right to heaven, any way."

"I do not know where they are going, Mrs. Grier," Helen said wearily; "for all I know, there is no heaven, either. I only know that God — if there is a God who has any personal care for us — could not be so wicked and cruel as to punish people for what they could not help."

"Good land!" cried Mrs. Grier, really frightened at such words, and looking about as though she expected a judgment as immediate as the bears which devoured the scoffing children.

"If you would rather not go," John answered, "if you are tired, wait for me here. I am sure Mrs. Grier will let you lie down and rest until it is time to start for home?"

"Oh, of course," responded Mrs. Grier, foreseeing a chance for further investigation, for she, too, was to be at home.

But Helen did not invite her to come into the spare room, when she went to lie down, after John's departure for church. She wanted to be alone. She had much to think of, much to reconcile and explain, to protect herself from the unhappiness which John's sermon might have caused her. She had had an unmistakable shock of pain and distress as she realized her husband's belief, and to feel even that seemed unloving and disloyal. To Helen's mind, if she disapproved of her husband's opinions on what to her was an unimportant subject, her first duty was to banish the thought, and forget that she had ever had it. She sat now by the open window, looking out over the bright garden to the distant peaceful hills, and by degrees the pain of it began to fade from her mind, in thoughts of John himself, his goodness, and their love. Yes, they loved one another, — that was enough.

"What does it matter what his belief is?" she said. "I love him!"

So, by and by, the content of mere existence unfolded in her heart, and John's belief was no more to her than a dress of the mind; his character was unchanged. There was a momentary pang that the characters of others might be hurt by this teaching of the expediency of virtue, but she forced the thought back. John, whose whole life was a lesson in the beauty of holiness — John could not injure any one. The possibility that he might be right in his creed simply never presented itself to her.

Helen's face had relaxed into a happy smile; again the day was fair and the wind sweet. The garden below her was fragrant with growing things and the smell of damp earth; and while she sat, drinking in its sweetness, a sudden burst of children's voices reached her ear, and Ellen and the two little boys came around the corner of the house, and settled down under the window. A group of lilacs, with feathery purple blossoms, made a deep, cool shade, where the children sat; and near them was an old grindstone, streaked with rust, and worn by many summers of sharpening scythes; a tin dipper hung on the wooden frame, nearly full of last night's rain, and with some lilac stars floating in the water.

This was evidently a favorite playground with the children, for under the frame of the grindstone were some corn-cob houses, and a little row of broken bits of china, which their simple imagination transformed into " dishes." But to-day the corn-cob houses and the dishes were untouched.

" Now, children," Ellen said, " you sit right down, and I 'll hear your catechism."

" Who 'll hear yours ? " Bobby asked discontentedly. " When we play school, you 're always teacher, and it 's no fun."

" This is n't playing school," Ellen answered, skillfully evading the first question. " Don't you know

it's wicked to play on the Sabbath? Now sit right
down."

There was a good deal of her mother's sharpness
in the way she said this, and plucked Bobby by the
strings of his pinafore, until he took an uncomfortable seat upon an inverted flower-pot.

Ellen opened a little yellow-covered book, and
began.

"Now answer, Jim! How many kinds of sin are
there?"

"Two," responded little Jim.

"What are these two kinds, Bob?"

"Original and actual," Bob answered.

"What is original sin?" asked Ellen, raising one
little forefinger to keep Bobby quiet. This was too
hard a question for Jim, and with some stumbling
Bobby succeeded in saying, —

"It is that sin in which I was conceived and
born."

"Now, Jim," said Ellen, "you can answer this
question, 'cause it's only one word, and begins with
'y.'"

"No fair!" cried Bob; "that's telling."

But Ellen proceeded to give the question : " Doth
original sin wholly defile you, and is it sufficient to
send you to hell, though you had no other sin?"

"Yes!" roared Jim, pleased at being certainly
right.

"What are you then by nature?" Ellen went on
rather carelessly, for she was growing tired of the
lesson.

"I am an enemy to God, a child of Satan, and an
heir of hell," answered Bobby promptly.

" What will become of the wicked ? " asked the little catechist.

Bobby yawned, and then said contemptuously, " Oh, skip that, — cast into hell, of course."

" You ought to answer right," Ellen said reprovingly, but she was glad to give the last question, " What will the wicked do forever in hell ? "

" They will roar, curse, and blaspheme God," said little Jim cheerfully ; while Bobby, to show his joy that the lesson was done, leaned over on his flower-pot, and tried to stand on his head, making all the time an unearthly noise.

" I 'm roarin' ! " he cried gayly.

Ellen, freed from the responsibility of teaching, put the little yellow book quickly in her pocket, and said mysteriously, " Boys, if you won't ever tell, I 'll tell you something."

" I won't," said Jim, while Bobby responded briefly, " G'on."

" Well, you know when the circus came, — you know the pictures on the fences ? "

" Yes ! " said the little boys together.

" 'Member the beautiful lady, ridin' on a horse, and standin' on one foot ? "

" Yes ! " the others cried, breathlessly.

" Well," said Ellen slowly and solemnly, " when I get to be a big girl, that 's what I 'm going to be. I 'm tired of catechism, and church, and those long blessings father asks, but most of catechism, so I 'm going to run away, and be a circus."

" Father 'll catch you," said Jim ; but Bobby, with envious depreciation, added, —

"How do you know but what circuses have cate-chism?"

Ellen did not notice the lack of sympathy. "And I'm going to begin to practice now," she said.

Then, while her brothers watched her, deeply interested, she took off her shoes, and in her well-darned little red stockings climbed deliberately upon the grindstone.

"This is my horse," she said, balancing herself, with outstretched arms, on the stone, and making it revolve in a queer, jerky fashion by pressing her feet on it as though it were a treadmill, "and it is bare-backed!"

The iron handle came down with a thud, and Ellen lurched to keep from falling; the boys unwisely broke into cheers.

It made a pretty picture, the sunbeams sifting through the lilacs on the little fair heads, and dancing over Ellen's white apron and rosy face; but Mrs. Grier, who had come to the door at the noise of the cheers, did not stop to notice it.

"Oh, you naughty children!" she cried. "Don't you know it is wicked to play on the Sabbath? Ellen's playing circus, do you say, Bobby? You naughty, naughty girl! Don't you know circus people are all wicked, and don't go to heaven when they die? I should think you'd be ashamed! Go right up-stairs, Ellen, and go to bed; and you boys can each learn a psalm, and you'll have no supper, either, — do you hear?"

The children began to cry, but Mrs. Grier was firm; and when, a little later, Helen came down-

stairs, ready for her ride, the house was strangely
quiet. Mrs. Grier, really troubled at her children's
sinfulness, confided their misdeeds to Helen, and was
not soothed by the smile that flashed across her face.

" They were such good children to study their
catechism first," she interceded, " and making a
horse out of a grindstone shows an imagination
which might excuse the playing."

But Mrs. Grier was not comforted, and only felt
the more convinced of the lost condition of Mrs.
Ward's soul. The conviction of other people's sin
is sometimes a very pleasing emotion, so she bade
her guest good-by with much cordiality and even
pulled the skirt of her habit straight, and gave the
gray a lump of sugar.

Helen told John of the scene under the lilacs, as
they trotted down the lane to the highway, but his
mood was too grave to see any humor in it. Indeed,
his frame of mind had changed after he left his wife
for his second sermon. The exhilaration and triumph had gone, and the reaction had come. He
brooded over his sin, and the harassed, distressed
look of the last few days settled down again on his
face. But Helen had regained her sweet serenity
and content; she felt so certain that the darkness
since Thursday had been the shadow in which his
sermon had been conceived that her relief brought
a joy which obscured any thought of regret that he
should hold such views.

John's head was bent, and his hands were clasped
upon his saddle-bow, while the reins fell loosely
from between his listless fingers.

"You are so tired, John," Helen said regretfully.

He sighed, as though rousing himself from thought.
" A little, dearest," and then his sorrowful eyes
smiled. " You look so fresh and rested, Helen. It
was wise for you to lie down this afternoon."

"Oh, but I didn't," she said quickly. "I was
busy thinking."

He looked at her eagerly. " Yes," she continued,
" I think I know what has distressed you so these
last few days, dear. It is this thought of the suffering of mankind. If you have felt that all the
heathen who have died are in hell, I don't wonder
at your sorrow. It would be dreadful, and I wish
you did not think it. But we will not talk about it,
— of course you would rather not talk about it, even
to me, but I understand."

She bent forward, and smiled brightly, as she
looked at him. But his face was full of grief.

" It was not that, Helen," he said ; " it was something nearer than that. It was remorse, because of
late, for nearly a year, I have neglected my people.
I have not admonished them and warned them as I
ought. And nearer still, because I have neglected
you."

" Me !" she cried, too much astonished to say
more.

" Yes," he answered, his head bent again upon
his breast, " you, my dearest, my best beloved, —
you, who are dearer than my life to me, dearer
than my happiness. I have known that you have
been far from truth, that you have not believed, and
yet I — I have been silent."

Helen looked at him, and the sudden awful thought flashed into her mind that he did not know what he was saying, and then she said with a gasp: " Oh, John, is that all? Have you been so unhappy just because of that? Oh, you poor fellow!"

She brought her horse close beside his, and laid her hand on his arm. " Dear, what does it matter what I believe or do not believe? We love each other. And where is your tolerance, John?" She laughed, but the look of terrible concern in his face frightened her.

" Ah, Helen," he said, " such tolerance as you would have me show would be indifference."

" Oh, John!" she said, and then began resolutely to speak of other things.

But soon they fell into silence, Helen longing to get home and brush this useless and foolish anxiety from her husband's heart, and he agonizing for his sin towards her and towards his people.

The late afternoon sunshine gilded the tender green of the fields, and slanting deep into the darkness of the woods, touched the rough trunks of the trees with gold. Long shadows stretched across the road, and the fragrance which steals out with the evening dews began to come from unseen blossoms, and early clover; and a breath of the uncertain night wind brought hints of apple orchards or the pungent sweetness of cherry-blossoms. They had gone more than half-way home when they drew rein to water their horses, under a whispering pine by the roadside. The trough, overflowing with sparkling water, was green with moss and lichen, and was

so old and soft that a bunch of ferns had found a home
on its side. The horses thrust their noses down into
it, blowing and sputtering with sheer delight in the
coolness. John made a cup of a big beech leaf, and
filled it for his wife. As he handed it to her, they
heard steps, and in a moment more Mr. Grier came
around the curve of the road. His horse, too, was
thirsty, and he let the reins fall on its neck while he
greeted them both with formal and ministerial dignity, saying he " wished they might have tarried
until he came home, and perhaps he could have persuaded them to stay the night."

The horses pounded and splashed in the pools
about their feet, and were impatient to be off, but
Mr. Grier delayed. He spoke of church matters,
and General Assembly, and their respective con-
gregations ; and then, with a little hesitation, he
said : —

" I had almost hoped, Mrs. Ward, that you would
have been in Brother Ward's church to-day, even
though Mrs. Grier had much pleasure in seeing you
under our roof. I had you in my mind in the preparation of my sermon."

Mr. Grier was a tall, thin man, with watery
blue eyes, and a sparse sandy beard growing like a
fringe under his chin from ear to ear. He moved
his jaws nervously as he waited for her answer, and
plucked at his beard with long, lean fingers.

Helen smiled. " Did you think I should be a
large contributor to foreign missions, Mr. Grier?"

" No, ma'am," he answered solemnly, " I was not
thinking of any benefit to the heathen. I had some-

what to say which I felt might be for the good of
your own soul."

Helen flushed, and flung her head back with a
haughty look. " Ah,— you are very good, I 'm sure,"
she said, " but " —

Mr. Grier interrupted her, wagging his head up
and down upon his breast : " Brother Ward will
forgive me for saying so, ma'am, but I had your welfare at heart.   Brother Ward, you have my prayers
for your dear wife."

" I — I thank you," John said, " but you must not
feel that my wife is far from the Lord.   Have you
been told that the truth is not clear to her eyes ?
Yet it will be ! "

" I hope so, — I hope so," responded Mr. Grier,
but with very little hope in his voice ; and then,
shaking the reins, he jogged on down the shadowy
road.

" What does he mean ? " cried Helen, her voice
trembling with anger, and careless whether the retreating minister overheard her.   John gave her a
long, tender look.

" Dearest," he said, " I am sorry he should have
spoken as he did, but the prayers of a good man " —

" I don't want his prayers," she interrupted, bewildered ; " it seems to me simply impertinence ! "

" Helen," he said, " it cannot be impertinence to
pray for a soul in danger, as yours is, my darling.
I cannot tell how he knew it, but it is so.   It is
my sin which has kept you blind and hidden the
truth from you, and how can I be angry if another
man joins his prayers to mine for your eternal salvation ? "

"You say this because I do not believe in eternal punishment, John?" she asked.

"Yes," he answered gently, "first because of that, and then because of all the errors of belief to which that leads."

"It all seems so unimportant," she said, sighing; "certainly nothing which could make me claim the prayers of a stranger. Ah, well, no doubt he means it kindly, but don't let us speak of it any more, dearest."

Their horses were so close, that, glancing shyly about for a moment into the twilight, Helen laid her head against his arm, and looked tenderly into his face.

He started, and then put a quick arm about her to keep her from falling. "No," he said, "no, I will not forget." It was as though he answered some voice in his soul, and Helen looked at him in troubled wonder.

The rest of the ride was very silent. Once, when he stopped to tighten her saddle-girth for her, she bent his head back, and smiled down into his eyes. He only answered her by a look, but it was enough.

CHAPTER XIX.

GIFFORD WOODHOUSE was not quite honest with himself when he said that he felt it was time to go back to Ashurst to make his aunts a visit. He had been restless and absent-minded very often since that flying trip in the early spring. In spite of his sternest reasoning, hope was beginning to grow up in his heart again. Dick Forsythe had not come to Ashurst, and Helen said plainly that she knew Lois was not engaged to him. So why should not Gifford himself be on the spot?

"Not that I would bother Lois," he argued in his own mind, "but just to know if" — And besides, he really ought to see the two little ladies.

He left Lockhaven a few days after John Ward had preached his sermon on foreign missions at Chester. It was reported to have been "powerful," and Elder Dean said he wished "our own people could have been benefited by it."

"I thought the heathen were expected to be benefited by such sermons," Gifford said, twisting a cigarette between his fingers, as he leaned over the half-door of the elder's shop, lazily watching a long white shaving curl up under his plane. "I thought the object was a large contribution."

The elder looked up solemnly, and opened his lips with vast deliberation. " Lawyer Woodhouse," he said, "that's your mistake. They're fer the purpose of instructing us that the heathen is damned, so that we will rejoice in our own salvation, and make haste to accept it if we are unconverted."

He looked hard at the young man as he spoke, for every one knew Lawyer Woodhouse did not go regularly to church, and so, presumably, was not a Christian.

Then Mr. Dean, while he pulled the shavings out of his plane, and threw them on the fragrant heap at his feet, said one or two things which made Gifford stop lounging and forget his cigarette while he listened with a grave face. "Unbelief in the church," "the example for our youth," "the heresy of the preacher's wife."

This was not the first time Gifford had heard such comments, but there was a threat in Mr. Dean's voice, though he did not put it into words, which made the young man carry a growing anxiety about Helen away with him. He could not forget it, even in the rejoicings of his home-coming, and he gave guarded answers about her which were unlike his usual frankness.

Lois noticed it, and wondered a little, but was perhaps more annoyed than troubled by it.

The shyness of her welcome Gifford quite misunderstood.

"After all," he thought, "what was the use of coming? Whatever Forsythe's chances are, there is one thing sure,—she does not care for me. She used to have that old friendly way, at least; but even that is gone, now. I might have known it.

I was a fool to run into the fire again. Thank Heaven, that cad is n't here. When he comes, I 'll go ! "

And so he wandered forlornly about, his hands in his pockets, and a disconsolate look on his face which greatly distressed his aunts. Somehow, too, the big fellow's presence for any length of time embarrassed them. They had been so long without a man in the house, they realized suddenly that he took up a great deal of room, and that their small subjects of conversation could not interest him.

" Perhaps," said Miss Ruth shrewdly, " he has found some nice girl in Lockhaven, and misses her. What do you think, sister ? "

" It is not impossible," answered Miss Deborah ; " but, dear me, sister, if only Helen Jeffrey had not married so young! I always felt that Providence pointed to her for dear Giff."

" Well," said Miss Ruth, a little color creeping into her cheek, " I think Providence does arrange such things, and as Helen seems much attached to Mr. Ward, no doubt that was meant. It is gratifying to think such things always are meant. I have even thought that when a person no longer very young, even quite advanced in life, remains unmarried, it was because the other, appointed by Heaven, died, no doubt in infancy."

Miss Deborah sniffed. " I should be sorry to think all marriages were planned by Providence," she said, " for it would seem that Providence showed very poor judgment sometimes. Look at Henry Dale. I 'm sure there were — *others*, who would have made him happier, and been quite as good housekeepers, too."

Miss Ruth mentioned her suspicion of the "nice girl in Lockhaven" to Lois, while Miss Deborah added that it was really no pleasure to cook for dear Giff; he was so out of spirits he did n't seem to care for anything; he did not even eat the whigs, and Lois knew how fond he was of whigs. Very likely dear Ruth was right.

This made Lois's interest in Gifford still deeper, though she said, tossing her head with airy impatience, that she did not believe there were any nice girls in Lockhaven; there were only working people there. Then she thought of that talk with Gifford at the stone bench, and recalled the promise she had made, and how she had sealed it. Her cheeks burned till they hurt her.

"He has forgotten it all, long ago," she said to herself; "men never remember such things. Well, he sha'n't think I remember!"

But how often Gifford remembered!

One afternoon he walked over to the stone bench, and sat down on the very same sunken step from which he had looked up into Lois's face that June evening. He saw a bunch of violets growing just where her foot must have rested, and what was more natural — for Gifford was still young — than that pencil and note-book should appear, and, with a long-drawn sigh, he should write hastily, —

> O Violet,
> Dost thou forget?

and then stop, perhaps to sharpen his pencil, and, if the truth be told, to cast about for a rhyme.

Alas, that love and poetry should be checked by anything so commonplace as syllables! Let — wet — yet, — one can fit in the sense easily when the proper rhyme has been decided upon; and who knows but that Gifford, lying there in the grass, with the old lichen-covered step for a desk, might have written a sonnet or a madrigal which would have given him his heart's desire before the moon rose! But an interruption came.

The rector and Mr. Denner were coming back from fishing, along the road on the other side of the hedge, and Dr. Howe turned in here to follow the garden path home, instead of taking the longer way. Both pushed through a gap in the hedge, and discovered Gifford lying in the grass by the stone bench.

"Hello!" said the rector. "Working up a case, young man?"

Perhaps Gifford was not altogether displeased to be interrupted; the song we might have sung is always sweetest. At all events, he very good-naturedly put his note-book back in his pocket, and rolling over on his stomach, his elbows crushing down the soft grass and his fists under his chin, began to talk to the two elder men.

"Had good luck?"

The rector shook his head ruefully. "Denner has two trout. Fate was against me. Any fishing about Lockhaven, Gifford? Ward do any?"

Gifford laughed. "He only fishes for men," he said. "He devotes himself to it day and night. Especially of late; his fear of hell-fire for other people's souls has seemed to take great hold on him."

" Gad ! " said Dr. Howe.   " He 's a queer fellow."

" He 's a good fellow," Gifford answered warmly.
" And as to his belief, why, you believe in hell, don't
you, doctor ? "

" Oh, bless my soul, yes," said Dr. Howe, with a
laugh, and with a twinkle in his eyes.   " I must, you
know, and it 's well to be on the safe side, Giff ;
if you believe it here, theoretically, it is to be supposed you won't believe it there, experimentally ! "
He laughed again, his big, jolly laugh.   " Good-by,
Denner.   You took all the luck."

Then he trudged whistling up the path, striking
at the hollyhocks with his rod, and wondering how
long it would take Sally to brush the mud off his
corduroys.

But Mr. Denner delayed.   He laid his rod tenderly down on the grass, and his fishing-basket on
the stone bench beside him.   Gifford's sense of
humor padded a good many of the sharp points of
life ; he had to look less doleful when he saw that
the lawyer had chosen Lois's seat, and even her attitude ; his little shriveled hands were clasped upon
his knees, and he was bending forward, looking at
the young man as he talked.   Gifford thought of a
sonnet in his left breast-pocket, beginning, " To one
who sat 'neath rustling poplar-tree," and smiled.

" Well, now," said Mr. Denner, " it is pleasant to
see you at home again, Gifford.   It must be a pleasure to your aunts."

" It is a great pleasure to me," the young man
replied.   " I only wish that I could carry them back
to Lockhaven with me."

" What, both of them?" Mr. Denner asked, in an alarmed way.

" Oh, of course," answered the other; "they could n't be separated. Why, you cannot think of one of them without thinking of the other!"

Mr. Denner sighed. " Just so, just so. I have observed that."

" But I'm afraid," Gifford went on, "they would n't be quite happy there. There's no church, you know, — I mean no Episcopal Church, — and then it is n't like Ashurst. Except Helen and Mr. Ward, there are only working people, though, for that matter, Ward works harder than anybody else. Yes, they would miss Ashurst too much."

" You really think they would miss — us?" said Mr. Denner eagerly.

" Yes," responded Gifford slowly. He was beginning to look at the bunch of violets again, and his aunts did not seem so interesting.

" Well, now," Mr. Denner said, " I am sure I am glad to hear you say that, very glad. We — ah — should miss them, I assure you."

Gifford reached out and plucked up the violets by the roots, to save them from Mr. Denner's drab gaiter, and planted them deep in a crevice of the steps.

" Ah — Gifford," said the lawyer, after he had waited a reasonable time for an answer, "a — a friend of mine is in some perplexity concerning an attachment; he wished my advice."

Gifford began to look interested.

" Foreclosure?"

"You — ah, you do not exactly catch my meaning," answered the little gentleman nervously. " I refer — he referred to an affair of — of the affections. Of course you are too young to really understand these things from a — a romantic point of view, as it were, but being a lawyer, your — a — legal training — would make you consider such a matter intelligently, and I might like your advice."

"Oh ! " said Gifford, seeming to grasp the situation. " Yes; I had one case of that kind in Lockhaven. Jury gave damages to my client ; seems they had been engaged twelve years when she jilted him. I detest those breach-of-promise suits ; they " —

Mr. Denner bounded from his seat. " My dear boy, my dear sir," he gasped, " not at all, not at all! You do not apprehend me, Gifford. My friend is in love, sir ; he wished my advice, not legally, you understand, but in regard to his choice! "

" Your advice ! " Gifford burst out, but instantly apologized by saying he believed it was not usual to ask advice in such matters, — a man usually knew. But perhaps he was mistaken.

" Yes — I am inclined to think you are," responded Mr. Denner, with a jauntiness which sat strangely upon his wrinkled face, — " I think you are. Being still a very young person, Gifford, you scarcely understand the importance of such matters, and the — ah — wisdom of seeking advice. I believe it is always said that youth does not realize the importance of advice. But the fact is, my friend has placed his affections upon two ladies. They are connections, and both he represents to be estimable persons ; both, as I understand it, equally admirable. Equally, you observe, Gifford. And he is unable to make up his mind which is the most — I should say the more — desirable. I, unfortunately, was unable to throw any light upon the subject."

" Do you know the young ladies? " asked Gifford.

"I — I may say I have met them," admitted Mr. Denner.

" And how did you advise him?" Gifford asked, his face preternaturally grave.

Mr. Denner looked anxious. "That is just it. I have been unable to come to any conclusion. I wondered if — if I spoke of their characteristics in a general way (they are both so truly estimable) you might have an opinion. He did think he could reach a decision, he tells me, for a friend of his thought he knew a proverb which would throw a light upon it."

" Settle it by a proverb! " cried Gifford.

"Yes," answered Mr. Denner firmly, " yes; and an excellent way it would be, if one could find the proverb."

The air of offended dignity in Mr. Denner's face sobered Gifford at once.

" I beg your pardon, sir," he said ; " the method was new to me, though it is, no doubt, excellent. May I ask the proverb? "

But the lawyer was hurt. " It is not worth while to mention it. It was not — not suitable. It did not enable my friend to reach a decision, after all ; it was merely something in regard to whist."

Gifford hid his face in the grass for a moment,

and then he said again, " I — I beg your pardon, Mr. Denner ; it struck me as an unusual way of settling a love affair. Your friend must have been much disappointed ? "

" He was, he was, sir," answered Mr. Denner, not knowing whether to be angry or injured, and picking up his reel and rod with trembling hands.

" Well, now," Gifford said, sitting up and leaning his arms upon his knees, the laughter still glimmering in his gray eyes, " I could give you a proverb, — unless they are twins ? "

Mr. Denner sat down again on the stone bench, and looked at him eagerly.

"No, Gifford, they are not twins, — no. There is a good ten years between them."

" Then," said the young man, " what does your friend want better than ' Age before beauty ' ? Let him propose to the elder."

Mr. Denner laid his rod down upon the grass, and, rising, extended his hand to his companion.

" Gifford," he said, " you are an intelligent young man, — a remarkable young man, sir. I knew it when I determined to ask your advice — for my friend. I thank you. My — my friend thanks you, Gifford. He will act upon this at once; he is forever indebted to you, sir."

It was all so solemn that Gifford's gravity lasted until the little gentleman had disappeared through the hedge, and was far down the road ; then he hid his face in the grass, and laughed aloud.

But Mr. Denner was happy. He fairly beamed as he walked along, repeating the proverb to himself. "Yes," he said, "nothing could be better — nothing. How strange that it has not occurred to me before, or that Henry should not have thought of it! 'Age before beauty!' Yes, just so, — just so!"

While he was meditating thus happily, he heard behind him that curious, irregular beat which only the hoofs of a runaway horse can make, and the whirl of flying wheels swinging from side to side. He sprang to one side of the road, his little heart pounding with sudden fright, and looked back to see the rectory phaeton, reeling and almost over-turning, dragged madly at the heels of the shaggy little pony. They came flying toward him. Mr. Denner caught a glimpse, through the cloud of dust, of Lois Howe's white face, and a shrinking figure clinging to her. A gray veil fluttered across the face, so that Mr. Denner could not tell who it was, but instantly it flashed through his mind, "It is one of them!" He threw down his basket and rod, and braced himself for the shock of the encounter with the plunging horse ; his little nerves, never very firm, were strung like steel. Somehow, in that in-stant of waiting, the proverb was forgotten ; he felt that fate would decide for him. "It shall be this one!" he said aloud, — "this one!" Then the horse seemed upon him ; he did not know when he made that jump at the bridle, or felt the iron hoof strike his breast ; he had only a confused sense of seeing the gray figure thrown out upon the ground just as he found himself falling backwards. Then he lost consciousness.

When he came to himself, and saw the trees and

bushes dance strangely about him for a moment, he found that he had been lifted over to the grass at the roadside, and that Gifford Woodhouse's arm was under his head. As his eyes grew steady, he saw that two men were holding the trembling, steaming horse, and that a little group of people were standing about the phaeton; but the gray figure had disappeared. Gifford was fanning him, and pressing something to his lips with a gentle, anxious hand.

"Gifford," he said faintly — "ah — which?"

"They are neither of them hurt, thank God," answered the young man reverently, "but they owe their lives to you, Mr. Denner."

"Yes — but " — he struggled to say — "which — which was it?"

"He means who was it," said the rector, who had taken his place on the other side of the injured man. "It was my daughter — God bless you, Denner! — and Mrs. Forsythe."

Mr. Denner groaned, and shut his eyes. "Oh, it wasn't either," he murmured; "that's always the way!"

"His mind is wandering," Gifford said, in a low voice. "I'm afraid this is very serious, doctor. Do you think he can be moved now?"

The lawyer did not try to prove his sanity; he only groaned again, but this time it was partly from pain. They lifted him gently, and carried him into his own house, which he had nearly reached when the runaway overtook him.

Both the women in the carriage had been thrown out, but Lois was able to walk, and so far as could be ascertained Mrs. Forsythe was unhurt, save for the shock, which sent her from one fainting fit into another until late that night. They had carried her back to the rectory, Lois clinging to one limp hand, and crying hysterically.

"Oh, she will die," she sobbed, "I know she will die ; and it is my fault, it is my carelessness! You need n't say it is n't, father. I know it is! Oh, what shall I do!"

But there was nothing to do ; and Mrs. Dale, who had been hastily summoned, — for her reputation for nursing was even wider than Miss Deborah's for housekeeping, — only put her to bed, "to get her out of the way," she said, but really because she was filled with sympathy for her niece's remorse, and felt that the forgetfulness of sleep was the only comfort for her.

"I 'll tell you what it is, brother," she said, — she had quietly settled herself in authority at the rectory, despite Jean's air of contemptuous dignity — "I believe Arabella Forsythe will have a chance to die, at last. She 's been looking for it these ten years, and as soon as she stops fainting it will be a positive satisfaction to her. I 'm afraid she is really a very sick woman."

But no such thought did she impart to Lois, when she tucked her up in bed, giving her a hearty kiss with her soothing draught, and bidding her have some sense and stop crying, for Mrs. Forsythe would be all right in the morning. But the morning brought no comfort ; the doctor, who had come from Mercer as quickly as Mrs. Dale's horses could bring him, was very grave.

"The shock to the nervous system," he said, — "we cannot tell what it will do."

Lois was so prostrated by grief at Mrs. Forsythe's condition, no one dared tell her that Mr. Denner was the immediate anxiety. There was an injury to the spine, and the plunging hoofs had done more harm than was at first supposed; things looked very serious for the little gentleman.

The lawyer had fainted when he was lifted over his gloomy threshold, where Mary stood waiting and wringing her hands, and had struggled back to consciousness to find himself on the big, slippery horsehair sofa, in his dusky library. Dr. Howe was standing at his side, looking anxiously down at him, and a neighbor was trying to slip a pillow under his head. Gifford had gone to help Mary bring a bed downstairs, for the slightest movement caused Mr. Denner pain, and they dared not lift him, even to take him up to his bedroom.

"What is the matter?" Mr. Denner tried to say. "I seem to be giving trouble. Ah — pray do not mind me, doctor."

"You were hurt, you know, Denner," said the rector, whose feet were planted wide apart, and his hands thrust down in his pockets, and who felt oppressed by the consciousness of his own superabundant vitality, for the lawyer looked so small and thin, and his voice was hardly more than a whisper. "You've been a little faint. You'll be all right soon. But Giff's going to put a bed up in here for you, because you might find it uncomfortable to try to get up-stairs, you know."

Mr. Denner looked anxious at this; he wondered if Mary would not be offended; but he was too strangely weary to talk, and his little twinkling eyes were dim and blurred.

Gifford and Mary had carried down the four big posts of Mr. Denner's bed, which looked like mahogany obelisks, and began to put it together, with many interruptions for Mary to wipe her eyes on the corner of her gingham apron, and remark it would soon be over, and she did not know where she would ever get such another place. Once the rector turned and sharply bade her hold her tongue. Mr. Denner opened his eyes at that, though he had scarcely seemed to hear her. Nor did he know why Gifford and the rector talked so long with the doctor on the broad flat stone at the front door, in the fragrant spring twilight. Afterwards he beckoned Gifford to him.

He did not quite like, he said, to leave his rod out over night; he could go and get it in the morning, he knew, but if it would n't be too much trouble, he would be obliged if Gifford would bring it in. And there were two trout in the basket: perhaps he would be good enough to present them, with his compliments, to the Misses Woodhouse. Gifford went for the rod, but could not go back without an inquiry at the rectory.

"Arabella Forsythe," said Mrs. Dale, — " well, as I told brother, I think this is her opportunity. She really is in a bad way, Giff. Lois was n't hurt at all, wonderful to say; but, naturally, she 's in great distress, because she blames herself for the whole thing."

" How so ? " asked Gifford.

" Well, of course," Mrs. Dale answered, rubbing
her little red nose with her handkerchief, and with
a suspicious mist in her eyes, — " of course it really
was her fault, only we must n't let her know we think
so. You see, she was driving. (I 've always said
women don't know how to drive ; they 're too incon-
sequent.) She was n't paying attention to her horse,
and let a rein slip. Before she could pick it up, the
horse shied at a newspaper blowing along the road.
Well, you know the rest. But Lois does not know
that we think it was her carelessness."

Gifford hesitated a moment, and then said slowly,
" But would n't it be better to help her face the truth
of it now? There is no use to try to escape self-
reproaches that have their root in facts."

" Nonsense ! " responded Mrs. Dale sharply. " I
thought you had more sympathy ! "

Gifford had told his aunts of the accident, when
he brought them the offering of the two small fishes,
and the ladies were full of distress and anxiety, and
the flutter of excited interest which would be sure
to be felt in a place like Ashurst. They had gone
at once to the rectory, to see if they could be of use,
though, as Miss Deborah said to her sister, " with
Adele Dale there, of course there is nothing more to
be desired." Nevertheless, the next morning, Miss
Ruth ran over with a bowl of wine jelly from Miss
Deborah, and brought back word that Mrs. Forsythe
was " still breathing ; " and that the gravest appre-
hensions were felt for Mr. Denner.

Miss Deborah was waiting in the parlor to hear

the news; so important an occasion seemed to demand the dignity of the parlor, and in a high-backed
armchair, with her feet on a cricket and a fresh
handkerchief in her hand, she listened to Miss Ruth's
agitated and tearful story.

"I will make some whips for William Denner,"
she said promptly, as Miss Ruth finished, "and we
will take them to him this afternoon."

"Well, but, sister," said Miss Ruth, hesitating,
"do you think — we 'd better? Ought not we to let
Giff take them?"

"Why?" asked Miss Deborah. "He is able to
see us, is n't he?"

"It is not quite that," answered the younger sister nervously, taking off her bonnet, and beginning
to roll the strings tight and smooth between her fingers, "but — he is in — his chamber, sister. Would
it be quite — proper?"

"I think," said Miss Deborah, holding her head
very straight, "we are old enough to" —

"You may be," returned Miss Ruth firmly, "but
I am not."

Miss Deborah was silent for a moment; then she
said, "Well, perhaps you are right, dear Ruth;
though he is certainly very ill, and did n't you say
he was in the library?"

"Yes," said Miss Ruth, "he is very ill, but the
fact of his couch being in the library does not alter
it. If anything sad should be going to happen, —
it would be different, then."

"Of course," assented Miss Deborah.

"You see," Miss Ruth explained, "if we saw him,
and then he got well, it would be very awkward."

"True," said Miss Deborah. "And certainly single women cannot be too delicate in such matters. We will send the whips by Giff. Poor, poor William Denner! Let me see, — were you to be his partner on Saturday? Oh, no, I recollect: it was I, — it was my turn."

"I think not," Miss Ruth replied gently; "you played last week. I should have played with him this time."

"Not at all," said Miss Deborah firmly, "he was mine."

CHAPTER XX.

THE suspense was very hard for Lois Howe to bear.

When Mrs. Dale drove her from the sick-room for air and exercise, she wandered restlessly about the rectory, or went to Mr. Denner's door to beg a word of encouragement from Mary, or take a momentary comfort from the messages he sent her that he was better, and he begged she would not allow herself the slightest discomfort; it was really of no consequence, — no consequence at all.

Gifford was almost always with the little gentleman, and scarcely left him, even to walk through the garden to the grassy street with Lois. On Sunday, however, late in the afternoon, he went home with her; for Mr. Dale, with whom she had come, was going to sit awhile with Mr. Denner, and Gifford felt he could be spared.

The hour was full of that peculiar Sunday afternoon quiet which seems to subdue even the crickets and the birds. There was a breath of fragrance from some fresh-cut grass, still wet from a noon thunder shower, which had left the air crystal-clear and fresh. Their shadows stretched far ahead along the road, where the dust was still damp, though the setting sun poured a flood of yellow light behind them. Lois walked as though very tired; she scarcely noticed her companion, and did not speak except to answer his questions.

"Is n't there any change in Mrs. Forsythe?" he asked, with anxious sympathy.

Lois shook her head. "No," she said.

"Has n't the rector gotten word to her son yet?"

"No," Lois said again. "We telegraphed twice, but he seems to be out of town, and nobody knows his address."

Gifford made no comment.

"I wish he would come!" the girl cried passionately. "It would be a relief to have him reproach me."

"I hope there will be no need of reproaches. I do hope his mother will get well."

"Oh, no, no," Lois said, "she won't! I know it."

"Try to be more hopeful," he urged. "The doctor said there was absolutely no injury except the shock. I believe she will get well, Lois."

"Oh, you don't know her," Lois answered. "You don't know how frail she is. And then there's Mr. Denner! It is the responsibility of it that kills me, Giff! I cannot get away from it for one single minute."

They had walked along the road where the accident had taken place, and Lois shivered as she saw the trampled grass, though it had been her wish that they should come this way.

"Oh," she said, putting her hands over her eyes, "life can never look the same to me, even if they get well!"

"No," Gifford said, "I understand that. But it may have a new sweetness of gratitude, Lois."

When they came to the gap in the hedge which was the outlet for the rectory path, Gifford held aside the twigs for her to enter.

"Let us sit down on the stone bench a little while," he said. "This is where poor little Mr. Denner sat that afternoon. Oh," he added in a lower tone, "just think from what a grief he may have saved us! I feel as though I could never be able to show him my gratitude." Then he looked at the transplanted bunch of violets, which was fresh and flourishing, and was silent.

Lois sat down a little reluctantly. The memory of that June night, nearly a year ago, flashed into her mind ; she felt the color creep up to her forehead. "Oh," she thought, "how contemptible I am to have any thought but grief, — how shallow I am, how cruel!"

And to punish herself for this, she rushed into speaking of her responsibility again.

Gifford noticed her nervousness. "She is afraid of me," he said to himself. "She would n't be, if she cared."

"You see, Gifford," she began, "I keep saying to myself every moment, 'I did it — it was my carelessness — all, all my fault.' Father tried to comfort me, and so did Mrs. Forsythe as soon as she could speak, and Mr. Denner has sent word that I must not give him a thought (dear Mr. Denner!), but oh, I know!"

Gifford looked at her pale face, with the sweet trembling lip. "It is awfully hard for you," he said.

"Every one said I was not to blame," she went on unsteadily, "that it was not my fault; but, Gifford, if they die, I shall have been their murderer!"

She pressed her hands tight together to keep her self-control.

"No, Lois," he answered gently, "it is not right to feel that; your will would be to die now for either of them" ("Oh, yes, yes!" she said), "so don't blame yourself any more than you must."

"Than I must?" she repeated slowly, looking at him with questioning eyes. "How do you mean? They say there is no blame, Gifford."

He did not answer; his face was full of a grieved reluctance.

"Why," she said, with a quick breath, "do you blame me?"

Gifford put his strong, steady hand impulsively over hers. "I only know how you must blame yourself," he said pitifully. "I wish I could bear the pain of it for you."

"Then you say it is my fault?" she asked slowly.

"Yes, Lois," he answered, looking down at her with anxious tenderness. "I wish I did n't have to say it, but if it is true, if you were careless, it's best to meet it. I — I wish you would let me help you bear it."

Lois sat up very straight, as though bracing herself against a blow. "You are right. I knew it was all my fault; I said so. But there's no help. Let us go home now, please."

Gifford rose silently, and they went together between the sweet-smelling borders, up to the rectory. " I wish I could help you," he said wistfully, as she turned to say good-night at the foot of the steps.

" You cannot," she answered briefly. " No one can ; and there 's nothing I can do to make up for it. I cannot even die as an atonement. Oh, if I could only die ! "

Gifford walked back, distressed and shocked ; he was not old enough yet to know that the desire of death is part of youth, and it seemed as though he too had incurred a great responsibility. " What a brute I was to say it ! " he said to himself. " I feel as though I had struck a woman. And it made her wish she was dead, — good heavens ! How cruel I was ! Yet if it was true, it must have been right to tell her ; I suppose it was my brutal way ! "

Lois went at once to Mrs. Forsythe's bedside, eager to hear of some improvement, but the invalid only shook her head wearily.

" No, no better," she said ; " still breathing, that 's all. But you must not grieve ; it only distresses me."

Lois knelt down, and softly kissed her hand.

" My only trouble," Mrs. Forsythe continued, " is about my boy. Who will take care of him when I am gone ? "

She said much more than this, and perhaps even Gifford's persistent justice could not have sustained the conviction that he had done right to tell Lois that the blame of the accident rested upon her, if he had known the thoughts of a possible atonement

which passed through her mind when Mrs. Forsythe
spoke thus of her son. It was not the first time since
her injury that she had told Lois of her anxiety for
Dick's future, and now the girl left her with a dazed
and aching heart.

Mrs. Dale, full of importance and authority, met
her in the hall.

"I've got some beef-tea for Arabella Forsythe,"
she said, balancing the tray she carried on one hand,
and lifting the white napkin with the other to see that
it was all right, "if I can only persuade her to take
it. I never saw anybody who needed so much coax-
ing. But there! I must not be hard on her; she is
pretty sick, I must say, — and how she does enjoy it!
I said she would. But really, Lois, if we don't have
some word from that young man soon, I don't know
what we shall do, for she is certainly worse to-night.
Your father has just had a letter from somebody, saying that he went away with some friends on a pleasure trip, and did n't leave his address. I thought he
was so anxious to get to Ashurst, — well, that is
Arabella's story. I should n't wonder if he did n't
see his mother alive, — that 's all I 've got to say!"

She nodded her sleek head, and disappeared into
the sick-room. Lois had a sudden contraction of
the heart that made her lips white. "If aunt
Deely says Mrs. Forsythe is worse, it is surely very
bad."

She stumbled blindly up-stairs; she wanted to get
away from everybody, and look this horrible fact in
the face. She found her way to the garret, whose
low, wide window, full of little panes of heavy green-

ish glass, looked over the tree-tops towards the western sky, still faintly yellow with sunset light, and barred by long films of gray cloud. She knelt down and laid her cheek against the sill, which was notched and whittled by childish hands; for this had been a play-room once, and many a rainy afternoon she and Helen and Gifford had spent here, masquerading in the queer dresses and bonnets packed away in the green chests ranged against the wall, or swinging madly in the little swing which hung from the bare rafters, until the bunches of southernwood and sweet-marjoram and the festoons of dried apples shook on their nails. She looked at the stars and hearts carved on the sill, and a big " Gifford " hacked into the wood, and she followed the letters absently with her finger.

" He blames me," she said to herself ; " he sees the truth of it. How shall I make up for it ? What can I do ? "

She stayed by the window until the clouds turned black in the west ; down in the heavy darkness of the garden the crickets began their monotonous z-z-ing, and in the locust-trees the katydids answered each other with a sharp, shrill cry. Then she crept down-stairs and sat outside of Mrs. Forsythe's room, that she might hear the slightest sound, or note the flicker of the night-lamp burning dimly on the stand at the bedside.

Gifford, sitting in another sick-room, was suffering with her, and blaming himself, in spite of principle.

Mr. Denner lay in his big bed in the middle of

the library. The blinds were drawn up to the tops
of the long, narrow windows, that the last gleam of
light might enter, but the room was full of shadows,
save where a taper flickered on a small table which
held the medicines.

"I think," said Mr. Denner, folding his little
hands upon his breast, — "I think, Gifford, that the
doctor was not quite frank with me, to-day. I
thought it proper to ask him if my injury was at all
of a serious nature, if it might have — ah — I ought
to apologize for speaking of unpleasant things — if
it might have an untoward ending. He merely remarked that all injuries had possibilities of seriousness in them ; he appeared in haste, and anxious to
get away, so I did not detain him, thinking he might
have an important case elsewhere. But it seemed as
though he was not quite frank, Gifford ; as though,
in fact, he evaded. I did not press it, fearing to
embarrass him, but I think he evaded."

Gifford also evaded. "He did not say anything
which seemed evasive to me, Mr. Denner. He was
busy charging me to remember your medicines, and
he stopped to say a word about your bravery, too."

Mr. Denner shook his head deprecatingly at this,
but he seemed pleased. "Oh, not at all, it was
nothing, — it was of no consequence." One of the
shutters blew softly to, and darkened the room ; Gifford rose, and, leaning from the window, fastened it
back against the ivy which had twisted about the
hinge from the stained bricks of the wall. "I cannot claim any bravery," the sick man went on.
"No. It was, as it were, accidental, Gifford."

" Accidental ? " said the young man. " How could that be ? I heard the horse, and ran down the road after the phaeton just in time to see you make that jump, and save her."

Mr. Denner sighed. " No," he replied, " no, it was quite by chance. I — I was mistaken. I am glad I did not know, however, for I might have hesitated. As it was, laboring under a misapprehension, I had no time to be afraid."

" I don't think I quite understand," said Gifford.

Mr. Denner was silent. The room was so dark now, he could scarcely see the young man's face as he stood leaning against one of the huge bed-posts. Behind him, Mr. Denner just distinguished his big secretary, with its pigeon-holes neatly labeled, and with papers filed in an orderly way. No one had closed it since the afternoon that he had been carried in and laid on the horse-hair sofa. He had given Mary the key then, and had asked her to fetch the bottle of brandy from one of the long divisions where it stood beside a big ledger. The little gentleman had hesitated to give trouble in asking to have it locked again, though that it should be open offended his ideas of privacy. Now he looked at it, and then let his eyes rest upon the nephew of the Misses Woodhouse.

" Gifford," he said, " would you be so obliging as to take the small brass key from my ring," — here he thrust his lean hand under his pillow, and produced his bunch of keys, which jingled as he held them unsteadily out, — " and unlock the little lower drawer in the left-hand side of my writing-desk ? "

Gifford took the ring over to the candle, which made the shadow of his head loom up on the opposite wall, as he bent to find the little brass key among a dozen others of all shapes and sizes.

"I have unlocked it, sir," he said, a moment later.

" Take the candle, if you please," responded Mr. Denner, " and you will see, I think, in the right-hand corner, back, under a small roll, a flat, square parcel."

" Yes, sir," Gifford answered, holding the candle in his left hand, and carefully lifting the parcel.

" Under that," proceeded Mr. Denner, " is an oval package. If you will be good enough to hand me that, Gifford. Stay, — will you lock the drawer first, if you please, and the desk ? "

Gifford did so, and then put the package into Mr. Denner's hands. He held it a moment before he gently removed the soft, worn tissue paper in which it was wrapped ; his very touch was a caress.

" I was desirous," he said, " of having this by me. It is a miniature of my little sister, sir. She — perhaps you scarcely remember her ? She died when I was twenty. That is forty-one years ago. A long time, Gifford, a long time to have missed her. She is the only thing of — of that nature that I have loved — since I was twenty."

He stopped, and held the miniature up to look at it ; but the light had faded, and the ivory only gleamed faintly.

" I look at this every day when I am in health, and I like it by me now. No, not the candle, I thank you, Gifford. I called for it now (how tarnished these pearls are in the frame! If — if I should not recover, it must be reset. Perhaps you will see to that for me, Gifford?), — I called for it now, because I wished to say, in the event of my — demise, I should wish this given to one of your aunts, sir,"

Gifford came out from the shadow at the foot of the bed, and took Mr. Denner's hand. He did not speak; he had only the man's way of showing sympathy, and one weaker than Gifford could not have resisted the piteous longing for life in Mr. Denner's tone, and would have hastened to reassure him. But Gifford only held his hand in a firm, gentle grasp, and was silent.

"I should wish one of them to have it," he continued. "I have not provided for its welfare in my will; I had thought there was no one for whom I had enough — enough regard, to intrust them with it. I even thought to destroy it when I became old. Some people might wish to carry it with them to the grave, but I could not — oh, no, not my little sister! See, Gifford — take it to the light — not that little merry face. I should like to think it was with your aunts. And — and there is, as it were, a certain propriety in sending it to — her."

Gifford took the miniature from the lawyer's hand, and, kneeling by the candle, looked at it. The faded velvet case held only the rosy, happy face of a little child; not very pretty, perhaps, but with eyes which had smiled into Mr. Denner's for forty years, and Gifford held it in reverent hands.

"Yes," said the old man, "I would like one of them to have it."

"I shall remember it, sir," Gifford answered, putting the case down on the lawyer's pillow.

The room was quite still for a few moments, and then Mr. Denner said, "Gifford, it was quite accidental, quite by mistake, as it were, that I stopped the horse for Mrs. Forsythe and little Lois. I — I thought, sir, it was one of your aunts. One of your aunts, do you understand Gifford? You know what I said to you, at the stone bench, that afternoon? I — I alluded to myself, sir."

Gifford was silent, almost breathless; it all came back to him, — the warm, still afternoon, the sunshine, the faintly rustling leaves of the big silver poplar, and Mr. Denner's friend's love story. But only the pathos and the tenderness of it showed themselves to him now. He put his hand up to his eyes a moment; somehow, he felt as though this was something too sacred for him to see.

"I know, sir," he said; "I — I see."

"I trust," Mr. Denner continued, in a relieved voice, "there is no impropriety in mentioning this to you, though you are still a youth. You have seemed older these last few days, more — ah — sedate, if I may so express it. They — they frequently speak as though you were quite a youth, whereas it appears to me you should be considered the head of the family, — yes, the head of the family. And therefore it seemed to me fitting that I should mention this to you, because I wished to request you to dispose of the miniature. It would have been scarcely proper to do otherwise, scarcely honorable, sir." '

"I am grateful to you for doing so," Gifford replied gently. "I beg you will believe how entirely I appreciate the honor of your confidence."

"Oh, not at all," said Mr. Denner, waving his hand, "not at all, — pray do not mention it. And you will give it to one of them," he added, peering through the dusk at the young man, "if — if it should be necessary?"

"Yes, sir," he answered, "I will; but you did not mention which one, Mr. Denner."

Mr. Denner was silent; he turned his head wearily toward the faint glimmer which showed where the window was, and Gifford heard him sigh. "I did not mention which, — no. I had not quite decided. Perhaps you can tell me which you think would like it best?"

"I am sure your choice would seem of most value to them."

Mr. Denner did not speak; he was thinking how he had hoped that leap at the runaway horse would have decided it all. And then his mind traveled back to the stone bench, and his talk with Gifford, and the proverb. "Gifford," he said firmly, "give it, if you please, to Miss Deborah."

They did not speak of it further. Gifford was already reproaching himself for having let his patient talk too much, and Mr. Denner, his mind at last at rest, was ready to fall asleep, the miniature clasped in his feverish hand.

The next day, Gifford had no good news to carry

to the rectory. The lawyer had had a bad night, and was certainly weaker, and sometimes he seemed a little confused when he spoke. Gifford shrank from telling Lois this, and yet he longed to see her, but she did not appear.

She was with Mrs. Forsythe, her aunt said; and when he asked for the invalid, Mrs. Dale shook her head. " I asked her how she felt this morning, and she said, ' Still breathing!' But she certainly is pretty sick, though she 's one to make herself out at the point of death if she scratches her finger. Still — I don't know. I call her a sick woman."

Mrs. Dale could not easily resign the sense of importance which attends the care of a very sick person, even though Arabella Forsythe's appetite had unquestionably improved.

" We 've telegraphed again for her son," she went on, " though I must say she does not seem to take his absence much to heart. They are the sort of people, I think, that love each other better at a distance. Now, if I were in her place, I 'd be perfectly miserable without my children. I don't know what to think of his not writing to her. It appears that he 's on a pleasure party of some kind, and he 's not written her a line since he started ; so of course she does not know where he is."

But to Lois Mrs. Forsythe's illness was something beside interest and occupation. The horror of her possible death hung over the young girl, and seemed to sap her youth and vigor. Her face was drawn and haggard, and her pleasant gray eyes had lost their smile. Somehow Mr. Denner's danger, which to some extent she realized, did not impress her so deeply; perhaps because that was, in a manner, the result of his own will, and perhaps, too, because no one quite knew how much the little gentleman suffered and how near death he was.

Lois had heard Gifford's voice as she went into the sick-room, and his words of blame rung again in her ears. They emphasized Mrs. Forsythe's despair about her son's future. She spoke to Lois as though she knew there was no possible chance of her recovery.

"You see, my dear," she said, in her soft, complaining voice, which sometimes dropped to a whisper, "he has no aunts or uncles to look after him when I am gone; no one to be good to him and help him to be good. Not that he is wild or foolish, Lois, like some young men, but he's full of spirit, and he needs a good home. Oh, what will he do without me. He has no one to take care of him!"

Lois was too crushed by misery to feel even a gleam of humor, when the thought flashed through her mind that she might offer to take his mother's place; but she knew enough not to express it.

"Oh," Mrs. Forsythe continued, "if he were only married to some sweet girl that I knew and loved, how happy I should be, how content!"

"I — I wish he were," Lois said.

"My death will be so hard for him, and who will comfort him! I am sorry I distress you by speaking so, but, my dear child, on your death-bed you look facts in the face. I cannot help knowing his sorrow, and it makes me so wretched. My boy, —

my poor boy ! If I could only feel easy about him! If I thought, oh, if I could just think, you cared for him ! I know I ought not to speak of it, but — it is all I want to make me happy. I might have had a little more of life, a few months, perhaps, if it had not been for the accident. There, there, you must n't be distressed ; but if I could know you cared for him, it would be worth dying for, Lois."

" I do care for him ! " Lois sobbed. " We all do ! "

Mrs. Forsythe shook her head. " You are the only one I want ; if you told me you would love him, I should be happy, so happy ! Perhaps you don't like to say it. But listen : I know all about last fall, and how you sent the poor fellow away broken-hearted ; but I could n't stop loving you, for all that, and I was so glad when he told me he was going to try again ; and that is what he is coming down to Ashurst for. Yes, he is coming to ask you. You see, I know all his secrets ; he tells me everything, — such a good boy, he is. But I've told you, because I cannot die, oh, I cannot die, unless I know how it will be for him. If you could say yes, Lois, if you could ! "

Her voice had faltered again, and the pallor of weariness which spread grayly over her face frightened Lois. She shivered, and wrung her hands sharply together.

" Oh," she said, " I would do anything in the world for you — but — but " —

" But this is all I want," interrupted the other eagerly. " Promise this, and I am content to die.

When he asks you — oh, my dear, my dear, promise me to say yes ! "

Lois had hidden her face in the pillow. " It was all my fault," she was saying to herself ; " it is the only atonement I can make."

" I will do anything you want me to," she said at last.

Mrs. Forsythe, laid her shaking hand on the girl's bowed head. " Oh, look at me ! You give me life when you say that. Will you promise to say yes, Lois ? "

She lifted her head, but she would not look into Mrs. Forsythe's eyes.

" Yes," she answered, twisting her fingers nervously together. " I promise if — if he wants me."

" Oh, my dear, my dear ! " Mrs. Forsythe said, and then, to Lois's horror, she burst into tears. She tried to say it was joy, and Lois must not be frightened, but the young girl fled for Mrs. Dale, and then ran up to the garret, and locked the door.

She went over to the western window and threw herself upon the floor, her face hidden in her arms.

" He made me do it," she said between her sobs ; " he said it was my fault. Well, I have made up for it now. I have atoned. I have promised."

She was too miserable even to take the satisfaction which belongs to youth, of observing its own wretchedness. She sobbed and cried without consciousness of tears. At last, for very weariness and exhaustion, she fell asleep, and was wakened by hearing Mrs. Dale rap sharply at the door.

" Come, Lois, come ! " she cried. " What's the

matter? Dick Forsythe is here. Do have politeness enough to come down-stairs. I don't know but
that his mother is a shade better, but she has had a
chance to die twice over, the time he 's been getting
here!"

CHAPTER XXI.

THE news of the anxiety in Ashurst hurried Helen's visit. She might be of use, she thought, and she had better go now than a week later.

Perhaps, too, she felt the necessity of calm. She had been forced into a tumult of discussion and argument, which at last she had begun to meet with the silence of exhaustion. Elder Dean had come to see her, and she had received him at first with patience, and given him her reasons for not believing in hell. There had even been a moment when Helen fancied that she might convince him of what was so clear and simple to her own mind. But to each argument of hers he had but one reply, — "The Bible, ma'am, the Word of God, instructs us" thus or thus, — and he returned again and again with unwearied obstinacy to his own position. After a while Helen's annoyance at the man got the better of her judgment, and she wrote to him, saying she did not wish to argue with him again, and must beg him not to come to the parsonage to see her.

Mr. Grier, too, horrified at his wife's reports of what Mrs. Ward had said, hastened to Lockhaven to reproach and admonish John for permitting such heresy in his household; for Mr. Grier held with St. Paul that the husband was head of the wife, even to the extent of regulating her conscience.

John was not at home, so he turned his attack upon the real offender, assuring her that it was for her soul's sake that he thus dealt with her. Helen had brought the interview to a sudden close by refusing to hear further argument, and bowing Mr. Grier from the room, with a certain steady look from under her level brows and a compression of the lips which, greatly to his surprise when he thought it over, silenced him.

The talks with John could not, of course, be called painful, for they were with him, but they were futile.

When the last evening came before she was to leave home, Helen knew, with a dull pain of helpless remorse, that it was a relief to go; she was glad that she could not hear Elder Dean's voice for a fortnight, or even know, she said with a pathetic little laugh to her husband, that she " was destroying anybody's hope of hell, in the parish."

" Yes," John answered, " it will be good for you to be away from it all for a time. It is hard to think clearly, hurried by my impatient anxiety to have you reach a certain conclusion. I realize that. But I know you will try to reach it, dearest."

Helen shook her head wearily. " No, I am afraid I cannot promise that. You must not hope that I shall ever come to believe in eternal damnation. Of course I believe that the consequences of sin are eternal ; the effect upon character must be eternal, and I should think that would be hell enough, sometimes. But I shall never, never believe in it as you do."

"Oh, Helen," her husband said, "I cannot cease to hope while I have power to pray."

Helen sighed. "I wish you could understand how useless it is, dearest, or how it hurts me, this talk of hell. For people to be good for fear of hell is like saying 'Honesty is the best policy;' it is degrading. And it seems selfish to me, somehow, to think so much about one's own salvation, — it is small, John. The scheme of salvation that the elders talk so much about really resolves itself into a fear of hell and hope of heaven, all for the individual soul, and is n't that selfish? But after all, this question of eternal punishment is such a little thing, so on the outside of the great puzzle. One goes in, and in: Why is sin, which is its own punishment, in the world at all? What does it all mean, anyhow? Where is God, and why does He let us suffer here, with no certainty of a life hereafter? Why does He make love and death in the same world? Oh, that is so cruel, — love and death together! Is He, at all? Those are the things, it seems to me, one has to think about. But why do I go all over it? We can't get away from it, can we?"

"Those questions are the outgrowth of unbelief in justice," he said eagerly; "if you only realized justice and mercy, the rest would be clear."

She came over to him, and, kneeling down, put her head on his knee. "Oh, John, how can I leave you to-morrow?"

It was true that they could not drop the subject. Hour after hour they had sat thus, John instructing, proving, reasoning, with always the tenderest love and patience in his voice. Helen listening with a sweet graciousness, which kept her firm negations from making her husband hopeless. He had showed her, that Sunday evening after the sermon on foreign missions, what he felt had been his awful sin: he had deprived his people of the bread of life for her sake, and, for fear of jarring the perfect peace of their lives and giving her a moment's unhappiness, he had shrunk from his duty to her soul.

At first Helen had been incredulous. She could not realize that her mere unbelief in any doctrine, especially such a doctrine as this of eternal punishment, could be a matter of serious importance to her husband. It needed an effort to treat his argument with respect. " What does it matter ? " she kept saying. " We love each other, so never mind what we believe. Believe anything you want, darling. I don't care ! Only love me, John. And if my ideas offend your people, let us leave Lockhaven ; or I can keep silence, unless I should have to speak for what seems to me truth's sake."

And then John tried to show her how he had wronged his people and been false to his own vows and that he dared not leave them until he had rooted out the evil his own neglect had allowed to grow up among them, and that her mere silence would not reach the root of the evil in her own soul. And the importance of it!

" Oh," he cried, once, when they had been talking until late into the night, " is not your soul's life of importance, Helen ? When I see you going down to eternal death because I have failed in my duty to you, can I satisfy myself by saying, We love one another? Because I love you, I cannot be silent. Oh, I have wronged you, I have not loved you enough! I have been content with the present happiness of my love, — my happiness! I had no thought of yours."

So they had gone over and over the subject, until to Helen it seemed threadbare, and they sat now in the dusky library, with long stretches of silence between their words.

Alfaretta brought in the lamps. In view of Mrs. Ward's departure for a fortnight, her father, still with an eye to wages, deferred giving notice. " Besides," he thought, "Mrs. Ward may be convicted and converted after she 's been dealt with."

Helen had risen, and was writing some instructions for her maid : just what was to be cooked for the preacher, and what precautions taken for his comfort. As she put her pen down, she turned to look at her husband. He was sitting, leaning forward, with his head bowed upon his hand, and his eyes covered.

" Helen," he said, in a low, repressed voice, " once more, just once more, let me entreat you ; and then we will not speak of this before you go."

She sighed. " Yes, dearest, say anything you want."

There was a moment's silence, and then John rose, and stood looking down at her. " I have such a horror of your going away. I do not understand it ; it is more than the grief and loneliness of being

without you for a few days. It is vague and indefinable, but it is terribly real. Perhaps it is the
feeling that atonement for my sin towards you is
being placed out of my reach. You will be where
I cannot help you, or show you the truth. Yet you
will try to find it! I know you will. But now,
just this last night, I must once more implore you to
open your heart to God's Spirit. Ah, my Helen, I
have sinned against Heaven and before you, but
my punishment will be greater than I can bear if I
enter heaven without you! Heaven? My God, it
would be hell! The knowledge that my sin had
kept you out — yet even as I speak I sin."

He was walking up and down the room, his hands
knotted in front of him, and his face filled with
hopeless despair.

"Yes, I sin even in this, for my grief is not that
I have sinned against God in my duty to his people
and in forgetting Him, but that I may lose you
heaven, I may make you suffer!"

Helen came to him, and tried to put her arms
about him. "Oh, my dear," she said, "don't you
understand? I have heaven now, in your love.
And for the rest, — oh, John, be content to leave it
in Hands not limited by our poor ideas of justice.
If there is a God, and He is good, He will not send
me away from you in eternity; if He is wicked and
cruel, as this theology makes Him, we do not want
his heaven! We will go out into outer darkness
together."

John shuddered. "Lay not this sin to her
charge," she heard him say; "she knows not what

she says. Yet I — Oh, Helen, that same thought
has come to me. You seemed to make my heaven, —
you ; and I was tempted to choose you and darkness,
rather than my God. Sin, sin, sin, — I cannot get
away from it. Yet if I could only save you! But
there again I distrust my motive : not for God's
glory, but for my own love's sake, I would save you.
My God, my God, be merciful to me a sinner ! "

In his excitement, he had pushed her arm from
his shoulder, and stood in tense and trembling silence, looking up, as though listening for an answer
to his prayer.

Helen dared not speak. There is a great gulf
fixed between the nearest and dearest souls when in
any spiritual anguish ; even love cannot pass it, and
no human tenderness can fathom it. Helen could
not enter into this holiest of holies, where her husband's soul was prostrate before its Maker. In the
solitude of grief and remorse he was alone.

It was this isolation from him which broke her
calm. It seemed profane even to look upon his suffering. She shrank away from him, and hid her
face in her hands. That roused him, and in a moment the old tenderness enveloped her.

He comforted her with silent love, until she
ceased to tremble, and looked again into his tender
eyes.

" What I wanted to say," he said, after a while,
when she was leaning quietly against his breast,
" was just to tell you once more the reasons for believing in this doctrine which so distresses you, dearest. To say, in a word, if I could, why I lay such

stress upon it, instead of some of the other doctrines
of the church. It is because I do believe that salvation, eternal life, Helen, depends upon holding
the doctrine of reprobation in its truth and entirety.
For see, beloved: deny the eternity of punishment,
and the scheme of salvation is futile. Christ need
not have died, a man need not repent, and the whole
motive of the gospel is false; revelation is denied,
and we are without God and without hope. Grant
the eternity of punishment, and the beauty and order of the moral universe burst upon us: man is a
sinner, and deserves death, and justice is satisfied;
for, though mercy is offered, it is because Christ has
died. And his atonement is not cheapened by being forced upon men who do not want it. They
must accept it, or be punished."

Helen looked up into his face with a sad wonder.
"Don't you see, dear," she said, "we cannot reason
about it? You take all this from the Bible, because
you believe it is inspired. I do not believe it is.
So how can we argue? If I granted your premises,
all that you say would be perfectly logical. But I
do not, John. I cannot. I am so grieved for you,
dearest, because I know how this distresses you; but
I must say it. Silence can never take the place of
truth, between us."

"Oh, it did, too long, too long!" John groaned.
"Is there no hope?" and then he began his restless
walk again, Helen watching him with yearning eyes.

"I cannot give it up," he said at last. "There
must be some way by which the truth can be made
clear to you. Perhaps the Lord will show it to me.

There is no pain too great for me to bear, to find it out; no, even the anguish of remorse, if it brings you to God! Oh, you shall be saved! Do the promises of the Eternal fail?"

He came over to her, and took her hands in his. Their eyes met. This sacrament of souls was too solemn for words or kisses. When they spoke again it was of commonplace things.

It was hard for her to leave the little low-browed house, the next morning. John stopped to gather a bunch of prairie roses from the bush which they had trained beneath the study window, and Helen fastened them in her dress; then, just as they were ready to start, the preacher's wife ran back to the study, and hurriedly put one of the roses from her bosom into a vase on the writing-table, and stooped and gave a quick, furtive kiss to the chair in which John always sat when at work on a sermon.

They neither of them spoke as they walked to the station, and no one spoke to them. Helen knew there were shy looks from curtained windows and peeping from behind doors, for she was a moral curiosity in Lockhaven; but no one interrupted them. Just before she started, John took her hand, and held it in a nervous grasp. "Helen," he said hoarsely, "for the sake of my eternal happiness seek for truth, seek for truth!"

She only looked at him, with speechless love struggling through the pain in her eyes.

The long, slow journey to Ashurst passed like a troubled dream. It was an effort to adjust her mind to the different life to which she was going. Late in the afternoon, the train drew up to the depot in Mercer, and Helen tried to push aside her absorbing thought of John's suffering, that she might greet her uncle naturally and gladly. The rector stood on the platform, his stick in one hand and his glasses in the other, and his ruddy face beaming with pleasure. When he saw her, he opened his arms and hugged her; it would have seemed to Dr. Howe that he was wanting in affection had he reserved his demonstrations until they were alone.

"Bless my soul," he cried, "it is good to see you again, my darling child. We 're all in such distress in Ashurst, you 'll do us good. Your husband could n't come with you? Sorry for that; we want to see him oftener. I suppose he was too busy with parish work, — that fire has kept his hands full. What? There is the carriage, — Graham, here 's Miss Helen back again. Get in, my dear, get in. Now give your old uncle a kiss, and then we can talk as much as we want."

Helen kissed him with all her heart; a tremulous sort of happiness stole over the background of her troubled thoughts, as a gleam of light from a stormy sunset may flutter upon the darkness of the clouds.

"Tell me — everything! How is Lois? How are the sick people? How is Ashurst?"

Dr. Howe took up a great deal of room, sitting well forward upon the seat, with his hands clasped on his big stick, which was planted between his knees, and he had to turn his head to see Helen when he answered her.

"Mrs. Forsythe is better," he said; "she is certainly going to pull through, though for the first week all that we heard was that she was 'still breathing.' But Denner is in a bad way; Denner is a very sick man. Gifford has been with him almost all the time. I don't know what we should have done without the boy. Lois is all right, — dreadfully distressed, of course, about the accident; saying it is her fault, and all that sort of thing. But she was n't to blame; some fool left a newspaper to blow along the road and frighten the horse. She needs you to cheer her up."

"Poor little Mr. Denner!" Helen exclaimed. "I 'm glad Giff is with him. Has Mr. Forsythe come?"

"Yes," said the rector; "but they are queer people, those Forsythes. The young man seems quite annoyed at having been summoned: he remarked to your aunt that there was nothing the matter with his mother, and she must be moved to her own house; there was nothing so bad for her as to have a lot of old women fussing over her. I wish you could have seen Adele's face! I don't think she admires him as much as she did. But his mother was moved day before yesterday, and he has a trained nurse for her. Your aunt Adele feels her occupation gone, and thinks Mrs. Forsythe will die without her," the rector chuckled. "But she won't, — she 'll get well." Here he gave a heavy sigh, and said, "Poor Denner!"

"You don't mean Mr. Denner won't get well?" Helen asked anxiously.

"I 'm afraid not," Dr. Howe answered sadly.

They were silent for a little while, and then Helen said in a hushed voice, "Does he know it, uncle Archie ?"

"No," said the rector explosively, "he — he does n't ! "

Dr. Howe was evidently disturbed ; he pulled up one of the carriage windows with some violence, and a few minutes afterwards lowered it with equal force. " No, he does n't," he repeated. " The doctor only told me this morning that there was no hope. Says it is a question of days. He 's very quiet ; does not seem to suffer ; just lies there, and is polite to people. He was dreadfully troubled at breaking up the whist party last Saturday ; sent apologies to the other three by Gifford." Dr. Howe tugged at his gray mustache, and looked absently out of the window. "No, I don't believe he has an idea that he — he won't get well." The rector had a strange shrinking from the word " death."

" I suppose he ought to know," Helen said thoughtfully.

" That is what the doctor said," answered the rector; " told me he might want to settle his affairs. But bless my soul, what affairs can Denner have ? He made his will fifteen years ago, and left all he had to Sarah Denner's boy. I don't see what he has to do."

" But, uncle," Helen said, " might n't he have some friends or relatives to whom he would want to send a message, — or perhaps see ? People you never heard of ? "

" Oh, no, no," responded Dr. Howe. " I 've

known William Denner, man and boy, these sixty
years. He has n't any friends I don't know about;
he could not conceal anything, you know; he is as
simple and straightforward as a child. No; Willie
Denner 'll have his money, — there 's not too much
of it, — and that 's all there is to consider."

" But it is not only money," Helen went on slowly :
" has n't he a right to know of eternity ? Not just
go out into it blindly ? "

" Perhaps so, — perhaps so," the rector admitted,
hiding his evident emotion with a flourish of his big
white silk handkerchief. " You see," he continued,
steadying his cane between his knees, while he took
off his glasses and began to polish them, " the doctor
wants me to tell him, Helen."

" I suppose so," she said sympathetically.

" And I suppose I must," the rector went on, " but
it is the hardest task he could set me. I — I don't
know how to approach it."

" It must be very hard."

" Of course it seems natural to the doctor that I
should be the one to tell him. I 'm his pastor, and
he 's a member of my church — Stay! is he ? "
Dr. Howe thrust out his lower lip and wrinkled his
forehead, as he thought. " Yes, oh yes, I remember.
We were confirmed at the same time, when we
were boys, — old Bishop White's last confirmation.
But he has n't been at communion since my day."

" Why do you think that is, uncle Archie ? " Helen
asked.

" Why, my dear child, how do I know ? " cried
the rector. " Had his own reasons, I suppose. I

never asked him. And you see, Helen, that 's what
makes it so hard to go and tell Denner that —
that he 's got to die. Somehow, we never touched
on the serious side of life. I think that 's apt to be
the case with friends in our position. We have
gone fishing together since we were out of pinafores,
and we have played whist, — at least I 've watched
him, — and talked politics or church business over
our pipes ; but never anything like this. We were
simply the best of friends. Ah, well, Denner will
leave a great vacancy in my life."

They rode in silence for some time, and then
Helen said gently, " Yes, but uncle, dear, that is
the only way you are going to help him now, — with
the old friendship. It is too late for anything
else, — any religious aid, I mean, — when a man
comes to look death in the face. The getting ready
for death has gone, and it is death itself, then.
And I should think it would be only the friend's
hand and the friend's eyes, just the human sympathy, which would make it easier. I suppose all one
can do is to say, ' Let my friendship go with you
through it all, — all this unknown to us both.' "

Dr. Howe turned and looked at her sharply ; the
twilight had fallen, and the carriage was very dark.
" That 's a heathenish thing to say, Helen, and it is
not so. The consolations of religion belong to a man
in death as much as in life ; they ought not to belong more to death than to life, but they do, sometimes. It is n't that there is not much to say to
Denner. It is the — the unusualness of it, if I can
so express it. We have never touched on such

things, I tell you, old friends as we are; and it is awkward, you understand."

They were very quiet for the rest of the long drive. They stopped a moment at Mr. Denner's gate; the house was dark, except for a dim light in the library and another in the kitchen, where Mary sat poring over her usual volume. Gifford came out to say there was no change, and opened the carriage door to shake hands with Helen.

"He would have prayers to-night," he said to the rector, still talking in a hushed voice, as though the spell of the sick-room were on him out under the stars, in the shadows of the poplar-trees. "He made Willie read them aloud to Mary, he told me; he said it was proper to observe such forms in a family, no matter what the conditions might be. Imagine Willie stumbling through Chronicles, and Mary fast asleep at her end of that big dark dining-room!"

Gifford smiled, but the rector was too much distressed to be amused; he shivered as they drove away.

"Ah," he said sharply, "how I hate that slam of a carriage door! Makes me think of but one thing. Yes, I must see him to-morrow. I must tell him to-morrow."

The rector settled back in his corner, his face darkening with a grieved and troubled frown, and they did not speak until they reached the rectory gate. As it swung heavily back against the group of white lilacs behind it, shaking out their soft, penetrating fragrance into the night air, some one sprang towards the carriage, and almost before it stopped stood on the steps, and rapped with impatient joy at the window.

It was Lois. She had thrown a filmy white scarf about her head, and had come out to walk up and down the driveway, and listen for the sound of wheels. She had not wanted to stay in the house, lest Mr. Forsythe might appear.

Lois had scarcely seen him since he arrived, though this was not because of his devotion to his mother. He spent most of his time lounging about the post-office, and swearing that Ashurst was the dullest, deadest place on the face of the earth. He had not listened to Lois's self-reproaches, and insisted that blame must not even be mentioned. He was quite in earnest, but strangely awkward. Lois, weighed down by the consciousness of her promise, felt it was her fault, yet dared not try to put him at his ease, and fled, at the sound of his step, to her refuge in the garret. She did not feel that her promise to Mrs. Forsythe meant that she must give opportunity as well as consent. But Dick did not force his presence upon her, and he was very uncomfortable and *distrait* when at the rectory.

She need not have feared his coming again that evening. He was in the library of his mother's house, covering many pages of heavy crested note-paper with his big, boyish writing. Strangely enough, however, for a young gentleman in love with Miss Lois Howe, he was addressing in terms of ardent admiration some one called " Lizzie."

But in the gladness of meeting Helen, Lois almost forgot him. Her arms around her cousin's neck, and Helen's lips pressed against her wet cheek, there was nothing left to wish for, except the recovery of the two sick people.

" Oh, Helen! Helen! Helen!" she cried hysterically, while Dr. Howe, flourishing his silk handkerchief, patted them both without discrimination, and said, "There, my dear, there, there."

CHAPTER XXII.

AFTER Helen had gone, John Ward went back to the parsonage, dazed and stupefied by the exhaustion of the moral conflict which for nearly a month had strained every fibre of his soul.

The house seemed dark and empty. His face brightened a moment, as he sat wearily down at his writing-table and saw the prairie rose in the slender vase. He leaned his head on his hand, and drew the flower towards him, touching it with gentle fingers, as though he caressed the bloom of Helen's cheek. Then he pushed it in front of her picture which stood always on the same table, and thought vaguely that he would leave it there until she put a fresh one in its place.

And so his thoughts came heavily back to the old grief and anxiety. He went over all the arguments he had used, and saw new points and reasons which he had neglected to give, and he even drew his pen and paper towards him, and began to make some notes. He would send them to her; and, away from him, surely what he should say would have an added force.

Yet he could not fix his mind upon his subject. He found himself heavily conscious of the silence of the house; and by and by he rose and went upstairs to their bedroom, standing drearily in the cen-

tre of the floor, and looking about at his own loneliness. He lifted a bit of lace upon her dressing-
table, and smoothed it between his fingers, noting
the faint scent of orris which it held. Again that
strange, unreasonable fear of her absence seized him,
and he was glad to go out and find some pressing
occupation to forget it.

When he started (as he had had to do of late),
alone, for prayer-meeting, his mind was dulled by its
own pain of anxiety, and he went absently through
the services, saying little, and " opening " the meeting as soon as he could. After that, he sat with
head bent and arms folded, scarcely hearing what
was said.

Just before he pronounced the benediction, however, Elder Dean rose, and, stepping with elaborate
quiet to the pulpit, handed him a note, and sat
down again, covering his face with a big horny
hand, and swinging one foot nervously. John
opened the folded paper, and held it up to one of
the tall lamps beside his desk, for the writing was
dim and crabbed, and the light poor, and then read
a call that the Session should meet immediately
after the prayer-meeting. No object for consideration was named, and the paper was signed by Mr.
Dean and another elder. John put it down, and,
noticing that his four elders sat together on one of
the bare settees, omitted the usual request that they
should all remain.

The little congregation gradually dispersed. Then
Elder Dean arose, and, creaking heavily down the
aisle, closed and locked the front door, and put out

four of the lamps in the back of the room for economy's sake. After that he sat down again on the
settee beside the three other elders, and the lecture-
room was silent.

John looked up, and waited for some one to
speak, then, suddenly recalling his duty of moderator, he called the Session to order, and asked the
reason for meeting.

Mr. Johnson, who was the youngest elder in the
church, shuffled his feet under the bench, coughed
slightly, and looked at his colleagues. Mr. Bent and
Mr. Smith kept their eyes upon the ground, and
Mr. Dean folded and unfolded his arms several
times.

"Brethren," said the preacher, "we have asked
the blessing of God upon the deliberations of this
Session; it now remains to bring the business before it."

Mr. Dean poked Mr. Smith furtively, who replied in a loud whisper, "It is your place, Brother
Dean."

The elder's face turned a dull mottled red; he
felt John's surprised eyes upon him. Under cover
of blowing his nose violently, he rose, and, shifting
from one foot to the other, he glanced imploringly
at his companions. But no one spoke.

"Brother Ward," he began at last, opening and
shutting his mouth until his upper lip looked like a
hooked beak, "this Session has been called for the
consideration of — of the spiritual condition of this
church. The duties of the elders of a church are
heavy, and painful — and — and — large. But they

are discharged, — they are always," said Mr. Dean, inflating his chest, and raising one hand, " discharged! The church expects it, and the church is not disappointed. Yet it is most terribly painful, sometimes — most awful, and — unpleasant."

Here Mr. Dean stopped, and coughed behind his hand. Mr. Johnson crossed his legs, and glanced back at the door as though calculating his chances of escape. The other two men did not look up. Elder Dean had no reason to fear that he had not the attention of the moderator. John was watching him with burning eyes.

" Proceed," he said.

" Well," he continued, " as we always perform our painful, most painful duties, we are here to-night. We are here to-night, Mr. Moderator, to consider the spiritual welfare of the church, and of one especial soul connected with the church. This soul is — is far from grace; it is in a lost condition; a stranger to God, an alien from the commonwealth of Israel. But that is not all. No. It is — ah — spreading its own disease of sin in the vitals of the church. It is not only going down to hell itself, but it is dragging others along with it. It is to consider the welfare of that soul, Brother Ward, that this Session has been convened. It is a very difficult task which is set before us, but we are sustained by duty, — by duty, sir! We will not have to reproach ourselves for neglect of an immortal soul. We wish to summon " —

" Do you refer," said John Ward, rising, his hands clenched upon the pulpit rail, his face rigid and his teeth set, — " do you refer to my wife?"

The three men on the bench started as though they had received a galvanic shock. Elder Dean, with his lips parted, looked at his minister in silence.

"Answer me," said John Ward.

"Mr. Moderator," replied the elder in a quavering voice, "if I do refer to your wife, that is not the way it is to be considered. I refer to a sin-sick soul. I refer to a — a cause of falling from grace, in this church. I refer to a poor neglected sinner, who must be saved ; yes, sir, saved. If she happens to be your wife, I — I — am sorry."

The room was very silent. The flaring lamps shone on the bare, whitewashed walls and on the shamed faces of the four men ; the shadows in the corners pressed upon the small centre of light. One of the lamps smoked, and Mr. Bent rose to turn it down, and a deeper gloom settled upon the group. Mr. Johnson nervously opened a hymn-book, and began to turn the pages. For a moment the rustle of the paper was the only sound that broke the quiet.

John Ward, appalled and angry, humiliated that his most sacred grief was dragged from his heart to be gazed at and discussed by these men, was yet silenced by his accusing conscience.

"There is no need," he said at last, with painful slowness, and breathing hard, " to bring this matter before the Session. As preacher of this church, I prefer to deal with that soul according to the wisdom God gives me. I neither ask nor desire your advice."

Elder Dean turned to his companions, and raised his hands slightly. Mr. Smith responded to his look by rising and saying, still gazing fixedly upon the floor, " This ain't the way, Brother Ward, to consider this matter. Your wisdom ain't enough, seein' that it has allowed things to get to this pass. All we desire is to deal with Mrs. Ward for her own good. Brother Dean speaks of the evil in the church, — ain't it our duty to check that? It appears, sir, that, preacher of this church or not, you 've allowed her sin of unbelief to remain unreproved, and the consequence is its spread in the church : that 's what we 're responsible for; that 's our duty. If you 've neglected your duty, we ain't a-goin' to neglect ours." He wagged his head emphatically, and then sat down.

John Ward was too entirely without self-consciousness to feel the change in the tone of these men. Their old sincerely felt admiration and awe of their preacher was gone. The moment they became his critics, they ceased to feel his superiority. Disapproval was power, and their freedom from the trammels of respect made them cruel. But the outcry of John's conscience made him deaf to smaller things. He sat bending forward, his hands locked together, and the vein in his forehead standing out like whip - cord ; his lips were white and compressed.

Mr. Dean got on his feet again, with much less embarrassment in his manner. Mr. Smith's share in the responsibility was a great relief.

" It is exactly as Brother Smith says," he said.

"If it was just — just her, we would n't, perhaps, meddle, though I ain't sure but what it would be our duty. But the church, — we have got to protect it. We would wish to summon her, and see if we can bring her to a realizing sense of her condition before proceeding to any extreme measure. If she remained in a hardened state, it would then be our duty to bring charges and proof. And we should do it, bein' supported by a sense of duty — and by the grace of God."

Here Mr. Johnson rose, rather noisily, and Mr. Dean looked at him impatiently.

"He 'll spoil it all," he muttered, as he sat down between Mr. Smith and Mr. Bent.

"I just want to say," said Mr. Johnson, in a quick, high voice, "that I 'm not in sympathy with this meeting."

John looked at him eagerly.

"It is my idea that these sort of things never do. The day has passed for forcing people into believing things, — yes, sir, — and it does n't do any good, anyhow. Now, my advice would be, don't disturb things, don't break up the peace. I 'm for peace and quiet and a happy life, before anything else. Just let 's not say anything about it. There 's nothing, brethren, like argument for disturbing a church or a home. I know it; I 'm a married man. And I just advise you to keep quiet. Use your influence in a quiet, easy way, but nothing else. May be it will come out all right, after all."

He sat down again, and Mr. Dean and Mr. Smith began to whisper to him with evident indignation.

But the preacher's face was full of doubt and grief. "No," he said at last, moving his dry lips with a visible effort, "we cannot conquer sin by hiding it or forgetting it, and I believe that this Session has the welfare of the church sincerely at heart ; but I do not believe the plan you propose will profit either the church or the soul of whom you speak. Her absence at present would, at all events, make it necessary to defer any action. In the mean time, I believe that the Lord will teach me wisdom, and will grant grace and peace to her whose welfare is the subject of your prayers. If I reach any conclusion in the matter which you ought to know, I will communicate with you. If there is no further motion, this meeting is adjourned."

The elders rose, and with the exception of Mr. Johnson, retreated in embarrassed haste. They ducked their heads, and made a guttural noise in their throats, as though to say good-night ; but they were ashamed to speak to him, though Mr. Bent said as he turned his back on the preacher, "We 'll — ah — pray for her."

Mr. Johnson stopped to justify his presence, and say again, " Don't notice it, Mr. Ward. I 'd just gently like bring her round some time ; keep on prayin', an' all that, but don't force it. It will only make trouble for you."

John hurried away from him, stung to the quick. This, then, was his own real attitude ; this was what his plea of wisdom had meant this last year. His own deceit loomed up before his soul, and the sky of faith grew black. One by one, the accusations of the elders repeated themselves to him, and he made no protest. His assenting conscience left him absolutely defenseless.

CHAPTER XXIII.

THERE was a strange unreality about Helen's wakening, the first morning in Ashurst.

The year in Lockhaven seemed to have made as little change as a dream. Here she was, back in her old room. How familiar everything looked! Her little white bed; the old cherry-wood dressing-case, with its shining brass rings and spotless linen cover; the morning sunshine dancing with the shadows of the leaves, and falling in a golden square upon the floor; the curtains at the south window blowing softly to and fro in the fresh wind, and the flutter of wings outside in the climbing roses; even the bunch of white lilacs on the little table, apparently all just as she had left them nearly a year ago. Lockhaven and theology were behind her, and yet in some indefinable way she was a stranger in a strange land.

The consciousness of a difference had come the night before, when Lois poured out her fears and griefs to her cousin (all except her promise to Mrs. Forsythe) as soon as they were alone.

Lois felt no difference. Helen had been away for a long time, but she was still the same Helen to her; strong, and true, and gentle, with perhaps a little more gravity in her eyes, but Lois was so grave herself she did not notice that. Whereas with Helen

there was a dual life : the one, absorbing, passionate, and intense ; the other, a memory; a tender,
beautiful past, no longer a necessity.

Helen's joys had come between her and this once
dear home life, and even while Lois was telling her
of her cruel anxiety, and Helen was listening with
a face full of sympathy, her thoughts were following John on his lonely walk back from prayer-meeting, and greeting him in the doorway of the empty
house.

Of course the consciousness of the difference and
the strangeness wore off in a few days; perhaps if
Ashurst had been its usual quiet self, it would have
lasted longer, but there was so much to do, and so
little appreciation of change in the mind of any one
else, she almost forgot to notice it herself, but only
knew that all the time, under all her sympathy with
Ashurst joys and sorrows, — mostly sorrows, now, —
was a deep, still current of thought flowing towards
her husband.

Mrs. Dale had been the first one to come in, in
the morning.   They had scarcely finished breakfast
when they heard her decided voice in the hall, re-
proving Sally for some careless sweeping.   A little
while ago, Lois would have resented this as inter-
ference ; but she had too many real troubles now to
take Mrs. Dale's meddling to heart.

" Well, Helen, my dear," she said, " I 'm glad to
see you."   Mrs. Dale turned her cheek to her niece,
under the impression that she was kissing her.
" It is high time for you to be home again.   You
must keep this foolish child in order ; she hardly

eats or sleeps. I suppose you 've sent to know how
Arabella Forsythe is to-day, Lois ? "

Lois looked anxious. " I thought she really was
better last night, but she sent word this morning
there was no change."

" Fudge ! " cried Mrs. Dale. " I brought her
round all right before that nurse came. She can't
have killed her in this time. The fact is, brother,
Arabella Forsythe is n't in any hurry to get well ;
she likes the excitement of frightening us all to
death. I declare, Helen, she made her death-bed
adieux six times over ! I must say, nothing does
show a person's position in this world so well as
his manner of leaving it. You won't find poor
William Denner making a fuss. He is n't Admiral
Denner's great - grandson for nothing. Yes, Arabella Forsythe has talked about her soul, and made
arrangements for her funeral, every day for a week.
That 's where her father's money made in buttons
crops out ! "

" But aunt Deely," Helen said, " is n't there any
hope for Mr. Denner ? Ashurst would n't be Ashurst without Mr. Denner ! "

" No, not a bit," Mrs. Dale answered promptly.
" I suppose you 'll go and see him this morning,
brother, and tell him ? "

" Yes," replied Dr. Howe, sighing, " I suppose I
must, but it does seem unnecessary to disturb him."

" He won't be disturbed," said Mrs. Dale stoutly ;
" he is n't that kind. There, now," she added, as
Dr. Howe took up his hat and stick and went gloomily out into the sunshine, " I should n't wonder if

your father left it to Gifford to break it to him, after
all. It is curious how Archibald shrinks from it,
and he a clergyman! I could do it, easily. Now,
Lois, you run along; I want to talk to Helen."

But the rector had more strength of purpose than
his sister thought. His keen eyes blurred once or
twice in his walk to the village, and his lip almost
trembled, but when he reached Mr. Denner's bedside he had a firm hand to give his friend. The
doctor had left a note for him, saying the end was
near, and he read this before he went into the sick-
room.

Mr. Denner had failed very perceptibly since the
day before. He looked strangely little in the great
bed, and his brown eyes had grown large and bright.
But he greeted the rector with courteous cordiality,
under which his faint voice faltered, and almost
broke.

"How are you to-day, Denner?" his friend said,
sitting down on the edge of the bed, and taking the
sick man's hand in his big warm grasp.

"Thank you," replied Mr. Denner, with labored
breath, "I am doing nicely."

"Has Giff been here this morning?" asked Dr.
Howe.

"Yes," the lawyer answered. "He has gone
home for an hour. Mary takes excellent care of me,
and I felt I was really keeping him too much from
his aunts. For his stay is limited, you know, and I
am afraid I have been selfish in keeping him so
much with me."

"No, no," the rector said, "it is a pleasure for him

to be with you ; it is a pleasure for any of us. Poor little Lois is dreadfully distressed about you, — she longs to come and nurse you herself; and Helen, — Helen came last night, you know, — she wants to be of some use, too."

"Oh, well, now, dear me," remonstrated Mr. Denner feebly, "Miss Lois must not have a moment's uneasiness about me, — not a moment's. Pray tell her I am doing nicely; and it is really of no consequence in the world, — not the slightest."

Then Mr. Denner began to speak of Gifford's kindness, and how good every one in the village had been to him; even Mary had softened wonderfully in the last few days, though of this the sick man did not speak, for it would seem to imply that Mary had not always been all she might be, and, in view of her present kindness, it would have been ungracious to draw attention to that.

"Yes," Mr. Denner ended, folding his little hands on the counterpane, "it is worth while to have had this indisposition (except for the trouble it has given others) just to see how good every one is. Gifford has been exceedingly kind and thoughtful. His gentleness — for I have been very troublesome, doctor — has been wonderful. Like a woman's; at least so I should imagine."

The rector had clasped his hands upon his stick, and was looking intently at Mr. Denner, his lower lip thrust out and his eyebrows gathered in an absent frown.

"William," he said suddenly, "you've seen the doctor this morning?"

"Yes," Mr. Denner answered, "oh, yes. He is very kind about getting here early; the nights seem quite long, and it is a relief to see him early."

"I have not seen him to-day," said Dr. Howe slowly, "but yesterday he made me feel very anxious about you. Yes, we were all quite anxious, William."

The lawyer gave a little start, and looked sharply at his old friend; then he said, hesitating slightly, "That — ah — that was yesterday, did I understand you to say?"

Dr. Howe leaned forward and took one of Mr. Denner's trembling little hands in his, which was strong and firm. "Yes," he said gently, "but, William, my dear old friend, I am anxious still. I cannot help — I cannot help fearing that — that " —

"Stay," interrupted Mr. Denner, with a visible effort at composure, "I — I quite understand. Pray spare yourself the pain of speaking of it, Archibald. You are very kind, but — I quite understand."

He put his hand before his eyes a moment, and then blindly stretched it out to his friend. The rector took it, and held it hard in his own. The two men were silent. Mr. Denner was the first to speak.

"It is very good in you to come and tell me, Archibald. I fear it has discomposed you; it was very painful for you. Pray do not allow yourself to feel the slightest annoyance; it is of no consequence, I — ah — assure you. But since we are on the subject, perhaps you will kindly mention — how — how soon?"

" I hope, I trust," answered the rector huskily, " it may not be for several days."

" But probably," said Mr. Denner calmly, " probably — sooner ? "

Dr. Howe bowed his head.

" Ah — just so — just so. I — I thank you, Archibald."

Suddenly the rector drew a long breath, and straightened himself, as though he had forgotten something. " It must come to us all, sooner or later," he said gently, " and if we have lived well we need not dread it. Surely you need not, of all the men I have ever known."

" I have always endeavored," said Mr. Denner, in a voice which still trembled a little, " to remember that I was a gentleman."

Dr. Howe opened his lips and shut them again before he spoke. " I — I meant that the trust in God, William, of a Christian man, which is yours, must be your certain support now."

The lawyer looked up, with a faint surprise dawning in his eyes. " Ah — you are very good to say so, I 'm sure," he replied courteously.

Dr. Howe moved his hands nervously, clasping and re-clasping them upon the head of his stick. " Yes, William," he said, after a moment's silence, " that trust in God which leads us safely through all the dark places in life will not fail us at the end. The rod and the staff still comfort us."

" Ah — yes," responded Mr. Denner.

The rector gained confidence as he spoke. " And you must have that blessed assurance of the love of

God, William," he continued; "your life has been so pure and good. You must see in this visitation not chastisement, but mercy."

Dr. Howe's hand moved slowly back to the big pocket in one of his black coat-tails, and brought out a small, shabby prayer-book.

" You will let me read the prayers for the sick," he continued gently, and without waiting for a reply began to say with more feeling than Dr. Howe often put into the reading of the service, —

" ' Dearly beloved, know this, that Almighty God is the Lord of life and death, and of all things to them pertaining ; as ' " —

" Archibald," said Mr. Denner faintly, " you will excuse me, but this is not — not necessary, as it were.'"

Dr. Howe looked at him blankly, the prayer-book closing in his hand.

" I mean," Mr. Denner added, " if you will allow me to say so, the time for — for speaking thus has passed. It is now, with me, Archibald."

There was a wistful look in his eyes as he spoke.

" I know," answered Dr. Howe tenderly, thinking that the Visitation of the Sick must wait, " but God enters into now ; the Eternal is our refuge, a very present help in time of trouble."

" Ah — yes " — said the sick man ; " but I should like to approach this from our usual — point of view, if you will be so good. I have every respect for your office, but would it not be easier for us to speak of — of this as we have been in the habit of speaking on all subjects, quite — in our ordinary way, as it were ? You will pardon me, Archibald, if I say anything else seems — ah — unreal ? "

Dr. Howe rose and walked to the window. He stood there a few minutes, but the golden June day was dim, and there was a tightening in his throat that kept him silent. When he came back to the bedside, he stood looking down at the sick man, without speaking. Mr. Denner was embarrassed.

"I did not mean to pain you," he said.

"William," the rector answered, "have I made religion so worthless? Have I held it so weakly that you feel that it cannot help you now?"

"Oh, not at all," responded Mr. Denner, "not at all. I have the greatest respect for it, — I fear I expressed myself awkwardly, — the greatest respect; I fully appreciate its value, I might say its necessity, in the community. But — but if you please, Archibald, since you have kindly come to tell me of this — change, I should like to speak of it in our ordinary way; to approach the subject as men of the world. It is in this manner, if you will be so good, I should like to ask you a question. I think we quite understand each other; it is unnecessary to be anything but — natural."

The clergyman took his place on the side of the bed, but he leaned his head on his hand, and his eyes were hidden. "Ask me anything you will. Yet, though I may not have lived it, William, I cannot answer you as anything but a Christian man now."

"Just so," said Mr. Denner politely — "ah — certainly; but, between ourselves, doctor, putting aside this amiable and pleasing view of the church, you understand, — speaking just as we are in the habit of doing, — what do you suppose — what do you think — is beyond ? "

His voice had sunk to a whisper, and his eager eyes searched Dr. Howe's face.

" How can we tell ? " answered the rector. " That it is infinitely good we can trust : ' Eye hath not seen, nor ear heard ' " — He stopped, for Mr. Denner shook his head with a fine sort of impatience.

" If you please, doctor ! "

The rector was silent.

" I have wondered about it often," the other continued. " I have expected — this, for some days, and I have wondered. Think how strange : in a few days — almost a few hours, I shall know all, or — nothing ! Yes, the mystery of all the ages will be mine ! " There was a thrill of triumph in his feeble voice. " Think of that, doctor. I shall know more than the wisest man that lives, — I ! I was never a very clever person, never very wise ; and yet, here is a knowledge which shall not be too wonderful for me, and to which I can attain."

He held up his little thin hand, peering at the light between the transparent fingers. " To think," he said slowly, with a puzzled smile, " to think that this is going to be still ! It has never been any power in the world ; I don't know that it has ever done any harm, yet it has certainly never done any good ; but soon it will be still. How strange, how strange ! And where shall I be ? Knowing — or perhaps fallen on an eternal sleep. How does it seem to you, doctor ? That was what I wanted to ask you ; do you feel sure of anything — afterwards ? "

The rector could not escape the penetrating gaze of those strangely bright brown eyes. He looked into them, and then wavered and turned away.

" Do you? " said the lawyer.

The other put his hands up to his face a moment.

" Ah ! " he answered sharply, " I don't know — I can't tell. I — I don't know, Denner ! "

" No," replied Mr. Denner, with tranquil satisfaction, " I supposed not, — I supposed not. But when a man gets where I am, it seems the one thing in the world worth being sure of."

Dr. Howe sat silently holding the lawyer's hand, and Mr. Denner seemed to sink into pleasant thought. Once he smiled, with that puzzled, happy look the rector had seen before, and then he closed his eyes contentedly as though to doze. Suddenly he turned his head and looked out of the window, across his garden, where a few old-fashioned flowers were blooming sparsely, with much space between them for the rich, soft grass, which seemed to hold the swinging shadows of an elm-tree in a lacy tangle.

" ' The warm precincts of the cheerful day,' " he murmured, and then his eyes wandered about the room : the empty, blackened fireplace, where, on a charred log and a heap of gray ashes, a single bar of sunshine had fallen ; his fiddle, lying on a heap of manuscript music ; the one or two formal portraits of the women of his family ; and the large painting of Admiral Denner in red coat and gold lace. On each one he lingered with a loving, wondering gaze. " ' The place thereof shall know it ' " — he began to say. " Ah, doctor, it is a wonderful book ! How

it does know the heart! The soul sees itself there.
'As for man, his days are as grass; as a flower of
the field, so he flourisheth. For the wind passeth
over it, and it is gone; and the place thereof shall
know it no more' — no more. That is the wonder
of it! How strange it is; and I had such plans for
life, now! Well, it is better thus, no doubt, — no
doubt."

After a while he touched the little oval velvet
case which lay on the table beside him, and, taking
it up, looked long and earnestly at the childish face
inside the rim of blackened pearls.

"I wonder" — he said, and then stopped, laying
it down again, with a little sigh. "Ah, well, I
shall know. It is only to wait."

He did not seem to want any answer; it was
enough to ramble on, filled with placid content, between dreams and waking, his hand held firm in
that of his old friend. Afterwards, when Gifford
came in, he scarcely noticed that the rector slipped
away. It was enough to fill his mist of dreams with
gentle wonderings and a quiet expectation. Once
he said softly, "'In the hour of death, and in the
day of judgment'" —

"'Good Lord, deliver us!'" Gifford finished
gently.

Mr. Denner opened his eyes and looked at him.
"Good Lord," he said, "ah — yes — yes — that is
enough, my friend. *Good* Lord; one leaves the
rest."

Dr. Howe walked home with a strange look on
his face. He answered his daughter briefly, that

Mr. Denner was failing, and then, going into his library, he moved a table from in front of the door, which always stood hospitably open, and shut and locked it.

"What's the matter with the doctor?" asked Dick Forsythe, lounging up to the rectory porch, his hands in his pockets and his hat on the back of his head. "I walked behind him all the way from the village; he looked as though some awful thing had happened, and he walked as if he was possessed."

"Oh, Mr. Denner's worse," Lois answered tearfully.

Mr. Forsythe had found her on the porch, and, in spite of her grief, she looked nervously about for some one to save her from a *tête-à-tête*.

Dick seemed as anxious as she. "No, I won't sit down, thank you. Mother just wanted to know if you'd run in this afternoon a few minutes," and any one less frightened than Lois must have seen that he wished his mother had chosen another messenger.

"Is she — is she pretty comfortable?" the girl said, pulling a rose to pieces, and looking into the cool, dark hall for a third person; but there was only Max, lying fast asleep under the slender-legged table, which held a blue bowl full of peonies, rose, and white, and deep glowing red.

Dick also glanced towards the door. "Oh, yes, she'll be all right. Ah — unfortunately, I can't stay very long in Ashurst, but she'll be all right, I'm sure. You'll cheer her up when I'm gone, Miss Howe?"

Lois felt herself grow white. A sudden flash of hope came into her mind, and then fear. What did it mean? Was he going because he dared not ask her, or would his mother tell him that he would surely succeed? Oh, her promise!

Her breath came quick, and Mr. Forsythe saw it. "Yes," he said, stammering with embarrassment, "I — I fear I shall have to go — ah — important business."

Just then both these unhappy young people caught sight of Helen coming serenely across the lawn.

"There's my cousin," said Lois; "let us go and meet her."

"Oh, yes, do!" Dick answered fervently; and presently greeted Helen with a warmth which made her give Lois a quick, questioning look from under her straight brows, and sent her thoughts with a flash of sympathy to Gifford Woodhouse.

When the young man had gone, Helen said to her cousin, "Lois, dear — ?"

But Lois only threw herself into her arms with such floods of tears Helen could do nothing but try to calm her.

Lois was not the only one who heard of Dick's plan of leaving Ashurst with mingled joy and dread. Gifford knew that Mr. Forsythe was going away, and seeing the distress in Lois's face, in these sad days, he put it down to grief at his departure. It was easier to give himself this pain than to reflect that Lois was trembling with anxiety about Mr. Denner, and was still full of alarm for Mrs. Forsythe.

"If that puppy neglects her," he thought, "if she

cares for him, and if he grieves her, I vow I'll have a word to say to him! Now why should she cry, if it isn't because he's going away?"

Though he was glad Ashurst would see the last of this objectionable young man, Lois's grief turned his gladness into pain, and there was no hope for himself in his relief at Dick's departure. Miss Deborah, with the best intentions in the world, had made that impossible.

The day after Dr. Howe had told Mr. Denner that he must die, Gifford had come home for a few minutes. He had met the little ladies walking arm in arm up and down one of the shady paths of their walled garden. Miss Ruth still held her trowel in her hand, and her shabby gloves were stained by the weeds she had pulled up.

"Oh, there you are, dear Giff," she cried; "we were just looking for you. Pray, how is Mr. Denner?"

Gifford's serious face answered her without words, and none of the group spoke for a moment. Then Gifford said, "It cannot last much longer. You see, he suffers very much at night; it does n't seem as though he could live through another."

"Oh, dear me," said Miss Ruth, wiping her eyes with the frankest grief, "you don't say so!"

"Have n't you just heard him say so, sister?" asked Miss Deborah, trying to conceal an unsteady lip by a show of irritation. "Do pay attention."

"I did, dear Deborah," returned Miss Ruth, "but I cannot bear to believe it."

"Your believing it, or not, does n't alter the case,

unfortunately. Did he like the syllabub yesterday, Gifford ? "

" He could n't eat it," her nephew answered, " but Willie seemed to enjoy it."

" Poor child," cried Miss Deborah, full of sympathy, " I 'm glad he had anything to comfort him. But Gifford, do you really feel sure Mr. Denner cannot recover ? "

" Too sure," replied the young man, with a sigh.

" There 's no doubt about it, — no doubt whatever ? " Miss Ruth inquired anxiously.

Her nephew looked at her in surprise. " I wish there were."

" Well, then, sister ? " said Miss Ruth.

Miss Deborah nodded and sighed. " I — I think so," she answered, and the two sisters turned to go into the house, importance and grief on both their faces ; but Miss Deborah suddenly recollected something she wished to say.

" Do you know, Gifford," she said, letting Miss Ruth get a little ahead of her, " I really think that that young Forsythe is without proper feeling ; and I am surprised at dear Lois, too. I cannot say — I am not at liberty to say anything more, but at such a time " —

Gifford gave her a quick look. " What do you mean, aunt Deborah ? "

But his aunt seemed reluctant to speak, and looked after Miss Ruth, who was walking slowly up the mossy path, flecked here and there by patches of sunshine that fell through the flickering leaves above her. When she was quite out of hearing, Miss Deborah said mysteriously, —

" Well, perhaps I might tell you ; you are not like any one else. Ruth thinks I cannot keep a secret, but then you know your dear aunt Ruth does not discriminate. You are quite different from the public."

" Well, and what is it ? " he said impatiently, and with a horrible foreboding.

" Why, it is settled," answered Miss Deborah ; " it is all settled between Lois and young Forsythe. Arabella Forsythe told Adele Dale, and Adele Dale told me ; quite privately, of course. It was n't to be mentioned to any one ; but it was only natural to speak of it to dear Ruth and to you."

Gifford did not wait to hear more. " I must go," he said hurriedly. " I must get back to Mr. Denner," and he was off.

" Oh, dear Giff ! " cried Miss Deborah ; taking little mincing steps as she tried to run after him. " You won't mention it ? You won't speak of it to any one, or say I — I " —

" No ! " he called back, — " no, of course not."

" Not even to your aunt Ruth would be best ! " But he did not hear her, and Miss Deborah went back to the house, annoyed at Gifford, because of her own indiscretion.

Miss Ruth had gone to her own bedroom, and some time after Miss Deborah had disappeared in hers, the younger sister emerged, ready to go to Mr. Denner's.

Miss Ruth had dressed with great care, yet with a proper sense of fitness, considering the occasion. She wore a soft, old - fashioned lawn with small bunches of purple flowers scattered over it, and gathered very full about the waist. But, before the swinging mirror of her high bureau, she thought it looked too light and bright for so sad a visit, and so trotted up-stairs to the garret, and, standing on tiptoe by a great chest of drawers, opened one with much care, that the brass rings might not clatter on the oval plates under them, and disturb Miss Deborah. The drawer was sweet with lavender and sweet clover, and, as she lifted from its wrappings of silvered paper a fine black lace shawl, some pale, brittle rose-leaves fell out upon the floor. That shawl, thrown about her shoulders, subdued her dress, she thought; and the wide-brimmed black hat of fine Neapolitan straw, tied with soft black ribbons beneath her little round chin, completed the look of half mourning.

Miss Deborah answered her sister's knock at her bedroom door in person. She was not dressed to make calls, for she wore a short gown over her red flannel petticoat, and on her feet were large and comfortable list slippers. Miss Deborah's eyes were red, and she sniffed once, suspiciously.

"Why, Ruth Woodhouse!" she cried. "Have you no sense? Don't, for pity's sake, dress as though you had gone into mourning for the man, when he's alive. And it is very forward of you, too, for if either of us did it (being such old friends), it should be I, for I am nearer his age."

But Miss Ruth did not stop for discussion. "Are you not going?" she said.

"No," Miss Deborah answered, "we'd better go

to-morrow. You might just inquire of Mary, this afternoon, but we will call to-morrow. It is more becoming to put it off as long as possible."

Miss Ruth had her own views, and she consented with but slight demur, and left Miss Deborah to spend the rest of the afternoon in a big chair by the open window, with Baxter's "Saints' Rest" upon her knee.

When Gifford had gone back to the lawyer's house, he found the little gentleman somewhat brighter. Mary had put a clean white counterpane on the bed, and buttoned a fresh valance around it; and on the small table at his side Willie had placed a big bunch of gillyflowers and lupins, with perhaps less thought of beauty than of love.

"Gifford," he said, "I am glad to see you. And how, if you please, did you leave your aunt? I hope you conveyed to her my thanks for her thoughtfulness, and my apologies for detaining you as well?"

"Yes, sir," the young man answered, "I did. They are both rejoiced that I can be of any service."

Gifford had come to the side of the bed, and, slipping his strong young arm under Mr. Denner's head, lifted him that he might take with greater ease the medicine he held in a little slender-stemmed glass. "Ah," said Mr. Denner, between a sigh and a groan, as Gifford laid him down again, "how gentle you are! There is a look in your face, sometimes, of one of your aunts, sir; not, I think, Miss Deborah. I have thought much, since

I — I knew my condition, Gifford, of my wish that your aunt Deborah should have the miniature of my little sister. I still wish it. It is not easy for me to decide a momentous question, but, having decided, I am apt to be firm. Perhaps — unreasonably firm. I would not have you imagine I had, in any way, changed my mind, as it were — yet I have recurred, occasionally, in my thoughts, to Miss Ruth. I should not wish to seem to slight Miss Ruth, Gifford ? "

" She could not feel it so, I know," the young man answered.

But Mr. Denner's thoughts apparently dwelt upon it, for twice again, in intervals of those waking dreams, or snatches of sleep, he said, quite to himself, " It is decided ; yet it would seem marked to pass over Miss Ruth." And again he murmured, " I should not wish to slight Miss Deborah's sister."

Later in the afternoon he wakened, with a bright, clear look in his face. " It occurs to me," he said, " that I have another portrait, of no value at all compared with the miniature (and of course it is becoming that the miniature should go to Miss Deborah), which I might give to Miss Ruth. Because she is the sister of Miss Deborah, you understand, Gifford. Perhaps you will be so good as to hand me the square package from that same little drawer ? Here is the key."

Gifford brought it : it was a daguerreotype case, much worn and frayed along the leather back, and without the little brass hooks which used to fasten it ; instead, a bit of ribbon had been tied about it to keep it closed. Mr. Denner did not open it; he patted the faded green bow with his little thin fingers.

"It is a portrait of myself," he said. "It belonged to my mother. I had it taken for her when I was but a boy; yes, I was only thirty. She tied the ribbon; it has never been opened since."

He put it down on the stand, by the miniature, under the gillies and lupins.

So it happened that when Miss Ruth Woodhouse came to inquire for him, she had been in Mr. Denner's thoughts all the afternoon. "Not," he kept assuring himself, "not that I have changed my mind, — not at all, — but she is Miss Deborah's sister."

It was after five when Mary pushed the library door open softly, and looked in, and then beckoned mysteriously to Gifford.

"It is your aunt; she wants to know how he is. You'd better come and tell her."

Mr. Denner heard her, and turned his head feebly towards the door. "Miss Woodhouse, did you say, Mary? Which Miss Woodhouse, if you please?"

"It's the young one," said Mary, who spoke relatively.

"Miss Ruth?" Mr. Denner said, with an eager quaver in his voice. "Gifford, do you think — would you have any objection, Gifford, to permitting me to see your aunt? That is, if she would be so obliging and kind as to step in for a moment?"

"She will be glad to, I know," Gifford answered. "Let me go and bring her."

Miss Ruth was in a flutter of grief and excite‧ment. "I'll come, of course. I — I had rather hoped I might see him; but what will Deborah say? Yet I can't but think it's better for him not to see two people at once."

Mr. Denner greeted her by a feeble flourish of his hand. "Oh, dear me, Mr. Denner," said she, half crying, in spite of Gifford's whispered caution, "I'm so distressed to see you so ill, indeed I am."

"Oh, not at all," responded Mr. Denner, but his voice had a strange, far-away sound in his ears, and he tried to speak louder and more confidently, — "not at all. You are very good to come, ma'am;" and then he stopped to remember what it was he had wished to say.

Miss Ruth was awed into silence, and there was a growing anxiety in Gifford's face.

"Ah — yes" — Mr. Denner began again, with a flash of strength in his tone, "I wished to ask you if you would accept — accept" — he reached to-wards the little table, but he could not find the leather case until Gifford put it into his hand — "if you would be so good as to accept this; and will you open it, if you please, Miss Ruth?"

She did so, with trembling fingers. It was a daguerreotype of Mr. Denner; the high neckcloth and the short-waisted, brass-buttoned coat and waist-coat showed its age, as well as the dimness of the glass and the fresh boyish face of the young man of thirty.

"What — what was I speaking of, Gifford?" said Mr. Denner.

" You gave my aunt Ruth the picture, sir."

"Oh, yes, just so, just so. I merely wished to add that I desired to present it to Miss Deborah's sister, — though it is of no value, not the least value; but I should be honored by its acceptance. And perhaps you will be good enough to — to con· vey the assurance of my esteem to Miss Deborah. And Gifford — my friend Gifford is to give her the miniature of my little sister."

" Yes," said Miss Ruth, who was crying softly.

" Not that I have — have changed my mind," said Mr. Denner, " but it is not improper, I am sure, that Miss Deborah's sister should give me — if she will be so good — her hand, that I may say good-by ? "

Miss Ruth did not quite understand, until Gifford motioned to her to lay her little hand in that feeble one which was groping blindly towards her.

Mr. Denner's eyes were very dim.

" I — I am very happy," he murmured. " I thank you, Ruth ; " and then, a moment after, " If you will excuse me, I think I will rest for a few moments."

Still holding Miss Ruth's hand, he turned his head in a weary way towards the light, and softly closed his eyes.

Mr. Denner rested.

CHAPTER XXIV.

PERHAPS the majesty of Death is better understood when some little soul is swallowed up in the
great Mystery than when one is taken on whom
Life has laid her bright touch, and made famous
and necessary.

Even in quiet Ashurst, Mr. Denner was, as he
himself would have said, of no consequence, and his
living was not felt in any way; yet when he was
gone, a sudden knowledge came of how much he
was to them, and how great a blank he left. So
Death creates greatness.

It was well for Lois Howe, in those first sad days,
that her cousin was with her, or the reaction from
the excitement of anxiety into hopeless grief might
have been even more prostrating than it was. All
the comfort and tenderness Helen could give her in
her helpless self-reproach were hers, though she as
well as Gifford never sought to make the sorrow
less by evading the truth. But Helen was troubled
about her, and said to Dr. Howe, "Lois must come
to see me for a while; she does need a change very
much. I'm afraid she won't be able to go with me
next week, but can't she come as soon as she is
strong enough to travel?"

And so it was decided that she should come with
Gifford, who would go back to Lockhaven in about

a fortnight. Business, which never reached Mr. Denner in Mercer, had been offered the young lawyer,
and he had been willing to stay in Ashurst a little
longer, though he had told himself he was a fool.

Lois looked forward to the visit with feverish
anxiety. Mr. Forsythe, perhaps to please his mother,
but certainly with rather an ill grace, had lingered
in Ashurst. But he had not been very much at the
rectory ; perhaps because it was not a time to make
visits, or be careless and light-hearted, while little
Mr. Denner was fading out of life, and his mother
felt herself trembling on the edge of the grave. This,
at least, was what Mrs. Forsythe said to Lois more
than once, with an anxious, troubled look, which
perhaps explained more than her words did.

She had accepted very complacently Lois's pro-
testations of joy and gratitude that she was no
longer, as she expressed it, in immediate danger,
but she did not apparently feel that that altered
at all the conditions of the promise Lois had given
her, which was evidently a very precious thing. Nor
did Lois remonstrate against being held by it. She
felt she deserved any grief that came to her, and it
would have been cowardly, she thought, to shrink
from what she had undertaken merely because she
had been so far mercifully spared the grief of Mrs.
Forsythe's death. And who could tell that she
would live, even yet ? Certainly Mrs. Forsythe
herself seemed to consider her recovery a matter of
grave doubt, and Lois's anxieties were quick to
agree with her.

So she went about with a white face and eyes from

which all the careless gayety had gone, simply bearing her life with a dull pain and in constant fear.
Gifford saw it, and misunderstood it; he thought,
in view of what Miss Deborah had told him and
what he knew of Mr. Forsythe's plans, that it was
natural for Lois to look unhappy. Anxieties are
very misleading; the simple explanation of remorse
for her carelessness did not come into Gifford's mind
at all.

One afternoon, — it was the day following Mr.
Denner's funeral, — Gifford thought this all over,
and tried to see what his life offered him for the future, now that the last faint hope of winning Lois's
love had died. Mr. Denner's will had been read
that morning in his dining - room, with only Dr.
Howe and Mary and Willie present, while the rain
beat persistently against the windows, and made the
room so dark that Gifford had to call for a candle,
and hold the paper close to his eyes to see to read.
Willie had shivered, and looked steadfastly under
the table, thinking, while his little heart beat suf-
focatingly, that he was glad there were no prayers
after a will. When that was over, and Dr. Howe
had carried Willie back with him to be cheered and
comforted at the rectory, Gifford had devoted himself to disposing of such small effects as Mr. Denner
had left as personal bequests.

They were not very many. A certain bamboo rod
with silver mountings and a tarnished silver reel,
were for Dr. Howe; and there were a few books to
be sent to Mr. Dale, and six bottles of Tokay, '52,
for Colonel Drayton. There was a mourning-ring,

which had been Mr. Denner's father's, for a distant cousin, who was further comforted by a few hundred dollars, but all the rest was for Willie.

Gifford had felt, as he sat at Mr. Denner's writing-desk and touched some small possessions, all the pathetic powerlessness of the dead. How Mr. Denner had treasured his little valueless belongings! There was a pair of silver shoe-buckles, wrapped in chamois skin, which the little gentleman had faithfully kept bright and shining; they had belonged to his grandfather, and Mr. Denner could remember when they had been worn, and the knee-breeches, and the great bunch of seals at the fob. Perhaps, when his little twinkling brown eyes looked at them, he felt again the thrill of love and fear for the stately gentleman who had awed his boyhood. There was a lock of faded gray hair in a yellow old envelope, on which was written, in the lawyer's precise hand, " My mother's hair," and a date which seemed to Gifford very far back. There were one or two relics of the little sister: a small green morocco shoe, which had buttoned about her ankle, and a pair of gold shoulder-straps, and a narrow pink ribbon sash that had grown yellow on the outside fold.

There was a pile of neatly kept diaries, with faithful accounts of the weather, and his fishing excursions, and the whist parties; scarcely more than this, except a brief mention of a marriage or a death. Of course there were letters; not very many, but all neatly labeled with the writer's name and the date of their arrival. These Gifford burned, and the blackened ashes were in the wide fireplace, be-

hind a jug of flowers, on which he could hear, down
the chimney, the occasional splash of a raindrop.
There was one package of letters where the name
was " Gertrude ; " there were but few of these, and,
had Gifford looked, he would have seen that the last
one, blistered with tears, said that her father had
forbidden further correspondence, and bade him,
with the old epistolary formality from which not
even love could escape, " an eternal farewell." But
the tear-stains told more than the words, at least of
Mr. Denner's heart, if not of pretty sixteen-year-
old Gertrude's. These were among the first to be
burned ; yet how Mr. Denner had loved them, even
though Gertrude, running away with her dancing-
master, and becoming the mother of a family of
boys, had been dead these twenty years, and the
proverb had pointed to Miss Deborah Woodhouse !

Some papers had to be sealed, and the few pieces
of silver packed, ready to be sent to the bank in
Mercer, and then Gifford had done.

He was in the library, from which the bed had
been moved, and which was in trim and dreary order. The rain still beat fitfully upon the windows,
and the room was quite dark. Gifford had pushed
the writing-desk up to the window for the last ray
of light, and now he sat there, the papers all arranged and nothing more to do, yet a vague, tender
loyalty to the little dead gentleman keeping him.
And sitting, leaning his elbows on the almost un-
spotted sheet of blue blotting-paper which covered
the open flap of the desk, he fell into troubled
thinking.

"Of course," he said to himself, "she's awfully distressed about Mr. Denner, but there's something more than that. She seems to be watching for something all the time; expecting that fellow, beyond a doubt. And why he is not there oftener Heaven only knows! And to think of his going off on his confounded business at such a time, when she is in such trouble! If only for a week, he has no right to go and leave her. His business is to stay and comfort her. Then, when he is at the rectory, what makes him pay her so little attention? If he wasn't a born cad, somebody ought to thrash him for his rudeness. If Lois had a brother! — But I suppose he does not know any better, and then Lois loves him. Where's Helen's theory now, I wonder? Oh, I suppose she thinks he is all right. I'd like to ask her, if I had n't promised aunt Deborah."

Just here, Gifford heard the garden gate close with a bang, and some one came down the path, holding an umbrella against the pelting rain, so that his face was hidden. But Gifford knew who it was, even before Mary, shuffling asthmatically through the hall, opened the door to say, "Mr. Forsythe's here to see you."

"Ask him to come in," he said, pushing his chair back from the secretary, and lifting the flap to lock it as he spoke.

Dick Forsythe came in, shaking his dripping umbrella, and saying with a good-natured laugh, "Jove! what a wet day! You need a boat to get through the garden. Your aunt — the old one, I think it was — asked me, if I was passing, to bring you these overshoes. She was afraid you had none, and would take cold."

He laughed again, as though he knew how amusing such nonsense was, and then had a gleam of surprise at Gifford's gravity.

" I 'd gone to her house with a message from my mother," he continued ; "you know we get off to-morrow. Mother 's decided to go, too, so of course there are a good many things to do, and the old lady is so strict about Ashurst customs I 've had to go round and ' return thanks ' to everybody."

Gifford had taken the parcel from Dick's hand, and thanked him briefly. The young man, however, seemed in no haste to go.

" I don't know which is damper, this room or out-of-doors," he said, seating himself in Mr. Denner's big chair, — though Gifford was standing — and looking about in an interested way; "must have been a gloomy house to live in. Wonder he never got married. Perhaps he could n't find anybody willing to stay in such a hole, — it 's so confound-edly damp. He died in here, did n't he ? " This was in a lower voice.

" Yes," Gifford answered.

" Should n't think you 'd stay alone," Dick went on ; "it is awfully dismal. I see he cheered himself once in a while." He pointed to a tray, which held a varied collection of pipes and a dingy tobacco pouch of buckskin with a border of colored porcu-pine quills.

" Yes, Mr. Denner smoked," Gifford was con-strained to say.

" I think," said Dick, clapping his hand upon his breast-pocket, " I 'll have a cigar myself. It braces one up this weather." He struck a match on the sole of his boot, forgetting it was wet, and vowing good-naturedly that he was an ass. " No objection, I suppose ? " he added, carefully biting off the end of his cigar.

" I should prefer," Gifford replied slowly, " that you did not smoke. There is an impropriety about it, which surely you must appreciate."

Dick looked at him, with the lighted match flaring bluely between his fingers. " Lord ! " he said, " how many things are improper in Ashurst ! But just as you say, of course." He put his cigar back in an elaborate case, and blew out the match, throwing it into the fireplace, among the flowers. " The old gentleman smoked himself, though."

Gifford's face flushed slowly, and he spoke with even more deliberation than usual. " Since you have decided not to smoke, you must not let me detain you. I am very much obliged for the package."

" You 're welcome, I 'm sure," Dick said. " Yes, I suppose I 'd better be getting along. Well, I 'll say good-by, Mr. Woodhouse. I suppose I sha' n't see you before I go ? And Heaven knows when I 'll be in Ashurst again ! "

Gifford started. " Sit down a moment," he said, waving aside Dick's hand. " Surely you are not leaving Ashurst for any length of time ? "

" Length of time ? " answered the other, laughing. " Well, I rather think so. I expect to go abroad next month."

A curious desire came into Gifford Woodhouse's strong hands to take this boy by the throat, and shake him until his ceaseless smile was torn to pieces. Instead of that, however, he folded his arms, and stood looking down at his companion in silence.

Dick had seated himself again, and was twirling his wet umbrella round and round by the shiny end of one of the ribs. "Yes," he said, "this is a long good-by to Ashurst."

"Mr. Forsythe," said Gifford, with an edge of anger in his voice which could not have escaped even a more indifferent ear than Dick's, "may I ask if Dr. Howe knows of your plans?"

Dick looked up, with a sudden ugly shadow coming across the sunny brightness of his face. "I don't know what I've done to deserve this concern on your part, Mr. Woodhouse; but, since you ask, I have no objection to saying that Dr. Howe does not particularly interest himself in my affairs. I don't know whether he's aware of my plans, and I care less."

He rose, and stood grasping his wet umbrella midways, looking defiantly into Gifford's face. It was singular how instantly, in some wordless way, he appreciated that he had been blamed.

Gifford began to speak in the slow, measured tone which showed how he was guarding his words. "You may not care for his interest," he said, "but you can scarcely expect that he would not notice your absence."

"I cannot see that my movements are of so much importance to Dr. Howe," Dick answered, "and he certainly has never taken it upon himself to meddle in my affairs to the extent of asking me about them."

"Nevertheless," said Gifford, with ominous gentleness, "he must feel — surprise at your departure. That your business should take you away at this time, Mr. Forsythe, is unfortunate."

"I know my business, at least," cried the other loudly, his voice trembling with anger, "and I 'm capable of attending to it without suggestions from you! I 'll trouble you to speak plainly, instead of hinting. What right have you to question my leaving Ashurst?"

"No right," Gifford said calmly.

"Why don't you speak out like a man?" Forsythe demanded with a burst of rage, striking the table with his fist. "What do you mean by your damned impudence? So you dare to question my conduct to Lois Howe, do you? — you confounded prig!"

"Be silent!" Gifford said between his teeth. "Gentlemen do not introduce the name of a woman into their discussions. You forgot yourself. It is unnecessary to pursue this subject. I have nothing more to say."

"But I have more to say. Who gave you the right to speak to me? The lady herself? She must be indeed distressed to choose you for a messenger."

Gifford did not answer; for a moment the dark room was very still, except for the beating rain and the tapping of the ivy at the south window.

"Or perhaps," he went on, a sneer curling his handsome mouth, "you will comfort her yourself, instead? Well, you 're welcome."

Gifford's hands clenched on the back of the chair in front of him. "Sir," he said, "this place protects you, and you know it."

But Dick Forsythe was beside himself with anger. He laughed insultingly. "I 'll not detain you any longer. Doubtless you will wish to go to the rectory to-night. But I 'm afraid, even though I 'm obliging enough to leave Ashurst, you will have no" — He did not finish his sentence. Gifford Woodhouse's hand closed like a vise upon his collar. There were no words. Dick's struggles were as useless as beating against a rock; his maddest efforts could not shake off that relentless hand. Gifford half pushed, half carried, him to the door, and in another moment Dick Forsythe found himself flung like a·snapping cur in the mud and rain of Mr. Denner's garden.

He gathered himself up, and saw Gifford standing in the doorway, as though to offer him a chance of revenge.

"Damn you!" he screamed, furious with passion. "I 'll pay you for this! I — I" — He choked with rage, and shook his fist at the motionless figure on the steps. Then, trembling with impotent fury, oaths stumbling upon his lips, he turned and rushed into the gathering darkness.

Gifford watched him, and then the door swung shut, and he went back to Mr. Denner's library. His breath was short, and he was tingling with pas-

sion, but he had no glow of triumph. " I 've been
a fool," he said, — " I 've been a fool ! I 've made
it worse for her. The hound ! "

But in spite of his genuine contrition, there was
a subtile joy. " He does not love her," he thought,
" and she will forget him."

Yet, as he sat there in Mr. Denner's dark library,
filled with remorse and unabated rage as well, he
began to realize that he had been meddlesome ; and
he was stung with a sudden sense that it was not
honorable to have pushed his questions upon Forsythe. Gifford's relentless justice overtook him.
Had he not given Forsythe the right to insult him ?
Would not he have protected himself against any
man's prying ? Gifford blushed hotly in the darkness. " But not to use Lois's name, — not that!
Nothing could justify the insult to her ! "

Mary came in to lock up, and started with fright
at the sight of the dark, still figure. " Lord ! it 's
a ghost ! " she cried shrilly.

" I am here, Mary," he said wearily. " I 'm going
home now."

And so he did, walking doggedly through the
storm, with his head bent and his hands in his
pockets, forgetful of Miss Deborah's thoughtfulness
in the way of rubbers, and only anxious to avoid any
kindly interruption from his aunts, which their anxiety concerning damp clothes might occasion. But
he could not escape them. Miss Deborah met him
at the door with a worried face. " My dear boy ! "
she said, " no umbrella? Pray go to bed directly,
and let me bring you a hot drink. You will surely

have a cough to-morrow." But the little lady came back to the parlor with an aggrieved face, for he had answered her with quiet determination not to be fussed over. The sisters heard him walk quickly up-stairs and lock his door. They looked at each other in astonishment.

" He feels it very much," said Miss Ruth.

" Yes," returned Miss Deborah; " he has been sorting the papers all the afternoon. I must go and see Willie to-morrow."

" Oh, I 'll do that," Miss Ruth answered. " I cannot help feeling that it is — my place."

" Not at all," replied Miss Deborah firmly; " the miniature shows plainly his sentiments towards me. I know he would wish me to look after Willie. Indeed, I feel it a sacred duty."

Miss Deborah moved her hands nervously. Mr. Denner's death was too recent for it to be possible to speak of him without agitation.

" Well," said Miss Ruth, " perhaps, after all, you are right, in a way. The miniature is childish. Of course a portrait of himself has a far deeper meaning."

" Ruth Woodhouse," cried the other, " I 'm ashamed of you! Did n't you tell me yourself he said it was of no value? And you know how much he thought of the little sister! "

" But that was his modesty," said Miss Ruth eagerly. However, both ladies parted for the night with unaltered convictions, and the younger sister, opening the daguerreotype for one last look by her bedroom candle, murmured to herself, "I wonder

what Deborah would think if she knew he said
' Ruth ' ? "

The Forsythes went away the next morning.
Perhaps it was the early start which prevented Dick
from seeing Gifford again, and finishing the so sum-
marily ended quarrel, or possibly it was recollection
of the weight of Gifford Woodhouse's hand. Yet
he thought he had found a means of revenge.

In spite of the rain, he had gone to the rectory.
Helen was writing to her husband, and Dr. Howe
was reading. "You'll have to see him in the parlor,
Lois," her father said, looking at her over his paper,
as Sally announced Mr. Forsythe.

" Oh, father ! " she said.

" Nonsense," replied the rector impatiently, " you
know him well enough to receive him alone. I can't
be interrupted. Run along, child."

" Will you come in, Helen, dear ? " she pleaded.

" Yes," Helen said, glancing at her with absent
eyes ; it was hard to leave the intricacies of a theological argument to think of a girl's lover. " I'll
come soon."

But in a letter to John she forgot every one else,
and when Lois went tremblingly out of the room
both the rector and his niece lost themselves in their
own interests.

" Good-evening, Miss Lois," Dick said, coming
towards her with extended hand.

She could hardly hear her answer for her beating
heart.

" I came to say good-by," he went on, his bright
blue eyes fastened angrily upon her ; but she did
not see him.

"You go to-morrow?" she faltered.

"Yes," he answered; "but I could not leave Ashurst without — one more look at the rectory."

Lois did not speak. Oh, why did not Helen come?

"A different scene this from that night after the dinner party," Dick thought, looking at her down-cast eyes and trembling hands with cruel exultation in his face. "If I cared!"

"How I have adored Ashurst!" he said slowly, wondering how far it would be safe to go. "I have been very happy here. I hope I shall be still hap-pier, Lois?"

Still she did not answer, but she pressed her hands hard together. Dick looked at her critically.

"When I come again, — oh, when I come again, — then, if you have not forgotten me — Tell me you will not forget me, until I come again?"

Lois shook her head. Dick had drawn her to a seat, and his eager face was close to hers.

"I said good-by to the rector this afternoon," he said, "but I felt I must see you again, alone."

Lois was silent.

"I wonder if you know," he went on, "how often I shall think of Ashurst, and of you?"

He had possessed himself of her hand, which was cold and rigid, but lay passively in his. She had turned her face away from him, and in a stunned, helpless way was waiting for the question which seemed on his lips. "And you know what my thoughts will be," he said meaningly. "You make Ashurst beautiful."

He saw the color, which had rushed to her face when he had begun to talk, fade slowly; even her lips were white. But she never looked at him.

"You were not always kind to me," he continued, "but when I come back" —

She turned with a sudden impulse toward him, her breath quick and her lips unsteady. "Mr. Forsythe," she said, "I" —

But he had risen. "I suppose I must go," he said in his natural voice, from which sentiment had fled, and left even a suggestion of alarm. "It is late, and mother may need something, — you know she's always needing something. We never can forget your kindness, Miss Lois. Good-by, — good-by!"

Though he lingered on that last word and pressed her hand, he had gone in another moment. Lois stood breathless. She put her hands up to her head, as though to quiet the confusion of her thoughts. What did it mean? Was it only to let her see that he still loved her? Was he coming again?

When Helen, remembering her duties, came into the parlor, it was deserted, and Lois was facing her misery and fright in her own room, while Dick Forsythe, raging homeward through the rain, was saying to himself, "I've put an end to your prospects! She'll wait for me, if it is six years. It is just as well she does n't know I'm going abroad. I'll tell mother not to mention it. Mother was right when she said I could have her for the asking!"

CHAPTER XXV.

HELEN's desire to get back to John made her decide to start on Monday, instead of waiting until Wednesday, when the fortnight she had planned for her visit ended.

"I must go," she said, smiling at Dr. Howe's railings. "I cannot stay away from home any longer. And you'll come soon, Lois, dear!"

Even daily letters from John had not saved her from homesickness. They were a comfort, even though they were filled with pleadings and prayers that, for her soul's sake, she would see the error of her belief. Such tenderness struggled through the pages of argument, Helen would lay her cheek against them, and say softly, "I'll come home to you soon, dear."

One of these last letters had entreated her to write immediately upon its receipt, and answer it point by point. She did so, saying at the last, "Now let us drop the whole subject. I will never, as long as I have reason, believe this terrible doctrine, — never. So why need we ever speak of it again? I know it is your fear of eternity which leads you to try to make me believe it, but, dearest, if eternity depends on this, it is already settled; let us just be glad together while we can, in this beautiful time. Oh, I shall soon be home; I can think of nothing else."

And she counted the hours until she could start. When the morning came, with its clear June sky, and great white clouds lying dreamily behind the hills, her face was running over with gladness, in spite of her sympathy for Lois's grief.

"How happy you look!" Lois said wistfully, as she sat watching Helen put on her bonnet before the swinging mirror in its white and gold frame, on her dressing-table.

Helen had not known how her eyes were smiling, and she looked with quick compunction at Lois's white face. "I shall see John so soon," she answered contritely. "I can't help it."

"I shall miss you awfully," Lois went on, leaning her forehead against the edge of the bureau, and knotting the long linen fringe of the cover with nervous little fingers.

"But think how soon I'll have you in Lockhaven, dear; and you will be a little stronger then, and happier, too," Helen said, brightly.

For Lois was so worn and tired that a less active person would have called herself ill; as it was, she was not able to bear the long ride to Mercer and back, and Helen was to go alone, for Dr. Howe had to go out of Ashurst a little way, to perform a marriage ceremony.

"You'll have rain before the day is over, my dear," he said, as he put her into the carriage, "and that will make it better traveling, no dust. It's a shame that I should have to go in the other direction. Why could n't those people get married to-morrow instead of to-day, I should like to know?

Or why could n't you stay twenty-four hours longer? Could not stand it to be away from home another minute! Well, well, that's right,— that's the way it should be. Hope Ward is as anxious to get you back as you are to run off and leave us; perhaps he does n't want you, young lady." The rector laughed at Helen's confident look. "I don't half like your going to Mercer by yourself," he added.

"Oh, I shall get along very well," said Helen cheerily. "I have no doubt there 'll be a letter for me from John at the post-office, and I will get it as we go through the village. I 'll have that to read."

"It will hardly last all the way to Lockhaven," Lois commented.

"Oh, yes, it will," answered Helen, with a ripple of joy in her tone, which, for pure gladness, was almost laughter. "You don't know, Lois!"

Lois smiled drearily; she was sitting on the steps, her arms crossed listlessly on her knees, and her eyes fixed in an absent gaze on the garden.

"Here's Giff," Helen continued, arranging her traveling-bag and some books on the opposite seat of the carriage. "I shall just have time to say good-by to him."

"That is what I came for," Gifford said, as he took her hand a moment. "I will bring Lois safely to you in a fortnight."

Mrs. Dale was on the porch, and Sally and Jean stood smiling in the doorway; so, followed by hearty good-bys and blessings, with her hands full of flowers, and the sunshine resting on her happy face and glinting through her brown hair, Helen drove away.

Mr. Dale was at the post-office, and came out to hand her the letter she expected.

"So you 're off ?" he said, resting his hand on the carriage door, and looking at her with a pleasant smile. "You 've made me think of the starling, this last week, — you remember the starling in the Bastile? 'I can't get out,' says the starling, — 'I can't get out.' Well, I 'm glad you want to get out, my dear. My regards to your husband." He stood watching the carriage whirl down the road, with a shade of envy on his face.

When Helen had gone, and the little group on the porch had scattered, Lois rose to go into the house, but Gifford begged her to wait.

"You stay too much in-doors," he remonstrated; "it has made your face a little white. Do come into the garden awhile."

"She does look badly," said Mrs. Dale from the top of the steps, contemplating her niece critically. "I declare it puts me out of all patience with her, to see her fretting in this way."

Mrs. Dale was experiencing that curious indignation at a friend's suffering which expends itself upon the friend; in reality her heart was very tender towards her niece. "She misses the Forsythes," Mrs. Dale continued. "She 's been so occupied with Arabella Forsythe since the accident, she feels as if she had nothing to do."

There was no lack of color in Lois's face now, which did not escape Gifford's eye.

"Go, now, and walk with Gifford," said Mrs. Dale coaxingly, as though she were speaking to a child.

Lois shook her head, without looking at him. " I don't believe I will, if you don't mind."

But Mrs. Dale was not satisfied. " Oh, yes, you 'd better go. You 've neglected the flowers dreadfully. I don't know how long it is since your father has had any fresh roses in the library."

" I 'll get the garden scissors," Gifford pleaded ; " it won't take long just to cut some roses."

" Well," Lois said languidly.

Gifford went through the wide cool hall for the shears and the basket of scented grass for the po-sies ; he knew the rectory as well as his own home. Mrs. Dale had followed him, and in the shadowy back hall she gave him a significant look.

" That 's right, cheer her up. Of course she feels their going very much. I must say, it does not show much consideration on the part of the young man to leave her at such a time, — I don't care what the business is that calls him away ! Still, I can't say that I 'm surprised. I never did like that Dick, and I have always been afraid Lois would care for him."

" I think it is a great misfortune," Gifford said gravely.

" Oh, well, I don't know," demurred Mrs. Dale. " It is an excellent match ; and his carelessness now — well, it is only to be expected from a young man who would carry his mother off from — from our care, to be looked after by a hired nurse. He thought," said Mrs. Dale, bridling her head and pursing up her lips, "that a lot of ' fussy old wo-men ' could n't take care of her. Still, it will be a good marriage for Lois. I 'm bound to say that, though I have never liked him."

The young people did not talk much as they went down into the garden. Lois pointed out what roses Gifford might cut, and, taking them from him, put them into the little basket on her arm.

" How I miss Helen!" she said at last.

" Yes, of course," he answered, " but think how soon you 'll see her in Lockhaven;" and then he tried to make her talk of the lumber town, and the people, and John Ward. But he had the conversation quite to himself. At last, with a desperate desire to find something in which she would be interested, he said, " You must miss your friends very much. I 'm sorry they are gone."

" My friends?"

" Yes, Mr. Forsythe — and his mother."

" Oh, no!" she answered quickly.

" No?" Gifford said, wondering if she were afraid he had discovered her secret, and hastening to help her conceal it. " Oh, of course you feel that the change will be good for Mrs. Forsythe?"

" Oh, I hope it will!" cried Lois, fear trembling in the earnestness of her voice.

Gifford had stepped over the low box border to a stately bunch of milk-white phlox. " Let 's have some of this," he said, beginning to cut the long stems close to the roots; " it always looks so well in the blue jug."

His back was toward her, and perhaps that gave him the courage to say, with a suddenness that surprised himself, " Ah — does Mrs. Forsythe go abroad with her son?"

Even as he spoke he wondered why he had said it ; certainly it was from no interest in the sick lady. Was it because he hoped to betray Lois into some expression of opinion concerning Mr. Forsythe's departure ? He despised himself if it were a test, but he did not stop to follow the windings of his own motives.

"Abroad ? " Lois said, in a quick, breathless way. "Does he go abroad ? "

Gifford felt her excitement and suspense without seeing it, and he began to clip the phlox with a recklessness which would have wrung Dr. Howe's soul.

"I — I believe so. I supposed you knew it."

"How do you know it ? " she demanded.

"He told me," Gifford admitted.

"Are you sure ? " she said in a quavering voice.

Gifford had turned, and was stepping carefully back among the plants, sinking at every step into the soft fresh earth. He did not look at her, as he reached the path.

"Are you sure ? " she said again.

"Yes," he answered reluctantly, "yes, he is going ; I don't know about his mother."

Here, to his dismay, he saw the color come and go on Lois's sad little face, and her lip tremble, and her eyes fill, and then, dropping her roses, she began to cry heartily.

"Oh, Lois ! " he exclaimed, aghast, and was at her side in a moment. But she turned away, and, throwing her arm about an old locust-tree in the path, laid her cheek against the rough bark, and hid her eyes.

"Oh, don't cry, Lois," he besought her. "What a brute I was to have told you in that abrupt way! Don't cry."

"Oh, no," she said, "no, no, no! you must not say that — you — you do not understand " —

"Don't," he said tenderly, "don't — Lois!"

Lois put one hand softly on his arm, but she kept her face covered. Gifford was greatly distressed.

"I ought not to have told you in that way," — Lois shook her head, — "and — and I have no doubt he — they 'll come to Ashurst and tell you of their plans before they start."

Lois seemed to listen.

"Yes," Gifford continued, gaining conviction from his desire to help her, "of course he will return."

Lois had ceased to cry. "Do — do you think so?"

"I 'm sure of it," Gifford answered firmly; and even as he spoke, he had a mental vision, in which he saw himself bringing Dick Forsythe back to Ashurst, and planting him forcibly at Lois's feet. "I ought to have considered," he went on, looking at her anxiously, "that in your exhausted state it would be a shock to hear that your friends were go- ing so far away; though Europe is n't so very far, Lois. Of course they 'll come and tell you all about it before they go; probably they had their own rea- sons for not doing it before they left Ashurst, — your health, perhaps. But no doubt, no possible doubt, that Mr. Forsythe, at least, will come back here to make any arrangements there may be about his house, you know."

This last was a very lame reason, and Gifford felt

it, for the house had been closed and the rent paid, and there was nothing more to do; but he must say something to comfort her.

Lois had quite regained her composure; even the old hopeless look had returned.

"I beg your pardon," she said. "I am very — foolish. I don't know why I am so weak — I -- I am still anxious about Mrs. Forsythe, you know; the long journey for her " —

"Of course," he assured her. "I know how it startled you."

She turned to go into the house, and Gifford followed her, first picking up the neglected roses at her feet.

"I do not know what you think of me," she said tremulously.

" I only think you are not very strong," he answered tenderly, yet keeping his eyes from her averted face; he felt that he had seen more than he had a right to, already. His first thought was to protect her from herself; she must not think she had betrayed herself, and fancy that Gifford had guessed her engagement. He still hoped that, for the sake of their old friendship, she would freely choose to tell him. But most of all, she should not feel that she had shown despairing love for a man who neglected and slighted her, and that her companion pitied her. He even refused to let his thought turn to it.

"You must not mind me, Lois. I quite understand — the suddenness of hearing even the most — indifferent thing is enough to upset one when one is so tired out with nursing, and all that. Don't mind me."

"You are so good, Gifford," she said, with a sudden shy look from under her wet lashes, and a little lightening of her heavy eyes.

It was at least a joy to feel that he could comfort her, even though it cut his own heart to do so, and the pain of it made him silent for a few minutes.

When they had reached the steps, Lois's face had settled into its white apathy, which was almost despair. "I think I'll go in, Giff," she said. "I am so tired."

"Won't you fix the roses?" he asked.

She shook her head. "No, I — I don't care anything about them; Sally can do it. Just leave them on the steps."

She gave him a wan little smile, and went into the house. Gifford stood in the sunshine, with the roses and the white phlox, and looked after her retreating figure. But in spite of his heartache, he would not leave the flowers to die, so he went hunting about for something to put them in, and finding the India china punch-bowl, with its soft blues and greens of enamel, and twists of roses and butterflies over groups of tiny mandarins, he brought it out, and laid his flowers in it, a little clumsily, perhaps, and heedless that some of the stems stuck out ; but as he forgot the water, this did not so much matter. Then he carried it into the hall, and put it down on the table under the square window, and plodded home alone.

The noon sunshine poured hot and bright through

the little panes of glass, and when Lois, later in the day, found the withered, drooping roses and the hanging heads of the white phlox, she felt they were only in keeping with all the rest of life.

Even the sparkling day had darkened, and Dr. Howe's prophecy of rain had been fulfilled.

CHAPTER XXVI.

It grew quite chilly towards dusk, which gave Dr. Howe an excuse for putting a match to the dusty pile of logs in the library fireplace. He liked the snap and glow of the flames, and did not object to the mild, soft heat; so he sat there long after Lois had gone wearily up-stairs to bed, and the rectory was full of drowsy silence.

Outside, the tree which leaned toward the house bent and swayed in the wind, and scratched against the weather boards, while the rain came in a quick dash against the glass, and then seemed to listen for an answer, and waver, and retreat, and go sweeping down among the bushes in the garden.

The rector had not lighted his lamp; the faint, still light from two candles in the row of silver candlesticks on the tall mantel was all he wanted until he began to read. He was ready to do that later. A church journal, with an account of a quarrel between a High-Church clergyman and his Low-Church Bishop, was within reach of his hand, and the "Three Guardsmen," in a ragged yellow cover, was astride his knee, but now he was content to sit and think. He made a prosperous and comfortable figure, reflected in the dim, dark mirror over the mantel, where the candles shone back like stars in a pool at night. A white moth had found

its way into the house, and fluttered back and forth
between the candles, its little white ghost following
it in the glass. The rector watched it placidly.
Even his thoughts were tranquil and comfortable,
for he was equally indifferent both to the bishop
and his rebellious clergyman. There was a cup of
mulled wine simmering by the brass dogs, and the
fire sputtered and sung softly. Max, with his nose
between his paws, watched it with sleepy eyes. The
little tinge of melancholy in Dr. Howe's face did
not interfere with a look of quiet satisfaction with
life ; perhaps, indeed, it gave an added charm to his
ruddy, handsome features. At first he had been
thinking of Mr. Denner ; not of that distressing
day when he had told him of approaching death,
— that was too painful for such an hour, he meant
to meet it later, — but of the sad vacancy the little
gentleman had left.

Perhaps the consciousness of the thought from
which he was hiding turned his mind to Helen, and
here all was satisfactory. There had been no discussion, none of the theological argument that her
letters had given him cause to dread, which had
made him feel a quiver in that solid rock of custom
that a long-quieted earthquake had once shaken to
its centre. He felt in a vague way that his niece
was not quite so near and familiar, and there was
a subtile reserve, which did not show itself in words
or any check in the expression of her love, but which
was certainly there. Yet he did not analyze it ; he
did not care to realize that perhaps she feared to
speak of what was so real to her, because she knew

he had no help for her. Dr. Howe would have perfectly understood that this must inevitably create a
distance between them ; but it would have been
extremely painful to have let this creep into his
thoughts, just as it would have been painful for him
had she spoken of it ; so he preferred to say to himself that all was well. The child had gotten over all
that foolishness; he would have disliked to find fault
with her, as he must have done had she mentioned
it ; he was glad it was all forgotten. He was glad,
too, Lois was going to Lockhaven to see her. Poor
little Lois ! Ah, poor Denner ! Well, well, there
are some very sad things in life. And he lifted
his mug of mulled wine, and drank thoughtfully,
and then crossed his legs again on the fender ; and
the rain beat and sobbed outside.

He wondered if Lois's pale face had any connection with the departure of the Forsythes. Mrs.
Dale had hinted at it, though she had not dared to
quote Arabella Forsythe's triumphant secret. Then
he remembered how disappointed he had been that
nothing came of that affair. But on the whole it
would have been very lonely at the rectory without
Lois. It was just as well. Dr. Howe generally found
that most things were "just as well." Indeed, he had
been heard to say that, with a good digestion, any
sorrow showed itself to have been best inside three
years. Perhaps he had forgotten for the moment
that he was a widower ; but at all events, he said it.

So he blew his logs to a brighter blaze, and drank
the rest of his mulled wine, stirring it round and
round for the nutmeg and spice, and said to himself,

listening to the beat of the rain as he pulled Max's silky ears, that it was the worst June storm he remembered. Perhaps that was why he did not hear the front door open and close with a bang against the gust which tried to force its way into the house, blowing out the hall lights, and sending a dash of rain into Sally's face.

" Lord !" cried Sally, with a shrill scream, " it 's Miss Helen's ghost ! "

The face she saw was ghost-like indeed. It was wet and streaming with rain, and the dark eyes were strange and unseeing.

" Do not tell Miss Lois I am here," the pale lips said. " Where is my uncle ? I must see him."

Sally could only point speechlessly to the library door. Helen went swiftly towards it. She seemed to hesitate a moment before she entered, and then she opened it, and closed it again behind her, standing silently in front of it.

Dr. Howe looked up calmly, expecting to see Sally ; but the sight of that still figure, with eyes which looked at him with a curious fixedness, sent the color from his face in one moment of actual fright. " Helen !" he cried, springing to his feet. " Good heavens ! child, what is it ? What is the matter ? "

" I have come back," she answered, uttering each word with that peculiar slowness one notices in a very sick person, who tries to hear himself speak.

Dr. Howe had turned to light the lamp, but his hand shook, and Helen absently steadied the shade until he raised the wick, and then fumbled for his glasses, and turned to look at her. It was a relief to hear her speak.

"My dear," he said, his voice still tremulous, "you alarmed me terribly. Why, how wet you are!" He had laid his hand upon her shoulder to help her take off her wraps. "Bless my soul, child, you're drenched! Did you come in an open carriage? But why are you here? Did you miss your train?"

Even as he spoke, before she silently shook her head, he knew she would have been back by noon had she missed her train.

Max had come and sniffed suspiciously at her skirts before he recognized her, and then he rubbed his head against her knee, and reached up to be patted. She let her hand rest a moment on his head, and then with cold, stiff fingers tried to help her uncle take off her cloak, and lift her bonnet from her dripping hair. She made no effort to wipe the rain from her face, and Dr. Howe, with his big handkerchief, tried clumsily to do it for her.

"What is the matter, my dear?" the rector was saying nervously. "Is anything wrong with Mr. Ward? Have you had bad news? Tell me, my darling; you distress me by your silence."

Helen's throat seemed dry, and she moved her lips once or twice before the words came. "I have come back," she answered slowly, looking with absent eyes at Max, who was furtively licking her hand. "I have had a letter from John. So I have come back. I am very tired."

She looked wearily around, and swayed a little

from side to side. Dr. Howe caught her in his
arms. " My dear," he said, in a frightened voice,
" my dear — you are very ill. I 'll fetch Jean —
I 'll send for Adele ! "

Helen laid her shaking hand upon his arm. " No,
no, — I am not ill. I am only tired. I walked
from Mercer, I think; I don't quite remember.
Please do not call any one, uncle."

In spite of the wildness of her words, it was not a
delirious woman who was speaking to him, as he had
thought. " Try and tell me, then, what it all means,"
he said; " or stay, — first let me get you a glass of
wine."

He went shuffling along in his slippers to the
dining-room, and came back with a wineglass and
the little fat decanter, with the silver collar clinking
about its neck. He filled the glass, and held it to
her lips, and then stood and looked at her as she
drank, his lower lip thrust out, and perplexity and
anxiety written on every feature.

Helen handed the glass back to him, and rose.
" Thank you, uncle Archie," she said. " I — I must
go up-stairs now. I am tired."

" But, my dear child," he remonstrated, " my dear
Helen, you must tell me what all this means, first."

She looked at him entreatingly. "Not now, —
oh, not to-night."

" But, Helen," he said, " I can't be kept in suspense, you know."

He tried to put his arm about her, but she pushed
it a little aside and shook her head. " I will tell
you," she said, while Dr. Howe, not understanding

his repulse, stood with parted lips and frowning eye-brows, polishing his glasses on the skirt of his dress-ing-gown. Helen rubbed her hand across her fore-head.

"I am a little confused," she began, "but — there is not much to say. John has written that I must not come back to Lockhaven. I shall never see my husband again, uncle Archie," she added piteously.

"Why — why — why!" cried Dr. Howe. "Bless my soul, what's all this? Mr. Ward says my niece is not to return to her husband! Oh, come, now, come!"

"Need we say anything more to-night?" Helen said. "I — I cannot talk."

Nothing could have shown Dr. Howe's affection for his niece more than the way in which he said, looking at her in silence for a moment, "My child, you shall do just what you please. Come up-stairs now, and get to bed. It will be a mercy if you're not laid up with a cold to-morrow. Would you rather not see Lois? Well, then, Jean shall come and make you comfortable."

But Dr. Howe, shuffling over the bare stairs, and fuming to himself, "What's all this! Nonsense, I say, perfect nonsense!" could not fail to arouse Lois, and she called out drowsily, "Good-night, father, dear. Is anything the matter?"

"Nothing, — nothing!" cried the rector testily. "Go to sleep. Come, Helen, take my arm, and let me help you."

"Helen!" Lois exclaimed, wide awake, and

springing from her bed to rush to her cousin. " What is it?" she gasped, as she caught sight of the group.

" Nothing, I tell you," said the rector. " Go to bed at once; you 'll take cold."

But Helen, seeing the distressed face, put her hands on Lois's shoulders, and pushed her gently back into her room. " I had to come back, Lois," she said. " I will tell you why, to-morrow. I am too tired, now. Don't speak to me, please, dear."

The rector had hurried down the entry to find Jean, who indeed needed no rousing, for Sally had told her who had come. " Let me know when Miss Helen is comfortable," he said.

And when the old woman, awed by Helen's still, white face, told him his niece was in bed, he came up again, holding the decanter by the throat, and begging her to take another glass of wine. But she only turned her head away and asked to be alone. She would not say anything more, and did not seem to hear his assurances that it would be " all right in the morning," and that " she must not worry."

It was the kindest thing to her, but it was very hard for the rector to go down to his library still in ignorance. The spell of peace had been rudely broken, and his fire was out. He lifted Helen's bonnet, still heavy with rain, and laid it on the cloak she had thrown across a chair, and then stood and looked at them as though they could explain the mystery of her return. The tall clock on the stairs struck eleven, and outside the storm beat and complained.

Dr. Howe was up early the next morning. He went through the silent house before Sally had crept yawning from her room, and, throwing open the doors at each end of the hall, let a burst of sunshine and fresh wind into the darkness and stillness. Then he went out, and began to walk up and down the porch as a sort of outlet to his impatience. Over and over he said, "What can it be?" Indeed, Dr. Howe had asked himself that question even in his dreams. "I hope there's no woman at the bottom of it," he thought. "But no; Ward's a fool, but he is a good man."

He stopped once, to lift a trailing vine and twist it about a support. The rain had done great damage in the night: the locust blossoms had been torn from the trees, and the lawn was white with them; the soft, wet petals of the climbing roses were scattered upon the path by the side of the house; and a long branch of honeysuckle, wrenched from its trellis, was prone upon the porch. These small interests quieted the rector, and he was able soon to reason himself into the belief that his niece's return was a trifling affair, perhaps a little uncomfortable, and certainly silly, but he would soon make it all right; so that when he saw her coming slowly downstairs, with Lois creeping after her, almost afraid to speak, he was able to greet her very tranquilly.

"Are you rested, my child? After breakfast, we'll have a good talk, and everything shall be straightened out."

Breakfast was a dreary affair. Helen's abstraction was too profound for her to make even the pretense of eating. Once or twice, when Lois's voice pierced through the clouds and reached her heart, she looked up, and tried to reply. But they were all glad when it was over, and the rector put his arm gently over his niece's shoulders, and drew her into the library.

"If any one comes, Lois," he said, "you had better just say Helen changed her mind about going yesterday, and has come back for a few days."

"No," interrupted Helen slowly. "You had better say what is the truth, Lois. I have come back to Ashurst to stay."

"Now, my dear," remonstrated the rector when they were in the library, and he had shut the door, "that is really very unwise. These little affairs, little misunderstandings, are soon cleared up, and they are even forgotten by the people most interested in them. But outsiders never forget. So it is very unwise to speak of them."

Helen had seated herself on the other side of his writing-table, brushing away the litter of papers and unanswered letters, so that she could lean her elbow on it, and now she looked steadily across at him.

"Uncle," she said, calmly "you do not know. There is no misunderstanding. It is just what I told you last night: he thinks it best that I should leave him indefinitely. I know that it is forever. Yes, it seems to him best. And I am sure, feeling as he does, he is right. Yes, John is right."

Dr. Howe threw himself back in his revolving chair, and spun half-way round. "Helen," he said, "this is folly; you must talk like a sensible woman.

You know you cannot leave your husband. I suppose you and Ward, like all the rest of the world that is married, have had some falling out; and now, being young, you think your lives are over. Nonsense! Bless my soul, child, your aunt and I had dozens of them, and all as silly as this, I'll be bound. But I'm sure we did not take the public into our confidence by declaring that we would live apart. I should have given you credit for more sense, indeed I should."

Helen did not notice the reprimand.

"Now tell me all about it," he continued. "You know you can trust me, and I'll write your husband a letter which will make things clear."

Helen shook her head wearily. "You will not understand. Nothing can be done; it is as fixed as — death. We can neither of us alter it and be ourselves. Oh, I have tried and tried to see some way out of it, until it seems as if my soul were tired."

"I did not intend to be severe, my child," the rector said, with remorseful gentleness, "but in one way it is a more serious thing than you realize. I don't mean this foolishness of a separation; that will all be straightened out in a day or two. But we do not want it gossiped about, and your being here at all, after having started home, looks strange; and of course, if you say anything about having had a — a falling out with Ward, it will make it ten times worse. But you have n't told me what it is?"

"Yes, I'll tell you," she answered, "and then perhaps you will see that it is useless to talk about it.

I must just take up the burden of life as well as I can."

"Go on," said the rector.

"John has been much distressed lately," Helen began, looking down at her hands, clasping each other until the skin was white across the knuckles, "because I have not believed in eternal punishment. He has felt that my eternal happiness depended upon holding such a belief." Dr. Howe looked incredulous. "Some weeks ago, one of his elders came to him and told him I was spreading heresy in the church, and damning my own soul and the souls of others who might come to believe as I did, — you know I told Mrs. Davis that her husband had not gone to hell, — and he reproached John for neglecting me and his church too; for John, to spare me, had not preached as he used to, on eternal punishment. It almost killed him, uncle," she said, and her voice, which had given no hint of tears since her return, grew unsteady. "Oh, he has suffered so! and he has felt that it was his fault, a failure in his love, that I did not believe what he holds to be true."

"Heavens!" cried the rector explosively, "heresy? Is this the nineteenth century?"

"Since I have been away," Helen went on, without noticing the interruption, "they have insisted that I should be sessioned, — dealt with, they call it. John won't let me come back to that; but if that were his only reason, we could move away from Lockhaven. He has a nobler reason: he feels that this unbelief of mine will bring eternal misery to my soul, and he would convert me by any means.

He has tried all that he knows (for oh, we have discussed it endlessly, uncle Archie!), — argument, prayer, love, tenderness, and now — sorrow."

The rector was sitting very straight in his chair, his plump hands gripping the arms of it, and his lips compressed with anger, while he struggled for patience to hear this preposterous story through.

"He makes me suffer," Helen continued, "that I may be saved. And indeed I don't see how he can do anything else. If a man believes his wife will be damned for all eternity unless she accepts certain doctrines, I should think he would move heaven and earth to make her accept them. And John does believe that. In denying reprobation, I deny revelation, he says, and also the Atonement, upon which salvation depends. So now you see why he says I shall not come back to him until I have found the truth."

Then Dr. Howe burst into a torrent of indignant remonstrance. A clergyman send his wife from him because she does not believe some dogma! Were we back in the dark ages? It was too monstrously absurd! If the idiots he preached to forced him to do it, let him leave them; let him come to Ashurst. The rector would build him a meeting-house, and he could preach his abominable doctrine to anybody who was fool enough to go and hear him.

Dr. Howe was walking hastily up and down the room, gesticulating as he talked. Helen's patient eyes followed him. Again and again she tried to point out to him her husband's intense sincerity, and the necessity which his convictions forced upon him.

But the rector refused to think Mr. Ward's attitude worthy of serious consideration. "The man is insane!" he cried. "Send his wife away from him to force her into a certain belief? Madness, — I tell you, madness!"

"I cannot hear you speak so of my husband," Helen said very quietly, but it caused Dr. Howe to conceal his wrath.

"He'll think differently in a day or two," he said. "This nonsense won't last."

Then Helen, having exhausted all her arguments to show that John was immovable, said, "Let me read you what he says himself; then you will understand, perhaps, how real it all is to him, and how he cannot help it."

"Bah!" cried Dr. Howe, and certainly it was trying to have Helen attempt to excuse such folly. "I've no patience with — There, there! I didn't mean to lose my temper, but bless my soul, this is the worst thing I ever knew. See here, Helen, if the man is so determined, you'll have to change your views, or go back to your old views, I mean, — I don't know what you do believe, — that's all there is about it."

Helen was unfolding John's letter, and she looked up at her uncle with a fleeting smile. "Change my views so that I can go back? Do you think that would satisfy John? Do you think I could? Why, uncle Archie, do you believe in eternal damnation? I know you pray to be delivered from it in the Litany, but do you believe in it?"

"That has nothing to do with the question,

Helen," he answered, frowning, " and of course I believe that the consequences of sin are eternal."

" You know that is not what the prayer means," she insisted; " you have to put your private interpretation upon it. Well, it is my private interpretation which John thinks is sin, and sin which will receive what it denies."

" Well, you must believe it, then," the rector said, striking his fist on the arm of his chair; " it is the wife's place to yield ; and while I acknowledge it is all folly, you must give in."

" You mean," she said, " that I must say I believe it. Can I change a belief ? You know I cannot, uncle Archie. And when you hear what John says, you will see I must be true, no matter where truth leads me."

Helen knew every word of that letter by heart. She had read it while she drove towards the depot, and when she dismissed the carriage it was with a vague idea of flying to Lockhaven, and brushing all this cobweb of unreason away, and claiming her right to take her place at her husband's side. But as she sat in the station, waiting, every sentence of the letter began to burn into her heart, and she slowly realized that she could not go back. The long day passed, and the people, coming and going, looked curiously at her ; one kindly woman, seeing the agony in her white face, came up and asked her if she were ill, and could she help her ? Helen stared at her like a person in a dream, and shook her head. Then, in a numb sort of way, she began to understand that she must go back to Ashurst.

She did not notice that it had begun to rain, or think of a carriage, but plodded, half blind and dazed, over the country road to her old home, sometimes sitting down, not so much to rest as to take the letter from its envelope again and read it.

She looked at it now, with a sudden gasp of pain; it was as though a dagger had been turned in a wound. It seemed too sacred to read to Dr. Howe, but it was just to John that it should be heard, even if only partly understood; and it was also just to her — for Helen had one of those healthy souls which could be just to itself. With the letter had come a clear and logical statement of the doctrine of reprobation, together with the arguments and reasons for holding it; besides this, there was a list of books which he meant to send her. All these she handed to her uncle.

" I will not read you all he writes," she said, " but even a little will show you the hopelessness of thinking I can ever go back to him. He tells me first of a meeting of his Session, where the elders told him they wished to have me summoned before them, and of another visit from Mr. Dean, of whom I spoke to you, insisting that John had been faithless in his duty to his church and me. 'I could only listen,' he writes, 'in assenting anguish, when he charged me with having been careless of your spiritual life; and when he said that the sin of your unbelief had crept from soul to soul, like an insidious and fatal disease unseen by the eyes of the church, until spiritual death, striking first one and then another, roused us to our danger. How can I write that word " us," as though I arrayed myself with them against you, dearest! Yet it is not you, but this fatal unbelief! They charged me, these elders, whose place it is to guard the spiritual life of the church, with having preached peace to them, when there was no peace, and leaving unspoken the words of warning that eternal death awaits unrepented sin. They told me Davis had died in his sin, not having had the fear of hell before his eyes to convert his soul. And, Helen, I know it is all true! When they insisted that you, like any other member of the church, should be brought before the Session, that they might reason with you, and by the blessing of God convert your soul to a saving knowledge of the truth, or at least bind you to silence for the sake of others, I would not listen. Here I felt my right was greater than theirs, for you are like my own soul. I told them I would not permit it; I knew it would but drive you further from grace. I cannot think I sinned in this, though I apparently neglect a means of salvation for you; but I could not subject you to that, — I could not put your soul into their hands. I distrust myself (I have need, having loved earthly happiness more than your immortal peace, and called it wisdom), yet I think I am right in this. God grant that the means of grace which I choose instead, which will crucify my own heart, may, by his blessing, save your soul. And I have faith to believe it will. The promises of God fail not.

. . . .

" ' Oh, Helen, if I loved you less! Sometimes, in

these two weeks, while this purpose has been growing up in my mind, I have shrunk back, and cried
that I could not drink of the cup, and in the depth
of human weakness I have felt, If I loved her less, I
could not do what I have to do, and so the pain
would be spared. But love is too mighty for me. I
shall save you! When I think of the months since
we were married, which I have kept unruffled by a
single entreaty that you would turn from darkness
into light, my eyes are blasted by the sight of my
own sin; despair and death lay hold upon me. But
He has had mercy upon me. He has shown me one
way in which you shall be saved, and by his strength
I am not disobedient to the heavenly vision. Reason
and argument have not shown you the light. Joy
and peace have not led you to it. There is one
other path, beloved, which I have faith to believe
shall not fail. It is sorrow. Sorrow can bring the
truth home to you as no other thing will. The relentless pressure of grief will force you to seek for
light. It will admit of no evasion; it will receive
no subtilty; it will bring you face to face with the
eternal verities; it will save your soul. And what
sorrow, Helen, can come to you such as making me
suffer? And is there a pang which can tear my soul
in this world like absence from my beloved? I tram-
ple my own happiness under my feet. Too long
I have been weak, too long I have loved you with but
half my nature; now I am strong. Therefore I say,
before God, for your soul's sake, you shall not see
my face until you have found the truth. This pain,
which will be to me but the just punishment for

my sin, will be to you like some sharp and bitter
medicine which shall heal you of what would otherwise bring eternal death. Even as I write I am
filled with strength from God to save you. For God
has shown me the way. And it shall be soon, — I
know it shall be soon. The Lord's hand is not
shortened that it cannot save. He has revealed to
me the one last way of showing you the truth, and
He will lighten your eyes. Yet, oh, my love, my
wife, help me to be strong for you, — my Helen,
help me in these days or weeks of waiting.

. . . .

"'There is one mercy vouchsafed to me who am all
unworthy of the least favor : it is the knowledge of
your understanding it all, — the bitter distress, the
absolute conviction, and the necessity which follows ·
it. You see what the temptation was to fly with you
to some spot where your unbelief could not injure
any one, and there work and pray for your salvation ; leaving these souls, which my neglect of you
and so of them, has allowed to drift deep into sin.
You will understand that, believing (oh, knowing,
Helen, knowing) that salvation depends upon a
right conception of truth, I have no choice but to
force you by any means to save your soul. This
knowledge makes me strong. So I am set, with
strength which you yourself give me, to inflict this
suffering upon you. Take this absence and use its
bitterness to sting you to search for truth. Take its
anguish to God. Pray for light, pray for the Spirit
of God. And when light comes — Oh, love, the
thought of that joy seems too great to bear except

before the throne of God! I shall not write again; you will meet this grief in the solitude of your own soul, where even I dare not come to break the silence which may be the voice of God. Write me any questionings, that I may help those first faint stirrings of the Holy Spirit, but unless questionings come I shall be silent.' "

Helen had not read all of this aloud, and there was yet more, on which she looked a moment before she folded the letter. The closing words were full of a human tenderness too divine and holy for any heart but her own; a faint smile crept about her lips for a moment, as she leaned out of her distress to rest upon her husband's love, and then she woke again to the present.

CHAPTER XXVII.

But the rector was not softened by John's letter; there was a curl of contempt upon his lip which colored his words, though with Helen's quiet eyes upon him he forced himself to speak calmly.

"You see he expects you to return. This idea of yours, of a separation, is nonsense. I told you so, in the first place. Now the only thing to do is to go to Lockhaven, and just say that your convictions are immovable (if they are, though it would be wiser to make a concession, Helen), so there is no use in experimenting in this absurd way. Absurd? Why it is — it is" —

Dr. Howe's face was crimson, and he could find no epithet strong enough to use.

"Do you suppose I have not told John that I could not change?" Helen said sadly, ignoring the suggestion of a concession; "and to go back, uncle Archie, — you don't know John! He thinks I will come back, — you are right there, — but only because he thinks this plan of his is an inspiration from God, and will lead me to believe as he wishes. It will not, and you know it. But John would feel that he was doubting God to let me come, if the promise were unfulfilled. So I shall never return. Oh, must we discuss it? It is fixed; it can never be changed. If only it could be understood at once! There is no hope."

Dr. Howe rose, and walked about the room a moment, breathing hard, and swallowing once or twice, as though to choke some hot words. Then he sat down, and began to argue.

First, he tried to prove to Helen that there was a hell, but unconsciously he veered to assertions that it made no difference, anyhow; that of course the doctrine of eternal damnation was preposterous, and that she must persuade Mr. Ward to drop the subject. He reasoned and threatened, then he expostulated and implored, ending all with, " You must go back, and at once."

Helen had been silent, but when he finished she said, so absently that he knew she had not been listening, " Shall I explain why I have come back, or would you prefer to do it ? "

" Explain ? " cried the rector. " What are you thinking of ? Of course not! It is not to be known."

" It must be known, I think," Helen answered calmly. " I am here, and I shall stay here, so it seems to me better to disarm gossip by telling the truth at once."

Dr. Howe sunk back in his chair, and looked at his niece in speechless annoyance.

" You had better let me tell them, uncle Archie," she said simply; " it will be less unpleasant for you."

Then he regained his voice: " It is not to be told, Helen. I shall not allow it. If you have no sense, I 'll take the matter into my own hands. If people choose to gossip about your being here a few

days or a week, — it may take a week for this folly
to blow over, — why, they can, that's all. I will
not — you hear me, Helen? — I will not enter into
any absurd explanations."

Helen lifted her heavy eyes, and looked at him
a moment, and then she said, " Aunt Deely ? "

Dr. Howe suffered a sudden collapse. " Well,
I — ah — well, perhaps Adele. I suppose Adele
must know it. I don't know but what her common
sense may be good for you, my dear. Yes, I'll tell
Adele."

" I should like to have Lois understand it," Helen
said.

" Well," Dr. Howe conceded, " yes — I suppose
you might mention it to Lois — because " —

" I don't want her to think anything wrong of
John," Helen explained.

Dr. Howe stared at her blankly, but did not
burst into wrathful exclamations ; he was actually
exhausted in mind and body; this controversy had
been too much for him. But that remark of Helen's
ended it. She went slowly up-stairs, clinging to
the balustrade as though she needed some support,
yet she had not spoken of being tired. She passed
Lois, sitting on the window - seat which ran across
the broad landing, but did not seem to see her,
and there was something in her cousin's face which
kept the young girl dumb.

Dr. Howe did not go to Dale house until the next
day ; he vaguely hoped something would turn up
before his sister discovered Helen's presence at the
rectory, which would make this humiliating confes-

sion unnecessary. But nothing happened except the arrival of a letter from John Ward to Dr. Howe, explaining his convictions and reiterating his determination.

Helen kept in her own room that day and the next, so Gifford Woodhouse, who came to the rectory, did not guess her presence, since Lois had been admonished to be silent concerning it, and no one else chanced to call. Of course the servants knew. Dr. Howe ground his teeth as he reflected that Sally would probably tattle the whole thing; the more so, if she were charged not to mention it. Yet he was rather relieved, when he went to tell his sister, to find that she knew the main fact already.

"Helen's back again!" she cried as soon as she saw him.

He found her in the big cool dining-room, cutting out pieces of paper for the tops of her pots of strawberry jam, and fringing them delicately with a little pair of shining scissors.

"Well, Archibald," she said, looking at him over her glasses, as he sat down at the other end of the polished table, "this is pretty hot, isn't it? I'll have Betty bring you a sangaree; there's a fan on the window-sill, if you want it; I never have patience to use a fan. Henry's in his library. I declare, it is as cold as a vault in that room; but you'd better not go down. We Howes are too rheumatic for such damp places."

Betty brought the sangaree, and the rector diverted himself while he put off the evil moment of explanation, by clinking the ice against the glass.

" Betty was down in the village last night," Mrs. Dale was saying, " and she saw your Sally, and she told her Helen did not get off on Monday. What in the world does that mean ? I do dislike to see the child so changeable. I suppose she wants to wait and go with Lois, after all ? But why did n't she make up her mind before she started ? And all this talk about getting back to her husband! Oh, these young wives, — they don't mind leaving their husbands!"

" Yes, she 's back," said the rector gloomily.

" What do you mean ? " Mrs. Dale asked quickly, for his tone did not escape her.

Then he told her the whole story. There was a moment's silence when he had finished. At last Mrs. Dale said violently, " Well! " and again, " Well! " After that she rose, and brushing the clippings of paper from her black silk apron, she said, " We will go and talk this over in the parlor, Archibald."

The rector followed her, miserably. Though he had a clear conscience, in that he had treated the ridiculous affair with the utmost severity, and had done all he could to make Helen return to her husband, he yet trembled as he thought how his sister would reproach him. (" Though I can't help it! " he said to himself. " Heaven knows I used every argument short of force. I could n't compel a reluctant wife to return to an unwilling husband, especially when she thinks the husband is all right.") " You see, she approves of Ward," he groaned.

Mrs. Dale sat down, but the rector walked nervously about, jingling some keys in his pocket.

" It is very distressing," he said.

" Distressing ? " cried Mrs. Dale. " It is worse than distressing. It is disgraceful, that's what it is, — disgraceful ! What will Deborah Woodhouse say, and the Draytons ? I tell you, Archibald, it must be put a stop to, at once! "

" That is very easy to say," began Dr. Howe.

" It is very easy to do, if there's a grain of sense in your family. Just send your niece " —

" She's your niece, too, Adele," he interrupted.

But Mrs. Dale did not pause — " back to her husband. You ought to have taken her yesterday morning. It is probably all over Ashurst by this time! "

" But you forget," objected Dr. Howe, " he won't let her come ; you can't change his views by saying Helen must go back."

" But what does it matter to her what his views are ? " said Mrs. Dale.

" It matters to him what her views are," answered Dr. Howe despondently. Somehow, since he had begun to talk to his sister, he had grown almost as hopeless as Helen.

" Then Helen must change her views," Mrs. Dale said promptly. " I have no patience with women who set up their own Ebenezers. A woman should be in subjection to her own husband, I say, — and so does St. Paul. In my young days we were taught to love, honor, and obey. Helen needs to be reminded of her duty, and I 'll see that she is."

" Well, I wish you success," said the rector grimly.

" And I 'll have it ! " Mrs. Dale retorted.

" But you don't take into consideration," Dr.

Howe said, " that Helen will not say one thing when she thinks another. How can you change a person's belief? I have been all over it, Adele. It is perfectly useless ! "

The brother and sister looked at each other a moment silently ; then Mrs. Dale said, " Well, if you ask my advice " —

" I did n't ; there 's no use. Helen will be her own adviser, you can depend upon that. I only just wanted you to know the facts. No outsider can direct the affairs of a man and woman who are entirely determined."

" I am not an outsider," returned Mrs. Dale, " though you can call yourself one, if you choose. And I am going to give you advice, and I hope you 'll be sensible enough to take it. You have just got to go and see this Mr. Ward, and tell him he must take Helen back; tell him we cannot have such things in our family. A wife separated from her husband, — why, good gracious, just think of it, Archibald ! "

" Do you suppose I have n't thought of it ? " demanded the rector.

" And Helen must go," continued Mrs. Dale, " belief or no belief."

Her brother shook his head, and sighed.

" I don't believe it will do any good for me to see him, but of course I shall go to Lockhaven unless I get a favorable answer to my letter. I wrote him yesterday. But do you imagine that any talk of our feelings is going to move a man like Ward ? His will is like iron. I saw that in his letter to Helen. I sup-

pose it pains him to do this. I suppose he does suffer, in a way. But if he can contemplate her distress
unmoved, do you think anything I can urge will
change him? He'll wait for her conversion, if it
takes her whole life."

" But Helen has been confirmed," said Mrs. Dale,
in a bewildered way ; " what more does he want ? "

" He wants her to be converted, I tell you," cried
her brother, " and he's bound to bring it about!
He uses the illustration of giving medicine to a sick
child to insure its recovery, no matter at what cost
of pain to the child or the giver."

" But isn't it the same thing ? " persisted Mrs.
Dale : " converted — confirmed ? We don't use such
expressions in the Church, but it is the same thing."

" ' Experience a change of heart,' Ward says in
his letter; 'be convicted of the sin of unbelief'!" the
rector said contemptuously, and ignoring his sister's
question ; " but conversion with him merely means a
belief in hell, so far as I can make out."

" Well, of course Helen is all wrong not to believe
in hell," said Mrs. Dale promptly; " the Prayer-
Book teaches it, and she must. I'll tell her so.
All you have to do is to see this Mr. Ward and tell
him she will ; and just explain to him that she has
been confirmed, — we don't use those Methodistical
expressions in the Church. Perhaps the sect he belongs to does, but one always thinks of them as
rather belonging to the lower classes, you know. I
suppose we ought not to expect anything else from
such a person, — who ever heard of his people? I
always said the marriage would turn out badly," she

added triumphantly. "You remember, I told you so?"

The rector sighed. After all, Mrs. Dale did not help him. It was useless to try to impress her with the theological side of the matter, as she only returned with fresh vigor to the charge that it was a disgrace to the family. So he rose to go, saying, "Well, I 'll wait for Ward's letter, and if he persists in this insanity I 'll start for Lockhaven. You might see Helen, and see what you can do."

As Mrs. Dale began in her positive way to say how he ought to talk to " this man," Mr. Dale came in.

"I thought I heard your voice," he said to his brother-in-law, " and I came up " — he looked deprecatingly at his wife — " to ask you to step down and have a pipe. I want to speak to you about Denner's books."

But before Dr. Howe could answer, Mrs. Dale poured forth all the troublesome and disgraceful story of the " separated husband and wife." Mr. Dale listened intently ; once he flourished his red handkerchief across his eyes as he blew his nose. When he did this, he scattered some loose tobacco about, and Mrs. Dale stopped to reprimand him. " I tell you, " she ended emphatically, " it is this new-fangled talk of woman's rights that has done all this. What need has Helen of opinions of her own? A woman ought to be guided by her husband in everything! "

"You see it is pretty bad, Henry," said the rector.

" It is, — it is," said the older man, his mild eyes glistening; " but oh, Archibald, how he loves her! "

" Loves her ? " cried the other two together.

" Yes," continued Mr. Dale slowly ; " one feels as if we ought not even to discuss it, for we are scarcely capable of understanding it. The place whereon we stand is holy ground."

" Henry," said his wife, " there 's no fool like an old fool. You don't know what you are talking about."

But when Dr. Howe, softening a little since Mr. Dale did not abuse John Ward, said he must tell Helen that, — it would please her, — Mrs. Dale begged him to do nothing of the sort.

" It would be just like her to consider the whole affair a unique mode of expressing affection. We had better try to show her it is a disgrace to the family. Love, indeed! Well, I don't understand love like that! "

" No," Mr. Dale responded, " no, I suppose not. But, my dear, don't you wish you did ? "

When Dr. Howe told Helen of his plan of going to Lockhaven, she tried to show him that it was useless; but as she saw his determination, she ceased to oppose him. She would have spared John if she could (and she knew how impossible it was that the rector could move her husband), yet she felt that her family had a right to insist upon a personal explanation, and to make an effort, however futile, to induce her husband to take her home. In the mean time, they waited for an answer to the rector's letter. Helen had written, but she knew no answer would come to her. She understood too well that sweet and gentle nature, which yielded readily in small things, and was possessed of invincible determination in crises, to hope that John could change. Yet she had written; she had shared her hopelessness as well as her grief with him, when she told him how impossible it was for her to think as he did. She showed how fast and far she had drifted into darkness and unbelief since she had left him, yet she held out no hope that a return to him could throw any light into those eternal shadows. " I understand it all," she had written, stopping to comfort him even while she told him how futile was his pain and hers, " and oh, how you must suffer, my darling, but it cannot be helped unless you free yourself from your convictions. Perhaps that will come some time; until then, you can only be true to yourself. But I understand it all, — I know."

Those days of waiting were hard to bear. The distance between her uncle and herself had suddenly widened; and she could not see that beneath his irritation there was really a very genuine sympathy.

She had vaguely hoped that Lois would comfort her, for one turns instinctively in grief to the nearest loving thing, and she knew her cousin loved her. Yet Lois had not been able to understand, and Helen would hear no words of sympathy which were not as much for John as for herself.

It was not until Thursday that she had told Lois why she had come back. They were in their pleasant sitting-room, Lois walking restlessly about, with such puzzled expectation on her face that its white

sadness was almost banished. Helen sat with her
hands clasped loosely in her lap, and leaning her
head against the window. Below, there was the
bloom and glory of the garden, butterflies darted
through the sunshine, and the air was full of the
honeyed hum of the bees. But the silence of the
room seemed only a breathless anxiety, which forbade rest of mind or body; and so Helen had
roused herself, and tried to tell her cousin what it
all meant; but even as she talked she felt Lois's unspoken condemnation of her husband, and her voice
hardened, and she continued with such apparent indifference Lois was entirely deceived. "So you
see," she ended, "I cannot go back to Lockhaven."

Lois, walking back and forth, as impatient as her
father might have been, listened, her eyes first fill-
ing with tears, and then flashing angrily. She
threw herself on her knees beside Helen, as she
finished, and put her arms about her cousin's waist,
kissing her listless hands in a passion of sympathy.
"Oh, my dear!" she cried, her cheeks wet with
tears, "how dreadful — how horrible! Oh, Helen,
darling, my poor darling!"

Lois did not stop to consider the theological side
of the matter, which was a relief to Helen. She
tried to quiet the young girl's distress, holding her
bright head against her breast, and soothing her
with gentle words.

"If I were you," Lois said at last, "I would go
back to Lockhaven; I would *go*, if it had to be in
disguise!" —

"Not if you loved John," Helen answered.

"How can you bear it?" Lois whispered, look-ing up into the calm face with a sort of awe which checked her tears. " It is so cruel, Helen, you can-not forgive him."

" There is nothing to forgive; I hoped you would understand that, Lois. John cannot do anything else, don't you see? Why, I would not love him as I do, if, having such convictions, he was not true to them. He must be true before anything else."

Lois was sitting on the floor in front of her, clasping her knees with her arms, and rocking back and forth. " Well," she cried hotly, " I don't un-derstand anything about his convictions, but I tell you what it is, Helen, I do understand how hard it is for you! And I can never forgive him, if you can. It is all very well to think about truth, but it seems to me he ought to think about you."

" But don't you see," Helen explained, still vaguely hoping that Lois would understand, " he thinks only of me? Why, Lois, it is all for me."

Lois's face was flushed with excitement. "I don't care! " she cried, " it is cruel — cruel — cruel! "

Helen looked at her steadily a moment, and then she said patiently, " The motive is what makes cruelty, Lois. And can't you see that it is only be-cause of his love that he does this? If he loved me less, he could not do it."

" Heavens! " Lois exclaimed, springing to her feet, " I wish he loved you less, then! No, there is no use saying things like that, Helen; he is narrow and bigoted, — he is a cruel fanatic." She did not see that Helen had half risen from her chair, and

was watching her with gleaming eyes. " He actually prides himself on being able to make you suffer, — you read me that yourself out of his letter.
He 's a bad man, and I 'm glad you 've done with
him " —

She would have said more, but Helen had followed her swiftly across the room, and grasping
her arm until the girl cried out with pain, she put
her hand over those relentless young lips. " Hush ! "
she cried, in a terrible voice ; " do not dare to speak
so to me ! If I hear such words again, I shall leave
this house. You may not be able to see my husband's nobleness, but at least you can be silent."

Lois pushed her hand away, and stared at her in
amazement. " I did n't mean to offend you," she
stammered. " I only meant that he " —

" Do not speak of him ! " Helen said passionately,
her breath still quick, and her face white to the
lips. " I do not wish to hear what you meant ! Oh,
Lois, Lois, I thought that you " — She turned away,
and pressed her hands hard on her eyes a moment ;
then she said, " I understand — I know — your affection for me prompted it — but I cannot listen, Lois,
if you have such feelings about him. I will take
your sympathy for granted after this. I do not want
to talk about it again."

Lois went silently out of the room, her heart overflowing with love for her cousin, and added rage at
the man who had come between them. She found
Gifford walking about in the hall down-stairs, and,
forgetful of her father's injunction, she went quickly
up to him, trembling with excitement, and half sobbing.

"Giff — oh, Giff — that man, that John Ward, has sent Helen back! She's here — she can't go home!"

Gifford was too astounded to speak.

"Yes," Lois cried, clinging to his arm, her eyes overflowing, "he is a wicked man — he is cruel — and she thinks I am, Giff, just because I said he was!"

Lois's agitation drove him into his most deliberate speech.

"What do you mean? I do not understand."

"Of course not! Nobody could think of anything so awful. Come into the library, and I'll tell you. Father does not want it spoken of, Gifford, but since you know she's here, I might as well explain."

The room was deserted, except for Max, who was stretched on the cool hearthstones; it was full of dusky shadows lurking in the wainscoted corners; the outside shutters were bowed, and only two thin streaks of sunshine traveled in from the warm sweet garden outside. Some roses in a bowl on the table filled the air with fragrance.

Lois hurried nervously through the story, breaking into angry grief that John Ward should have made Helen angry at her. For she had told Gifford how she had tried to console her cousin.

"It makes me hate John Ward more than ever!" she said, striking her hands passionately together. "Oh, Giff, isn't it awful?"

"Poor fellow!" said the young man, deeply moved, "poor Ward! It is worse for him than it is for Helen."

" Oh, how can you say so ? " she cried ; " but I 'm
sure I hope it is ! "

" He won't weaken," Gifford went on slowly.
" He will stand like a rock for what he believes is
right, and he will be more apt to believe it is right
if it nearly kills him."

" I wish it would ! And Helen, poor darling,
thinks he loves her.   What sort of love does he call
this ? "

" Oh, it is love," Gifford answered ; " and I tell
you, Lois, it is a height of love that is ideal, — it is
the measure of Ward's soul."   They were both so
much in earnest, there was not the slightest self-consciousness in this talk of love, even though Gifford
added, " I never knew a man capable of such devotion, and there are few women like Helen, who could
inspire it."

" But, Giff," Lois said, not caring to discuss John
Ward's character, " did you suppose anybody could
be so narrow ?   Think how bigoted he is !   And
nobody believes in hell now as he does."

"I don't know about that, Lois," Gifford responded
slowly.   " Lots of people do, only they don't live up
to their belief.   If the people who say they believe
in hell were in dead earnest, the world would have
been converted long ago."

" He is a wicked man ! " Lois cried inconse-
quently.

But Gifford shook his head.   " No, he is not.   And
more than that, Lois, you ought to consider that this
belief of Ward's, if it is crude, is the husk which
has kept safe the germ of truth, — the consequences

of sin are eternal. There is no escape from character."

"Oh, yes," she answered, "but that is not theology, you know : we don't put God into that."

"Heaven help us if we do not!" the young man
said reverently. "It is all God, Lois; perhaps not
God as John Ward thinks of Him, a sort of mag-
nified man, for whom he has to arrange a scheme of
salvation, a kind of an apology for the Deity, but the
power and the desire for good in ourselves. That
seems to me to be God. Sometimes I feel as though
all our lives were a thought of the Eternal, which
would have as clear an expression as we would let it."

Lois had not followed his words, and said impatiently as he finished, "Well, anyhow, he is cruel,
and Helen should not have felt as she did when I
said so."

Gifford hesitated. "She could not help it. How
could she let you say it ? "

"What ! " cried Lois, "you think he's not
cruel ? "

"His will is not cruel," Gifford answered, "but
I meant — I meant — she could n't let you speak as
you did of John Ward, to his wife."

Lois flung her head back. "You think I said too
much ? " she asked. "You don't half sympathize
with her, Gifford. I did n't think you could be so
hard."

"I mean it was not quite kind in you," he said
slowly.

"I suppose you think it was n't right ? "

"No, Lois, it was not right," he answered, with
a troubled face.

" Well, Gifford," she said, her voice trembling a
little, " I 'm sorry. But it seems I never do do anything right. You — you see nothing but faults.
Oh, they 're there ! " she cried desperately. " Nobody knows that better than I do ; but I never
thought any one would say that I did not love
Helen " —

" I did n't say so, Lois," the young man interrupted eagerly ; " only I felt as though it was n't
fair for me to think you did not do just right, and
not tell you so."

" Oh, of course," Lois said lightly, " but I don't
think we are so very friendly that I can claim such
consideration. You are always finding fault — and
— and about Helen you misunderstand ; we can
say anything to each other. I am afraid I exag-
gerated her annoyance. She knew what I meant, —
she said she did ; she — she agreed with me, I 've
not a doubt ! "

" I always seem to blunder," Gifford said, his
face stinging from the cut about friendship. " I
never seem to know how to tell the truth without
giving offense — but — but, Lois, you know I think
you are the best woman in the world."

" You have a pretty poor idea of women, then,"
she responded, a lump in her throat making her
voice unsteady, " but I 'm sure I don't care what you
think. I have a right to say what I want to
Helen."

She ran out of the room, for she would not let
Gifford see her cry. " I don't care what he thinks ! "
she said, as she fled panting into the attic, and

bolted the door as though she feared he would follow her. But then she began to remember that he had said she was the best woman in the world, and to her dismay she found herself smiling a little. "What a wretch I am!" she said sternly. "Mr. Denner is dead, and Helen is in such distress, and — and Dick Forsythe may come back! How can I be pleased at anything?"

CHAPTER XXVIII.

OF course it was soon known that Helen Ward was at the rectory, but to the Misses Woodhouse, at least, her presence was not of enough importance to speculate or gossip about. Gifford had merely said Helen had changed her mind about going, and would be in Ashurst a few days longer, and the little ladies had such an absorbing interest of their own they did not ask many questions. Miss Ruth only remarked that she wondered how she could be satisfied to stay away from her husband so long, and Miss Deborah replied that the young did not understand serious attachment.

To both sisters a vague happiness had come in these last few weeks, and a certain sense of importance. Each felt it for herself, but was unable to realize it for the other, yet constantly encountered it with irritated astonishment, when the desire to confide was strong.

Once Miss Ruth, tearful with the memory of that last look from Mr. Denner's dying eyes, tried to approach the subject delicately, but was met with such amazing certainty on the part of Miss Deborah, and a covert allusion to the value of the miniature, that she was silenced. And again, — on Dr. Howe's return from Lockhaven, — Miss Deborah's condescension in telling Miss Ruth she might accompany her

to the graveyard fell somewhat flat when she found
that her sister had intended going, and had even
picked some flowers to put on Mr. Denner's grave.
However, they went together, a gentle seriousness on
each face, and in an unusual silence.   Their parents
were buried here, so that it was not altogether sentiment which made them sad.

A white, dusty road climbed the hill which overlooked the village on the east, and on its brow,
facing the sunrise, was the little group of Ashurst's
dead.

The blossoming grass grew long and tangled here ;
the gray headstones slanted a little, or had even
fallen, and some of the inscriptions were hidden by
moss.   The place was full of shadowy silence, only
broken by the rustle of the leaves and small bird-
cries, or, from down in the valley, the faint tinkle of
a cow-bell.   Cypresses stood dark against the blue
sky, swaying a little in the soft wind, and from the
top of one of them flew suddenly a brown hawk, his
shadow floating from the green dusk under the trees
out over the sunny meadow below.

The two sisters went to the graves of their father
and mother first, and laid some flowers on them,
and stood a moment looking at them silently.   Their
sighs were rather a reverent recognition of an old
grief than real sorrow, for it was many years ago
that these two had been laid here ; the simple souls
were too happy to understand the pathos of a forgotten grief, indeed, they did not even know that
they had forgotten it.

As they turned away, Miss Ruth said in a hushed

voice, "It is over by Dr. Howe's lot, sister. You can see it under that larch." So they went towards this one new grave, stepping softly, and stopping by some familiar name to brush away the grass that hid the inscription, or lay a blossom against the stone. They spoke once or twice of those who lay there, calling them by their first names, yet with that curious lowering of the voice which shows with what dignity death has invested what was once familiar.

They were silent as they laid their flowers on the fresh earth of Mr. Denner's grave, over which the kindly grass had not yet thrown its veil; and Miss Deborah stopped to put a single rose upon the sunken, mossy spot where, forty years before, the little sister had been laid to rest. Both the little ladies frankly wiped their eyes, though with no thought except for the old friendship which had ended here. They would have turned to go, then, but Miss Deborah laid her hand on Miss Ruth's arm. "Why, sister," she said, "who is that by Mary Jeffrey's grave?"

Some one was lying upon the grass, her cheek resting against the small marble cross at the head of the grave, and one arm thrown around it.

"It must be Helen!" answered Miss Ruth anxiously. "How imprudent!"

They went towards the prostrate figure, — there were no divisions in the Ashurst burying-ground, — and Miss Deborah stooped and touched her on the shoulder, saying in a shocked voice, for Helen was shaken with sobs, "Why, my dear child, what is the matter?"

Helen started violently, and then sat up, brushing the tears away, and struggling to speak calmly. " I — I did not know any one was here."

" We were just going," Miss Ruth replied in her kind little voice, " but we were grieved to see you troubled, my dear ? "

Miss Ruth could not help saying it in a questioning way, for, in spite of Ashurst traditions of parental love, it could hardly be imagined that Helen was crying for a mother she had never known.

" You are very kind," Helen said, the tears still trembling in her eyes. " Something did trouble me — and — and I came here."

The sisters spoke some gentle words of this young mother, dead now for more than twenty years, and then went softly away, full of sympathy, yet fearing to intrude, though wondering in their kind hearts what could be the matter. But their curiosity faded ; Mr. Denner's grave was a much more important thing than Helen's unknown grief.

" I dare say she misses her husband ? " Miss Ruth suggested.

But Miss Deborah thought that quite improbable. " For she could go home, you know, if that was the case."

And here the sisters dropped the subject.

As for Helen, she still lingered in the silent graveyard. She felt, with the unreasoning passion of youth, that the dead gave her more comfort than the living. Lois had scarcely dared to speak to her since that talk in their sitting-room, and Dr. Howe's silence was like a pall over the whole house. So

she had come here to be alone, and try to fancy
what her husband and her uncle had said to each
other, for Dr. Howe had refused to enter into the details of his visit.

His interview with her husband had only resulted
in a greater bitterness on the part of the rector. He
had waited for John Ward's answer to his letter,
and its clear statement of the preacher's position,
and its assertion that his convictions were unchangeable, gave him no hope that anything could be accomplished without a personal interview.   Discussion
with a man who actually believed that this cruel and
outrageous plan of his, was appointed by God as a
means to save his wife's soul, was absurd and undignified, but it had to be.   The rector sighed impatiently as he handed her husband's letter to Helen.

" He is lost to all sense of propriety ; apparently
he has no thought of what he owes you. Well, I
shall go to Lockhaven to-morrow."

" It is all for me ! " Helen said.   " Oh, uncle
Archie, if you would just understand that ! "

Dr. Howe gave an explosive groan, but he only
said, " Tell Lois to pack my bag. I 'll take the
early train.   Oh, Helen, why can't you be like other
women?   Why do you have to think about beliefs ?
Your mother never doubted things; why do you ?
Is n't it enough that older and wiser people than
you do not question the faith ? "

At the last moment he begged her to accompany
him. " Together, we can bring the man to his
senses," he pleaded, and he secretly thought that
not even the hardness and heartlessness of John

Ward could withstand the sorrow in her face. But she refused to consider it.

"Have you no message for him?" he asked.

"No," she answered.

"Sha'n't I tell him how you — miss him, Helen?"

A light flashed across her face, but she said simply, "John knows," and her uncle had to be content with that.

Dr. Howe grew more intolerant with each mile of his journey. Every incident touched him with a personal annoyance at the man he was going to see. The rattling, dingy cars on the branch railroad afflicted him with an irritated sense of being modern; the activity about the shabby station jarred upon his remembrance of Ashurst's mellow quiet; the faces of the men in the lumber-yards, full of aggressive good-nature, offended his ideas of dignity and reserve. A year ago, Dr. Howe would have thought all this very entertaining, and simple, and natural. Now, that a man who lived in such a place, among such people, should have it in his power to place the Howes in a conspicuous and painful position was unbearable!

By the time he reached the parsonage, to which an officious young person of whom he had inquired his way conducted him, he had attained a pitch of angry excitement which drove all theological arguments out of his mind. Alfaretta greeted him with a blank stare, and then a sudden brightening of her face as he gave his name.

"You 're her uncle!" she cried. "How is she? and when is she comin' back? She ain't sick?" —

this with quick alarm, for Dr. Howe had not answered her questions.

"No, no, my good woman," he said impatiently, "certainly not. Where is your master?"

"The preacher's not home," the girl answered coldly. She was not used to being called "my good woman," if she did live out. "You can wait, if you want to;" but there, her anxiety getting the better of her resentment, she added, "Is she comin' back soon?"

"I'll wait," said Dr. Howe briefly, walking past her into John Ward's study.

"Insufferable people!" he muttered. He looked about him as he entered the room, and the poverty of the bookshelves did not escape his keen eyes, nor the open volume of Jonathan Edwards on the writing-table. There was a vase beside it, which held one dried and withered rose; but it is doubtful if the pathos of the flower which was to await Helen's return would have softened him, even if he could have known it. He stopped and glanced at the book, and then began to read it, holding it close to his eyes, while, with his other hand behind him, he grasped his hat and stick.

He read the frequently quoted passages from Edwards, that God holds man over hell as a man might hold a spider or some loathsome insect over the fire, with the satisfaction one feels in detecting a proof of the vicious nature of an enemy. "Ward is naturally cruel," he said to himself. "I've always thought so. That speech of his about slavery showed it."

He put down the book with an emphasis which argued ill for his opinion of a man who could study such words, and began to pace up and down the room like some caged animal, glancing once with a smothered exclamation at the old leather-covered volume, which had fallen upon the floor; he even gave it a furtive kick, as he passed.

He was so occupied with his own thoughts, he did not see John Ward come up the garden path and enter the parsonage, and when, a moment afterwards, the preacher came into the room, Dr. Howe started at the change in him. These weeks of spiritual conflict had left their mark upon him. His eyes had a strained look which was almost terror, and his firm, gentle lips were set in a line of silent and patient pain. Yet a certain brightness rested upon his face, which for a moment hid its pallor.

Through fear, and darkness, and grief, through an extraordinary misconception and strange blindness of the soul, John Ward had come, in his complete abnegation of himself, close to God. Since that June night, when he met the temptation which love for his wife held out to him, he had clung with all the passion of his life to his love for God. The whole night, upon his knees, he besought God's mercy for Helen, and fought the wild desire of flight, the longing to take her and go away, where her unbelief could not injure any one else, and devote his life to leading her to light; go away from his people, whom God had committed to him, and whom he had betrayed, leave them, stained with the sin he had permitted to grow unchecked among them, and give his very soul to Helen, to save her. But the temptation was conquered. When the faint, crystal brightness of the dawn looked into his study, it saw him still kneeling, his face hidden in his arms, but silent and at peace. God had granted his prayer, he said to himself. He had shown him the way to save Helen. At first he had shrunk from it, appalled, crying out, "This is death, I cannot, I cannot!" But when, a little later, he went out into the growing glory of the day, and, standing bare-headed, lifted his face to heaven, he said, "I love her enough, thank God, — thank God." A holy and awful joy shone in his eyes. "God will do it," he said, with simple conviction. "He will save her, and my love shall be the human instrument."

After that had come the days when John had written those imploring letters to his wife, the last of which she had answered with such entire decision, saying that there was no possible hope that she could ever believe in what she called a "monstrous doctrine," and adding sorrowfully that it was hard even to believe in God, — a personal God, and she could be content to let doctrines go, if only that light upon the darkness of the world could be left her.

Then he had sent his last letter. He had written it upon his knees, his eyes stung with terrible tears; but his hand did not falter; the letter was sent. Then he waited for the manifestation of God in Helen's soul: he distrusted himself and his own strength, but he never doubted God; he never questioned that this plan for converting his wife was a direct answer to his prayers.

Now, when he saw Dr. Howe, he had a moment of breathless hope that her uncle had come to tell him that Helen had found the truth. But almost before the unreasonableness of his idea struck him, he knew from Dr. Howe's face that the time was not yet.

"I am glad to see you," he said, a little hurriedly; the thin hand he extended was not quite steady.

The rector's forehead was gathered into a heavy frown. "See here," he answered, planting his feet wide apart, and still holding his hat and stick behind him, "I cannot give you my hand while you are ignorant of the spirit in which I come."

"You come for Helen's sake," John replied.

"Yes, sir, I do come for Helen's sake," returned Dr. Howe, "but it is because of your conduct, because of the heartless way in which you have treated my niece. You cannot expect me to have a friendly feeling for the man who is cruel to her." For the moment he forgot that this was to be a theological dispute. "Now, sir, what explanation have you to give of this outrageous affair?"

"Helen's soul shall be saved," John said, his voice growing firmer, but losing none of its gentleness.

Dr. Howe made an impatient gesture. "Helen's soul!" he cried. "Is it possible that a sane man can seriously excuse his conduct on such a ground? Why, it is incredible! How do you suppose the world will regard your action?"

"What have you or I to do with the world?" the other answered.

" We live in it," said Dr. Howe, " and if we are wise men we will not, for a mad whim, violate its standards of propriety. When a man turns his wife out of his house, he must consider what meaning is attached to such an action by the world. You blast Helen's life, sir, and her family is necessarily involved in the same disgrace."

John looked at him with clear, direct eyes. " I save Helen's soul, and her family will rejoice with me when that day comes."

" Her family," the other replied contemptuously, " are not troubled about Helen's soul; they are quite satisfied with her spiritual condition."

" Do they know what it is ? " John asked.

" Certainly," answered the rector, " of course. But it is n't of the slightest consequence, anyhow. The main thing is to cover up this unfortunate affair at once. If Helen comes back right away, I think no one need know what has happened."

" But there is nothing to cover up," John said simply ; " there is no shame that Helen should accept God's way of leading her to himself."

" Lord ! " exclaimed Dr. Howe, and then stopped. This would never do; if Ward became angry, he would only grow more obstinate.

" If you are so troubled about her unbelief," the rector said, feeling that he was very wily, " I should think you would see the need of daily influence. You could accomplish more if she were with you. The constant guidance of a clergyman would be of the utmost value. I suppose you think she is with me, but I doubt " — his lip curled a little — " if I can give her quite the instruction you desire."

"Oh, I had not hoped for that," John answered. "But her surroundings will not influence Helen now. Impelled by my grief, she must search for truth."

Dr. Howe was too much excited to notice the reproof in John's words. "Well, it will teach her to think; it will push her into positive unbelief. Agnosticism! — that's what this ' search for truth' ends in nowadays! Come, now, be reasonable, Ward; for Heaven's sake, don't be a — a — don't be so unwise. I advise this really in your own interests. Why, my dear fellow, you'll convert her in half the time if she is with you. What? And don't you see that your present attitude will only drive her further away? You are really going against your own interests."

"Do not play the part of the Tempter," John said gently; "it ill becomes Christ's minister to do that. Would you have me pray for guidance, and then refuse to follow it when it comes? God will give me the strength and courage to make her suffer that she may be saved."

Dr. Howe stared at him for a moment. Then he said, "I — I do not need you to teach me my duty as Christ's minister, sir; it would be more fitting that you should concern yourself with your duty as a husband." The vein in his forehead was swollen with wrath. "The way in which you pride yourself upon devising the most exquisite pain for your wife is inhuman, — it is devilish! And you drag her family into the scandal of it, too."

John was silent.

Again Dr. Howe realized that he must control

himself; if he got into a passion, there would be an end of bringing about a reconciliation.

"You made me forget myself," he said. "I did n't mean to speak of my own feelings. It is Helen I want to talk about." Perhaps some flash of memory brought her face before his eyes. "Sit down," he added brusquely, — "you look tired;" and indeed the pallor of John's face was deadly.

The rector, in his impatience, sat on the edge of his chair, one plump fist resting on the table, and the other hand clenched on the head of his cane. His arguments and entreaties were equally divided, but he resolutely checked the denunciations which trembled upon his lips. John answered him almost tenderly; his own grief was not so absorbing that he could be indifferent to the danger of a man who set the opinion of the world before the solemn obligations of his profession. Carefully, and fully, and very quietly, he explained his position in regard to his parish; but when Dr. Howe urged that Helen might observe all proper forms, and yet keep silence on what was, after all, a most immaterial difference, John roused to sudden passion. Here was an old temptation.

"God forbid!" he said. "Observe forms, and let her hope of spiritual life die? No, no, — not that. Form without soul is dead. You must have seen that too often."

"Well, I'll tell you what to do," said the rector, in his eagerness pulling his chair closer to John's, and resting his hand almost confidentially upon his knee: "if you fear her influence in your parish, —

and of course I understand that, — why, give her a letter to another church."

John half smiled, but did not answer. The room had grown dark as they talked, and now Alfaretta brought a lamp, looking curiously at the rector, as she passed him. "Supper's ready, Mr. Ward," she said.

"Yes," John said. "Dr. Howe, I hope" —

But the rector plunged again into argument. Once he stopped, and said, "So, surely, she can return?"

"It is impossible," John answered quietly.

And again, "You will let me send her back?"

And he said, "No."

At last, wearied and baffled, Dr. Howe rose. He leaned heavily forward on the table, his open palm resting on the volume of sermons, which Alfaretta had lifted from the floor, and he looked steadily at John. "Then, sir," he said slowly, "I am to understand, for my niece, that this monstrous decision of yours is fixed and unchangeable? We cannot hope that her love, or her youth, or your duty, or the miserable scandal of the affair, will ever move your cruel determination?"

John rose, too. The interview had been a terrible strain. His courage was unshaken, but his strength was leaving him; a pathetic desire for sympathy and understanding seized him. "I love her too much to change. Don't you understand? But I cling to more than human strength, when I say, I will not change."

"Then, by Heaven," cried the rector, "neither

shall she! With my consent she shall never return
to a man who reads such books as those," and he
pointed to the row of Edwards, — "a man who denies good in anything outside his own miserable conception of religion ; the very existence of whose faith
is a denunciation and execration of every one who
does not agree with him. You are firm, sir? So
is she! I bid you good-day."

He turned to the door, breathing hard through his
shut teeth. John Ward followed him, and laid his
hand upon his arm. "Do not go," he said ; "there
is much I would like to say ; and you will spend the
night here with me? I beg that you will not go."

"The roof which refuses to shelter my niece," answered Dr. Howe, his voice shaking with anger,
"shall not be over my head!"

"Then," said John slowly and gently, "you must
listen now to what I have to say."

"Must!" cried the rector.

"Yes, for it is your duty to listen, as it is mine to
speak. I dare not hear a servant of God set the
opinion of the world above a conception of duty —
no matter how strained and unnatural the duty may
appear to him — and keep silence. I cannot listen
when you urge Helen's temporal happiness, and refuse to consider her eternal welfare, and not tell you
you are wrong. You evade the truth ; you seek ease
in Zion. I charge you, by the sacred name of Him
whose minister you are, that you examine your own
soul."

Dr. Howe looked at him, his face crimson with
anger. "Sir," he stammered, flinging the detaining

hand from his arm, — " sir ! " And then, for the first time since Archibald Howe took orders, an oath burst from his lips ; he struck his stick madly against the table, and rushed from the room.

Alfaretta was lying in wait for him at the garden gate, a large and rustic bunch of flowers in her hand, which she hoped he would carry to Helen.

" How's Mrs. Ward ? " she said, trying to detain him. " When will she be home ? "

" Get out of my way, girl ! " he cried, and, slamming the gate behind him, he strode down the street.

CHAPTER XXIX.

When Dr. Howe reached his own door, Helen was waiting for him.

She had been sitting on the porch alone for more than an hour. She had been very quiet; there was none of that restlessness which excitement produced in her uncle or cousin; but when she saw Dr. Howe, she rose, and stood trembling at the head of the steps. The rector flung himself out of the carriage almost before it stopped.

"I want to see you, Helen," he said. "I have something to say to you. Come into the library."

She followed him silently, and when he had closed the door he turned and looked at her. "Now, my child," he began, "you must listen to what I have to say."

He stood with one hand on his hip, and lifted the forefinger of the other as he spoke. "I have seen that man. I have been insulted by him. He is as firm as the devil can make him that you shall not return to him. Now, I have no right to interfere between husband and wife; you are entirely free at any moment to follow any course you may wish. At the same time, I must tell you that I shall respect you more if you do not return to him. And I want to add one other thing: from this time, his name is not to be spoken in my presence."

Helen's face had grown slowly whiter. " Oh, you will not understand! " she said hoarsely ; but he interrupted her.

" I am sorry for you, my darling. Oh, what a blow this would have been for your mother! Poor Mary felt any family trouble so deeply. But you must be a woman, you must bear it bravely. Yes, your marriage with this fanatic was a terrible mistake, but we must bear it."

Helen shook her head ; she could not speak. She had not known that she had hoped anything from her uncle's visit, but this final despair almost overpowered her.

" He thinks you are going to change your mind in a week or two," he went on. " I 'd say he was insane if he were not so cruel! There is too much method in his madness. There! I cannot speak of it; let us drop the subject. Your place in my heart is secure ; I trust you will never leave me ; but on this one topic we cannot meet." Then with a sudden tenderness, " Oh, Helen, how hard this is for you! You must try to forgive him, — I cannot."

" Forgive him ? " she said, almost in a whisper, her beautiful eyes dilating and her lips white. " Oh, John, how I have wronged you, if they think I have anything to forgive! "

Dr. Howe looked at her, and seemed to swallow a sob ; then he opened his arms, and, drawing her head down on his shoulder, " Poor child," he said, " poor child ! "

But this softening on his part met no response from Helen. " You do not understand John," she said, " and so — so please do not think about me."

The rebuff sent the rector back to his own resentment. " Remember, I do not wish to speak of him
again, Helen. I have nothing more to say."

Nor would he say more to Lois and Mrs. Dale
than that John Ward was inflexible, and he wished
no further discussion upon the subject; he also forbade any urging that Helen should return to her
husband.

" Well, but, brother, what explanation shall we
give of her being here?" asked Mrs. Dale anxiously.

" I 'm sure I don't know," he answered impatiently; " anything but the truth."

" Why, Archibald ! " his sister cried, in a shocked
tone.

" Oh, well, you know what I mean," he said;
" make some sort of an excuse. Of course, don't
say anything which is untrue, but don't tell people
our private affairs."

" Do you think she 'll ever go back to him?"
Mrs. Dale inquired, looking at him meditatively over
her glasses.

" I hope not! " he said savagely. " Now stop,
Adele, stop! I will not discuss that man ! "

" Where did she get her obstinacy?" Mrs. Dale
sighed. " I suppose it was from her father's side.
And the whole affair is so ill-bred; one would know
Helen was not all a Howe. I always felt there was
something lacking in Charles Jeffrey, though poor
dear Mary was so infatuated. Yes, I remember,
when that sister of his came here to visit us, I did
not feel sure, not at all sure, that the Jeffreys were

really well-born people. She used to sit up straight and uncomfortable in a carriage. I never saw her lean back, and I always said that that girl's grandmother was n't used to riding in carriages! So you see, that 's where Helen gets her — her bad taste."

" Well, don't talk about it," said Dr. Howe, walking restlessly back and forth.

Mrs. Dale took off her glasses, and rubbed them on the corner of her black silk apron. " It would never have happened," she said positively, " if they had had children. I declare, I " — and she stopped, as though about to suggest that Helen should adopt a child at once. Mrs. Dale usually blamed John and Helen with equal impartiality, but to-day the fault seemed to belong entirely to her niece. She was very much puzzled to know how she was to " make excuses " without telling an untruth. " I 'll just speak to Giff about it," she thought; " it all depends on the way Deborah Woodhouse hears it, and Giff is really quite sensible, and can advise me what to tell her."

She saw him that afternoon, but, as she said afterwards in reluctant confidence to her husband, " Giff has n't much sense, after all. He thought it was best to just tell the truth about it."

"Yes? " responded Mr. Dale. " Well, I have often noticed, I am only apt to admire the good sense of people who agree with me. Gifford doubtless has not the advantage of feeling sure that his wishes constitute the standards of right and wrong."

" Nonsense," said Mrs. Dale; " I am sure I don't know what you are talking about."

" Well, what are you going to do ? " asked her
husband.

" Oh," Mrs. Dale answered, " Gifford will tell
Deborah Woodhouse the truth (Helen wants him
to), but he will do it as carefully and as mildly as
possible. And he will make her promise to keep it
to herself. But you know Deborah Woodhouse ;
she trickles — there is no other word for it — everything. She could n't keep a secret to save her life.
But Helen will have it so. Oh, dear, dear, dear !
Heaven save us from willful women ! "

Gifford broke the news to his aunts as wisely as
he knew how, but he did not hide the truth. It was
not until the day before he went back to Lockhaven
that he told them ; he had put it off as long as he
could, hoping, as Dr. Howe had done, that John
Ward would see how useless it was to carry out his
plan. Gifford had found the sisters together. Miss
Ruth was at work in her studio, while Miss Deborah
sat in the doorway, in the shadow of the grape-vines,
topping and tailing gooseberries into a big blue
bowl. She had a handful of crushed thyme in her
lap, and some pennyroyal.

"It is n't roses," Miss Deborah remarked, " but
it is better than Ruth's turpentine. And so long as
I have got to sit here (for I will sit here while she 's
copying the miniature ; it is a sacred charge), the
pennyroyal is stronger than the paint."

Miss Ruth, her hands neatly gloved, was mixing
her colors a little wearily ; somehow, on her canvas,
the face of the little sister lost what beauty it had
ever known.

"I can't get the eyes," Miss Ruth sighed. "I have a great mind to help you with your preserving, sister."

"My dear Ruth," said Miss Deborah, with much dignity, "do I try to do your work?"

"But you know you could n't paint, dear Deborah," said the younger sister eagerly. The round china-blue eyes of the little sister stared at her maliciously.

"Well," returned Miss Deborah, running her small hand through the gooseberries in the bowl, "neither could you make gooseberry jelly, or even a tart." Then seeing her nephew lounging down the flagged path to the door of the studio, his straw hat pushed back and his hands in his pockets, she was suddenly reminded of his packing. "I hope, Giff, dear," she cried, "you left plenty of room in your trunk? I have a number of articles I want you to take."

"There's lots of room, aunt Deborah," he answered. "You know I had to put in a bag of straw to fill up, when I came on, — I could n't have things rattle around."

Miss Deborah laughed. "You need your aunt to look after you, my dear."

"Or a wife," said Miss Ruth, looking up at him over her gleaming spectacles.

"Nonsense," replied her sister vigorously; "don't put such ideas into his head, if you please. I must say such jokes are not in good taste, dear Ruth."

But Miss Ruth was more anxious about her light than Gifford's marriage. "You are really so big,

Giff," she complained mildly, "you darken the whole studio, standing there in the doorway. Do pray sit down."

Gifford obediently took his seat upon the step, and this brought his face on a level with Miss Ruth's.

"Oh, that is nice," the little lady said, with gentle enthusiasm. "I shall have your eyes to look at. I have not been able to get the little sister's eyes just to suit me."

It made no difference to Miss Ruth that Gifford's eyes were gray and full of trouble. "Aunt Deborah," he said abruptly, "Helen Ward is not going back to Lockhaven for the present. Indeed, I do not know when she will go."

Miss Deborah forgot her gooseberries, in her surprise. "Not going back!" she cried, while her sister said, "Is Mr. Ward coming here?"

Then Gifford told them the story as briefly as he could, interrupted by small cries of amazement and dismay. "Well," exclaimed Miss Deborah, her delicate hands uplifted, "well! I never heard of such a thing! How shocking, how ill-bred! And she is going to be at the rectory? Ruth, my dear, you must never go there without me, do you hear? It is not proper. A wife separated from her husband! Dear me, dear me!"

"How can she leave him?" gasped Miss Ruth. "Married people ought to love each other so that they could not be parted."

"You have never been in a position to judge how they ought to love each other," said Miss Deborah sharply. " But this is what comes of youthful marriages, Gifford. A person should have reached years of maturity before thinking of marriage. Such things do not happen when people are reasonably old " —

" But not too old, sister," Miss Ruth interrupted, a little color creeping into her faded cheek.

Miss Deborah did not notice the amendment; she was anxious to hear the practical side of the matter, and had questions to ask about Helen's money, and whether Gifford supposed that that man would do anything for her; but except their grave disapproval that Helen should differ from her husband, nothing was said of theology. As they talked, the sisters grew full of sympathy, which waxed and waned as they thought of Helen's sorrow, or the impropriety of her action.

" I shall make her some jelly directly," said Miss Deborah, " and put in plenty of Madeira; the poor thing needs strength."

" This must be the reason," Miss Ruth said, — she had put her brushes down some time ago, — " that she was in such distress that day at her mother's grave. Oh, how trying this is for her! Indeed, I am sure death is easier to bear, when one — loves — than a parting like this."

" Really, dear Ruth," returned her sister, holding her head very straight, " you would not say that if you knew what it was to lose a — friend, by death. At least Mr. Ward is alive, even if Helen cannot see him. Ah, dear me! Well, I wonder how Adele Dale feels now? I should be miserable if we had

such a thing happen in our family. A husband and
wife quarrel, and separate ! Shocking ! "

" But there is no quarrel, you know," Gifford protested slowly, and for the third or fourth time.

But Miss Deborah brushed this aside. " They
are separated ; it is the same thing. In our family,
an unhappy marriage was never known. Even when
your grandfather's sister married a Bellingham, —
and of course everybody knows the Bellingham temper, — and they quarreled, just three weeks to a day
after the wedding, she never thought of such a disgraceful thing as leaving him. I have heard dear
mamma say she never spoke to him again, except
when she had to ask for money ; that almost killed
her, she was so proud. But she never would have
lowered herself by leaving him. Yes, this is really
most improper in poor dear Helen."

Miss Deborah's feelings vibrated, even while she
was making the jelly, and though it was finally sent,
she balanced her kindness by saying to Mrs. Dale
that it did not seem just right for a young thing
like Lois to know of such a painful affair. It gave
Miss Deborah so much pleasure to say this to her
old enemy that she made excuses for Helen for a
whole day afterwards.

Late that afternoon Gifford went to say good-by
at the rectory. It was a still, hazy August day,
with a hint of autumn in the air ; sometimes a yel-
lowing leaf floated slowly down, or one would notice
that the square tower of St. Michael's could be seen,
and that the ivy which covered its south side was
beginning to redden.

Miss Helen was not at home, Jean said. She
thought she'd gone up to the graveyard, — she most
always went there.

So Gifford started in search of her. " She ought
not to be alone so much," he thought, and he wondered, with a man's dullness in such matters, why,
if she and Lois had made up after that one quarrel,
they were not the same tender friends. He met
Lois at the rectory gate. She was coming from the
village, and there was a look in her face which gave
him a sudden jealous pain. She held a letter in her
hand, and her eyes were running over with happiness ; her lips smiled so that they almost broke into
laughter as she spoke.

" Something seems to make you very happy,
Lois ? " he said.

" It does," she cried, — " very, very ! "

" I am glad," he said, wishing she could find it in
her heart to tell him of her joy.

" Forsythe has come to his senses," he thought.
" I suppose he has been unusually loving, confound
him ! "

The two young people parted, each a little graver
than when they met. " How he does like to be with
Helen ! " Lois thought, as she went on, and Gifford
sighed impatiently as he wished Forsythe were more
worthy of her.

He found Helen walking wearily home alone.
" I wanted to say good-by," he said, taking her
hand in his big warm grasp, " and just tell you that
I'll look after him, you know, in any way I can.
I'll see him every day, Helen." She looked at him

gratefully, but did not speak. " I wish," Gifford
continued, hesitating, " you would not take such
long walks by yourself. Why don't you let Lois
come with you ? "

" She would not care to," she answered briefly.

" Oh, I think you are wrong there," he remonstrated. " She is lonely, too." Helen seemed to consider. " You know it has been an unhappy summer
for Lois, and if you shut her out of your sorrow " —

" I did not mean to be selfish," she replied, not
seeing how much Gifford spoke for her own sake,
" and I do not shut her out; but so long as she only
sympathizes with me, and not with John too, I cannot let her talk to me about it."

" That is not quite just, Helen," he said ; and
afterward, Helen acknowledged this.

She put her hands into his, when he turned to go
home, and searched his face with sad, eager eyes.
" You are going to see him, — oh, Giff, you'll see
John ! " she said.

Lois saw them talking, as they came to the rectory door, with a dull feeling of envy. Gifford
never seemed to care to talk much to her. What
was that Miss Deborah had said of his once caring
for Helen ? She had the good sense to be ashamed
of herself for remembering it, but a thought which
comes even into an unwilling mind cannot be driven
away without leaving its impress ; the point of view
is subtilely and unconsciously changed. She was not
altogether cordial to Gifford, when he said good-by
to her, which he was quick to feel. " He thinks
only of Helen," she said to herself. " I suppose he

has forgotten anything he ever said to me, and my promise, too. I 'm ready enough with promises," she thought, with a bitter little smile. But even this memory could not keep that happiness which Gifford had seen from shining in her eyes; and when she went up-stairs, Helen noticed it.

Perhaps because of Gifford's gentle reproof, she roused herself to say, as he had done, " You are very happy, Lois ? "

" Oh, I am, I am ! " she cried impulsively. " Oh, Helen, I have something to tell you." A very little sympathy in her cousin's voice brought her eager confidence to her lips. " Oh, Helen, a letter has come ! "

" John ? " she hardly breathed. For one exquisite moment, which had yet its background that he had not been strong, Helen misunderstood her.

" No, it 's only something about me," Lois answered humbly.

" Tell me," Helen said gently. " If anything makes you happy, you know I 'll be glad."

Lois twisted her fingers together, with a nervous sort of joy. " I 've just heard," she said; " Mrs. Forsythe has just written to me."

" And she is very well ? " Helen asked. She had almost forgotten her cousin's grief and anxiety about Mrs. Forsythe. It all seemed so long ago and so unimportant.

" No, no," Lois said, " she says she 's very sick ; but oh, Helen, Dick Forsythe is engaged to be married ! "

Helen looked puzzled. " I don't understand."

" Never mind," Lois cried joyously, " he is, and I am so happy ! "

CHAPTER XXX.

WHEN the summer had faded into autumn, Ashurst had not yet recovered from the social earthquake of discovering that it had the scandal of an unhappy marriage within its decorous borders. There had been nothing which had so shaken the foundation of things since Gertrude Drayton had run away with her dancing-master, who, it was more than suspected, had left a wife in France. That sensation lasted a long time, for William Denner's face was a constant reminder of his grief; but by and by it faded, and, as Gertrude never came back to Ashurst, people even said very kindly things about her.

But Helen Ward continued to live among them.

Indeed, the excitement was so great at first that Miss Deborah did not remember for some time to write to Gifford that Dick Forsythe was engaged to a New York girl. "She really could scarcely blame him," she had added, "for he could hardly be expected to keep his engagement with Lois after this disgraceful affair in her family."

Gifford read that part of the letter again, dizzy with happiness and pain. "How she must suffer!" he said to himself. "The cur! Ah, she never could have married him; she must have discovered his contemptible nature."

His first impulse was to hurry to Ashurst. " Not for my own sake," he reasoned, " but just to be there. I would never show that I knew how he had treated her. She should not have an instant's mortification in my presence. But she might just see, without being told, that I loved her through it all."

He even rose, and began to study a time-table; but he frowned a little and put it down, and went and looked out of the window a while. " Helen would be more unhappy if she thought I were not here to look after Ward. Yes, I must wait till he gets stronger. Perhaps next month " —

Then, shaking himself together, with a revulsion of common sense, " As she is unhappy, she won't care whether I'm there or not, or may be she'd rather I was n't ! "

Yet, though he could not easily subdue the desire to rush to Ashurst, the thought that Helen's sorrow would be a little greater if she could not think of him as near her husband, helped to keep him at his post.

But it might have been good for Helen to have had the young man's frank and healthy understanding of her position. She was growing every day more lonely and self-absorbed ; she was losing her clear perceptions of the values of life ; she became warped, and prejudiced, and very silent. She even fancied, with a morbid self-consciousness which would have been impossible before, that she had never possessed the love of her uncle and cousin, and had always been an alien. This subtile danger to her generous nature was checked in an unexpected way.

One afternoon, late in September, she went as usual, alone, to the graveyard on East Hill. The blue haze lay like a ribbon through the valley and across the hills; the air was still, and full of the pungent fragrance of burning brush, and yellow leaves rustled about her feet. The faded grass had been beaten down by the rain, and was matted above the graves; here and there a frosted weed stood straight and thin against the low soft sky; some late golden-rod blazed along the edge of the meadow among the purple asters, and a single stalk of cardinal flowers flashed out beside the lichen-covered wall; but all the rest of the world was a blur of yellow and gray. Helen sat down on a stone, and listened to the small wood sounds around her. A beech leaf, twisted like the keel of a fantastic boat, came pattering down on the dead leaves; a bird stirred in the pine behind her, and now and then a cricket gave a muffled chirp.

It was here Mr. Dale found her, her head resting forlornly on her hands; she was absently watching a gray squirrel who had ventured from his covert in the wall, and was looking at her with curious, twinkling eyes.

" My dear," said Mr. Dale gently, " they told me at the rectory they thought you were up here, so I came to see if you would let me walk home with you."

Helen started as he spoke, and the squirrel scampered away. " Did you come for that ? " she said, touched in spite of her bitter thoughts.

Mr. Dale pushed his broad-brimmed hat back on his head, so that his face seemed to have a black aureola around it. " Yes," he replied, regarding her with anxious blue eyes, — " yes. I am grieved to have you so much alone ; yet I know how natural it is to desire to be alone."

Helen did not answer.

" I hope," he went on, hesitating, " you will not think I intrude if I say — I came because I wanted to say that I have a great respect for your husband, Helen."

Helen turned sharply, as though she would have clasped his hands, and then put her own over her face, which was quivering with sudden tears.

Mr. Dale touched her shoulder gently. " Yes, a great respect. Love like his inspires reverence. It is almost divine."

Helen's assent was inaudible.

" Not, my dear," the old man continued, " that I do not regret — yes, with all my heart I deplore — the suffering for you both, by which his love is proved. Yet I recognize with awe that it is love. And when one has come so near the end of life as I have, it is much to have once seen love. We look into the mysteries of God when we see how divine a human soul can be. Perhaps I have no right to speak of what is so sacredly yours, yet it is proper that you should know that the full meaning of this calamity can be understood. It is not all grief, Helen, to be loved as you are."

She could not speak ; she clung to him in a passion of tears, and the love and warmth she had thought she should never feel again began to stir about her heart.

"So you will be strong for him," Mr. Dale said gently, his wrinkled hand stroking her soft hair. "Be patient, because we have perhaps loved you too much to be just to him; yet your peace would teach us justice. Be happier, my dear, that we may understand him. You see what I mean?"

Helen did see; courage began to creep back, and her reserve melted and broke down with a storm of tears, too long unshed. "I will try," she said brokenly, — "oh, I will try!" She did not say what she would try to do, but to struggle for John's sake gave her strength and purpose for all of life. She would so live that no one could misunderstand him.

Mr. Dale walked home with her, but he did not speak to her again of her sorrow. The impulse had been given, and her conscience aroused; the harder struggle of coming back to the daily life of others she must meet alone. And she met it bravely. Little by little she tried to see the interests and small concerns of people about her, and very gradually the heavy atmosphere of the rectory began to lighten. Dr. Howe scarcely knew how it was that there was a whist party in his library one Friday evening; rather a silent one, with a few sighs from the Misses Woodhouse and a suspicious dimness in Mr. Dale's eyes. The rector somehow slipped into the vacant chair; he said he thought he was so old whist would not hurt him, if they were willing to teach him. But as he swept the board at the first deal, and criticised his partner's lead at the second, instruction was deemed superfluous.

By degrees, Lois and Helen came nearer together. There was no explanation : the differences had been too subtile for words, at least on Lois's side, and to have attempted it would have made a vague impression harden into permanence.

No one recognized an effort on Helen's part, and she only knew it herself when she realized that it was a relief to be with Mr. Dale. He understood ; she could be silent with him. So she came very often to his little basement office, and spent long mornings with him, helping him label some books, or copying notes which he had intended "getting into shape" these twenty years. She liked the stillness and dimness of the small room, with its smell of leather-covered volumes, or whiff of wood smoke from the fireplace.

Mrs. Dale rarely disturbed them. " If Helen finds any pleasure in that musty old room," she said, one cold January morning, " I 'm sure I 'm glad. But she would be a great deal more sensible and cheerful if she 'd sit up in the parlor with me, if she did n't do anything more than play patience. But then, Helen never was like other people."

And so she left her niece and her husband, with a little good-natured contempt in her eyes, and went up to her own domains. Mr. Dale was arranging some plants on a shelf across one of the windows, and Helen was watching him. " They generally die before the winter is out," he said, " but perhaps with you to look after them they 'll pull through."

He was in his flowered dressing-gown, and was standing on tiptoe, reaching up for one of the mildewed flower-pots. "These are orange plants," he explained proudly. "I planted the seeds a month ago, and see how they 've grown." He put his glasses on and bent down to examine them, with an absorbed look. The pot that held the six spindling shoots had streaks of white mould down its sides, and the earth was black and hard with the deluge of water with which Mr. Dale's anxious care usually began the season. He began now to loosen it gently with his penknife, saying, "I 'm sure they 'll flourish if you look after them."

"I will if I 'm here, uncle Henry," she replied.

"Ah, my dear," he said, looking at her sharply, "you are not thinking of that hospital plan again?"

"Yes," she answered, "I cannot help it. I feel as though I must be of some use in the world." She was standing in the stream of wintry sunshine which flooded the narrow window, and Mr. Dale saw that some white threads had begun to show in the bronze-brown waves of her hair. "Yes," she continued, "it is so hard to keep still. I must do something, and be something."

Mr. Dale stopped digging in his flower-pots, and looked at her without speaking for a moment; then he said, "I wonder if you will not be something nobler by the discipline of this quiet life, Helen? And are you not really doing something if you rouse us out of our sleepy satisfaction with our own lives, and make us more earnest? I know that cannot be your object, as it would defeat itself by self-consciousness, but it is true, my dear."

She did not speak.

"You see," he went on, in his gentle voice, "your life cannot be negative anywhere. You have taken a stand for a vital principle, and it must make us better. Truth is like heat or light; its vibrations are endless, and are endlessly felt. There is something very beautiful to me, Helen, speaking of truth, that you and your husband, from absolutely opposite and extreme points, have yet this force of truth in your souls. You have both touched the principle of life, — he from one side, you from the other. But you both feel the pulse of God in it!"

"You know," she said gratefully, "you understand" — She stopped abruptly, for she saw Lois coming hurriedly along the road, and when she opened the gate she ran across the snowy lawn to Mr. Dale's office, instead of following the path. There was something in her face which made Helen's heart stand still.

She could not wait for her to reach the door, but went out bareheaded to meet her.

Lois took her hands between her own, which were trembling. "Gifford has sent a dispatch. I — I came to bring it to you, Helen."

Her cousin put out her hand for the telegram.

"I'm afraid John is ill," Lois said, the quick tears springing to her eyes.

"Give it to me," said Helen.

Reluctantly Lois gave her the dispatch, but she scarcely looked at it. "Uncle Henry," she said, for Mr. Dale had followed her, and stood in speechless sympathy, his white hair blowing about in the keen wind, "I will go to Mercer now. I can make the train. Will you let me have your carriage?"

Her voice was so firm and her manner so calm Lois was deceived. " She does not understand how ill John is," she thought.

But Mr. Dale knew better. " How love's horror of death sweeps away all small things," he said, as he sat alone in his study that night, — " time, hope, fear, even grief itself ! "

His wife did not enter into such analysis; she had been summoned, and had seen to wraps and money and practical things, and then had gone crying up-stairs. "Poor child," she said, " poor child! She does n't feel it yet."

A calamity like this Mrs. Dale could understand; she had known the sorrow of death, and all the im-patience which had stood between Helen and herself was swept away in her pitying sympathy.

As for Lois, Helen had not forbidden her, and she too had gone to Mercer. Helen had not seemed even to notice her presence in the carriage, and she dared not speak. She thought, in a vague way, that she had never known her cousin before. Helen, with white, immovable face, sat leaning forward, her hand on the door, her tearless eyes straining into the distance, and a tense, breathless air of waiting about her.

" May I go to Lockhaven with you ? " Lois asked softly; but Helen did not answer until she had re-peated the question, and then she turned with the start of one suddenly wakened, and looked at her.

" Oh, you are here ? " she said. " You were good to come, but you must not go further than Mercer." Then she noticed that the window beside Lois was open, and leaned forward to close it. After that, she lapsed again into her stony silence.

When they reached the station, it was she who bought the ticket, and then again seemed startled to find the girl by her side. "Good-by," she said, as Lois kissed her, but there was no change in her face, either of relief or regret, when her cousin left her.

How that long slow journey passed Helen never knew. She was not even conscious of its length. When Gifford met her, she gave him one questioning look.

"Yes," he said tenderly, "you are in time. He would not let me send before, Helen; and I knew you would not come unless I said, 'John sends for you.'"

"No," she answered. He told her, in their quick ride to the parsonage, that this had been the third hemorrhage, and John had not rallied; but it was not until the night before that he had known the end was inevitable and near, and had sent for his wife.

Oh, the strangeness of those village streets! Had she ever been away? These months in Ashurst were a dream; here only was reality and death.

Alfaretta could not speak as she met them at the gate, but ran by Helen's side, and furtively kissed her hand. There was a light burning in the study, but Helen stood at the table in the hall and took off her bonnet and cloak.

"I will go and tell him you are here," Gifford said, trying to detain her as she turned to go upstairs.

" He knows," she said calmly, and left Gifford and the servant standing in the entry.

She did not even pause at the door ; there seemed no need to gather strength for the shock of that meeting; she was all strength and love.

The room was lighted only by the fire, and the bed was in shadow.

There were no words ; those empty, dying arms were stretched out to her, and she gathered him close to her heart.

The house was strangely silent. Again and again Gifford crept up to the door, but all was quite still ; once he heard that soft sound which a mother makes when she soothes her baby on her breast, and again a low murmur, which died away as though even words were an intrusion.

All that long winter day, Gifford, in his intense anxiety lest Helen should not come in time, and his distress for the sorrow of this little household, had been calmed and comforted by John's serene courage. He knew that death was near, but there was an exultant look in his fading eyes, and sometimes his lips moved in grateful prayer. Perhaps his physical extremity had dulled his fears for his wife's salvation into a conviction that his death was to be the climax of God's plans for her. He was bewildered at the temptation of greater joy at the prospect of her presence than gratitude that God should save her soul alive. But he never for one moment doubted she would come to tell him she had found the light.

The night wore heavily on. Gifford stationed

himself upon the stairs, outside the door; the doctor came, and then went quietly down to John's study, and found a book to while away the time. And then they waited.

When the first faint lightening of the sky came, and the chill of dawn began to creep through the silent house, Helen came out of the closed room. She put her hand upon Gifford's shoulder. " Go and rest," she said; " there is no need to sit here any longer. John is dead."

CHAPTER XXXI.

AFTER it was all over, they begged her to go back to Ashurst.

"You can't stay here," Lois entreated — she had come with Mr. Dale as soon as the news of John Ward's death reached Ashurst — "you can't live among these people, Helen."

But Helen shook her head. "They are John's people. I cannot go yet."

Lois thought with a shiver of the exhortations of the clergymen who had come to the funeral to officiate. She wondered how Helen could stay where every one had heard her sin of unbelief publicly prayed for; yet, with her cousin's brave sad eyes upon her, she dared not give this as a reason why Helen should leave Lockhaven.

Mr. Dale did not urge her to return; he knew her too well. He only said when he went away, holding her hands in his and looking at her, his gentle old face quivering with tears, "He is all yours now, my dear; death has given you what life could not. No matter where you are, nothing can change the perfect possession."

There was a swift, glad light in the eyes she lifted to his for a moment, but she did not answer.

At first she had been stunned and dazed; she had not realized what her sorrow was; an artificial courage came to her in the thought that John was free, and the terrible and merciful commonplace of packing and putting in order, hid her from herself.

She had stayed behind in the small brown parsonage, with only Alfaretta for a companion, and Gifford's unspoken sympathy when he came every day to see her. Once she answered it.

"I am glad it is John instead of me," she said, with an uplifted look; "the pain is not his."

"And it is so much happier for him now," Gifford ventured to say, — "he must see so clearly; and the old grief is lost in joy."

"No," Helen answered wearily; "you must not say those things to me. I cannot feel them. I am glad he has no pain, — in an eternal sleep there is at least no pain. But I must just wait my life out, Gifford. I cannot hope; I dare not. I could not go on living if I thought he were living somewhere, and needing me. No, it is ended. I have had my life."

She listened in eager and pathetic silence to every detail of John's life since she had left him which Alfaretta or Gifford could give her. A little later, she asked them both to write out all that they remembered of those last days. She dared not trust the sacred memory only to her heart, lest the obliterating years should steal it from her. And then, by and by, she gathered up all her power of endurance, and quietly went back to Ashurst. That last night in the little low-browed parsonage not even Alfaretta was with her. Gifford left her on the threshold with a terrible fear in his heart, and he came to the door again very early in the morning; but she met him calmly, with perfect comprehension of the anxiety in his face.

"You need not be afraid for me," she said. "I do not dare to be a coward."

And then she walked to the station, without one look back at the house where she had known her greatest joy and greatest grief.

.   .   .   .

The summer had left spring far behind, when Gifford Woodhouse came to Ashurst.

He could not stay in Lockhaven; the tragedy of John Ward had thrown a shadow upon him. The people did not forget that he was Mrs. Ward's friend, and they made no doubt, the bolder ones said, that Lawyer Woodhouse was an infidel, too. So he decided to take an office in Mercer. This would make it possible for him to come back to Ashurst every Saturday, and be with his aunts until Monday.

Perhaps he did not know it, but Lockhaven shadows seemed deeper than they really were because Mercer was only twelve miles from Lois Howe. Not that that could mean anything more than just the pleasure of seeing her sometimes. Gifford told himself he had no hope. He searched her occasional letters in vain for the faintest hint that she would be glad to see him. "If there were the slightest chance of it," he said, with a sigh, "of course I'd know it. She promised. I suppose she was awfully attached to that puppy."

However, in spite of hopelessness, he went to

Mercer, and soon it became a matter of course that he should drop in at the rectory every Sunday, spending the evening with Helen after Dr. Howe and Lois had gone to church.

Helen never went. " I cannot," she said to Gifford once ; " the service is beautiful and stately, and full of pleasant associations, but it is outside of my life. If I had ever been intensely religious, it would be different, I suppose, — I should care for it as a sacred past ; but it was never more than pleasant. What I called my spiritual life had no reality to me. And now, surely, I cannot go, when I have no faith at all."

" I think you will go, some day, Helen," Gifford said thoughtfully ; " the pendulum has to swing very far away from the extreme which you have seen before the perfect balance comes. And I think you make a mistake when you say you have no faith. Perhaps you have no creed, but faith, it seems to me, is not the holding of certain dogmas ; it is simply openness and readiness of heart to believe any truth which God may show."

They were sitting on the porch at the rectory ; the fragrant dusk of the garden was beginning to melt into trembling light as the moon rose, and the last flush of sunset faded behind the hills. Helen had a soft white wrap over her black dress, but Gifford had thought it was cool enough to throw a gray shawl across her feet ; he himself was bareheaded, and sat on the steps, clasping his knees with his hands.

" Perhaps so," Helen said, " but I think I am like

a person who walks along in the dark, yet looks toward the east. I will not comfort myself with little candles of memory or desire, and say, ' This is light ! ' Perhaps light will never come to my eyes, but I will wait, for I believe there is light somewhere."

It was much for Helen to say this. No one had guessed what was behind her reserve on such subjects ; perhaps no one had very greatly cared.

" Gifford ! " she said suddenly. He looked up, surprised at her tone.

" Yes, Helen ? "

" I wish," she said, " I wish you were as happy as you deserve to be."

He knew what she meant, and would not repay her confidence by pretending not to understand. " Well, I 'm not as happy as I desire, perhaps, but no doubt I 'm as happy as I deserve."

" No," she answered, " you are not. And oh, Gifford, there is so much sorrow in the world, the only thing which makes life possible is love, because that is the only thing which does not change."

" I am afraid it can never be for me," he said, after a moment's silence, " except the joy of giving love."

" Why ? " she asked gently.

Gifford did not speak ; he rose, and began to pace up and down in front of the porch, crossing and recrossing the square of light which fell from the open hall door. " I ought not to talk about it," he said at last. " I 've got it down at the very bottom of my life, a sort of foundation stone on which to build

noble things. Your words make it spring up into
a whole palace of beauty ; but it is in the air, — it is
in the air ! You know what I mean : it must always
be giving with me ; she will never care. She never
could, having loved once. And it is curious, Helen,
but in a certain paradoxical way I 'm content she
should n't. She would not be the woman she is, if
she could love twice."

Helen smiled in the darkness. " Gifford " — she
began.

But he interrupted her, flinging his head back, in
impatient despair. " No, it cannot be, or it would
have been, don't you see ? Don't encourage me,
Helen ; the kindest thing you can do is to kill any
hope the instant it shows its head. There was a
time, I was fool enough to think — it was just after
the engagement was broken. But I soon saw from
her letters there was no chance for me."

" But Gifford," — Helen almost forgot to protect
Lois, in her anxiety to help him, — " you must not
think that. They were never engaged."

Gifford stood still and looked at her ; then he said
something in a low voice, which she could not hear.

" I must not say another word," she said hurriedly.
" I 've no right even to speak as I did. But oh,
Gifford, I could not see you lose a chance of happi-
ness. Life is so short, and there is so much sorrow !
I even selfishly wanted the happiness of your joy,
for my own sake."

Still Gifford did not speak ; he turned sharply on
his heel, and began his restless walk. His silence
was getting unbearable, when he stopped, and said

gently, " I thank you, Helen. I do not understand
it all, but that's no matter. Only, don't you see,
it does n't make any difference? If she had been
going to care, I should have known it long ago."

This was very vague to Helen; she wondered if
Lois had refused him again. But Gifford began to
talk quietly of his life in Mercer, and she did not
venture to say anything more. "After all, they
must work out their own salvation," she thought.
"No one can help them, when they both know the
facts."

She listened a little absently to Gifford, who was
speaking of the lack of any chance for advancement
in Mercer. "But really," he added, " I ought not
to go too far away from my aunts, now; and I believe that the highest development of character can
come from the most commonplace necessities of life."
Helen sighed; she wondered if this commonplace
of Ashurst were her necessity? For again she was
searching for her place in the world, — the place that
needed her, and was to give her the happiness of
usefulness; and she had even thought vaguely that
she might find some work in Lockhaven, among
John's people, and for them. They both fell into the
silence of their own thoughts, until the rector and his
daughter came back from church, and Gifford went
home.

That next week was a thoughtful one with Gifford
Woodhouse; Helen's words had stirred those buried
hopes, and it was hard to settle back into a life of
renunciation. He was strangely absent-minded in
his office. One day Willie Denner, who had come

to read law, and was aspiring to be his clerk, found him staring out of the window, with a new client's papers lying untouched before him. After all, he thought, would it be wrong, would it trouble Lois (he had said he should never trouble her), if he just told her how the thought of her helped him, how she was a continual inspiration in his life? "If I saw it bothered her, I could stop," he argued.

And so, reasoning with himself, he rode over from Mercer late that Saturday night. The little ladies were, as usual, delighted to see him. These weekly visits were charming; their nephew could be admired and fussed over to their hearts' content, but was off again before they had time to feel their small resources at an end. The next morning he dutifully went to church with them. Sunday was a proud day for the Misses Woodhouse; each took an arm of the young man, whose very size made him imposing, and walked in a stately way to the door of St. Michael's. They would gladly have been supported by him to their pew, but it would have been, Miss Deborah said, really flaunting their nephew in the faces of less fortunate families, for Ashurst could not boast of another young man.

Miss Ruth wore her new bonnet that day in honor of his presence. She had taken it from the bandbox and carefully removed its wrapping of tissue paper, looking anxiously at the clouds as she smoothed the lavender strings and pinched the white asters on the side, before she decided that it was safe to wear it.

Gifford looked up the rectory lane as they drew near the church, and Miss Deborah noticed it. "Giff, dear," she asked, "did you observe, last Sunday, how ill poor little Lois looked?"

" No," he said, somewhat startled.

" Ah, yes," said Miss Ruth, nodding her head so that the white asters trembled, " she has never really gotten over that disappointment about young For- sythe."

" But she was not engaged to him," responded Gifford boldly.

" Not engaged," Miss Deborah admitted, " but she fully expected to be. He did not treat her honor- ably; there is no doubt of that. But her affections were unalterably his."

" How do you know that?" demanded her nephew.

" Why, my dear child," said Miss Ruth, " there is no doubt of it. Adele Dale told dear Deborah the whole story. Of course she had it from Lois."

" Not that it makes the slightest difference in my position," Gifford thought, as he sat crowding down the pain of it, and looking at Lois, sitting in the rosy light of the window of the left transept. " I am just where I was before, and I'll tell her, if it does not seem to bother her."

After church, there was the usual subdued gossip about the door, and while Gifford waited for his aunts, who had something to say to the rector, he lis- tened to Mrs. Dale, who said in her incisive voice, " Isn't it too bad Helen isn't here? I should think, whether she wanted to or not, she'd come for her husband's sake." Even the apology of death had not made Mrs. Dale pardon John Ward.

But Mr. Dale mildly interjected, — " She would

stay away for his sake, if she did not really want to come."

To which Mrs. Dale responded, " Fudge ! "

Miss Deborah also spoke of her absence to Lois. " Sorry dear Helen is not here, but of course Gifford will see her to-night. He does so enjoy his evenings with her. Well, they are both young — and I have my thoughts! "

So, with the utmost innocence, Miss Deborah had planted the seeds of hopelessness and jealousy in the hearts of both these young people. Gifford spent the rest of the long, still Sunday wandering restlessly through the house, and changing his mind about speaking to Lois every few minutes. Lois was very distant that evening at the rectory, so Gifford talked mostly to Helen. There was no chance to say what he had intended, and he made none.

" Well," he said to himself as he went home, not caring to stay and talk to Helen when Lois had gone to church, — " well, it is all a muddle. I don't understand about there being no engagement, but I cannot help remembering that she cared, though I have no business to. And she cares yet. Oh, what a confounded idiot I am ! "

He told his aunts he was going to make an early start the next morning. " I shall be off before you are up. I guess Sarah will give me something to eat. And, aunt Deborah, I don't know that I can get over next week."

The little ladies protested, but they were secretly very proud that his business should occupy him so much.

There was a silver mist across the hills, when Gifford led his horse out of the barn the next morning, and the little sharp paving-stones in the stable-yard, with thin lines of grass between them, were shining with dew. The morning-glories about the kitchen porch had flung their rosy horns toward the east, as though to greet the sunrise. Sarah stood under them, surveying the young man regretfully. " Your aunts won't half like it, Mr. Gifford," she said, " that you would n't eat a proper breakfast."

But he put his foot in the stirrup, and flung himself into his saddle. He was too much absorbed in his own concerns to reflect that Miss Deborah would be distressed if her Scotch collops were slighted, and that was not like Gifford. However, he was young and a man, so his grief did not prevent him from lighting a cigarette. The reins fell on the horse's neck as he climbed East Hill, and Gifford turned, with one hand on the bay's broad flanks, to look down at Ashurst. The valley was still full of mist, that flushed and trembled into gold before it disappeared at the touch of the sun. There was a flutter of birds' wings in the bushes along the road, and the light wind made the birch leaves flicker and dance; but there was hardly another sound, for his horse walked deliberately in the grass beside the road, until suddenly a dog barked. Gifford drew his rein sharply. " That was Max ! " he said, and looked about for him, even rising a little in his stirrups. " How fond she is of the old fellow ! " he thought.

In another moment the dog ran across the road, his red coat marked with dew ; then the bushes were pushed aside, and his mistress followed him.

" Why, Gifford ! " she said.

" Why, Lois ! " he exclaimed with her, and then they looked at each other.

The young man threw away his cigarette, and, springing from his horse, slipped the reins over his arm, and walked beside her.

" Are you going away ? " Lois asked. " But it is so early ! "

She had her little basket in her hand, and she was holding her blue print gown up over a white petticoat, to keep it from the wet grass. Her broad hat was on the back of her head, and the wind had blown the curls around her face into a sunny tangle, and made her cheeks as fresh as a wild rose.

" You are the early one, it seems to me," he answered, smiling.

" I 've come to get mushrooms for father," she explained. " It is best to get them early, while the dew is on them. There are a good many around that little old ruin further up the road, you know."

" Yes, I know," he said. (He felt himself suddenly in a tumult of uncertainty. " It would be no harm just to say a word," he thought. " Why should n't she know — no matter if she can never care herself — that I care? It would not trouble her. No, I am a fool to think of it, — I won't.") " But it is so early for you to be out alone," he said. " Do you take care of her, Max ? "

" Max is a most constant friend," Lois replied ; " he never leaves me." Then she blushed, lest Gifford should think that she had thought he was not constant.

But Gifford's thoughts were never so compli-
cated. With him, it was either, " She loves me,"
or, " She does not ;" he never tormented himself,
after the fashion of women, by wondering what this
look meant, or that inflection, and fearing that the
innermost recesses of his mind might be guessed
from a calm and indifferent face.

" You see the old chimney ? " Lois said, as they
drew near the small ruin. " Some mushrooms grow
right in on the hearth."

It was rather the suggestion of a ruin, for the
walls were not standing ; only this stone chimney
with the wide, blackened fireplace, and the flat doorstones before what was once the threshold. Grass
and brambles covered the foundations ; lilacs, with
spikes of brown dead blossoms, grew tall and thick
around it, and roses, gone back to wild singleness,
blossomed near the steps and along a path, which was
only a memory, the grass had tangled so above it.

Max kept his nose under Lois's hand, and the
horse stumbled once over a stone that had rolled
from the broken foundation and hidden itself beneath a dock. The mushrooms had opened their
little shining brown umbrellas, as Lois had said, on
the very hearth, and she stooped down to gather
them and put them in her basket of sweet grass.
From the bushes at one side came the sudden note
of a bob-white ; Max pricked his ears.

" Lois," Gifford said abruptly, still telling himself that he was a fool, — but then, it was all so commonplace, so free from sentiment, so public, with
Max, and the horse, and the bob-white, it could not

trouble her just to — "Lois, I 'd like — I 'd like to tell you something, if you don't mind."

"What?" she said pleasantly; her basket was full, and they began to walk back to the road again.

Gifford stopped to let his horse crop the thick wet grass about a fallen gate-post. He threw his arm over the bay's neck, and Lois leaned her elbows on the other post, swinging her basket lightly while she waited for him to speak. The mist had quite gone by this time, and the sky was a fresh, clear blue. "Well," he began, suddenly realizing that this was a great deal harder than he had supposed ("She 'll think I 'm going to bother her with a proposal," he thought), — "well, the fact is, Lois, there's something I want you to know. Perhaps it does n't really interest you, in one way; I mean, it is only a — a happiness of my own, and it won't make any difference in our friendship, but I wanted you to know it."

In a moment Miss Deborah's suggestion was a certainty to Lois. She clasped her hands tight around the handle of her grass basket; Gifford should not see them tremble. "I 'm sure I 'll be glad to hear anything that makes you happy."

Her voice had a dull sound in her own ears.

"Helen put it into my head to tell you," Gifford went on nervously. "I hope you won't feel that I am not keeping my word " —

She held her white chin a little higher. "I don't know of any ' word,' as you call it, that there is for you to keep, Gifford."

"Why, that I would not trouble you, you know, Lois," he faltered. "Have you forgotten ?"

" What ! " Lois exclaimed, with a start, and a thrill in her voice.

" But I am sure," he said hurriedly, " it won't make you unhappy just to know that it is still an inspiration in my life, and that it always will be, and that love, no matter if " —

" Oh, wait a minute, Giff ! " Lois cried, her eyes shining like stars through sudden tears, and her breath quick. " I — I — why, don't you know, I was to — don't you remember — my promise ? "

" Lois ! " he said, almost in a whisper. He dropped the bay's rein, and came and took her hand, his own trembling.

" I know what you were going to say," she began, her face turned away so that he could only see the blush which had crept up to her temple, " but I " — He waited, but she did not go on. Then he suddenly took her in his arms and kissed her without a word ; and Max, and the horse, and the bob-white looked on with no surprise, for after all it was only part of the morning, and the sunrise, and Nature herself.

" And to think that it 's I ! " Lois said a minute afterward.

" Why, who else could it be ? " cried Gifford rapturously.

But Lois shook her head ; even in her joy she was ashamed of herself. " I won't even remember it," she thought.

Of course there were many explanations. Each was astonished at the other for not having understood ; but Lois's confession of her promise to Mrs.

Forsythe made all quite clear, though it left a look that was almost stern behind the joy in Gifford's eyes.

"You know I could n't help it, Giff," she ended.

But he did not speak.

"It was n't wrong," she said. "You see how it was, — you don't think it was wrong?"

"Yes, I do, Lois," he answered.

"Oh!" she cried; and then, "But you made me!"

"I?" he exclaimed, bewildered.

And then she told him how his acknowledgment of her fault drove her into a desire for atonement. "You know, you think I'm wrong pretty often," she added shyly; and then they mutually forgave each other.

"I suppose I did find a good deal of fault," Gifford admitted, humbly, "but it was always because I loved you."

"Oh!" said Lois.

But there was so much to say they might have talked until noon, except that, as they had neither of them breakfasted, and happiness and morning air are the best sort of tonics, they began to think of going to the rectory. Gifford had quite forgotten the business in Mercer which needed him so early.

"Father won't have mushrooms with his steak to-day," Lois commented, looking ruefully at the little basket, which she still held in her hand.

They stopped at the roadside, walking hand in hand like two children, and looked back at the ruin. "It was a home once," Gifford said, "and there was love there ; and so it begins over again for us, — love, and happiness, and all of life."

" Oh, Giff," the girl said softly, " I don't deserve " —

But that, of course, he would not hear. When they came to the rectory gate, — and never did it take so long to walk from East Hill to the rectory, — Gifford said, " Now let's go and tell Helen ; we've kept her out of our joy too long." They met her in the cool, dusky hall, and Gifford, taking her hand, said gently, " Be glad, too, Helen ! "

Lois had put her arms about her cousin, and without further words Helen knew.

.   .   .   .

And so Helen Ward's duty came to her, the blessedness and helpfulness of being needed ; when Lois went to her new home, Helen would be necessary to her uncle, and to be necessary would save her life from hardness. There need be no thought of occupation now. When Mr. Dale heard the news, he said his congratulations were not only for Lois and Gifford, but for Helen, and after that for Ashurst.

.   .   .   .

A genuine Ashurst engagement was a great thing, and the friends of the young people received it in their several ways. Dr. Howe was surprised, but disposed to make the best of it. " This is always the way," he said, with his big, jolly laugh : " a man brings up his girls, and then, just as soon as they get old enough to amount to something and be a comfort to him, some other man comes along and carries them off. What ? Mind, now, Gifford, don't you go further away than Mercer ! "

As for Mrs. Dale, she was delighted. "It is what I have always wanted; it is the one thing I've tried to bring about; and if Lois will do as I tell her, and be guided by a wiser head than her own, I have no doubt she will be very reasonably happy."

"Does n't a woman expect to be guided by her husband?" Mr. Dale asked.

"When he has sense enough," responded his wife significantly.

Miss Deborah and Miss Ruth were greatly pleased. "Of course they are very young," said Miss Deborah, "but I 'll have an eye to the housekeeping until Lois gets older. Fortunately, they 'll be so far away from dear Adele, she cannot interfere much. Even with the best intentions in the world, a girl's relations should n't meddle."

"They seem very much in love, sister," said Miss Ruth thoughtfully.

"Well, really, dear Ruth," replied her sister, "you are hardly capable of judging of that; but you happen to be right; they are as much attached as one can expect young people to be."

But Miss Ruth, as she stood that night before her cherry-wood dressing-table, its brass rings glimmering in the candle-light, opened Mr. Denner's daguerreotype, and, looking wistfully at the youthful face behind the misty glass, said softly to herself, "Ah, well, it 's good to be young."

THE END.